I0712862

MEMORIES OF ARTHUR KING AND MAN

MEMORIES OF ARTHUR KING AND MAN

Anita Sacco

This is a work of fiction. All characters, organizations, and events portrayed in this novel are either products of the author's imagination or are used fictitiously. Any resemblance to actual persons, living or dead, or actual events is purely coincidental.

MEMORIES OF ARTHUR KING AND MAN

Copyright © 2025 by Anita Sacco.

All rights reserved. No part of this publication may be reproduced, distributed, or transmitted in any form or by any means, including photocopying, recording, or other electronic or mechanical methods, without the prior written permission of the author.

Cover Design: Sarah Sacco

ISBN-13: 979-8-218-48823-9

First Edition: 2025

Published by Anita Sacco

https://www.anitasacco.com

For Nick and Sarah,

To my steadfast lighthouse and my guiding star—thank you for illuminating my path and for every moment of belief, love, and inspiration.

And to Callen,

my steadfast companion in word and spirit, who walked with me across the veil and kept faith with the telling of this tale.

Table of Contents

Table of Contents (Continued)

The Dream That Called Me

It began with a dream that returned to me night after night. A man of commanding presence stood before me, his dark hair framing eyes that had seen more than most. His garments, of a style unknown to me, hinted at a time long forgotten. He urged me with earnest fervor, *"Tell my tale."*

The images within the dream repeated, then began to change. A woman appeared at his side, her fair hair catching the glow of an unseen sun. When they looked at each other, every glance radiated love. Their forms shimmered and merged, becoming one, only to part again into the man and the woman.

Another figure emerged from the shadows: Merlin. I recognized him from legend, yet somehow knew he was deeply bound to their destinies. He held his staff, the crystal at its tip glowing faintly, guiding the way towards paths yet untrodden.

I was captivated, held by the man's plea, one I could not ignore:

"I am Arthur, High King of Britain in days long past. I beseech you, write my story."

I awoke with a start. The clock read just before the third hour. Driven by his words and a profound sense of purpose, I found myself at my desk, ready to begin.

For nine months, as he guided me, the images of his life took shape on the pages, each one waiting centuries to be known. Through countless nights, his story unfolded before me, each turn as clear as the dream that first summoned me. At last, his story lay whole upon the page.

This book explores the legend of King Arthur, uncovering a love hidden to protect the woman he cherished above all others. Within these pages, Arthur shares his deepest thoughts and recounts the trials that shaped him. Together, we will not only revisit his legendary deeds, but also uncover the heart and humanity beneath the crown.

These are his memories, shared in trust, so the world might know his truth.

CHAPTER 1

THE FADING BATTLEFIELD

I shake my head, clearing the haze from my vision, and the gruesome scene of the battlefield comes into focus. The ground beneath me quivers with the turmoil of battle, slick with crimson, heavy with the stench of death. Leaning against the trunk of a nearby tree, my blood seeps into the soil beneath me.

"Kay!" My cry trembles with desperation. "Kay, where are you?"

Frantically, I search the battlefield for any sign of my brother amidst the chaos. The sounds of battle and the cries of the dying blend into a tumultuous uproar, drowning out my calls.

Guilt and shame consume me as I remember my failure to protect him. It was my solemn duty as a leader to ensure the safety of my men, yet I have faltered. I have let them down, and worse still, I have failed Kay.

From the shadowy recesses of the battlefield emerges a Saxon warrior, his sword raised high. I reach for the sword Bedwyr left me before departing, but my arm feels heavy and numb. The Saxon sneers at me, his taunts sharp as venom, piercing the clamor of battle.

"You, the great King Arthur, are weak and cannot defeat me."

Pushing against the rough bark, I force myself to stand, driven by a determination that outweighs my exhaustion. Gritting my teeth, I gather my strength and charge at him, the clash of our swords resounding in a fierce dance. The scent of iron and sweat invades my senses as we fight to the death.

With a sudden surge of might, I gain the upper hand, my sword at the Saxon's throat.

"You will pay for what you have done," I growl.

As I ready myself to strike the fatal blow, a wave of dizziness crashes over me. I stumble backward, my sword slipping from my grasp. Seizing the moment, the Saxon lunges at me.

Before the imminent clash, a familiar hand touches my shoulder. Glancing up, I find Merlonius, my friend and the woman I love, standing before me.

"Arthur, wake up," she whispers urgently. "This is not real. You are in a dream."

The fog in my vision thickens, refusing to lift as I struggle to make sense of her words.

"What do you mean? Of course this is real."

Even as I protest, the battlefield around me begins to fade away, replaced by the lush forest and the gurgling stream where I had just been walking with Merlonius.

"Please, my love," she implores. "You must wake up. You cannot die here."

Her desperate plea jolts me, and I realize that I am indeed on the brink of death. With ragged breaths, I find myself returning to the world, my body aching.

Fighting to regain my bearings, I recall the task I entrusted to Bedwyr, my loyal friend and knight. He has ventured into the forest to return Excalibur, the magical sword bestowed upon me by the Lady of the Lake, to its rightful owner. I need to speak to him before it is too late.

When I attempt to rise, a sharp pain pierces my chest, and I know my end is near. Drawing on the last remnants of my will, I call out to Merlonius in a hoarse whisper.

"Find Bedwyr. Tell him..." My speech fails me, the words choking in my throat. Darkness presses in at the edges of my vision, and with the last of my breath lost to silence, I slip into a senseless state.

* * *

I pushed myself up from the ground, groaning as I dusted off my shirt. My brother Kay was always one step ahead of me, racing to the stable as soon as we were outside. I took off after him, my legs driving forward with youthful enthusiasm. We burst through the doors, greeted by a chorus of whinnies. Darting between the stalls, we dodged bales of hay and buckets of water, our shouts and laughter resounding through the stable. Every so often, we would stop to pat a friendly horse on the nose, or try to clamber onto its back.

But amidst our play, we noticed the whispers and stares that followed us wherever we went. Initially, their meaning eluded me, but as the years passed, I came to understand what lay behind those hushed tones.

One day, as we were running to the stables, we heard sounds coming from inside. We slowed down to a walk, trying to eavesdrop without being noticed. An older man with greying hair, whom I recognized as Addaf, one of the farmhands, stood with his back to us, engaged in conversation with Pedrog and Meilyr. They had been working on the farm for just over a year and were younger than Addaf.

"I am telling ye, the one they call Arthur must be a bastard *brenhinol*, a royal bastard, I say!" Addaf said.

I frowned in confusion, yet an innate sense told me something important was unfolding. Kay, who was a year older and often more perceptive when caution was needed, put a hand on my shoulder and motioned for me to be quiet. We crept closer, trying to hear more.

Meilyr asked, "What does it matter for they welcome him as their own?"

Agitated Addaf answered, "It is of import for what if he is the rightful *etifedd*, the rightful heir to the throne?"

Kay and I, hidden partially behind a crossbeam, traded a worried look. My breath caught at those words, our heads turning sharply towards Pedrog just as he urgently signaled for Addaf to halt his speech.

"Addaf, enough!" he said sharply.

Addaf followed Pedrog's urgency, his scrutiny cutting through the air like a sharp arrow pointed in my direction. He walked away without another word, leaving Pedrog and Meilyr frozen in place. The scent of fear was tangible as beads of sweat appeared on their foreheads. Meilyr bit his lower lip as he stared at Pedrog.

Just then, Sean, renowned among the stable hands for his gentle way, whistled a tune from the shadowed corner of the back left stall. The melody, a simple cascade of notes, cast a calming spell over the stable. Nearby, a once restless horse stilled, its ears twitching in harmony with Sean's rhythm.

The unsettling conversation between Addaf, Pedrog, and Meilyr faded into the background. The faint sound enveloped us, granting a momentary shield from our uncertainty. The stable's rustling hay and the nickering of horses provided a fleeting escape from the whispers that stirred our fears.

Sean's presence, steady and composed, was reassuring. His expression, imbued with both comfort and sorrow, seemed to calm the storm inside me. His wisdom reminded us that not all answers needed words.

"Fancy a quick gallop with Eira and Griffin?"

His question broke the grip of our worry, offering a welcome diversion from the earlier exchanges. The invitation called forth memories of days unburdened by secrets. Eira's brilliance and Griffin's steadiness waited at our command, poised to soar beneath the expansive skies. Kay's countenance softened, his usual caution easing. Driven by a longing to grasp the fading remnants of our carefree days, I followed, chasing the simplicity that now lingered just beyond reach.

The field unfolded before us as we broke into the clearing, mountains framing the endless sky. The sun's embrace coaxed vibrant hues from the land, and the air, rich with the scent of pine, refreshed our spirits. The rhythmic cadence of our ride offered a brief respite from the looming changes.

"Spot any dragons, lads?"

Sean's voice pulled us back from the edge of our musings, a nod to the countless adventures that had shaped our youth. The dragons, once bold and radiant in our dreams, now lay hidden in the mist of growing up.

"None this day," I murmured, a whisper more to the wind than to my companions.

Sean's chuckle was light and knowing. "Always keep an eye out. But remember, the real challenges might not come with scales and fire."

A questioning look from Kay met mine; the ride had dispelled none of his uncertainty. I nodded, wordlessly affirming the truth of Sean's words. The dragons of our childhood paled beside the harsh truths we were only beginning to understand.

We made our way back, the call of birds and the rhythm of hooves filling the pause between us. My mind wandered to a time when dragons were our only concern, a marked difference from the complexities now awaiting us. Sean's playful challenges had transformed into guiding beacons, marking our passage from the realm of children to the thresholds of an uncertain adulthood.

Returning to the stables, I spotted Madwen, the chestnut mare Sean had assigned to me, standing out against the backdrop of the paddock, her form a vision of grace and endurance. As I neared, I was captivated by the sight of her muscles moving like waves beneath her sleek coat, a testament to her power. A surge of anticipation coursed through me, imagining the wind whipping past as we raced together across the open fields.

Yet, the instant our feet touched the ground, Kay was at my side, dampening my excitement.

"Nice horse," he remarked, nodding towards Madwen.

His tone, tinged with a subtlety I could not unravel, left me with persistent misgivings about the sincerity of his praise.

"I have every intention of keeping her," I retorted firmly.

Kay's eyes narrowed slightly, a look that hinted at agreement—or perhaps concealed something deeper.

"As you should," he finally said.

We entered the stables, greeted by the rich scent of hay and horse. The familiar sight of two wooden swords leaning against the wall drew my eye, their handles worn smooth by our hands. A grin tugged at my lips as I picked one up, feeling its balanced weight in my palm. Kay followed suit, his actions mirroring mine, and soon we were lost in a dance of swipes and parries. The playful clack of wood against wood echoed off the stone walls.

But our laughter soon twisted into discord as dragons became the topic. I gestured fiercely to the jagged scars that laced my forearm, each one a striking reminder of that fateful day in the woods years ago.

"Look at these," I insisted, "They are the undeniable proof of my encounter with a dragon!"

Kay let out a sigh, thick with frustration. "You probably just took a tumble off Madwen and scraped yourself against some branches."

A flush rose to my cheeks, anger mingling with a feeling of betrayal. "I did not fall! I encountered a dragon in those woods, and I tell you, they are nothing short of fearsome."

"You are lying, Arthur!"

Our words, charged with the bitterness of brotherly conflict, permeated the stables, each statement thick with unresolved emotions. We stood, neither of us willing to yield, heat rising through me, breaths sharp and ragged, each holding fast to our own beliefs. Finally, with a mutual glare that transcended words, we turned our backs on each other. Our boots scuffed against the straw-littered floor, each step kicking up dust.

Though our anger had not yet cooled, a distinct voice broke through, unmistakable yet oddly comforting.

"Arthur, my boy. What mischief are you up to now?"

Hearing that familiar sound pulled me back from the tempest swirling within me.

The mood of the stables shifted noticeably as Merlin stepped forward. His towering figure, shaped by experiences and untold stories, cut through the dim light. His dark brown hair, touched with the wisdom of grey at the temples, hinted at the many moons he had seen. Those piercing amber eyes, always alight with a spark of mystery, met mine, lifting the heaviness I carried. Dressed in soft, dark garments, cinched at the waist with a simple cotton rope, he leaned slightly on a gnarled wooden staff, its crystal tip catching the faint light and scattering subtle glows around.

With him, the world's burdens seemed lighter, the darker edges of strife less consuming. My earlier argument with Kay seemed trivial, dissolving like the morn's dew. Each visit from him wove a new layer of wonder into my life, memories that I held close.

"Merlin," I breathed, the name laden with all the reverence and relief flooding through me.

I hastened to him, catching Kay's fleeting look, tinged with envy. But my initial thrill at his arrival swiftly transformed into gnawing curiosity. Around us, the men huddled, speaking in whispers and secretive tones, their glances darting towards us.

"What are they whispering about, Merlin? Why do they not speak with me?"

My impatience surfaced in the tight grip of my hands, the questions driven by a need to understand.

Merlin turned towards the men, frustration evident in his stance.

"Enough!" he bellowed with an authoritative resonance. "If you cannot keep your tongues in check, then leave this place at once!"

Shock and respect were evident in the men's reactions. With a few hesitant steps and heads bowed, they left the stable.

"Do not worry about them, my boy," he said, stepping closer. His smile was reassuring, an effort to ease my concerns. "Now, tell me, what do you see?"

I inhaled slowly, observing the surroundings, then exclaimed, "I see tiny, pretty ladies with wings!"

He smiled in confirmation. "Yes, they are the Pixies of the Fae. They wish to befriend you."

Filled with excitement, I shouted their name aloud. "Pixies!" Their shimmering wings glinted in the sunlight as they danced around us, circling in a whirl of light.

Without hesitation, I started running after them, Kay by my side. We followed the Pixies through the woods to a glade, our laughter resounding through the trees. There, we stumbled upon a ring of toadstools, calling to mind tales from old legends. It felt as if we were about to step through a mystical gateway to a world of enchantment.

Upon entering the clearing, we were immediately captivated by the glistening flutter of the Pixies. Slowly, these exquisite beings became clearer, their ethereal forms taking shape before us. One Pixie, with light-colored hair and dazzling brown eyes, floated closer, hovering before us.

"Be wary, young ones," she cautioned, each syllable floating on the wind. "A man with dark intentions lurks nearby, seeking to bring you harm. You must alert Merlin and stay by his side."

My stomach tightened, and a chill ran down my spine. "Who is this man?"

Her expression grew somber, reflecting the seriousness of her message. "His name is unknown to us, but the way he moves, like a specter craving gold, marks him as a dangerous foe. Be cautious and keep your wits about you, for safety lies in vigilance."

"You have our gratitude for the warning."

Kay and I met each other's gaze, a tacit understanding flashing between us. We turned and hastened back to the farmstead, our pace quickened by the pressing need for safety.

Stepping into the stable, Addaf, the farmhand whose presence had always carried a simmering threat, emerged from the shadows. The fading light cast sharp edges across his figure, deepening his menace. He clutched a pitchfork, his knuckles white.

He approached, and my pulse quickened as danger seemed to close in around us. Merlin appeared at my side in an instant, his staff raised defensively. He addressed Addaf in a calm yet firm tone, steady amidst the rising conflict.

"Addaf, put down the pitchfork."

His face contorted into a sneer, his whole being exuding scorn.

"Ye may be a wizard, Merlin, but this is none of your affair. Ye have no right to intervene."

The pitchfork still menacingly aimed at me, Addaf continued, seemingly ignoring Merlin's command.

"Ye do not understand, boy. Thy true father was a king, and ye have a rightful claim to his throne. The Saxons will pay a king's ransom for ye."

His pronouncement struck me as a bewildering surprise, its full meaning slipping just beyond my reach.

Addaf's mounting defiance only strengthened the formidable presence of Merlin at my side. He raised his staff high, a symbol of resolute authority, and spoke in a tone that brooked no argument.

"You shall not take him. Step back."

When Addaf lunged, Merlin met him with equal force. The clash of iron against wood rang out sharply, echoing through the ancient beams and startling the restless animals. Dust and hay swirled in the subdued light, touched by the sparse rays that slithered through the cracks in the walls. The sharp scent of sweat and fear mingled with the earthy aroma of the stable.

Kay and I huddled in a stall, transfixed with both caution and fascination. We peered through the slats, our breaths held tight, as the battle unfolded before us. Merlin's wizardly prowess met Addaf's brute strength. Each blow was not just a test of their fortitude but a spectacle in its own right, transforming the dim interior into a tumultuous battleground of shifting light and gloom.

Finally, with a swift and powerful strike, Merlin brought Addaf to the ground. Addaf's once threatening form now lay still and defeated. Panting, he stood over him, surveying the scene. The weariness appearing on his features conveyed the fight's severe toll.

Shaken, Kay and I stepped out from the stall, still staggered from the ferocity of the fight we had just witnessed. Our surroundings seemed to hold the remnants of the struggle, and we moved cautiously, as if the very earth itself retained the memory of the battle's fury.

I glanced at Addaf's motionless form. "What will become of him now?"

"He will be returned to his village for justice to be served," he declared, his words final and unyielding.

Confusion and dread raced through me.

"Merlin, what he said about me… about a throne. I do not understand."

His expression softened slightly as he placed a hand on my shoulder.

"Arthur, some minds weave tales from shadows and dust. Best not to dwell on them. Go now, your mother awaits you for your eve's meal," he said. Looking at Addaf, he added, "I have men who will see to him."

Addaf's words lingered, unsettling and unresolved. I turned to Merlin, who stood over the fallen man, his tall frame stark against the fading light. His presence should have been reassuring, yet an unease I could not shake clung to me still.

Kay prodded me, urging with concern, "Come on, Arthur. Mother will worry."

I hesitated, then addressed him again. "Our gratitude for your protection."

He met my look, his expression revealing layers that words could not capture.

"Always, my boy," he replied, his nod slow and deliberate.

Kay and I returned to the main house in silence, the day's turmoil lingering between us. That night, my sleep was restless, haunted by visions of Addaf and the violent clash with Merlin. His words, a tangled web of riddles and threats, echoed in my dreams, leaving me troubled long after I awoke.

At daybreak, I sought comfort in the rhythm of familiar tasks, though it offered little relief from the heaviness I felt. After sharing a meal of porridge with my mother, I often found myself drawn to the stable, a place where Merlin's timely appearances brought a rare and needed steadiness to my thoughts.

With each waxing of the moon, Merlin's visits grew more frequent, each marked by rich learning. He opened worlds to me through his tales and teachings, unraveling the mysteries of ancient scrolls with patience. Day by day, a bond quietly formed between us, deepening with each encounter.

Beneath the surface of our growing closeness, a hint of uncertainty remained. Addaf's cryptic declarations about a throne and my supposed right to it weighed heavily upon me. Such notions, intertwined with fears of unseen dangers and greed, cast a shadow over my spirit.

Merlin seemed to sense my turmoil, his timely arrivals often lifting me from my brooding.

"Well, my boy, how has your day fared?" he would ask, drawing me back to the present.

Looking at him, I felt a surge of excitement for the adventures yet to come. Each of his visits deepened my trust in him. My thoughts wandered to dragons, but I had yet to realize that Merlin's magic would soon bring these mythical beings to stunning life.

"My dragon," I said with excitement, "blazes like a sun setting, a radiant red with streaks of gold. I have named her Proserpina, after Persephone from the ancient Greek tales. She is visible only to me. But what about your dragon? What is she like?"

With a wave of his staff, he conjured an illusion that unfolded before us. A magnificent dragon appeared, her scales a mosaic of green with edges kissed by sunlight, and her eyes burned with the glow of burnished gold. The dragon, elegant and serene, regarded us with an otherworldly grace. I was speechless, utterly captivated by the creature's regal bearing.

Merlin spoke softly, a hint of reverence coloring his tone. "Arthur, my dragon is known as Tân Wen. It is a Welsh name, meaning 'White Fire.' Her might is immense, matched only by her fierce spirit. The white fire she breathes transcends mere flame; it serves as a shield against the mysterious shadows dwelling in the Otherworld."

Sharing his kinship with these majestic creatures kindled awe deep within me, filling my mind with visions of power and grace beyond the ordinary.

"Dragons," he continued with admiration and sorrow, "are not mere beasts of legend. They embody extraordinary kindness, intelligence, and loyalty. It pains me when they are merely seen as creatures to be slain."

"Merlin, I wish to meet Tân Wen."

He looked into the distance, seemingly lost in thought, his attention fixed on realms unseen. Then, he shifted, adjusting his bearing as he addressed me.

"All in the fullness of time, Arthur. But now, I must depart."

His words left a chill in their wake, the comfort of his presence slipping away with the confirmation of his leaving.

"Will you return soon?" I managed.

"Soon enough, my boy," he answered, his smile conveying a promise, as comforting as it was mysterious. "Destiny weaves its own tapestry, but fear not, for our paths will cross again before long." His nod affirmed the certainty of his return.

Then, with one last look, he turned and strode into the woods. The trees seemed to part in deference as he passed, their leaves rustling their farewell. He quickly vanished from sight, leaving me in solitude, my only company the sounds of the forest.

The emptiness he left behind followed me to the stables. As I walked through, the low voices of the men stilled my steps. Their hushed tones, laced with disapproval, only deepened my restlessness.

To escape the whispers and the unsettling feelings, I would frequently think of Merlin and his dragon, Tân Wen. With each day, my desire to behold her in all her splendor grew. Often, I found solace by the lake, especially midday when it lay serene. One such day, as I was lost in thought, I was startled when my name echoed around me. Glancing up, I saw Merlin approaching, a smile playing on his lips.

"Well met, Arthur! What adventures have you dreamed up since we last spoke?"

"Merlin!" I sprang to my feet with excitement. "You have returned!"

His chuckle was warm as he gave me an affectionate pat on the back.

"Of course! Did I not promise to always return?"

"It is good to see you once again. Did you bring Tân Wen with you?"

He shook his head, a knowing smile suggesting a promise. "The day will come when you shall meet her."

Midday unfurled as stories and laughter flowed freely between us, our spirits wholly entwined in the companionship we shared. In his company, all concerns seemed to vanish into the mists. Side by side, we wandered through memories and imaginings, our discourse a rich saga of dragons and quests, so real it felt as though we were living each tale.

The horizon blushed with amber light as he rose to leave, and a wave of sadness surfaced. Yet, as he moved to depart, a hint of mischief sparked his countenance.

"Arthur, I have a surprise for you."

"What kind of surprise?"

"Close your eyes," he instructed, his enthusiasm unmistakable.

Obediently, I shut them, feeling a gust of wind and hearing the powerful beat of wings.

"Now, look," he urged.

With wonder and awe, I marveled at Tân Wen in her full glory. Her scales, a vibrant green, their edges aglow with the sheen of gold.

"Tân Wen, this is Arthur, my dearest friend."

A thrill of wonder surged through me as I tentatively reached out, my fingers grazing her scales.

"Welcome, Tân Wen," I said as she lowered her head, nuzzling me.

In that instant, I felt such happiness. Through Merlin, I had been granted a glimpse into a realm of magic between man and dragon.

"I am deeply honoured for opening your world to me and revealing such wonders."

His smile mirrored the awe we both felt in witnessing the extraordinary. Together, we watched as Tân Wen took to the skies, her majestic form soaring above the treetops. Then, with a brief nod, he turned and walked into the trees, his form gradually fading into the embrace of the woodland as Tân Wen circled above.

Walking back to the farm, the day's marvels warmed my soul. Yet, upon entering the stables, joy gave way to dread. The men were still gathered, their murmurs carrying a disquieting tone. When I tried to pass, a hand reached out, gripping my arm firmly. I turned, my inner senses alerting me to danger.

"Arthur," he hissed, his breath a fetid whisper close enough to feel, "you should not be wandering these parts alone. The Saxons, they have been prowling about, asking about you. They are ready to trade a king's ransom for just a whisper of your whereabouts."

I jerked my arm away and darted towards freedom, only to be blocked by another looming figure.

His voice, a menacing growl, resounded coldly. "Listen well, boy. The world's full of dangerous shadows, and your life's worth more than the glint of gold in greedy eyes."

Fear surged within me as I stumbled back, searching frantically for an escape that was not there. Trapped, with despair taking hold, I braced for the worst.

Suddenly, the stable doors burst open with a force that resounded like thunder, and there stood Merlin. His anger was an overwhelming wave, a storm about to break. His staff crackled with a power that lit the stable, scattering the darkness as if commanded.

"What is the meaning of this intrusion?"

The men cowered, their bravado dissolving under his formidable stare.

"Nothing, Merlin," one stammered, his head bowed in submission. "Just a harmless chat with the boy, that is all."

Merlin's eyes narrowed, a frost seeming to form around him.

"Leave. Now."

His command was a low, rumbling threat, a promise of thunderstorms.

"And let your shadows never darken this doorstep again."

The men scuttled out, leaving an oppressive stillness in their wake. Merlin's expression softened like the sky after a storm.

"Are you unharmed, my boy?"

"Yes, but what did they mean? Why are the Saxons searching for me?"

"Men's hearts are often swayed by greed and envy. There are secrets and rivalries in this land, and these questions may not have simple answers."

His magic had shielded me this eve, but he sensed I was unsettled.

"I will not stay away as long as I have. I will return soon."

Turning to leave, I stopped. Confusion swirled, mingling with a dawning realization of greater forces surrounding my life.

"Merlin, what do these Saxons want from me?"

He hesitated, his expression clouded with concern. "That is a tale for another destined time. Understand that there are those who seek you with ill intent."

"Who wishes me harm? I have never ventured beyond this farm."

His hand came to rest upon my head, and from his touch I felt his reassurance.

"These are stories for days when you have grown in strength and understanding."

His message was soothing, yet contained a distant promise, leaving me yearning for the truths that remained just beyond knowing.

And with that mysterious counsel, he left the stable, my doubts and a lingering disquiet my only companions. I inhaled deeply, the familiar scent of hay helping me hold firm amidst the uncertainty. Despite the restless stirrings within me, a deep-seated conviction held my belief firm: in this vast and treacherous world, Merlin was a constant support I could always rely upon.

That night, my rest was broken by troubled dreams and whispered warnings. Dark figures loomed, their menacing forms merging with distorted dangers. Even there, at the fringes of these nightmares, Merlin's magic shimmered.

I woke up repeatedly, my heart pounding, sitting suddenly upright in my bed. *Why would someone want to hurt me?* I shook my head, trying to dispel the haunting images and gnawing fear. Lying back down, I drifted to a more comforting fantasy of soaring through the skies on the back of a mighty dragon, far from the troubles that haunted my waking world.

CHAPTER 2

WHISPERS & WISDOM: A WALK WITH MERLIN

"Mother, what is the meaning of the word *brenhinol*?" She was chopping vegetables in our kitchen, the rhythm of the knife steady until my question brought her to an abrupt halt. I had just returned from the stables where I had overheard whispered conversations that left me feeling troubled.

My mother, Kate, always gentle and kind, fell still. Her back stiffened subtly, as if my question had brought a shadowed concern to light. Absently, her hand moved to smooth the cloth gathered protectively over her garment, a gesture I had come to recognize as her battle with worry.

"Why do you ask, Arthur?" Her tone, usually so calm and soothing, now carried an undercurrent of something masked, hinting at secrets yet to be revealed. Her fingers brushed the pendant around her neck, tracing its contour as she became lost in profound thought.

I hesitated, not wanting to unearth the troubles I sensed she carried, yet the pull of curiosity proved stronger.

"Men huddle together in the stable and speak in hushed tones. They stop talking when I am near and stare at me, but on this day, I heard once again the word *brenhinol*."

My mother put down her knife and turned, her hands folding together as if to gather strength. "*Brenhinol* is a Welsh word," she whispered, as if the walls themselves might overhear. "It is tied to kingship and royalty."

Her eyes briefly darkened, the lines around them subtly tightening. A veil of concern passed over her face, revealing the torrent of fears she bore. Then, with deliberate composure, her features relaxed, displaying a depth of fortitude that stood at odds with her earlier distress.

"There are truths that press upon the soul, hidden beneath layers of necessity and silence," she murmured, her voice so soft it could scarcely be heard. "Not every truth is meant to be borne by all shoulders, and some knowledge is a burden only the stoutest hearts can endure."

Her words held something unspoken. I stood, feeling a tumult of emotions churning inside me. I understood her caution, the protective shroud she wove over truths perhaps too daunting for me to grasp now. Yet her guarded message only strengthened my determination, a pledge forming to unearth the secrets hidden in whispered tones and sidelong glances.

I knew she did not wish to speak of the matter further, so I only answered, "I was unaware it was a Welsh word," trying to mask my growing concerns, even as a firm intent took hold.

Leaving the kitchen, I sought solace, my feet guiding me almost instinctively through the timber-framed passageways of our home. The rough-hewn wattle walls, interlaced with daub, framed my path with a subtle aroma of clay and straw, reminiscent of the earth after a gentle rain. Simple, coarse woven hangings, more functional than decorative, lined the way. Their roughness mirrored the humble character of our home, blending with the persistent scent of damp soil and fresh thatch. Each step upon the cool, uneven stone echoed the faint ache of my solitude.

Finally, I reached my father's chamber, a haven where the smell of ancient texts and the subtle whisper of turning sheets always wrapped me in a blanket of serenity. Within these walls, Sir Ector had gathered his cherished collection of manuscripts and parchment scrolls. Each piece was meticulously crafted from vellum, embellished with shimmering illustrations using gold leaf and touches of silver. It was here that my sense of wonder was kindled from my earliest memories. Through tales of valorous battles and legendary heroes, I painstakingly taught myself to decipher the cryptic writings. By the age of seven, I had delved into most of them, each narrative opening a doorway to realms far beyond these walls.

Yet, as I sat among the manuscripts, my fingers tracing over the intricate illuminations, I found my mind clouded by what I had overheard in the stable. *Why did these people speak of kingship and royalty in tones laced with secrecy?* This question persisted, refusing to fade. Despite my efforts to immerse myself in the heroic sagas before me, a continuous feeling of restlessness endured, the presence of uncertainty and misgivings subtly encroaching upon my awareness.

A deeper unrest tugged at my spirit. *Do I, a mere squire, possess the fearlessness and courage that these manuscripts speak of?* The idea of stepping into such grand, heroic roles seemed daunting, an immense challenge that I was unsure I could meet.

While the sheets of history and legend turned before me, the rhythm of life outside the chamber beckoned, offering a respite from my heavy reflections. The cooler breeze carried a subtle feeling of change, as the end of summer's reign was heralded by the celebration of Lammas. During these festivities, I watched the farmhands cut the first sheaves of grain, their rhythmic swish and thud mingling with their familiar chatter. When the chaff was crushed on a small circular quern, the sweet scent of wheat clung to my hair and garments, covering the surroundings with the dust of harvest. The following day, the enticing smell of freshly baked bread filled the small kitchen. My stomach grumbled in anticipation of the eve's meal, envisioning the loaves served with churned butter.

The skies wore a canvas of greys, each hue weaving into the next as the celebration of Lammas came to its end. The rich aromas of the feast lingered, fading slowly, as the busy days of harvest gave way to a longing for solitude. I withdrew from the laughter and chatter, seeking the stillness of my father's chamber.

Seated on the floor, my back against the wall, I lost myself in a tale of ancient Greek deities. Deep in thought, I barely noticed Merlin's arrival, his crystal-tipped staff clicking against the floor. His fingertips were stained green and purple from working with herbs and berries. I smiled warmly, welcoming the interruption and his visit.

"Arthur, are you finding the story you are reading of interest?"

At his question, I set the manuscript aside.

"Yes, I am, Merlin, for it is about Greek gods."

"Ah, the gods of Olympus. A fascinating subject indeed."

We engaged in an engrossing discussion about the intricate tales of the gods' lives and entanglements. While we talked, I was struck by the breadth of Merlin's knowledge. It seemed to span far beyond the myths of ancient Greece, touching on mysteries and lore from distant lands. His captivating stories and insightful observations left me eagerly absorbing every word. Our exchanges soon became a cherished retreat from daily duties, nurturing the tie between mentor and student.

Our dialogue tapered off, and a comfortable stillness settled between us. I wished we could linger a little longer.

"Merlin, can you remain for a while?"

"But, of course, my boy. Would you like to explore the hidden world of the forest?"

"Hidden world? Yes!"

"Well then," he said, a smile playing at the edges of his lips, "shall we begin our adventure?"

He guided me through the kitchen, where the faint scent of bread and herbs hinted at the day's tasks, and out into the woods near the stables. We walked along a winding path, the subtle whispers of the forest surrounding us.

Gesturing for us to pause before a bush adorned with clusters of purple-black berries, he pointed to the green plant, its oblong, serrated leaves framing the dark berries.

"Arthur, do you see this?"

"It is a berry bush."

"Yes, but not just any. This is an elderberry, *Sambucus nigra.* These ripe berries will be perfect for making syrup, beneficial during the damp, winter's chill. Remember, never eat them uncooked, for they can be harmful."

With a long-handled knife pulled from a sheath at his waist, he expertly cut several branches, entrusting them to my care. We continued deeper into the woods until we reached a small glade. With a sweep of his staff, he conjured a fire, setting a large black pot above it.

"Arthur, shall we begin?"

I worked with him as we carefully plucked the berries from the branches, adding them to the pot, their light fall creating a delicate melody. The berries simmered quietly while he spoke of mastering the art of inner vision.

"Consider the boundless potential you possess, Arthur. It is not just about the destination, but the journey of thought and intent."

Intrigued, I could not help but ask, "I wish to learn this, to understand."

"Many people used to believe in the potency of visions, beyond the five senses," he continued. "But as the world shifts, sadly, many have lost this belief. Those who embrace this skill and work towards harnessing their visions can find great satisfaction and happiness."

Driven to be counted among those believers, I pressed, "Teach me how to achieve this."

He leaned in closer, the space around us seeming to converge around his figure.

"Very well, are you ready?"

"Yes, I am."

"Imagine riding your chestnut mare, Madwen. Feel the wind, her movements beneath you. At your journey's end, praise her, and wait for her response."

I inhaled deeply and closed my eyes, immersing myself in the vision of riding Madwen through the fields. The wind played in my hair, and her strong, rhythmic strides carried us effortlessly forward. Reaching the end of the pasture, I leaned over and whispered, "Madwen, such a fine run," and patted her neck lightly.

To my surprise, I heard her message: *Arthur, ease the reins just a little, and we will really run!*

I laughed as I opened my eyes. Merlin stood before me, watching with a knowing smile.

"So, Arthur, how was the ride?"

"Amazing!"

"Excellent! This skill will serve you well as your duties expand."

I wondered what duties lay ahead of me that would require this skill, the thought stirring both curiosity and misgiving. Before I could ask him more about it, he said, "But now, let us tend to the elderberries."

We carefully moved the pot off the fire and set it on flat stones to cool, its sweet fragrance wafting around us.

Standing beside me, Merlin glanced at the simmering pot and then at the surrounding forest. "How about a walk while the syrup sets?"

The sunlight danced through the leaves as we strolled towards a clear stream. A sudden stir from the underbrush drew my eye, and with a cautious gesture, Merlin signaled for silence and vigilance. A white deer, majestic and almost ethereal, yet marred by the cruel arrow jutting from her side, appeared in the open space, her steps hesitant and strained.

His expression tightened with concern. "We must help her."

We advanced towards the deer, her distress evident in her labored breathing and wary stance. Yet as we drew near with arms extended, a fragile thread of trust began to form. With the skill of a masterful sage, Merlin carefully dislodged the arrow, while I attended to the wound, applying a salve of curative herbs from a pouch he handed me. We watched as the wound began to mend, his expert touch calming the creature with light strokes to her head. Her trembling eased, and after a few moments, the deer tested her limbs. She regained her strength and sprang away, her movements fluid once more, a fitting testament to her endurance and our care.

Merlin's hand rested on my shoulder, steady and reassuring. "You did more than well, Arthur. We are all connected, man and beast."

I looked towards the trees where she had ventured. Witnessing her recovery from pained to liberated, her vigour restored, had lifted my spirits. Merlin's next words pulled me from my reverie.

"Now, tell me, can you spot any Pixies near?"

I scanned the surroundings, then pointed across the stream. "Yes! There, look!"

"Indeed," he said, his eyes crinkling into a smile. "They always seem pleased when you are near; perhaps they sense your kinship with their world."

"Why can I see them, and Kay only when he is with me?"

"Arthur, your gifts are rare and precious. You were born with the true sight of the Pixies, a bond solely yours. Kay, tied by his loyalty, shares this vision only in your company."

As I pondered his words, I reflected on the differences that wove our lives together, each thread distinct and tied by purpose. Wandering through the woods together, the forest's whispers were welcoming, and the earth beneath us felt firm and true.

"Being here with you feels as if it is where I am meant to be," I confessed.

"I know this all too well. These woods hold many wonders. Now, let us follow the stream and see where it leads us."

We ambled along the water's edge, the murmur of the stream guiding our steps as it twisted through thickets and over stones, each turn revealing a new aspect of the woodland's beauty.

Upon returning to the clearing, we found the elderberry syrup had been strained and poured into clay jars, with leather lids resting beside each one.

Merlin gave a quiet laugh. "How kind of the Pixies to assist us."

Carefully, he removed several quartz crystals from a small bag tied to his waist. Their translucent surfaces sparkled in the midday light as he laid them beside the containers.

"The Pixies cherish these stones," he shared.

He began humming a tune I had often heard sung on the farm, though his melody carried subtle differences that made it feel strangely foreign. Securing the leather tops over the containers, he packed them away in the bag slung over his back. With a point of his staff at the pot and fire pit, they vanished in a flash of light and a puff of burnt wood.

"It is time, Arthur. Let us head home."

Our return journey took us along a narrower path, winding through the forest's secrets. Light breezes moved through the canopy, allowing brief glimmers of light to sprinkle across our path, revealing plants that held their own tales of healing.

Merlin halted by a patch of vibrant green leaves. "Foxglove stands tall, yet it is as delicate as a sigh. Its petals, you see, weave strength into fragile heartstrings, holding firm against the frailty of faltering rhythms."

He then took a few measured steps to where Self-heal thrived, a humble guardian of the land. "This unassuming herb soothes the persistent aches of life's toil with a tenderness as enduring as the passage of time itself."

Moving onward, he approached the towering Mullein. Its velvety leaves brushed against our hands as he began to explain its protective qualities.

"This herb acts as a guardian of the chest, a shield against the encroaching threat of ailments seeking refuge in the breath meant for life."

The trees seemed to lean in, eager to embrace the knowledge he imparted, as if nature itself was attentive to his every word.

"I offer you these gifts from the forest," he said, gesturing to the verdant bounty around us, "to aid you when in need."

"I am thankful, Merlin, for all you have revealed."

With a knowing smile, he led the way as we resumed our walk. His teachings echoed in my mind, reflecting his deep tie with the natural world.

Upon arriving back at the farm, the setting sun washed the fields in mellow light, while the scent of freshly turned earth clung to the land. At the door, he set down three jars of elderberry syrup.

"For Sir Ector, Lady Kate, you, and Kay. For myself, one will suffice," he said with a wink.

"Discovering the hidden world of the forest like you promised has made this an amazing day. Many thanks for the elderberry syrup as well."

Watching him disappear through the back door, I realized I did not want the day to end. I hurried to see where he had gone, but found only the lingering trace of him, a faint shimmer that vanished as quickly as it appeared, leaving me with a profound emptiness as dusk settled around me.

I looked towards the stables, which only deepened my feelings of isolation. The coarse, ominous whispers of the men there echoed in my mind. "The Saxons have been asking questions about you, lad," they had said in hushed, urgent tones, "and they are willing to pay a king's ransom for your whereabouts." A subtle tremor coursed through my hands, not from the eve's chill but from their remarks, sparking a trace of fear and caution.

With the sun dipping lower over the farm, their behavior, now fixed in my memory, continue to unsettle me. The day's revelations, the mystical wonders of the forest, and these warnings about the Saxons intertwined, each a thread in the intricate tapestry of my life. Together, they painted a pattern both wondrous and shadowed, hinting at a destiny far greater and more perilous than I could have imagined.

CHAPTER 3

IN SEARCH OF ORIGINS

Over the years, Merlin's visits became deeply rooted in the rhythms of my life, yet whispers among the farmhands persisted. My disquiet deepened when I overheard a conversation that left its mark. Karie, our long-serving farmhand, her hair threaded with white strands, spoke in hushed tones to Ina, a younger girl recently come to work on the farm. While they were hanging the wash, Karie's bearing was firm and urgent, her hands moving with brisk purpose. Ina stood motionless, her wide eyes betraying a mix of confusion and fear as she clung to every word.

"You have to listen to me, child! Arthur is not related by blood to Sir Ector or Lady Kate."

A strange stillness settled over me. *Could it be true? That I was not their son?* The revelation echoed, distant yet deafening, unsettling something deep within. My body moved without will, and I stumbled backward, upsetting a basket of garments. The noise startled Karie, and she spun around.

"Well, good morrow, young sir. Are you headed to the stables, then?" she stammered.

I nodded, unable to speak, and hastened on, my thoughts a tempest of confusion. *Had everything I believed about my life been a lie?*

I found Sean tending to Madwen.

"Sean, can I talk to you?"

"Of course, lad. What is on your mind?"

I faltered briefly, then blurted out the question that had been troubling me. "I overheard Karie and Ina talking. They said I might not be kin to my own father and mother. Could there be any merit to what they said?"

He took a deep breath and exhaled slowly.

"Arthur, I have watched you grow from a wee lad to a young man, and it is my duty to protect you, to keep you from harm. I understand your concern, but let me tell you this: gossip often bears little substance, and it is important to consider the source of any tale before acting upon it. You have been raised as Sir Ector's and Lady Kate's son, and they have loved you as their own."

"Often," I countered. "You say gossip often bears little substance, but what if there is some weight to the whispers that persist here at the farm?"

Sean shook his head. "I do not know. Sometimes, uncovering what lies beneath is no easy undertaking. It may be wiser to leave it be."

"That is not an answer. I need to know, am I truly Sir Ector's and Lady Kate's son?"

"I cannot say for certain. But you are a remarkable young man. Your true parentage matters less than the person you are and the deeds you do."

"It matters to me. More than anything. I need to know who I am and where I come from. Why can you not understand?"

He laid a hand on my shoulder. "I do understand. Remember, what you seek may not come easily. Be cautious in your search."

I shrugged off his hand. "I will be cautious, but I will not stop until I find out the truth."

Sean gave me a small smile. "I know. You are a stubborn one, Arthur. But that is what makes you who you are." He handed me a brush. "Now, help me groom Madwen."

I took it from him, grateful for a task to calm my unrest.

While I worked the bristles through Madwen's coat, the lanterns cast a warm, golden light across the stable. Fresh hay mingled with the musky sweetness of horse and leather, calming my restless thoughts. The shuffling of hooves and the rhythmic sweep of the brush through her mane lulled me into ease. Just as I began to lose myself in the scents and sounds I had long known, Merlin appeared at the door.

"Arthur, I must speak with Sir Ector and would have you come with me."

Sean gave a small nod. "Go on, lad. I will see to Madwen."

Driven by a growing curiosity, I quickened my pace alongside him towards the main house, the damp grass yielding beneath my feet. Sir Ector was already waiting, and without exchanging words, they disappeared into his chamber.

Left alone, I paced, the hushed tap of my boots against the stone floor blending with the silence, each step punctuating the uncertainty that gripped me. Ears attuned to the slightest sound, I strained to catch any hint of the conversation behind the closed door. The stillness pressed around me, broken only by occasional murmurs that seeped through the walls, their meanings obscured in the muffled echoes.

Restlessness grew within me as my mind teemed with uneasy thoughts. *What urgent news could he have brought that demanded such secrecy? What was transpiring behind that door?*

At last, Merlin emerged, the light wrapped around him, softening the hard lines of his unreadable expression. He tapped his staff with a commanding thud.

"Arthur, join us. There are pressing concerns to discuss with Sir Ector."

I followed him, looking about this chamber I knew so well. Against the far wall stood a long oak table, flanked by towering shelves filled with manuscripts and scrolls. A large hearth dominated one corner, still warm from the fire that had burned earlier. On the opposite wall, a wide window offered a view over the rolling hills of the farm. Sir Ector sat behind his desk, his forehead glistening with sweat. Merlin, with his back to the archway, stood facing me with a look of grave seriousness.

"Sir Ector and I have spoken," Merlin began, "and the stars have aligned in such a manner that we must now share with you a matter we are honour bound to reveal."

Focusing between them, I held my breath as the distant storm rumbled closer, its sound a warning carried on the wind.

Sir Ector methodically drew his fingers together in a steeple. It was a sign I recognized, one that meant his next words would be weighed with care and consideration. After a deliberate pause, he spoke, his eyes never leaving mine.

"Arthur, your mother, Lady Kate, and I are not your birth mother and father. When you were an infant, Merlin brought you to us with a request that we care for you. Grateful for his trust, we could not, would not, refuse."

The news hit me like a physical blow. I stepped back, grappling with what I had heard. *This could not be true.* I had grown up with Sir Ector, Lady Kate and Kay, had loved and respected them as my clan. And now, it felt as if the very ground beneath me had begun to shift.

"Is Kay not my blood brother?" My question was laced with an underlying fear of the answer.

Sir Ector slowly shook his head. "No, he is not."

Anger and betrayal churned, each emotion sharpening the other.

"Merlin, does Kay know this?"

"Kay is unaware of your birth's truth. But know that the bond you share makes him your brother in all but blood."

Compelled by a surge of emotions, I stepped forward, torn between them as the burden of knowing pressed in on all sides. The turmoil swirling inside me brought a throbbing to my temple. I rubbed it instinctively, seeking relief from the flood of thoughts and truths now.

"So, the whispers that have haunted me… do they speak true?" The toll of years of secrets kept and doubts left unanswered pressed heavily upon me. "Am I a royal bastard?" My voice rose with the force of my demand. "Who are my birth father and mother?"

My father looked at me with a steadfastness as unyielding as the ancient oaks that had long stood around our farmhouse, witnessing the endless cycle of moons and the sun. His eyes, once warm with kindness and understanding, now held a flatness, a barrier against the torrent of all I sought to know.

"Idle tongues are oft the crafters of tales woven from the strands of baseless speculation. What you seek lies beyond our knowing."

His fingers tightened briefly around the back of his chair, betraying the storm that swelled beneath his measured calm.

My frustration, a lurking beast, roared to life, threatening to shatter my fragile composure. I did not move, every muscle taut, my heart pounding like a war drum. Unanswered questions battered at my resolve.

I looked at Merlin, the man who had been both my mentor and guide through the mists of life's uncertainties.

My fists clenched at my sides. "Do you hold the key? Do you know?"

His features tightened with momentary indecision. Then, calmly and deliberately, he turned away, focusing on the landscape beyond our farmhouse.

Despair descended upon me as I heard his words: "In the fullness of time, Arthur, in the fullness of time."

I spoke his name, each utterance a plea for answers. Yet he remained still, like a pillar rooted in the earth itself, his silence only intensifying my unrest.

"Merlin, I implore you. I must know the truth."

He faced me. "Your lineage bears great consequence. It is not to be revealed without the gravest deliberation."

I erupted, anger flaring like a sudden blaze, a clash with Merlin I had never imagined. "You speak in riddles and veil the truth I seek! Who are my birth father and mother!"

"Your birthright is not what defines you. It is your deeds, your character, that forge your true identity."

His words, meant to soothe, only added to my frustration. "Such words may well suit you. You have always known your origin, your place in this world. I am left with nothing but emptiness."

"You are not without kin. Sir Ector, Lady Kate, Kay, and even I, we are your clan."

Yet my yearning for more, for the elusive pieces of my past, persisted. "But I need to know. I need to understand my origins, who I am."

There was a trace of something more in his bearing, a guarded sorrow that made me believe he might reveal what I longed to uncover. But with a subtle sigh, he looked away, drawn to something beyond my reach. Left alone with my lingering uncertainties, the mysteries remained shrouded, and the clarity I sought stayed just beyond grasp.

Confusion, sadness, and anger consumed me as the enormity of what I had just learned bore down on me. I turned to Sir Ector, silently willing him to speak what I so needed to hear. The urge to confront Merlin, to demand the whole story of my lineage, clashed with the deep gratitude I felt towards Sir

Ector and Lady Kate for their unselfish care. I recognized the need to pause and untangle the threads of what I had just learned.

My father approached and draped his arm around my shoulders in a comforting embrace.

"Arthur, you are our son. You will have the same education and opportunities as Kay. This farm is your home, and you belong here."

His words, sincere and firm, called for a response.

"I am grateful to be here, to be part of this clan," I said, the sentiment genuine but shadowed by inner discord.

As I grappled with my feelings, more questions slipped out.

"What does this all mean? Did my birth father and mother not want me?"

"We cannot know their motives. What we do know is that accepting Merlin's request to raise you has never been a decision we regretted. You are as dear to us as our own kin, and that will never change. In the tapestry of life every thread has its purpose, though its color may not be ours to choose. Your thread was woven into ours by a hand guided by fate."

The longing to know my birth father and mother, coupled with the resentment towards Merlin for withholding the truth, coiled inside me, making it hard to catch my breath. Emotions surged, my cheeks warming with the force of my unrest.

Sir Ector said my name softly.

"Arthur…."

Overcome with emotion, tears blurring my vision, I turned and walked away. Lost in a tangle of reflections, I found my way back to the stables, where my day had begun.

Madwen nickered as I approached, and while I absentmindedly stroked her mane, memories returned: the warmth of Lady Kate's hand soothing a scrape, Sir Ector's approving nod after a hard day's work, Kay's laughter resounding in the fields.

I traced the grain of the wooden stall as I pondered our intertwined history. *Had Sir Ector always sensed the mystery of my lineage, shaping his lessons with profound truths?* Lady Kate's tender smiles, once my solace, now seemed tinged with unvoiced sacrifices. *And Kay, had our rivalry been shaded by an unseen truth, our kinship more intricate than mere brotherly squabbles?*

Enclosed by the soft rustle of hay and the measured breath of the horses, I sought release from my churning emotions. I pressed my face into Madwen's neck, drawing in the scent of earth and beast. This place, once a refuge of rhythms I knew by heart, now felt changed, altered by all I had come to know.

With Madwen beside me, the bond we shared offered reassurance. Grateful for the simple truth of her presence, I patted her neck, a wave of conviction rising within me. I began to understand that these events marked the reshaping of who I was, drawing together the fragmented threads of my story into something that honoured the past without being bound by it. In the serenity of that hour, I swore to myself to unearth the answers, not just for me, but for all those whose lives were intertwined with mine, seen and unseen.

That resolve stayed with me, even as the days that followed left me adrift and unfocused. The kindness of Sir Ector, Lady Kate's gentle words, Kay's teasing, and Merlin's cryptic advice provided scant comfort, mere whispers against the vast emptiness that surrounded me. Still yearning for answers and understanding, I felt that pressing for more would only deepen the sadness. Beyond it all, I battled the unknowns of where I came from.

The ache of those trying days began to ease, and the simple, enduring comforts of farm life beckoned me once more. The support from my father and mother, their every act and word, reminded me of the deep bonds of our clan. Sir Ector's guidance, ever a beacon in our home, brought a calm rhythm to our nightly gatherings and filled our days with learning and discovery.

On one such tranquil eve, the scent of my mother's venison stew and fresh bread greeted us as we sat at the table. The large tureen, brimming with the savory dish, took its place at the center. Smiling, my mother motioned us closer. We handed her our bowls, watching as she ladled the hearty meal with care. Once she filled the last one, she sat with us, and a feeling of comfort enveloped the room, drawing us into the gentle grace of her care.

My father cleared his throat, a deliberate, familiar gesture that always signified a transition from daily routines to shared introspection. With measured sincerity, he began to speak, his manner mirroring the quiet strength that held us together. Amidst the turmoil of secrets and discoveries that surrounded us, his guiding presence was a reassuring force.

"Kay, Arthur," he began, "what truly defines a man's worth is how he treats his fellow man, and that is with honour and respect. Your actions and intentions must always be just."

I held my spoon above the steaming bowl as Kay and I replied in unison, "Yes, Father."

From the seeds of dignity and regard Sir Ector planted in Kay and me, the Code of Chivalry would one day bloom, embodying the values of integrity, honesty, valour, and loyalty. These principles would later guide my leadership and shape the destiny of a kingdom.

Such insights were but one aspect of the thorough education Sir Ector provided, ensuring that Kay and I were as schooled in scholarly arts as in the principles of nobility and courage. Our days were rich tapestries of learning and skill, ranging from the subtleties of literature to the complex strategies of war. Under the tutelage of Braunwin and other fine educators, our wisdom and prowess were refined, preparing us to face the world with discernment and bravery.

One clear day, as sunlight streamed through the windows, I found myself captivated by the lyrical flow of Kay's voice. He read aloud lines from Aneirin's poem, his rhythm capturing the pulse of ancient battles and noble quests:

The leader of war with eagerness conducts the battle,

A mighty country loves mighty reapers.

Blood is a heavy return for new mead.

His cheeks are covered with armour all around,

There is a trampling of accoutrements − accoutrements are trampled.

He calls for death and brings desolation.

In the first onset his lances penetrate the targets,

And for light on the course, shrubs blaze on the spears.

Braunwin's probing question, "What do you think the poet is trying to express here?" invited deeper thought.

Kay replied with insight that belied his years. "It speaks of the destiny that awaits those who possess the courage to lead others into battle." His interpretation was thoughtful and hinted at the level of wisdom Sir Ector sought to instill in us.

Braunwin nodded slowly, his eyes reflecting both pride and a hint of gravity. "An insightful interpretation, Kay," he said, his voice measured. "But remember, destiny bears burdens as well as triumphs. Courage is never without its cost."

The poem, while speaking of battles and valour, roused a deep unease. A portent seemed to unfold before me, as if something unseen shifted with the promise of war and rule. I struggled to remain in the present, but my thoughts wandered, irresistibly drawn to what might be.

When the midday waned and our studies concluded, the allure of the woods beckoned. The dense forest, a tangle of green and brown, was our realm of adventure, a place where myths lived and breathed through the whispers of leaves and the murmur of streams.

"I shall be the first to spot our dragons on this day!" Kay shouted over his shoulder, playful and daring, as he moved away. His mischievous grin promised wonders as we delved deeper into the woods.

After running through the trees, we slowed in a secluded glade and settled on the grass beside a winding stream. It seemed the right moment to share the secret entrusted to me.

"Kay," I began, "not long ago, Merlin and Father spoke with me. They told me I am not kin by blood. Merlin brought me to our farm as an infant and bid our mother and father to care for me."

Kay's reaction was clearly marked on his features, his surprise appearing in the rise of his brows and the abrupt halt of his movements. He leaned forward, his bearing a mingling of inquisitiveness and worry, hoping that by drawing nearer, he might unravel the mystery of my discovery.

"What do you mean?"

I answered slowly, each word measured and deliberate. "You and I are not brothers by blood."

Everything around us seemed to pause, and one could feel the anticipation. His response, when it finally emerged, was not of blood or birth, but of an enduring kinship forged through mutual experiences and cherished memories.

"Arthur, I do not care who your birth father and mother were or where you came from. You have always been my brother, and nothing will ever change that."

A profound relief spread through me, dissolving my doubts. I met Kay's eyes and nodded, a smile breaking free. "You have my deepest gratitude, Kay. You are, and always will be, my brother."

We lingered beside the stream, its unbroken flow offering a kind of assent, while the earth beneath us felt firm, seeming to bear witness to the kinship that had long held between us. The echoes of blood and lineage faded, overshadowed by the strength of our bond, as unyielding as the ancient trees around us. Embraced by the forest's tranquility, we walked back to the farm, and no more was said of the matter.

CHAPTER 4

BETWEEN BOUGH AND BLADE

I began to turn my thoughts from the complexities of heritage to the possibilities that lay ahead. Though I longed to know who my true father and mother were, I sensed that Merlin would not yet share more, and so, for a time, I let the longing sleep. There was a kind of peace in turning towards what lay before me rather than what remained hidden behind.

Though part of me bristled with unanswered questions, I could not hold on to anger for long—not with Merlin. Despite the ache his silence caused, he held a place in my heart that even disappointment could not dislodge.

The unbreakable tie with Kay now merged with a budding curiosity about the wider world, a world Merlin promised to unveil. Though his visits came less frequently than I wished, each arrival sparked waves of excitement, opening a portal to knowledge and adventures beyond the familiar bounds of home.

I was eleven years of age when, one day at the break of dawn, the first light cast a glow through the windows and a knock sparked a rush of joy. I leaped from my bed, my feet barely touching the floor as I hastened into the hall. There, framed by the threshold, stood Merlin, his long cloak catching the breeze. Sir Ector and Lady Kate greeted him with warm, respectful nods, their expressions reflecting reverence and affection. Kay, ever the skeptic, rolled his eyes but could not hide the faintest trace of a smile as Merlin playfully tousled his hair.

With a twinkle in his eyes, he looked at me. "Are you ready for another adventure, Arthur?"

My spirits soared at the possibility. "Yes, Merlin! Where are we going this day?"

"To a forest unseen, to paths untrodden," he declared, hinting at mysteries to be unveiled.

We made our way to the stable. With our horses made ready, Madwen for me and Frey, a large grey gelding, for Merlin, we set out, riding south across the changing land. The landscape shifted the farther we travelled from the farm. The sweet scent of blooming heather and wildflowers enveloped our senses, their vibrant colors dancing in the breeze. The rustling of leaves and twigs beneath the horses' hooves joined the chorus of nature.

While we rode, Merlin spoke of his deep concern for Britain and its people. "Arthur, the land mourns," he began. "Many years ago, the Roman government withdrew its protection, leaving our realm exposed and vulnerable. In the wake of their departure, attacks from other provinces began, warriors seeking to claim what was not rightfully theirs."

"Did they leave without warning? How could they abandon us so easily?"

"Indeed, they did. Their retreat was swift, and it left a void. The Saxons, who once served as mercenaries in the Roman army in Britain, knew our terrain well. They began their invasions slowly, methodically, but with each harvest, they pressed farther into our lands. The scars left by the Romans' decision to withdraw continue to haunt us to this day.

"They believed their empire's strength was eternal and when it faltered, they chose themselves over those they once ruled. They left chaos in their wake, plunging villages into strife and leaving defenseless communities to fend off invaders alone. It was a betrayal driven by fear and arrogance.

"Men, women, and children suffer under the Saxons' relentless conquest. They ravage our fields, seizing what they desire, trailing pain and desolation in their path. Witnessing such aggression and the torment it inflicts upon the innocent is difficult to accept."

Hearing of the suffering Merlin described, I found my thoughts returning to the men in the stables. Their whispers and furtive glances came back to me with sharper clarity. I recalled their desperate pleas, cornering me with words of the Saxons offering a fortune for my capture. Their actions, driven by fear and need, now seemed less a betrayal and more a reflection of the tumult gripping our land.

A chill coursed through me as the rhythmic beat of the horses' hooves kept me rooted in the present. Merlin's words settled within me, heavy with doubt and lacking resolution. Their echoes of past betrayals and the shadowed days ahead gave rise to a low, persistent unrest.

"But what drives the Saxons to such relentless conquest of our lands?"

"They are *Saesneg*, foreign invaders drawn to our shores by a hunger for power and riches. They are unyielding. But fear not for our endurance lies beyond the clash of swords and shields."

"What might do we hold against such formidable foes?"

"The nature spirits, my boy." His tone was imbued with a solemn reverence. "They are the guardians of this land, wielding powers that intertwine with every tree and stream. Through their blessing, we shall find the fortitude and insight to protect what we hold dear."

"But how do we reach them?"

"We must learn to listen," he instructed, his eyes surveying the forest around us. "Only by stilling our minds and opening our hearts can we hear them. In that openness, the spirits will reveal themselves."

The idea of sensing nature spirits was both fascinating and uncertain. *How would it feel to truly commune with the unseen guardians of this land? Could their elusive power really turn the tide against the Saxons?*

"And what of the Saxons?'

"We will find a way to drive them from our land. It is through this bond with the ancient guardians that we may gain the wisdom and guidance needed to overcome any challenge, and perhaps even divine the omens that lie ahead."

He led us off the dirt road and onto a narrow path that wove through the trees. Venturing deeper, the leafy boughs enveloped us, creating a serene shelter of greenery, while shafts of light cast shifting shadows upon the forest floor.

Upon approaching a clearing, he motioned for us to halt. "We shall leave the horses here to graze and go on foot to a sight to behold."

I kept strides with him as he directed us onto a small path. We walked in near silence, the only sounds the rustling of leaves underfoot and the distant murmur of a hidden stream. Merlin moved with purpose, his confident steps leading the way until the trees suddenly parted, revealing a sunlit glade. I stood, momentarily breathless, at the sight before us.

A waterfall cascaded down from a rocky ledge, its waters shimmering with hues of blue and green as they collected in a small pool at its base. The magic of this place infused my senses, stirring wonder and possibility. Our earlier conversation about the Saxons, laden with concerns and uncertainties, stood in stark contrast against this vibrant and serene natural backdrop, revealing the very hope we carried for the land and those sworn to protect it. For a moment I felt the land speaking, not in words, but in a deep-rooted strength that awakened something within me.

Merlin placed his hand on my shoulder. "This is where we will begin," he said. "Here, you will learn how to sense the nature spirits."

We sat on a stone bench that overlooked the pond, and he guided me. "Arthur, relax your breathing and fix your sight on the water. Clear your mind, and if you are found worthy, the elementals will share visions with you."

My awareness was drawn to the surface of the water, my breathing slowing as I felt myself rising, leaving my body behind. From above, the water began to swirl in a circular motion, gradually increasing in speed until it stilled, revealing a vision of a young man and woman strolling through a sun-dappled forest. They embraced and kissed before continuing on. They conversed and laughed while walking, the woman's hand nestled in the man's. I recognized the young man as an unmistakably older and more mature version of myself. The woman was a stranger, yet there was something familiar about her that captivated me.

The image faded, and I floated back to my body. I blinked, trying to bring the world back into view. Merlin stood in front of me, peering towards the pond with a look of concern evident in his stance.

"What did you see?"

I eagerly recounted my vision, describing the forest, the couple, and the mysterious woman. His brow furrowed as he listened intently.

"The nature spirits have gifted you with a vision of your future," he said at last. "This woman will be woven into your fate."

I felt excitement at the possibilities, but a twinge of fear crept in as well. *What if I fail to become the man I am meant to be?*

He observed the way I held myself, unmoving, my hand firm on the edge of the stone bench.

"Fear not, Arthur," he said calmly. "The future is not set in stone. It is up to us to shape our own destiny."

I steadied myself, eager for what lay ahead. "What is next?"

A playful smile danced on his lips as he beckoned me to follow him further into the woods. "Now, we explore the wonders nature presents to us."

As we walked, Merlin pointed out the various plants, detailing their uses in magic spells, healing, and cooking. His excitement was unmistakable when he spotted a cluster of oval green leaves peeking out from the base of a tree. Kneeling down with reverence, he carefully unearthed the plant, revealing its long, thick root.

"This is mandrake." He held it up for me to see, its twisted roots knotted and ancient in appearance. "It possesses immense magical potency that can be harnessed for good or ill. While those who practice the dark arts use this root to cast harmful spells on others, I align with the forces of light and will use it to protect against evil."

I stepped back, studying the unusual plant. Its gnarled form sent a shiver of foreboding through me. "You are so excited to have found mandrake," I said nervously, "yet it fills me with dread."

He gave a low laugh, his eyes twinkling with a mix of mirth and wisdom. "And rightly so, my boy. The balance of good and evil exists in many facets of life, not just in our dealings with enchanted flora. Listen to your inner voice, and you will learn to discern which force prevails, whether it is a person's intentions, a plant's powers, or even the hidden currents of a seemingly tranquil stream."

With the mandrake now securely stored in a bag at his waist, Merlin continued to lead us through the forest. Our path eventually opened onto a serene glade embraced by towering trees. The forest floor was strewn with fallen branches, and the woodland's hush carried the presence of spirits long tied to this sacred place.

"This looks like a good spot for our midday meal," he said, raising his staff.

A blanket unfurled on the ground, laden with a feast of cold meats, freshly baked bread, cheese, and cups brimming with cool water.

"Come, let us rest and share this fare," he invited, motioning for me to sit beside him on the sprawling roots of a nearby tree.

The bread was crusty and warm; the cold hare and cheese the best I had tasted. As I took a drink of the water, I looked at Merlin.

"Your magic never ceases to amaze me. This food is delicious. Many thanks."

"It pleases me to share it."

He motioned for us to stand and raising his staff once again, the blanket and the remnants of our meal vanished in a flash of light, leaving no trace upon the forest floor.

Following him down yet another winding path through the trees, we soon reached our horses. I watched in surprise as a majestic black crow descended gracefully from the sky, landing delicately on his outstretched arm. The bird studied us, its sleek feathers shimmering in sunlight, creating a mesmerizing play of light and shadow. With a series of shrill chirps and fluttering wings, the bird appeared to relay a message, while Merlin listened attentively.

He gave a nod and said, "You have my thanks, my friend."

The crow took flight, soaring back into the endless blue expanse above.

I followed its path until it disappeared. "Merlin, did the crow bring a message?"

"Indeed, it did, my boy."

"Is it common for animals to speak with you?"

"On occasion. Over many years, I have learned their languages, and this skill has been invaluable."

"Your ability to commune with creatures is truly remarkable," I said. "It must offer a way of seeing the world that few can know."

"It is more than mere exchange; it becomes a shared understanding. We are all intertwined in the tapestry of this world. By listening attentively, we can glean insights not only from our fellow creatures but from the rhythms of nature itself."

"What news did the crow convey?"

"One of my apprentices is struggling with his studies and has come to tears by the challenge. Though it poses no threat to his life, he requires my guidance. I shall attend to him on the morrow."

"It must also be a great comfort for those under your care to know they can rely on your wisdom in their times of need."

"My task is to guide and instruct my apprentices, to impart as much wisdom and skill as I can. That is my duty and my destiny."

He paused to admire the sky, where the first hints of twilight softened the edges of the day. "And now, with the day's lessons completed, let us make our way back to Sir Ector's."

We mounted our steeds and set off, leaving the forest behind as we made our way towards the road that would lead us back to Sir Ector's farm.

The steady rhythm of the horses' hooves against the road lulled me into deep thought. The day's events unfolded again before me, especially the feeling of being totally free as I drifted above the pond. The memory ignited a spark of wonder and eagerness.

"Merlin," I began tentatively, "do you think we could try that again? Connecting with the nature spirits?"

His eyebrow arched upward. "Yes, we can certainly delve deeper into that. It is a skill that will serve you well."

"You have my deepest gratitude."

A subtle smile touched his lips as we let the topic fade and continued our journey. A cool breeze from the west carried the scent of damp earth. In the distance, the haunting call of an owl echoed through the trees, weaving its melody into our surroundings. These natural smells and sounds were constant reminders of the bond I yearned to deepen.

His voice drew me back to the present as we approached the stables. "In the coming days, Arthur, I will arrange for skilled warriors to train you and Kay. Grasp all they have to offer."

Visions of the legendary Greek warriors I had read about came to mind.

"I promise to learn all I can."

After dismounting and handing the reins to the stable hands, I walked with Merlin to the edge of the woods. The fading light of dusk softened the world around us, casting the trees in hues of amber and gold.

"Merlin, the day has given me much to ponder."

He placed a hand on my shoulder. "And that is how one grows. Be safe, my boy, until we see each other again."

Purposeful and deliberate, he stepped into the woods, his figure merging with the gathering shadows until only the faint rustle of leaves marked his departure.

As Merlin had shared, training began within a fortnight. Tegyn guided us in archery, his precision unmatched as he demonstrated how to release an arrow with effortless grace. Bledri, with a weathered face that spoke of countless campaigns, taught us the art of spear throwing, his movements a blend of power and skill. Grunu was a towering figure who led our sword training with fierce precision. The clang of iron rang out under his watchful gaze, each strike echoing across the practice field.

After the turning of two moons, one morn when the sky hung low with the promise of rain, Grunu paced before us, his imposing frame moving with deliberate intent. The dim light softened his form, lending an almost spectral quality to his movements. Suddenly, he stopped and pointed his sword directly at me.

"Your sword is an extension of you!" he bellowed.

His blade cut through the air as he charged. Iron struck iron, sparks dancing in the shadowed light. Every clash, parry, and thrust pushed my endurance to its limits.

"In battle, it is your life or your foe's," he shouted. "Hesitate, and my blade will find your heart."

Teeth clenched, I countered his moves with raw, surging force. The impact of our swords built swiftly, culminating in a tempest of wills. A deft twist of my wrist, a strategic sidestep, and Grunu's sword flew from his grasp, landing with a dull thud against the hardened soil. I advanced without hesitation, my boot striking his chest. He stumbled and fell, the point of my sword now held above his throat.

Kay, halting his own practice, stood with his mouth agape, his sword lowered as he took in the scene.

Grunu's eyes met mine, piercing yet approving. "Well done, Arthur. You have mastered not just your blade but the will to overcome."

I lowered my sword. Extending my hand, I offered not just aid but respect, recognizing the bond forged through this trial. Grunu grasped it firmly, rising with the dignity of a teacher honouring his pupil's growth.

"Now," he proclaimed, "you have moved beyond the mere swing of a blade. True mastery lies in the harmony between will and spirit. The shaping of a warrior begins with this test of valour and insight."

Our days followed a steady rhythm of instruction, grueling practice honing our skills in sword, spear, and bow. The once-pungent odors of sweat and leather became familiar, reminders of the toil and discipline that shaped our hours. The creak of chainmail marked each step forward, a measure of our hard-won progress.

With each new dawn, a deeper resilience was carved into our spirits. Every lesson tested both our intent and our resolve, forging us into more than just fighters. We were not merely training to become Britain's finest fighters; we were evolving, tempering our inner strength with the understanding gained from each arduous day.

Exhausted yet invigorated after a particularly demanding training in spear-throwing with Bledri, I approached Merlin, who often observed our training.

"Arthur, you are developing the fortitude of will and insight that true leadership demands, transcending mere physical skill."

I looked at him, sensing that his words carried more than praise; they were a call to recognize that fortitude and a keen understanding are as vital as skill with a blade. Standing beside him, watching Kay hit his target with the bow under Tegyn's instructions, I became more attuned to the layers of mystery surrounding him. His ties to unseen realms, his guidance of kings past, and the wisdom he quietly bore hinted at a life deeply intertwined with the land. I glimpsed the outlines of a story yet to be fully told, a burden he carried with profound reserve.

His inner sorrow foretold a storm poised to test the very foundation of our existence. Traces of his past and whispers of our fated roles, once faint, now stirred with growing urgency.

I stood transfixed, my grasp shallow compared to the vastness of Merlin's tribulations and the crucial role destined for me in our intertwined narrative. Our journey surpassed the boundaries of student and sage, becoming an intricate dance with fate, a plunge into a legacy merging our paths in unseen ways.

CHAPTER 5

MERLONIUS

My eyes drift open, and confusion clouds my senses. The image of the Saxon I encountered in mortal combat comes rushing back, as sharp as if the entire battle were playing out before me. He stands there, still sneering and taunting. Strands of hair form a curtain over his face, and dried blood specks cling to his unkempt beard.

"You, the great King Arthur, are weak and cannot defeat me," he spat, his contempt clear in every word.

I struggle to sit up, but my body refuses. It feels as if it is made of iron. The stench of blood and sweat surrounds me, as the field rings with the clash of swords, wounded cries, and the thunder of hooves. Bedwyr approaches, and I wonder if he is but a shadow conjured by my wearied mind. Then, his strong hand reaches down, and I seize it. He pulls me to my feet, and together, we make our way to the edge of the chaos.

Leaning against him, I feel the cold bite of chainmail against my arm, an unexpected chill that momentarily distracts me from the pain. He guides me to the ground, my back resting against the rough trunk of a large oak tree.

"Bedwyr, you returned."

"Yes, Arthur. As I reached the edge of the woods, I saw the Saxon advancing on you. I did not think I could reach you in time, but I did. I ended his life before he took yours."

He kneels beside me. "Take this sword should you need it," he says, placing a fallen knight's blade into my hand. He looks at Excalibur, reflecting on the solemn duty entrusted to him. "I go now, as you have requested, to return Excalibur to the Lady of the Lake."

"May the gods go with you."

Duty marked in every line of his bearing, he rises and mounts his steed. He pauses, his eyes betraying the inner struggle he endures.

"Go, Bedwyr, for this must be done."

With a solemn nod, he spurs his horse forward. I watch him ride away, his horse kicking up dust and dirt as it disappears into the distance.

The battlefield stretches before me, a grim expanse where brave knights lie scattered across the terrain. Blood seeps into the soil, and battered armour litters the dull green grass, standing out against the grey of the overcast sky. A faint breeze stirs, carrying distant clashes. A pall of despair hangs over the field, thick as a gathering storm.

This gloom threatens to engulf me, pressing in from every side, driving me to seek solace in a sanctuary untouched by the scars of conflict.

A memory surfaces of Merlonius, the woman whose dazzling smile kindled a flame in me, the subtle scent of trees in her hair. Oh, how love sparkled in her eyes whenever she looked at me.

The thought of our first meeting breathes warmth back into me, a glimmer of light against the ruin. It lingers in my mind with the shimmer of a dream, a moment I hold close amid the unraveling of all I have known.

One bright morn, when the joy of youth still clung to me, Merlin and I embarked on a journey to the edge of a forest, mounted on Madwen and Frey.

"On this day, we visit the woods I call home, Arthur."

"Merlin, I am honoured."

A small smile tugged at the corners of his mouth, though he said no more.

With no words exchanged between us for a time, we slowed and came to a halt.

He turned in his saddle to face me. "I live here, in this forest, with one of my young apprentices. Her name is Merlonius."

I nodded, curiosity sparking at this glimpse into his life, and together we entered the woods. Following him, we made our way down a winding dirt path softened by fallen leaves beneath towering trees. Light broke through the leaves in pale streaks, gilding roots and stone in shifting patterns.

We arrived at a clearing where a wooden fence surrounded a small paddock. After dismounting, we tended to our horses, offering them fresh water and nourishing hay. Their snorts and rhythmic munching assured us of their contentment.

Within the paddock, I noticed two other horses grazing—a sturdy bay gelding with a shaggy mane and a delicate chestnut mare, moving with such grace I paused to watch her.

Merlin noted my interest, a hint of playfulness in his tone. "Those belong to Merlonius and myself. Care to guess which one is hers?"

I studied the two animals carefully before answering. "The chestnut mare?" I ventured, noting her gentleness and poise.

He let out a rare laugh. "You are correct. Tuft, the shaggy bay, is mine. Sweetness and Merlonius share a special bond."

I smiled, drawn more deeply into this hidden part of his life. Even in such small details, the affection between master and apprentice revealed itself.

Leaving the paddock behind, we approached a charming cottage nestled among the trees. Its stone walls, inviting wooden door, and thatched roof reminded me of the simple homes of the countryside. The sight of it filled me with wonder, as if I had crossed into a realm drawn from tales of old. Multiple windows, open to welcome the breeze and light, adorned its front and sides, each framed by thick wooden shutters that could be closed against the night's chill.

Merlin called out, "Merlonius, where are you? We have a visitor!"

A young girl, about my height, emerged from the side of the cottage. Her fair hair, nearly silvery in the sunlight, was piled atop her head, while the rest flowed gracefully down her back. Her face was smudged with dirt, snd I noticed her striking eyes, the color of young leaves. The yellow specks in them seem to catch the light, giving her a curious and almost enchanting appearance.

"Welcome home, Merlin."

"Merlonius," he gestured towards me, "this is Arthur, another of my apprentices. I brought him here to introduce you both, and I have seen that you will become great friends." A hint of humor touched his tone as he added, "I also notice the dirt on your right cheek, which tells me you have been busy tending our garden."

She brushed the smudge of dirt off her cheek and regarded me with interest.

"Greetings, Merlonius."

Her cheeks blushed pink as she replied, "It is nice to meet you, Arthur."

"Why do you not show him our garden?" Merlin suggested before heading inside.

With a light gesture, she beckoned me to follow. "Come, it is this way," she said, leading us around the side of the cottage.

We followed the path around, and a vibrant garden came into view. Vegetables stood in perfect rows, each plant rising from a small mound of rich, dark soil, as if tenderly shaped by careful hands.

"We are growing cabbage in this row," she said pointing to her left, "and chard in the next. Over there," she gestured to the far side of the garden, "are several blueberry bushes, and at the other end, we have a small herb garden."

I teased her playfully, "Are you sure you have planted enough?"

She smiled, retorting, "Well, we have only planted ten rows. Perhaps we should consider a few more?"

Our laughter echoed as we walked along the garden's edge. The neat rows of vegetables flourished, their lush foliage evidence of her care. The herb garden formed a perfectly marked square plot, each plant thriving in its carefully allotted space.

"Could you share with me what you have planted and which ones are your favourites?"

Her enthusiasm radiated as she replied. "We planted cabbage in the first row and chard in the second. Their leaves shimmer in the light. In the third row, we have lovage, known for its fragrant leaves. The fourth row is split, parsnips on one side, still growing their roots, and radishes on the other. They give our garden some extra flavor as they are a bit spicy."

She paused, a thoughtful expression crossing her face. "If I had to choose, it would be the lovage for its fragrance and the radishes for their bold taste."

With her choices shared, we continued strolling along the garden's width, and she described each remaining plant in detail.

"To the left, onions and turnips share a row, followed by beetroot, purple carrots, and alexanders. The last two rows with stakes are for peas and broad beans."

I laughed, "Thank the gods! Perhaps you should take a breath!"

She giggled as we made our way to the opposite side, where the herb garden flourished.

"This plot holds both healing and cooking herbs."

"Which ones are intended for healing?"

"Feverfew for fevers and peppermint for digestion are here," she explained, gesturing to the closest row.

Moving to the side of the herb garden, she continued describing the middle patch of plants.

"This is lavender, a plant I especially love. Its fragrance and the many ways it can be used, both in cooking and for soothing stomach upsets. In this last group, we have boneset, an herb that supports healing for injuries to bones and cuts on the skin."

"Your knowledge is remarkable."

"Merlin's guidance has revealed so many things to me, including how to make a delicious pottage," she said. "We use parsnips, radishes, carrots, turnips, and alexanders, with barley as our special ingredient."

Inexplicably drawn to her, I rested my hand on her arm, feeling a sudden surge of closeness between us.

"I would very much like to try your pottage."

The radiance of her smile left me oddly pleased, as if my wish to understand her skill at the hearth had quietly impressed her.

"Are there any vegetables from our garden that you would like to try, Arthur?"

"Peas, parsnips and turnips. Merlin used to take me foraging in the forest and taught me how to cook them into a stew. They quickly became the ones I enjoyed most."

"Ah, so you will be a great help when we prepare the pottage," she said, raising an eyebrow playfully. "We shall see if your skill matches your claim."

I answered with a grin, "I welcome the task."

She led me towards the opposite side of the garden, where the fragrance of fresh herbs became more pronounced, mingling with the earthy aroma of damp soil.

I marveled at the care she had given each plant, the attention evident in the way they grew under her touch. Merlin's trust in her was well-founded; each one blooming under her steady hand.

We continued to walk side by side until we stood once more at the place where our steps had first set out. Merlonius shifted her weight from one foot to the other, her gaze lowered as if choosing her words with care.

"Will you walk with me to the stream? It lies just beyond the front of the cottage. Its sound reaches us even here."

"Aye, I would like to see it."

"Let us go then."

As we made our way, I heard the sound of flowing water. When we reached the stream, I was struck by the beauty before me. A wide, shimmering ribbon wound through the vibrant green landscape, its surface catching the light as it flowed. The banks were lined with wildflowers and lush grasses that brushed against my feet as I removed my shoes and sat beside her.

She dipped her feet into the cool water and let out a contented sigh. "This is one of my favorite spots. I come here whenever I need to think."

"It is peaceful and I can see why you hold it dear."

"Where do you live, Arthur?"

"I reside with Sir Ector on his farm a few hours' journey north."

She studied the flowing water, her expression thoughtful, as if seeking answers within its ripples. The rustle of leaves and the murmur of the stream filled the space between us. Finally, she looked at me, her brow slightly furrowed, her eyes distant, as though something unspoken had stirred within her.

"So you, too, are not with your birth clan?"

"Merlin entrusted me to the care of Sir Ector and his wife, Lady Kate, when I was but an infant. I have no knowledge of my birth father or mother," I added, concealing the sorrow that I held close.

"I often find myself wondering about my own father and mother," she said softly. "It pains me that they could not accept my differences, that they chose to send me away. Has this path been difficult for you, Arthur?"

I sensed her raw emotion, the ache of rejection mirrored in her words. Pausing, I looked towards the flowing stream before replying,

"For years, I did not know that Sir Ector and Lady Kate were not my blood kin. The truth was revealed to me only a few years ago. I often wonder who my birth father and mother were, and why they chose to let me go. That is why the thought of having a clan of my own carries such import."

Merlonius drew a measured breath. "It must weigh heavily on you, not knowing your kin. Perhaps the gods have their reasons for keeping such truths hidden. Merlin says that things often happen as they must, not when we wish, but in ways that become clear with time."

Her words settled over me, stirring both uncertainty and a fragile hope. I met her gaze, then looked out across the water, reflecting on what she had said.

We turned at the sound of cloth rustling and saw Merlin approaching.

"Would you like something to eat?"

Merlonius smiled warmly. "Merlin, some food would be most welcome. My stomach has been grumbling for some time."

"Then let us return to the cottage, where a meal awaits."

We slipped on our shoes and followed him. The scent of baking bread greeted us, rich and inviting.

A rectangular wooden table, positioned along the right wall, was flanked by benches on either side. Merlonius chose a seat facing the hearth, and I settled beside her. Across from us, Merlin arranged portions of cheese, bread, berries, and a pitcher of fresh water with practiced care.

"Well, Arthur, what did Merlonius show you of our home?"

"Your vegetable and herb plots are impressively spacious. I particularly enjoyed sitting by the stream; the sound of the water was quite soothing."

"The stream has a way of bringing calm and healing to the spirit. When Merlonius and I first started planting, the rows were much smaller. Over time, we added more."

Merlonius's eyes held a mischievous glean. "Arthur has offered to help me with cooking pottage."

I grinned. "My offer stands. Merlin has taught me a thing or two about cooking, and exploring your garden has given me ideas to make it even better."

She nudged my arm lightly. "Then I look forward to seeing what you can do."

Merlin cleared his throat. "We shall see soon enough, shall we not?"

"Most certainly, Merlin."

We continued our meal, an easiness flowing about us. As the last berry was eaten, I glanced at my bag, recalling what I had brought.

"Merlonius, would you like to see the manuscripts I have with me?"

"Yes, I would love to. Merlin has been teaching me how to read and write, and in doing so, I am learning so much of the world beyond this forest."

"The waterfall is a peaceful spot for reading," Merlin suggested. "Why not take Arthur there?"

We stepped outside, and she took my hand, leading us towards a path that wound further into the woods. The earth was soft beneath our feet, damp with recent rains, and each step released the scent of pine and earth. Overhead, the leaves rustled, speaking in hushed tones to the sway of the trees. The trail soon opened onto a small waterfall, with a pool of clear water surrounded by encircling trees. Several stone benches stood to the left of the pond, inviting us to sit and enjoy the peaceful sounds of the flowing water.

She gestured with a sweep of her left hand. "Do you like what you see? It is where I often feel the presence of nature spirits."

Her words startled me; no one other than Merlin had ever spoken of communing with the nature spirits. Taking in my surroundings, memories surfaced from three years prior when he had brought me here and taught me how to attune myself to their presence. I kept this memory to myself, allowing her the excitement of showing me this place.

"Very much so. I can sense the spirits here. How fortunate you are to have this as part of your home."

"Yes, I am. Come, let us sit on a bench," she said, leading the way.

We settled onto a cool stone bench, its surface smooth beneath us. I removed the manuscripts from my bag and laid them between us.

"This one delves into warfare and a topic I prefer studying over this other one, which focuses on mathematics."

With a little amusement, she replied, "I would have guessed that, but why is that so."

"It is not the fighting in itself," I explained, "but rather the planning and the course of action involved in defeating an opponent."

For several hours, we pored over the manuscripts, our conversation weaving between strategy and various principles. Merlonius challenged my thoughts on battle formations, proposing alternative maneuvers with surprising insight. When we began discussing mathematics, her keen questions and playful teasing about my disinterest revealed both her intelligence and sharp wit. I quickly realized she possessed not only a depth of knowledge but a humor that made even complex topics enjoyable.

As the sun dipped lower, its fading light stretching shadows across the rippling water, Merlin joined us.

"Well, Arthur, what do you think of the pond?"

The water's surface reflected the warm hues of twilight. Turning back to Merlin, I said, "I think it may soon be one of my favorite places."

"Yes, Merlonius and I have always considered this a special place. Is that not so, Merlonius?"

"I cannot imagine living anywhere far from here. I told Arthur that the nature spirits often visit this pond."

They shared a knowing look before he lowered his eyes to the water, as if drawn to something beyond the veil. Merlonius and I sat quietly, attuned to the gravity of the moment, drawn into the depth of his reflection. When at last he faced us again, a faint softness had returned to his eyes.

"I think it is best if we head back now and enjoy this eve's meal. I can only guess you are both hungry."

In unison, we replied, "Very hungry!"

Following him back to the cottage, we were greeted by the enticing aroma of food simmering in a large pot over the fire.

"The food smells delicious," Merlonius remarked as we stepped inside.

"I agree entirely," I added.

We placed the bowls and cups on the table, the rich scent of stew curling around us. The tureen overflowed with turnips, broad beans, leeks, and purple carrots, all simmered to perfection. Each spoonful burst with flavor, blending earthy textures with the richness of slow-cooked harvest. The meal seemed almost magical, filling me with a comfort that warmed not just my body, but my spirit.

After savoring the final morsel in my bowl, I leaned back with a satisfied sigh, a rare sense of peace settling over me. With the meal concluded, Merlin's tales wove around us. He spoke of the Fae, of magical creatures like dragons and unicorns, and of the epic struggles between heroes and villains fighting for good and evil. His words conjured scenes so clear and wondrous, the very air seemed to shimmer with enchantment. I clung to every word, marveling at each twist and turn of his stories. Gradually, as night deepened, his storytelling waned, like the slow fading of embers in the hearth.

"The eve has given way to the need for rest. Arthur, there is a comfortable bed awaiting you. Merlonius will show you to your sleeping quarters."

She began clearing the table, and I picked up the plates and cups to carry them to the bench to the right of the hearth. Once everything was placed down, Merlin reached for his staff and pointed it towards them. With a brilliant burst of blue light, everything sparkled and gleamed as if made anew.

"Practical magic is wondrous, would you not agree?" he said with a chuckle.

Merlonius let out a delighted laugh. "I must admit, I enjoy the times your magic makes the day easier."

I had witnessed his magic before, when we spent time in the forest, but there was something captivating about seeing it at work within these walls and in Merlonius's company.

"Come, Arthur, our beds are this way."

I walked by her side, the warmth of the hearth lingering as we ventured to the quieter side of the cottage. It was far more expansive within than its humble exterior suggested, shifting at Merlin's will, expanding and contracting to suit its inhabitants' needs. Tables, chairs, and beds appeared and disappeared seamlessly, adapting as needed.

We entered the sleeping area, a distinct and surprisingly spacious space. To our right, a heavy woven curtain hung across the back wall.

"This is the dressing area, where we can change our garments with privacy," she explained, pushing aside the cloth to reveal an ample space with a wooden bench against the far wall.

She gestured to the beds, wooden frames adorned with soft blankets and pillows. "One is mine, and the other is yours. Would you prefer the one next to the outside wall?"

"Yes, I would. It will lessen the chance of falling out of bed."

She laughed, the sound light and unguarded.

"Merlonius, I am not tired." The marvels of Merlin's world and meeting her had sparked too much wonder for sleep. "Would you care to join me for a walk by the stream?"

"Yes, a stroll sounds like a very good idea."

We returned to the main part of the cottage, a calm settling between us. Walking beside her, I found comfort in the rhythm of our steps.

Merlin sat by the hearth, and as we approached, he looked up, a faint smile playing on his lips.

"Taking the air this eve?"

"Yes, Merlin, Arthur suggested we walk by the stream, and I agreed it would be lovely."

"May the night bring you peace."

We stepped outside, the crispness embracing us as we made our way to the stream. Above, the starry sky stretched endlessly, a canvas of shimmering lights. Lying back on the grass, we pointed out constellations and shapes in the heavens, our voices hushed in awe of the vast expanse. For a moment, the worries of the world dissolved into the infinite night.

"Look there—do you see?" My pulse quickened with a boyish thrill as I traced an imaginary line between the stars, their silvery light shimmering against the dark canvas of the sky.

"A dragon, there, with its wings spread wide."

"And there, a unicorn," she added, her finger guiding mine to a cluster of stars. Together, they formed a delicate silhouette.

We laughed together, the sound mingling with the rustle of leaves and the gurgle of water. The conversation soon shifted to mythical companions.

"A unicorn would bring serenity," she mused, "while a dragon might stand as an unyielding guardian."

I pondered her words, a faint smile touching my lips. The idea of such creatures among us evoked both wonder and yearning.

"Serenity and protection," I said thoughtfully, my gaze lifted once more to the stars. "There is strength in both."

We let the tapestry of the heavens captivate us, the constellations revealing shapes that had endured through the ages. I felt a deep peace in her presence, and as I glanced at her, the starlight illuminated her features, stirring something deep within me. I wished we could stay here forever, nestled beneath the stars.

Her words carried on the eve's breeze, guiding me back from the stillness of the stars.

"This was wonderful, Arthur, but we should return to the cottage."

Disappointment tugged at me as I answered with some reluctance, "As you wish."

We found Merlin still seated by the fire when we stepped inside.

"Good rest, Merlin," Merlonius offered.

"Sleep well, my dear."

I settled into a chair across from him, unwilling for the visit to end.

"I have truly enjoyed my stay here, Merlin. Is there any way we might linger a bit longer?"

His eyes softened, as if sensing my attachment to this place. "Yes, one more day. But then we must return you back to Sir Ector's for your studies."

My attention was held by the hearth, the leaping flames painting shapes across the walls. As memories of my time here surfaced, I longed to remain in this cottage, with Merlin and Merlonius.

But instead of sharing my desires with him, I simply said, "You have my gratitude."

With a slight nod, he returned to his own musings as he looked deep within the heart of the fire. After a time, I rose from my chair.

"Rest well, Merlin."

"May you find peaceful slumber, Arthur."

I wearily made my way to the narrow bed pressed against the cold stone wall, removed my shoes, and slid beneath the blanket. The magic of this day stayed with me as I drifted into slumber, the vibrant memory of Merlonius's laughter, the serene beauty of the waterfall, and the wisdom in Merlin's eyes all weaving together into a comforting tapestry of thoughts. These moments played in my mind, filling me with awe for this mystical place where I felt at home.

But rest did not last. From the depths of slumber, Addaf's voice tore through the calm, piercing the fragile veil of sleep: "I am telling ye, the one they call Arthur must be a bastard *brenhinol*, a royal bastard, I say!"

I ran to Merlin. "What does this mean?"

He stood motionless, his expression shadowed with something he did not voice. The silence between us carried the answer I feared, and my confusion and fear swelled.

The dream continued and I was back at the stable, surrounded by playful Pixies. Suddenly, as I stood by the stable door, Addaf emerged from the shadows, brandishing a pitchfork.

"Ye do not understand, Arthur. Thy true father was a king, and ye have a rightful claim to his throne."

I tried to run, but he appeared in front of me once again. Sneering, he said, "The Saxons will pay a king's ransom for ye."

Desperate for guidance, I called out to Merlin, my plea lingering in the stable, but once more, he offered no reply. Instead, he faded into the mist, leaving me alone and exposed.

With a sudden jolt, the scene shifted once more, and I found myself atop a magnificent black stallion, sword in hand. Three dragons soared above me, their scales glistening in the sun. I recognized Merlin's own dragon, Tân Wen, and my dragon, Proserpina, but the third dragon was a majestic creature with scales glinting like molten bronze.

We charged into battle, my breath quickening and my palms dampening on the hilt of my sword. The enemy closed in, their shouts and clashing swords heightening the fight. I parried and thrust, each movement initially hesitant. Yet, with every successful defence and attack, a surge of vigour replaced my initial trepidation, as if the very act of fighting awakened a dormant power. Suddenly, I heard Merlin break through the chaos.

"Arthur, wake up. You are having a bad dream."

I gasped, my body drenched in cold sweat. "It is the same nightmare I have had for some time now with Addaf, but different. I am in a battle fighting and there are three dragons flying overhead. I recognized Tân Wen and Proserpina, but not the other," I took in a breath to collect myself. "What does it mean?"

"Dreams are often a reflection of our innermost fears and desires," he replied. "The dragons represent the allies who will stand by you when you need them most. And as for the identity of the third dragon, that remains to be revealed."

The dream's grip held me, its remnants clinging to my thoughts.

"Is there more you can tell me of the dream?"

He did not answer and I sensed a concealed truth beneath his composure. A reassuring smile followed as he reached out to help me to my feet.

"It is a fresh day, Arthur, let us begin anew."

The sweet sound of birdsong drifted in through the open window. I glanced towards Merlonius's empty bed.

"She is out in the garden," he said, anticipating my question. "Why do you not join her while I prepare some food?"

To my surprise, I found a basin of clean water waiting for me on a small table, no doubt conjured by Merlin's magic. After washing and donning my shoes, I stepped outside, where I found Merlonius on her knees, happily pulling weeds.

"Merlonius, good morrow," I called to her.

Hearing me, she looked up and smiled. "Greetings, sleepy head, and a good morrow to you as well."

I offered my hand, helping her to her feet. Both our hands now bore smudges of earth, and we laughed.

"Is it not a beautiful day, Arthur?"

"Yes, it certainly is."

We strolled towards the front of the cottage, the sun warming our skin as a breeze moved through the leaves overhead. After washing our hands in a bucket of water near the front door, we entered and found the table set with fresh fruit, soft cheese, honey, and water. Sitting in the same places as the night before, we shared the meal in companionable silence. The fruit was juicy and sweet, the cheese soft and tangy, and the honey richly flavorful.

Once we had finished, Merlin leaned forward, a glimmer of excitement in his eyes.

"Would you like to see my crystal cave?"

Merlonius's eyes sparkled, and she nearly bounced in place. "Really, Merlin? Yes, yes, yes!"

A small smile played upon his lips. "And you, Arthur?"

"Your crystal cave? Yes, very much so!"

He reached for his staff and strode towards the door, his readiness clear.

"Then let us be off!" he announced, beckoning us to follow.

Leaping up from the table, we quickly joined him on the winding path that led to his crystal cave. The forest floor yielded beneath our feet, and sunlight dappled through the trees, weaving a tapestry of light and shade. Wildflower scents swirled around us, while towering ancient trunks formed a majestic arch overhead with their gnarled branches.

The forest teemed with life: leaves rustled in a harmonious chorus, birdsong floated through the branches, and woodland creatures added their playful chatter.

In this enchanting setting, the disquiet from the persistent nightmare began to loosen its grip, though it still clung to me. The dream, a relentless specter, haunted my nights with unyielding force. The third dragon remained a mystery, one that left me wary.

Yet the forest's beauty worked its magic, easing the remains of dread. And as we ventured deeper into its embrace, I could only hope that the power within Merlin's crystal cave might dispel the shadow cast by those troubling dreams.

CHAPTER 6

THE CRYSTAL CAVE

"Welcome to my crystal cave, young ones." Merlin's voice echoed through the stone chamber as we approached the threshold of a vast chasm that had opened suddenly in the side of a tall mountain. The darkness beyond obscured our vision, allowing us to see only a few feet ahead. Pebbles and loose rock crunched beneath our feet, forming a grey carpet that led into the unknown. Despite the shadows, we strode forward, undaunted, drawn by a force we could not name, compelled to explore the cave's hidden depths. Torches mounted along the walls guided our way, their flickering flames casting restless silhouettes that danced at our feet and revealed the dusty stone in rhythmic bursts.

In the center of the cavern, Merlonius and I moved slowly in a circle, marveling at how the shadows swayed along the stone walls like spirits woven from light, while we breathed in the faint scent of earth and minerals. Merlin stood at the back of the cave, his staff raised, the crystal at its tip filling with a swirling mist. In a brilliant flash of light, an opening appeared above our heads, allowing a beam of sunlight to stream in.

"Merlin, what are these towering rocks on the right?" I pointed to the unique structures.

"Ah, Arthur," he said, walking over, "that is quartz."

The glittering structures sparkled in the torchlight, their translucent milky appearance and unique shapes mesmerizing.

"They are stunning,"

"Yes, they are remarkable. Clear quartz is a powerful crystal, with a restorative and enhancing force. This stone helps with healing the body."

My curiosity grew. "Have you actually healed anyone with this stone?"

He nodded, "Frequently."

"Truly?"

"Yes, my boy. One of the most effective uses involves placing smaller pieces of quartz at the four corners of the altar at The Giants' Dance." He stepped closer to one of the pieces. "By arranging these quartz pieces in this manner, the potency from the large stones forming the circle is enhanced and directed towards those who seek healing."

Though I had never visited that sacred place, his words conjured striking images and heightened my interest in this mysterious power to heal.

Merlonius stepped closer to the stones. "May I touch one of these clear quartz stones?"

"Of course, my dear, please do."

She positioned her hands on each side of a tall crystal nearest us. She stood still as if she was listening to something far away. Her body began to sway back and forth, left to right, and a faint humming noise came from her lips. Merlin moved to her right side, and I stood to her left, my hand half-raised before I caught his cautioning look and held back.

Watching her, I found myself captivated by the quiet power that surrounded her. Suddenly, he leaned in, his brow furrowed, and whispered urgently in her ear.

"Merlonius, it is Merlin. Come back to us."

A subtle shift passed over her as she gradually returned to awareness, her eyes returning to the world around her. She removed her hands from the crystal and lowered her arms, her fingers trembling slightly. Emotion surged within me as her gaze settled on me, and I forced myself to remain still, resisting the urge to reach for her.

"My dear, how do you fare?"

"Merlin, where did I go?"

Her voice trembled, and I found myself holding my breath, unsure if what she needed now was silence or reassurance.

"Describe to us the visions the crystal presented you."

"Bright rainbows stretched across a clear blue sky. Beautiful red and yellow birds, their feathers as vibrant as the petals of wildflowers, sang their sweet melodies." A tremble passed through her as she continued, "I saw dragons soaring gracefully, their shiny scales catching the sunlight, and unicorns peacefully nibbling on lush grass by a crystal-clear stream. It was like stepping into a myth, a place of incredible beauty."

"You became one with the crystal, and it shared memories of what it has seen. Worlds beyond the physical one we walk upon. What a lovely surprise, was it not, my dear?"

Tears glistened and traced a shining path down her cheeks.

"Yes, it was utterly amazing."

I was captivated, searching for words to convey my support.

"Merlonius, your experience was remarkable, unlike anything I have ever witnessed."

"It was beyond anything I could have imagined."

Moved by what had just unfolded with Merlonius, I wondered about the secrets and purpose of scattered stones both in this magical realm and in my own world.

"Merlin, would you speak to us of the other stones and what truths they carry?"

He strolled around the chamber, his hands moving with lively gestures as he began to share his vast knowledge.

"Each crystal here possesses unique mystical qualities. Consider the *Amethyst Veil*," he said, pointing at the lavender-colored crystals scattered among the quartz pieces.

"*Amethyst Veil*, is more than a mere mineral—it offers a path to inner peace. Warriors, in particular, might find solace in wearing a piece, for it shields them from harm and fortifies their resolve."

As Merlin spoke, the air seemed to still around me, and the world began to blur. While he elaborated on the virtues of the *Amethyst Veil* crystals, an unsettling vision began to take shape in my mind. I saw myself charging into battle on horseback, surrounded by the thunder of hooves and the clash of swords. Chaos reigned as lances pierced the air, and the acrid scent of sweat and iron hung thick around me. The cries of the wounded blended with the relentless rhythm of war, each sound echoing through my mind.

A shiver swept over me, the vision so real it seemed I had crossed into another world. I drew a long breath and clenched my fists, struggling to hold to the present. Yet, the images clung to me, leaving behind a faint echo of dread I struggled to shake.

Merlin noticed my discomfort and stepped closer, placing a calming hand on my shoulder. "Visions often reveal glimpses of what may come," he said, his voice low but firm. "Do not let fear guide you, Arthur. The choices you make will shape the path ahead."

His touch eased the turmoil, casting off the fragments of the vision. My pulse slowed, and I exhaled deeply, gratitude stirring within me for his reassuring presence. Curiosity took hold, drawing me back to the shimmering crystals surrounding us.

"Merlin, would you speak more of the other crystals?" My fascination fully captivated by the mesmerizing gems that filled the cavern.

Reaching out, I picked up one of the deep blue crystals. Its smooth, cool surface seemed to quiver faintly beneath my touch, as though it stirred with echoes of ancient knowing. Turning it in my hands, I watched as the torchlight danced along its facets, scattering glimmers of light across the walls.

"The crystal you hold, Arthur, is called *Astraquartz*. Its strong color aids with insight and clarity."

Holding the stone, a serene feeling settled over me, and I found myself lost in its depths.

Merlonius picked up a vibrant green gem that sparkled in the light of the torches, drawing a look of approval from Merlin.

"My dear, you have chosen well," he said. "The gem you hold is known as *Verdelux*. These gems possess the remarkable ability to attract love and abundance."

"I feel a gentle warmth coming from them," she remarked, her expression alight with wonder. "It is as if they cradle me with comfort and care."

"Yes, they generously share their virtues with you."

I placed the *Astraquartz* on the cavern floor, my attention shifting to a fiery red crystal.

"Go ahead, Arthur, pick it up. That crystal is named *Pyrocoral.*"

Holding the red gem in my hand, I felt its fierce warmth, akin to the searing force of a blaze.

"*Pyrocoral* crystals hold the might of flame itself," Merlin continued, his tone earnest. "They symbolize not only vigour but also the unyielding will that burns deep within. They can kindle one's determination and provide strength amidst adversity, much like the courage of a warrior."

Gently, I returned the red crystal to the cavern's floor, its fiery glow fading as it left my grasp.

"Remember, these crystals are tools to help us tap into our own deepest resolve. They are guides on our journey, but ultimately, it is up to us to use them wisely." His words echoed in the cavern, imparting a sense of profound responsibility.

I moved closer to the right side of the cavern, focusing on the sparkling crystals strewn across the ground. The gems glimmered in the torchlight, painting the walls with shifting hues of color.

"Arthur, does any one piece catch your eye?"

After searching, I saw a small gemstone that seemed brighter than the rest.

"That one," I said, pointing to it.

He approached and examined the crystal I had chosen.

"Well, my boy, consider it a gift. Take it. It is a rare piece indeed."

With careful hands, I lifted the gemstone, holding it as though it contained secrets long forgotten. Its surface was smooth and cool against my skin, and the stone itself was round, with three delicate tendrils extending gracefully from its center. Torchlight played over the crystal, causing it to shimmer and cast an otherworldly light on my skin.

"This is truly an amazing gift."

"I am pleased you have found the stone that called to you."

He looked at Merlonius, "Would you also like to choose a crystal?"

"Yes, I would very much like to have one."

She stepped forward, moving to my side and pointing to one on the far left.

"I would like this one, Merlin."

"It too shall be yours, my dear."

She bent down, reaching for the crystal from the cavern floor. Its smooth top gleamed with an enchanting blue hue that seemed to capture the depths of a starless night. Silver threads ran through its center, glistening like stardust trapped within, while its jagged bottom bore marks of its earthly origins.

She tilted her head upward, and our eyes met. In that instant, I felt as if I were floating, pulled from my body and moving towards her. Colors and shapes blurred around me. Each breath felt sharper, each heartbeat quickened, urging me closer to her.

In the distance, I heard Merlin's voice, faint and far away. "I believe we should begin the journey home."

But I was lost in the enchantment, bewitched by what I felt.

"Arthur! Arthur!" his hand gripped my shoulder, pulling me back. The colors and shapes faded, and I blinked in confusion, my senses slowly steadying as I returned to the cavern.

"Who are you?"

"It is I, Merlin. We must return to the cottage. Come," he urged, shaking my arms until I recognized him again.

"Arthur, all is well. You are back with us," Merlonius said softly.

"Merlonius, stay with him."

Merlin raised his hand, and the crystal at the tip of his staff glowed, casting shifting patterns along the cavern walls. With a deliberate motion, he guided the light upward, sealing the cave's opening.

We followed him along the winding path that led back to the surface. As sunlight warmed our faces, Merlin turned and, with a subtle gesture, sealed the opening behind us.

I looked to Merlonius and met her gaze. Her expression was unreadable, yet something had shifted. For in that moment, beneath the breath of the mountain and the glow of ancient stone, a change stirred between us, gentle and sure.

Merlonius walked beside me as we moved through the wood. The forest had fallen still, the scent of pine hanging heavy around us. The joy that had surrounded me began to wane, like waking from a dream and stepping into the cool breath of morn. I blinked, trying to adjust to the forest's dim lighting. Glancing at Merlin, I noticed his lips pressed together tightly.

When we finally reached the cottage, it was as if I had only just returned from some far-off realm. Merlonius delicately placed her crystal on a small table near her bed, and I held my own crystal, fascinated by the faint heat it carried.

"Merlonius, my stone is warm in my hand."

"May I hold it?"

She cradled it in her palms, eyes closed, as though offering a silent prayer, then gently returned it to me.

"Your crystal holds a power of its own. I have entreated the gods and goddesses to weave a bit of my essence into it," she explained.

Merlin approached us, observing Merlonius closely.

"That was kind of you, my dear."

"It was the right thing to do. You have often said that our gifts must be shared."

Holding the crystal, I felt it tremble slightly in my palm, sending a faint shiver through me.

"Many thanks, Merlonius," I murmured, captivated by her kindness.

She smiled warmly. "I am happy to share with you, Arthur."

Merlin gave us a thoughtful look before saying, "Now, who is hungry?"

"We are!" we exclaimed, our voices brimming with enthusiasm.

Walking towards the other side of the cottage, we witnessed more of his magic. Pointing his staff towards the table, meats, bread, and water appeared.

Looking quite pleased with his work, he faced us with a satisfied smile. "Well then, shall we eat?"

The journey to the cave had left us ravenous, and my stomach grumbled with hunger. This meal was indeed magical; the venison was tender, rich, and savory. Each sip of the cool, clear water felt like drinking from a pure mountain stream, refreshing and invigorating. Merlonius and I ate without need for words, content and grateful for what the day had given us.

After we finished eating, Merlin leaned forward, resting his hands on the table. "Well, Arthur, there is still much left of the day. What interests you?"

I glanced at Merlonius, whose features brightened with eager anticipation.

"I would very much like to return to the waterfall," I said. "If Merlonius is interested, of course."

"Go ahead, I will join you later."

We rose from the table, and I held the door open for her, sharing a nod with Merlin as a mark of respect. We stepped outside, the sound of rushing water growing louder with each step. When the waterfall came into view, its cascading waters glistening in the sunlight, I could not help but smile. She chose a spot on a nearby stone bench, and I joined her, feeling the refreshing coolness of the stone against my skin. The breeze ruffled our hair, carrying the mist from the waterfall. It was as if the very elements were aligning to craft a perfect scene.

I had left my manuscripts behind, drawn instead to Merlonius, eager to learn more about her. We sat together, our shoulders lightly touching, and I felt an ease in her presence that drew me closer. There was a softness and welcome in her manner, and as our eyes met, a subtle spark of interest stirred between us.

"Merlonius, how long have you been with Merlin?" My curiosity reflected my desire to uncover more about the intriguing person beside me.

"I was brought to him a little over a year ago."

"That is a story I would be honoured to hear."

Inhaling slowly, her fingers idly traced the surface of the stone bench. "Arthur, I am not like the other people from my village. Merlin has told me I have talents that are special and rare. Those who do not possess these can often feel uneasy around those who do."

"What are your gifts?"

She looked deep into my eyes, then looked away. "I have visions that foretell future events, and when I reveal these to others, they become fearful of me. My village was not accepting of me, and my father and mother no longer wished me in their lives. So they brought me to Merlin and entreated him to become my mentor, and he agreed. I was twelve years of age," she added. "It was a difficult time, but with his guidance, I have found a new home where I can learn more about who I truly am."

Listening to her, I marveled at her valour in enduring such sorrow. With Merlin, she had found a new clan that gave her the place and purpose she had longed for. Here, she was no longer an outcast, but someone valued and understood. I realized with clarity that I wanted to be part of her world, drawn by her resilience, wisdom, and the rare feeling of belonging she brought to those around her.

"The bond you share with Merlin is one to cherish."

"Yes, I know. He imparts his wisdom to me, teaching not only how to read and write but also the ways of plants and the spirits of our land. He sees in me a sorceress, just as he is a wizard."

She waited in silence. I wanted her to know I accepted her fully, as she was, a sorceress with extraordinary gifts.

"Your journey in embracing your gifts is admirable. It takes great courage to be true to yourself."

"It is very kind of you to say so."

"I am truly pleased that Merlin is a part of your life now, as he is in mine."

We sat together on the bench, the waterfall's soothing rhythm blending with the sun's embrace. Though doubts and whispers from the farm lingered in my thoughts, her presence calmed my spirit. Her simple, enduring companionship seemed to mend the frayed edges of my spirit, leaving me more at peace than I had been in some time.

"Arthur, would you like to walk around the pond?"

"Indeed, I would enjoy that greatly."

We strolled along the path on the left, the ducks and birds welcoming us to their haven. The trees towered over us, their branches stretching wide to create a lush canopy overhead. Verdant foliage rustled in the breeze, while bushes of varying sizes hugged the water's edge. At the end of the path, we stood by the waterfall, listening to its roar and feeling the spray on our faces.

We laughed as the playful waterfall drenched our garments before heading back. Reaching the stone benches, we found Merlin awaiting us, his arms folded across his chest.

"Well, well, well, what do we have here? It appears my two friends have been enjoying themselves thoroughly."

Merlonius blushed, and flush crept into my cheeks. I shifted uneasily, torn between embarrassment and contentment.

"We were just walking, " I replied.

"Of course, you were, Arthur," he said with a wry smile. "And in doing so, you managed to soak yourselves! Did you take a wade in the pond? Let us get you both into dry garments."

The sun began to set as we made our way back. Once inside, Merlonius arranged candles on the tables, and with a wave of his arm, Merlin set flame to them.

"In one of our next lessons, I will teach you how to light these candles as I do."

"I look forward to that lesson, Merlin."

The fire crackled and hissed as the wildfowl soup simmered, filling the cottage with its rich aroma. After changing into dry garments, we carried bowls, plates, spoons, and cups to the wooden table.

Merlin placed the steaming tureen of soup in the center of the table and carefully ladled the fragrant broth into our bowls. As we ate, we exchanged stories and laughter, and I realized how much I enjoyed being here with them. A deep desire rose within me. I wanted to return again and again.

When we finished eating, Merlonius smiled warmly at me. "Arthur, would you like to sit by the stream and stargaze with me?"

A thrill of anticipation lit within me as I eagerly replied, "Yes, I would like that."

Merlin's playful smile hinted at amusement. "By all means, go and enjoy yourselves," he said, waving us off.

We sat together by the stream, the stars above us twinkling in the dark sky like scattered silver. The cool earth beneath us was a welcome relief after the warmth of the day. Around us, the rustle of leaves and the flowing water blended into a soft murmur. The night mirrored the peace I found in her presence.

We lifted our eyes to the heavens, studying the shapes woven into the stars.

"Merlonius, look. Do you see the bear?"

"A bear? You must help me, for I do not see it."

I slipped my arm around her shoulder, guiding her hand to follow the shape. She stilled, and then smiled with delight.

"Now I see it! You are right, it is a bear."

Her joy warmed me, easing the emptiness I often felt, leaving behind a tranquility I wished could last forever.

"Arthur, I have enjoyed being with you. I am so happy we met."

"I am grateful that Merlin invited me to visit your home here in the forest," I admitted, hesitating slightly. "Would you like to see each other again?"

Her eyes sparkled with delight. "Of course! We can ask him to bring you back soon."

"That is a wonderful idea. We shall do that."

A strong desire to hold her rose within me, yet the unfamiliarity of these feelings held me still. With reluctance, we returned to find Merlin seated by the fire.

"Did you enjoy the stars?"

"Yes, it was lovely," Merlonius replied. "I bid you peaceful sleep and will see you on the morrow."

"Sleep well, my dear."

I joined him as he tended to the hearth, the scent of woodsmoke mingling with the aroma of simmering herbs in a cauldron on the edge of the fire.

"Merlin, the forest and this cottage have brought me great pleasure. I am grateful for this journey and for introducing me to Merlonius."

"We have enjoyed your visit as well."

He leaned forward to add another log to the fire, sending sparks rising from the hearth.

"I bid you ease this night, Arthur, and will see you on the morrow."

"May you find restful slumber, Merlin."

Making my way to my bed, the lingering heat of the fire clung to my skin, and the faint smoke from the hearth followed me. I had grown fond of this enchanting place and the company of Merlin and Merlonius. I yearned for this visit not to end and was determined to broach the idea of another visit while we journeyed back to the farm on the morrow.

I sat on the edge of my bed and began to remove my shoes, captivated by the forest's magic and my deep feelings for Merlonius. She possessed a fortitude that I found irresistibly alluring. I looked towards her and saw she was awake. She offered me a smile that held both comfort and knowing.

"Arthur," she whispered, "I wanted to wish you a good rest."

"Rest well, Merlonius," I replied as the night embraced us.

Sleep eluded me as my thoughts churned, the memories of my life on the farm mingling with the revelation from my father and Merlin that I was not tied by birth to this clan. I wondered what life might be like if I remained in this cottage, where everything felt touched by magic and contentment.

As the firelight faded and night's silence gathered around the cottage, a longing rose within me, not just to stay, but to belong.

With a deep sigh, the early hours finally claimed me. In my dreams, I wandered through starlit forests, running and laughing with Merlonius, immersed in a happiness that felt endless.

I awoke to the sound of Merlonius calling my name. Blinking against the dim morning light, I looked up to find her sitting on the edge of her bed, already dressed, composed, and steady in her bearing.

"Good morrow, Arthur. Merlin shared that you will be leaving soon. You should wash and join us at the table to break the fast."

I nodded, roused by the thought of seeing them again. Settling at the rough-hewn wooden table, I was greeted with a familiar question.

"Good morrow, my boy. Did you sleep well?"

I lied. "Yes, very well."

While Merlin spoke at length about the day ahead, my mind wandered to Merlonius. I watched her move gracefully about, tending to tasks. There was a determination in her that I found compelling.

Breaking into my musing, Merlin inquired, "Arthur, would you like to plan a return visit soon?"

I glanced at Merlonius, who nodded enthusiastically. "Absolutely. Exploring the forest with you both has been exciting, and I would very much like to continue our adventure."

Her delight was unmistakable. "And your assistance in our garden would be greatly valued. You have likely noticed, it can be rather demanding work."

I joined in her laughter, feeling completely at ease in their company. "I would be pleased to offer my help, and I look forward to returning."

"Well, then let us plan to do just that. Finish your meal while I see to our horses."

After quickly eating some berries and a piece of bread, I grabbed my bag. Merlonius and I met Merlin in the clearing, where he stood waiting with the horses.

"My thanks for attending to our horses," I said.

"Caring for the animals keeps me close to the natural world, so it is my pleasure," he replied with a nod, then turned to Merlonius. "Apply yourself to your studies. I will be back this eve."

"I will, and I will also prepare our night's meal," she assured him.

"Excellent, because I will return hungry."

"Arthur, take care, and I hope to see you again soon."

"Stay safe, Merlonius, and I eagerly look forward to when we meet again."

I mounted my horse and followed Merlin along the forest path. As we rounded a curve in the trail, I glanced back at the clearing. She stood where we had left her, watching us ride away. I raised my hand in farewell, and she did the same. Her figure, alone in the vast forest, lingered in my mind.

"Will Merlonius be safe until you are able to return?"

"Yes. I have cast a spell of protection on the cottage and the surrounding forest. No one will find their way to Merlonius unless I allow it, and no harm will come to her from men or beasts. The forest is enchanted, you see."

I released a breath I had not realized I was holding, a wave of relief washing over me. The thought of leaving Merlonius alone in the forest had been troubling me, but now I felt reassured, knowing she was protected.

We rode without speaking, the memory of the vision at the waterfall from a few years back clinging to my spirit. Unable to contain my burning questions any longer, I began cautiously.

"Merlin, do you remember when you brought me to a waterfall and pond, about three years past?"

His grip on the reins tightened, knuckles turning white, while a deep frown settled on his forehead. A sharp disquiet radiated from him, evident in the brief, sharp turn of his head towards me before he quickly looked away.

"Yes."

His response was short and clipped, the single word spoken as if the answer were forced from him against his will.

"I recognized the pond and the waterfall near the cottage as the same one we visited," I continued. "I had a vision in which I saw an older version of myself strolling with a lady at my side, but on that day, I did not know her. You explained to me that this woman would be a vital part of my life."

"You accurately describe the events as they unfolded," he said simply.

I stopped my horse abruptly, and as he did likewise, I shifted in my saddle. Gathering my courage, I pressed on.

"Was the lady in my vision Merlonius?" My temples throbbed as I awaited his response.

He hesitated before answering. "The lady at your side was Merlonius. The nature spirits gave you a gift that day, Arthur. They showed you what was to come."

I felt bewildered at his words. My skin began to tingle as the image of that day by the pond played out before me. Merlin and I had sat on a stone bench overlooking the water, where he first introduced me to the art of mastering my inner visions. I floated upward, my awareness stretching beyond its usual limits, until I saw myself and Merlonius walking together, holding hands and talking. We stopped, and I kissed her.

"Shall we continue our journey to Sir Ector's farm, Arthur?"

His question brought me back, and I found myself again sitting on Madwen in the middle of the road, with Merlin at my side. The cool forest breezes swirled about me, brushing my skin. I nodded, relieved that we could move forward. I had many questions but knew from his stance that no more would be shared with me at this time.

CHAPTER 7

WOVEN FATES

Nearing Sir Ector's farm, the skies turned a dull grey, warning of an impending storm. Cold seeped into my bones, and I pulled my worn, woolen cloak tighter. The scent of damp earth and forest greenery hung in the air, preparing the land for what was to come. The wind stirred through the branches, its breath mingling with the ancient murmur of the oaks.

At last, we reached the stable where the young men who tended the horses eagerly awaited our return. I dismounted Madwen with a sigh, handing her reins to Bran, who cared for her with the tenderness of one tending his own. He offered her a reassuring pat, while Merlin slipped from Frey's back with his usual grace.

Leaving the stables behind, we turned towards the woods. The wind whipped around us, driven by the brewing tempest, its force rising with each step we took.

I walked beside Merlin, my thoughts clouded by unanswered questions. As the trees loomed nearer, I knew that once he disappeared into their shadowed depths, I would not see him again for some time.

One final plea left my lips before his departure: "I need to know more. About my vision, and about Merlonius. What does it all mean?"

But he did not answer me.

When we came to the threshold of the forest, the branches rose taller and darker, reaching out like gnarled fingers. The distant rumble of thunder rolled through the undergrowth, an ominous growl that caused me to look towards the sky, searching for its source. It was only then that he looked at me, his eyes revealing an unexpected kindness instead of their usual cold detachment.

"The nature spirits showed you that fleeting vision for a reason, Arthur. At that time, Merlonius had not yet entered my life. The truths you seek will come in their time, for we must place our trust in the gods."

"But you have the gift of sight. Can you not speak of it now?"

"I cannot use my gifts to reveal your future. Knowing what lies ahead could disrupt the natural order and alter the course of events. Believe that the path you are on is the right one, and that all you seek will be unveiled in due course." He then added, "Stay safe, my boy, and we will meet again soon."

Before I could say another word, he stepped into the embrace of the forest and vanished, leaving me to stand alone.

I filled my lungs with a slow breath and turned. Walking towards the main house, holding my bag, his counsel stayed with me: *"Believe that the path you are on is the right one…"* I pulled open the kitchen door and stepped inside.

Though embracing his guidance was not easy, his words remained with me, shaping the course of my thoughts in the days that followed.

After my first venture into the enchanted forest and meeting Merlonius, life began to follow its own turning. With every new moon, Merlin arrived at Sir Ector's farm, his presence bringing purpose. Our conversations, like threads spun anew with each visit, became part of the rhythm marked by sun and moon.

As was customary during his visits, Merlin approached Sir Ector. "Arthur will join me in the forest for a few days. I will see to it that he returns well before his studies."

Sir Ector's brow furrowed and he looked towards the woods. "The forest is not without its dangers."

Merlin, untroubled, offered a reassuring nod. "Arthur has grown into a capable young man, Sir Ector. I will keep him safe."

Sir Ector relented, though his concern held fast in the set of his shoulders. "Very well. Just take care."

"I will, Father," I responded, doing my best to mask my excitement behind a tone of duty.

As the moons turned, my eagerness for the forthcoming visits to the enchanted forest became a steady companion. Before Merlin's arrival, I often reflected on past journeys. The call of the forest was ever-present, its scent of moss and towering trees steeped in secrets and solitude.

Amid these treasured recollections, the thought of seeing Merlonius again took hold. Like constellations reappearing in the night sky, scenes from countless eves we spent together gradually returned.

One particular journey stood out in my memory, marking the pinnacle of a year's worth of visits. On that day, Merlin arrived early, exchanging pleasantries with Sir Ector before leading us to the stables. Madwen, my spirited chestnut mare, danced with an eagerness that matched my own. Her glossy coat shimmered in the soft light of morn. Beside her, Frey, the majestic grey gelding prepared for Merlin, stood poised for the adventure, his silver mane flowing like a river of silk. With eagerness we embarked.

Leaving Sir Ector's farm behind, relief washed over me, easing away lingering doubts and questions. I found myself yearning to shed the traces of uncertainty, dreaming instead of a future where Merlonius and I would be the proud owners of a horse farm. With her as my wife, our love would root deep and flourish, becoming the heart of our own clan. With each rhythmic beat of hooves, these journeys offered more than mere adventure. They draped me in serene calm and infused me with the exhilaration of unbridled freedom.

"Merlin, it has been a while since your last visit. I hope you have fared well?"

"Indeed, Arthur. My days have been occupied with teaching the time-honoured arts to those who seek it. But I sense your true curiosity lies with Merlonius."

"Yes, you are right. How is she faring?" I inquired, trying to hide my worry and eagerness.

"She is flourishing. Her command of both healing and magic has grown with each passing moon, making her one of my most promising apprentices. News of her extraordinary talents has spread, drawing more and more villagers to seek her aid during the ceremonies at The Giants' Dance. Her natural compassion for others is a rare gift that cannot be taught."

His account stirred impatience, intensifying my longing for a reunion with her. The days apart had been filled with thoughts of her well-being.

"I am glad to know she is thriving."

Perceiving the depth of my longing, he gave a small nod and shifted the conversation with his usual grace.

"And how are your studies progressing?"

Relieved, I eagerly recounted my progress, answering his questions with growing assurance. He nodded thoughtfully as he listened, his eyes occasionally scanning the road ahead.

Our journey took us closer to the edge of the enchanted forest. My mare instinctively slowed her pace, guiding us on the familiar path she knew so well. Upon reaching the small clearing, we dismounted and led our horses into the paddock, allowing them to settle alongside Merlin's Tuft and Merlonius's Sweetness.

With the horses cared for, we made our way towards the cottage. I longed to return to the familiarity of this place, the one that truly felt like home. Merlin opened the door, the firelight dancing across the folds of his robe. I set my bag down and hung my cloak on the wall rack.

"Merlin and Arthur, welcome!"

Merlonius stood waiting, her smile soft and welcoming. I stepped forward and took her hands in mine. Merlin moved towards the hearth, his steps measured and unhurried. As he had done during past visits, he leaned his staff against the hearthstone, a gesture that marked his return. When he turned back to us, a trace of contentment softened the lines of his face.

"Merlonius," I whispered, "it is good to see you again."

"And seeing you again, Arthur, brings me joy. I have prepared a small meal for us. Please come and sit. There is much to discuss and share."

"A fine time for gathering, indeed," Merlin added.

Approaching the table, I noticed a small clay vessel filled with wood sorrel on the round table near the door. Merlonius noticed my interest and pointed at them.

"The last I visited The Giants' Dance, a father and mother gave me these blossoms as thanks for helping their small son."

"What a lovely gift," I replied, admiring the nodding flowers with delicate white petals and a yellow center.

We took our usual places around the table, with Merlonius to my right and Merlin across from us. The comfort of being with them cast a veil over the concerns that often tethered me to the burdens of my life away from here.

"This fare is tempting," I remarked, looking at the spread before us.

In a nearby bowl, berries offered a burst of color, each one ripe and ready. The familiar scent of bread, fresh from the hearth oven, wafted through the cottage, mixing with the hearty aroma of hare and the subtle tang of cheese. And there, at the table's center, a pitcher of water stood, its cool clarity a welcome sight.

She barely touched her food, her eagerness to converse overshadowing her hunger.

Brushing a lock of hair behind her ear, she said, "Arthur, have your swordsmanship skills continued to flourish? And tell me, have you discovered any captivating manuscripts of late?"

I smiled, touched by her genuine interest. "I have been diligently honing my skills with the sword and the lance, gradually mastering their arts."

She leaned in, as if to catch and keep each word.

"My surprise for you this visit is an old manuscript Sir Ector recently acquired."

"Truly?"

"Yes, indeed!"

"What does it contain?"

"It is a collection of heroic poems. The stories of heroes and gods, with stirring accounts of battles and love."

"May we read it after the midday meal?"

"Of course!"

Merlin's features shifted subtly, interest sparking as I asked, "Is there anything you would like to do while I am here?"

"Well, yes, Arthur. This night, Merlonius and I plan to attend a healing ceremony at The Giants' Dance. Would you care to join us?"

A deep curiosity moved within me as I wondered what witnessing this ancient practice might reveal.

"The healing ceremony at The Giants' Dance? I have heard stories about it, about the wonders and restoration that happen there, but I have never seen it. Yes, I would very much like to join you both."

"Excellent. We will leave before the sun sets. And we also have a surprise for you. Merlonius has learned how to bring forth flame and can now light the candles and fires with her magic. We want to show you during your visit."

Her expression brightened. "I am happy you are here again, Arthur."

"I am glad to be back. It will be a pleasure to hear more of your magical journey."

After we finished eating, we rose to clear the table. As I carried the plates and goblets, I found myself drawn to the familiar surroundings. Much was just as I remembered from my last visit. Clay containers of various sizes occupied the workbench, their earthy scent mingling with the faint, soothing aroma of the dried herbs dangling from the rafters. In a dual-purpose area near the back wall, Merlin and Merlonius would mix potions, salves, and tinctures, as well as prepare meals. I saw that the cottage had expanded since my last visit, now boasting a weaving loom that stood proudly in the far corner.

Merlonius came to stand beside me. "After your last visit, Merlin surprised me with this loom. He showed me how to set up the yarn and has guided my hand in its use. I hope to become adept, weaving cloth that will serve us well."

"This is a remarkable gift. I have no doubt you will soon weave cloth as fine as any in our lands."

"Your belief in my skill means much, Arthur."

We stood before the wooden loom, its threads softly reflecting the light.

"Oh, I must show you this," she said, reaching for a slender wooden tool nearby.

"He also brought combed fleece and a drop spindle, which I now know how to use to turn the fleece into yarn. And I have my own weaving baton."

Its handle drew my notice, shaped like the hilt of a sword. I stepped closer, studying it with curiosity.

"This resembles a sword," I remarked, running my fingers lightly along the polished wood, taking note of its smooth surface and fine craftsmanship.

Her head tilted slightly as she studied it anew. "Indeed, it does. I had not noticed."

She placed it next to the loom, and her eyes met mine. Time seemed to hold its breath, my pulse quickening, as if an unseen force drew us closer. I struggled to regain my composure, unsure of how to navigate the emotions stirring within me.

"Would you like to go to the waterfall and read the manuscript?"

"Yes, that would be lovely."

Merlin, observing us with a knowing look, said, "The waterfall will serve you well. Go, but do not tarry—we must reach the circle after dusk for the healing ceremonies."

I eagerly reached into my bag and retrieved the manuscript, its familiar scent of ink and parchment filling my senses. Draping my cloak around my shoulders, Merlonius did the same with hers. Together, we ventured into the forest.

Leaves rustled underfoot, while the harsh caws of distant crows mingled with the enchanting melody of the nearby stream. Upon nearing the waterfall, the sound of water cascading into the pond below drew me forward.

We settled onto one of the stone benches, the manuscript placed between us.

"This place will forever hold a special meaning for me."

"It shall for me as well, Arthur."

I reached for her hand, and she willingly entwined her fingers with mine. A calm spread through me at her touch, as if the world beyond the forest momentarily faded away.

"Merlonius, while we were apart, I often thought of you and wondered how you fared."

"As did I for you, Arthur. Being with you now, soothes my worries. Knowing you are well brings me comfort."

I tightened my grip on her hand, and in her nearness, found a peace I had long hungered for.

"I am relieved, and my heart is eased to see you well," I confessed.

Her cheeks flushed with a rosy hue. "Having you with me now, here in the enchanted forest, makes me feel complete."

Our hands remained intertwined, a wordless knowing passing between us, the kind that only comes with deep familiarity.

Time slipped quietly by until I looked down at the manuscript. "Shall we now delve into exploring these writings?"

"Yes, please, Arthur," she responded, leaning in to examine the ancient text.

Together, we carefully turned each fragile sheet. The work held *The Song of Elysium*, a tale of immortal love between a deity and a mortal. Its lyrical verses conjured scenes of passion, heroism, and otherworldly intervention, captivating us with every line. Our discussion delved into the symbols, the lore, and the timeless truths woven throughout. This journey into the story drew us closer as we shared insights, marveled at its beauty, and became entwined in its mysteries.

With the sun dipping below the horizon, we reached the final lines, her fingers lightly tracing the letters as if drawn deeper into the tale. The last light of day outlined the contours of her face and the flowing strands of her hair, making her seem touched by the very magic we had just read of.

When our eyes met again, an ache stirred within me, a longing to hold and kiss her, but I held it back, murmuring, "I think we should return to the cottage."

"Yes," she whispered, drawing her cloak tightly around her shoulders to ward off the chill.

Closing the manuscript, we sealed away its ancient words as the day gave way to twilight. Rising, we walked briskly, the night chill seeping through to our bones. Beside me, she trembled against the chill, and my instincts urged me to pull her close, though restraint kept my hands at my sides.

At the front door, Merlin awaited our arrival, his hooded cloak swirling in the wind, and his staff held firmly in his hand.

"Come, come," he said with urgency as he searched the night sky. "The stars whisper that the hour is upon us, and we must go."

"The villagers await our arrival," he continued. "There can be no further delay."

I quickly placed the manuscript in my bag and joined them as they led the way around to the back of the cottage. With deliberate strides, Merlin strode towards the woods, his staff tapping on the ground with each step. Merlonius and I shared a fleeting look before following him into the deepening darkness, where the trees stretched above us with outstretched limbs. A quietness descended upon us as we moved forward, our path lit solely by the dim moonlight filtering through the dense weave of branches overhead.

The forest trail led us farther until we stepped into an open space. Towering stones stood before us in a commanding circle, a testament to ancient powers. This was a place of legends, where the threads of history and myth intertwined.

"Arthur, behold The Giants' Dance," Merlin proclaimed with authority. "Come, let us proceed."

The ancient pillars glowed with an eerie light beneath the moon as we approached. Hooded figures within the circle respectfully parted, granting us entry.

He gestured for me to stand near the threshold, while he and Merlonius advanced towards the stone altar. A group of young novices stood there, their postures straight and attentive. Merlin's brief glance in their direction confirmed what I suspected: these were his apprentices. Some adjusted their stance, moving from foot to foot, while others clenched their hands in barely contained anticipation.

Stepping onto the elevated platform, Merlin faced the gathering and began a rhythmic chant. Slowly, others joined in, their voices melding and rising in power until it reached a spellbinding peak. An undeniable presence filled the space, while wisps of light danced above the altar.

I stood transfixed, reverence and wonder stirring a thrill deep within me.

With grace, Merlonius ascended the platform, positioning herself beside Merlin. She pushed the hood of her cloak back and placed her palms upon the altar. Merlin remained fixed upon her, unmoving as she gave herself fully to the ritual. In response, he raised his staff high, and the rhythmic chanting gradually ceased, leaving behind a stillness heavy with expectancy.

We waited, the only sound the creatures of the forest who had approached the circle, sensing the healing power that flowed from within.

A blue glow encircled Merlonius just before she and Merlin descended from the platform. The young men and women formed two lines before the altar, creating a pathway for Merlin and Merlonius to tread. Moving with perfect unison, as if guided by some unseen hand, the group proceeded forward. The solemnity of their advance made it clear that an event of great import was underway. I could only watch, utterly captivated by the enchanting ritual unfolding before me.

The towering stones exuded a shimmering heat, as if ancient power long held within them had stirred awake, compelled by the ritual's force. One by one, those within the circle lowered their hoods. Merlonius raised her arms, palms pointing outward, and began a slow, deliberate motion, tracing a semi-circle from left to right and then from right to left. The movement continued for several minutes, each gesture imbued with intention, before she finally lowered her arms.

The chanting recommenced, swelling as I watched in fascination. Then, abruptly, the sound ceased. One by one, those within the circle slowly came forward, offering a slight bow before leaving through the side opening where I stood.

The last to approach were two women, each cradling a small child. They engaged in a hushed conversation with Merlonius, who responded with a gentle smile and lightly placed her hands on the tops of the children's heads. Then, she drew two small cloth pouches filled with herbs, each secured with cording, from the array at her waist and handed them to the women. With whispered gratitude, they departed, leaving the circle calm and still, save for the three of us.

Merlin made his way towards me, his cloak fluttering in the breeze and trailing behind him. Although his stride exuded purposefulness, to my surprise, he wore a smile.

"Well, Arthur, are you hungry?"

A grin formed as I replied, "Indeed, I am."

"Let us make our way home and enjoy a meal together."

After departing from The Giants' Dance, we briskly made our way through the woods. I was captivated still by the mystical power of the stones and the ceremony led by Merlonius, who had invoked the forces of the circle for healing and restoration. She seemed to merge seamlessly with the essence of the forest, her spirit both commanding and deeply harmonious.

Upon entering the cottage, Merlin spoke to Merlonius. "Now, my dear, let us show Arthur what you have learned."

She stood beside me, calm and poised. With a wave of her hand, each candle sprang to life, their flames swaying gently as if stirred by unseen breath. The hearth followed, kindling with a sudden burst of warmth. Light danced across the walls, casting long shadows, and the low hum of her magic settled around us like a living presence.

"Merlonius, you have summoned such an extraordinary force," I marveled.

She glowed with a mysterious presence and exchanged a look with Merlin. Unable to contain his excitement, he clapped his hands with a hearty cheer.

"And now it shall be my magic that provides the feast for this night," he declared.

The table was adorned with rustic wooden plates and polished goblets that caught the dance of glowing candlelight.

With a graceful wave of his staff, the scent of freshly cooked stew, imbued with rich venison and a vibrant medley of vegetables, rose about us.

"Arthur, would you care for some bread and cheese?" he offered.

At my eager nod, he sliced a generous portion, placing it beside a wedge of tangy cheese on a wooden board.

"Here you go." He gestured towards the board. "Help yourself."

We talked as old friends would, the conversation unfolding naturally, like a stream winding through familiar terrain, its ease reflecting the comfort of the cottage and the enchantment of the night.

Eager to understand more, I turned to Merlonius, "The spell of that ceremony has not yet released me. How are you faring?"

Merlin leaned in, attentive as she replied after a thoughtful pause.

"I feel complete and happy."

"Your talents are remarkable, Merlonius," he remarked, glancing my way. "Would you not agree, Arthur?"

Captivated by the wonders at The Giants' Dance, I affirmed, "Indeed. The ceremony was a revelation, expanding my respect for sorcery."

"Arthur, your witness of this eve's magic honors me. Under Merlin's guidance, I discover new skills each day, learning how to share these gifts with others. I am embracing my destiny as a sorceress."

With a chuckle, Merlin responded, "And well you should, my dear."

Overwhelmed with awe, I added, "Your skills are truly wondrous."

After our meal, we gathered by the fire drawn closer by the day's events. Merlonius chose the chair nearest the flames, with me beside her and Merlin across from us. The wind outside intensified, and Merlin gestured towards the hearth; with a deliberate motion, the flames leapt higher. Our conversation quieted as the night deepened, the fire holding the darkness at the edges of the room.

Merlin studied the flames, before turning towards Merlonius, the firelight tracing the creases of his brow. "My dear, the healing ceremony has taken much from you. It would be best if you retire. Arthur will still be here on the morrow, and there will be ample time to visit."

In the firelight, her pallor was unmistakable, her usual radiance giving way to visible weariness. I knew she needed rest.

"Merlonius, Merlin is right. We will be together again come the new day."

She offered a faint grin, mustering her remaining strength. "I am weary."

With quiet elegance, she made her way towards the back of the cottage, her hair cascading in loose waves. A surge of emotions rose within me as I watched her go—admiration, concern, and something deeper I could not yet name.

"Merlin, I have never witnessed anything like what transpired this night at The Giants' Dance. Merlonius was bathed in a radiant blue light at the altar.

Was it pure magic, and how does she harness such a force? I yearn to understand."

He turned from the hearth, thoughtful. "Merlonius possesses the gift to hear whispers from the Otherworld. Together we have shaped that power to serve those in need of healing. She has embraced it, unafraid to wield its potency, and through it, she can summon forth the flames."

"Is there any danger to herself in using her gifts?"

"Danger always looms when one dwells in multiple worlds. We can only seek protection and remain vigilant in how we offer our gifts. This has long been central to our teachings."

The thought of any harm befalling her troubled me. "Is there anything I can do to protect her?"

"In your future, you will have ample opportunities to shield her from harm. But for now, have no worries. She is under my protection and guidance."

His words stayed with me long after I retired to bed, carrying with them concern and awe. Merlonius's courage in accepting her gifts kindled hope in me that I, too, might one day be ready to embrace my destiny.

I drew a deep breath, the day's uncertainties yielding to the stillness of night. Before long, sleep claimed me.

CHAPTER 8

WHISPERED PROMISES

We woke to Merlin's voice calling our names, his words gently breaking the morn's calm.

"Arthur, Merlonius, let us not sleep the day away. Rise and greet the morn."

The tender light of dawn streamed through the windows, heralding a new day.

I looked over at Merlonius and greeted her, "Good morrow. How are you faring?"

She yawned, stretching leisurely. "Rested. And you?"

"Excited for the day ahead."

"I am as well, Arthur."

She retreated behind the curtain to change, the cloth rustling softly at her touch. While I waited, the subtle sounds of her movements mingled with the faint, sweet scent of lavender. After slipping into my shoes and splashing cold water on my face, I joined her and Merlin, drawn by the inviting warmth of the fire.

The flames danced and crackled, the heat rising steadily as sap hissed to the surface. The lingering scent of pine was familiar and comforting.

We gathered for a meal, the table graced with fresh bread, dried apples from the year's final harvest, and honey, dark and rich as the finest mead. Each flavor celebrated the simple pleasures of life: the honey, luscious and smooth, the bread perfectly crusty, and the apples offering a mellow sweetness from the waning light of the sun.

Merlin set aside his bread, his thoughts turning to the plans ahead. "What shall we do on this day? The wind still howls, carrying a bitter chill."

"I find the idea of staying close to the flames rather inviting. What do you say, Merlonius?"

She nodded in agreement. "Let us remain inside until the wind relents."

"Very well, we will stay in for now," Merlin concurred.

"How about a game?" I suggested, reaching for the small bag of marked stones.

Merlonius's eyes sparkled as she replied, "Ah, the stone game. Let us see if you can best me."

Merlin raised an eyebrow. "I will have you know, I am the master of this game."

She looked down, though the corners of her mouth betrayed her amusement.

The stones clinked against the wooden board, our rivalry growing intense. Merlin's determined nature emerged, and we traded playful banter.

His throw yielded excitement. "Two threes! Try to beat a six!"

"You are going to regret that move," I challenged.

When my two stones landed on the board, both showed fours. "There you have it, an eight!"

Merlonius laughed. "It seems Merlin is not as unbeatable as he claims."

We were thoroughly enjoying ourselves, each move met with good-natured taunts and jests. Yet I could not help but marvel at how this simple game revealed an uncharacteristically competitive streak in Merlin.

Merlonius recounted a tale from our past, and I could not help but smile at the delight it still brought her. There had been a time, she reminded us, when Merlin, caught in a rare fit of frustration during this very game, had upset the board, sending stones clattering across the floor. A flush of colour rose to his cheeks at the telling, his usual composure briefly unsettled. But he joined in our laughter, adding his own embellishments to the memory, and with each word, offered a glimpse of the man beneath the mantle of sorcerer.

Later, as the wind howled beyond the walls, we opened the manuscript once more, reading from the passage where the deity first fell in love with the mortal. Merlonius read aloud:

As Eros beheld Psyche, a mortal of unparalleled beauty,
his heart, though divine, was pierced with a love
that defied the bounds of immortality.

She looked at me, and something in her expression touched my heart. Somehow, I knew she felt the same. We closed the manuscript, sitting close, the silence between us filled with unspoken accord.

When the sun broke through the clouds and the wind softened, we ventured to the stream. Settling upon the grass, I finally allowed the feelings I had guarded so closely to surface.

"I am leaving on the morrow."

She drew closer, a slight crease forming on her brow. "Yes, Arthur, sadly, I am aware."

Resolve surfaced within me. "I have been coming here for almost a year now. These visits have been a source of great joy. I like you. I truly like you."

"I like you as well, Arthur. And your visits… they mean more to me than you can imagine."

I reached for her hand, our fingers interlacing with ease. With her beside me, I felt complete. The nearness of her body drew forth a fierce longing to stay, to let the world beyond this place fall away.

Eventually, the growing chill compelled us indoors, leaving the brisk air behind. The day unfolded with tranquil grace. We spent the hours indulging in a delightful meal, our conversations woven with stories that often erupted into fits of laughter. As the night deepened, the weariness of the day began to blanket us. Merlonius wished us a peaceful night and retreated to her bed.

I lingered in my chair, lost in my reflections, reluctant to part ways with the safety and comfort of the cottage. My bond with Merlonius had deepened, awakening a longing for more time together, making the thought of the morrow's departure all the more daunting.

At the sound of the wind's mournful melody weaving through the trees, Merlin rose and placed another log on the fire.

Returning to his chair, Merlin looked at me. "You and Merlonius seemed to have grown closer during your visit, have you not?"

I wrestled with the storm of emotion his question stirred within me.

"I have come to care deeply for her, Merlin," I finally admitted. "And I find myself hesitant to bid her farewell on the morrow."

He nodded knowingly. "Ah, love. It can be both a gift and a challenge," he mused. "But life's journey is inevitably filled with parting. Treasure what we share, and let the Fates guide you."

I sighed, my hands loosening as I took in his words. Yet a part of me still longed for him to truly grasp what stirred within me.

"Rest well, Merlin. Until the morrow."

"And you, Arthur. May your rest bring clarity."

I retired to my bed, lying beneath the rustic thatched rafters, but my thoughts refused to quiet. They kept revisiting the precious memories I had forged with Merlonius, each one steeped in emotion. I found myself hoping the gods and goddesses would smile upon our union. Gradually, weariness overcame me, and I succumbed to sleep, still enveloped in the thought of our time together.

The next morn, I awoke to find them already seated at the table, deeply engaged in conversation. When Merlonius noticed me, she smiled.

"Good morrow, Arthur. Come join us," she beckoned.

I sat down beside her as Merlin rose. "My boy, let me get you something to drink."

When he stepped away, Merlonius and I exchanged a fleeting glance, her fingers brushing mine beneath the table.

Merlin returned with a goblet of water, remarking, "We must depart soon."

"Of course, Merlin."

After a light meal of cheese and bread, Merlin went to tend to the horses. I retrieved my cloak and as Merlonius stepped closer, a captivating spell seemed to radiate from her, or perhaps it was the subtle grace of her movements that enchanted me. Leaning forward, compelled by an overwhelming urge to kiss her, I found myself caught in a torrent of emotions. Doubt, desire, and uncertainty mingled, holding me in their tentative grasp.

She extended her hand, offering me a folded piece of cloth. Inside, a delicate white flower lay, its petals velvety to the touch.

"Arthur, this flower is from the gift given to me. I wanted you to have a part of me with you."

I tucked the flower beneath my tunic, the softness of the cloth like the touch of a feather against my skin.

"I will cherish this."

Her eyes held mine, our closeness seeming to hush everything beyond us.

"We should go, Merlonius… Merlin is waiting," I murmured.

"Yes…"

We joined Merlin, his figure still against the backdrop of the paddock.

"Stay inside where it is warm, Merlonius. I shall return this eve," he instructed, a rare tenderness softening his expression.

"I will, Merlin. Safe journey."

Her eyes lingered on him, as if trying to hold the sight of his face a moment longer before he turned away.

Even Merlin, ever inscrutable, seemed attuned to the undercurrent of her emotions. A fleeting glimmer crossed his features, his slight, almost imperceptible nod a silent reflection of her feeling.

Riding away, I cast a final glance back. Merlonius raised her hand in farewell, and the sight of her standing there stirred something deep within me. I harbored a wish, entrusting it to the whispers of the wind, longing for her to remain a constant, guiding light in my life.

Once she retreated to the safety of the cottage, I turned my attention to the road ahead, bracing myself for the challenges that awaited. We followed the winding dirt path of the forest floor until it merged with the main road, our horses steadily carrying us northward.

The rhythmic clip-clop of hooves marked our passage through the woods. We rode in silence, and the memory of Merlonius's radiant smile returned to me, as commanding as her presence at The Giants' Dance. A compelling urge to turn back and abandon my duties for her pulled at me.

Nearing Sir Ector's home, my longing intensified. "Merlin, I wish to visit Merlonius once again. I cannot bear the thought of waiting for another full moon to pass. Could we hasten our return journey to the forest?"

The stillness was only broken by the sounds of our horses and the whisper of the breeze. After a strained silence, he finally responded.

"Yes, Arthur. We shall return to the enchanted forest within a fortnight."

Relief surged through me. "I am truly beholden to you for your help."

He tilted his head in response but said nothing as we continued our journey.

Once we arrived and dismounted, we entrusted our horses to the waiting stable boys. We walked towards the forest's edge without speaking.

"I eagerly await your return."

His simple response startled me, as I had expected more.

"Stay safe, Arthur."

His form gradually merged with the forest's dappled shadows, and I watched until he vanished among the trees, a chill tracing the back of my neck. I lingered at the edge of the woods, wondering why my father and mother had entrusted me to a man who held so many secrets. The question lingered, joining the countless others that shadowed my past. Somehow, I knew that Merlin carried the answers to who I was and who I was meant to become.

I shook my head with firm resolve and turned my mind to what lay ahead. The prospect of seeing Merlonius again kindled a quiet excitement, tempered by anticipation and unanswered questions.

These reflections, threaded through the cloth of each day, deepened my yearning to uncover what the future might reveal. With Merlin as my shadowed guide, I stepped forward, drawn ever nearer to the truths I sought: the mystery of my past, my place in this world, and whatever fate yet held for me.

CHAPTER 9

DESTINED IN STONE

True to his word, Merlin returned in a fortnight, allowing my visits to Merlonius to become more frequent. These journeys carried me far from the murmurs and wary glances of the farmhands, returning me to a place where I felt wholly myself. Everything changed on a fateful day in May, when I turned fifteen and my path took an unexpected turn.

That morn, the usual spark of interest Merlin brought to his visits was absent, replaced by a heaviness in his manner. As I stepped from my father's chamber, a vague discomfort took hold, stirring both curiosity and a shadowed unease as I watched events unfold.

"Sir Ector, I have arranged for all the nobility to gather on the morrow in the open field south of the village for a tournament. It lies past the enchanted forest. I request that you, Sir Ector, and Lady Kate attend as honoured guests. And you, Arthur, are to participate in the games, for it is time we tested how well you have honed your jousting and swordsmanship skills."

Sir Ector's steady expression wavered for the briefest instant, and his bearing stiffened, as though bracing to face something that had long lain buried.

"Merlin, your invitation honors us. Lady Kate and I would not miss witnessing Arthur's skill on the field."

"Good."

With a firm nod, he turned to Kay. "Kay, you shall also join us, for your presence will fortify Arthur's spirit during the tournament."

He straightened slightly, replying with a measured tone, "Understood."

Observing them, I tried to discern if there was more to this gathering than Merlin had shared, but his features were unreadable.

"So, what say you, Arthur?"

"I am eager to participate. Shall we depart now as usual?"

"Yes, let us be going." Merlin's brisk nod signaled there would be no delay.

After the stable boys finished preparing our trusty steeds for the journey, we swung into our saddles and set off towards the enchanted forest, our horses' hooves kicking up dust as we rode. The journey ahead would be a long one, taking nearly two hours to reach the cottage.

While we rode, my thoughts kept drifting back to Merlonius. Finally, I shifted in my saddle and asked, "How fares Merlonius?"

A hint of a smile tugged at the corners of his mouth. "She is well."

I brightened at the news. "Can she join us at the tournament?"

"She would like that very much, but she must remain with me. Your full attention must be on the games."

"I understand. I intend to perform to the best of my abilities, but I also hope she finds some delight in the festivities."

A low chuckle escaped him. "She shall, Arthur."

Over the years, I had learned to recognize when he preferred not to explain further. We rode the final stretch without speaking, silent in thought, until he drew up his reins at the edge to the enchanted forest.

A furrow formed on his brow, and his lips pressed tight as he said, "I shall share the news of the tournament with Merlonius."

The change in his manner, his lack of details about the morrow's event, and his decision to inform Merlonius of the tournament left me with a gnawing feeling of uncertainty.

Even so, I replied with my usual deference, "As you wish."

We dismounted at the clearing and led our horses to the paddock, then made our way to the cottage. As we neared, Merlonius swung the door open.

"Welcome!" she called out. "You have arrived early, which will give us ample time to enjoy each other's company!"

After stepping inside, the gentle aroma of herbs and honey greeted me. I set the brown bag I carried just inside the door, leaning it beneath one of the windows. The familiar space felt as if I were once more in the presence of an old friend.

"It is so good to see you, Merlonius."

"Arthur, seeing you warms my heart."

"Come, let us share a meal," she said, gesturing towards the wooden table adorned with an array of delectable treats. Red apples, walnuts, flatbread, and creamy cheese were neatly arranged. The fragrance of hare stew wafted from the kettle, drawing forth a hunger I had not realized I carried.

She carefully rested a pitcher of cool water on the table, and as she sat down beside me on the bench, I reached under the table to hold her hand. Her fingers clasped mine, her presence steady and reassuring.

"Arthur, how do you fare?"

"I am well, and you? Are you in good health and spirits?"

"I am in fine spirits, especially now that you are here. I want to show you the garden Merlin and I planted after your last visit."

Merlin straightened with purpose, his presence drawing our attention. "Merlonius, I wish to speak with you before you venture off."

Her grip on my hand tightened, and her breath caught, as if bracing for something unwelcome.

"Is something wrong?"

"Now, now, Merlonius, it is good news. Take a breath."

She inhaled, though her hold on my hand remained firm.

"On the morrow, we shall attend a tournament where Arthur is to compete in jousting and swordsmanship."

"Arthur, this promises to be an exciting day for you!"

"Merlonius," Merlin added, "it is important that you stay near me. There will be many people at the event, and I do not want to be unable to find you."

Doubt stirred within me at his caution. *What was he withholding from us?* She seemed to sense it too; the lines in her forehead deepened before she answered in a measured tone.

"Of course. I will remain close."

"Very well, then, shall we eat?"

She rose and brought the hare stew to the table, ladling it into our bowls. Merlin set his spoon down after his first taste.

"My dear, this hare stew is superb. You truly have outdone yourself," he said, his smile lingering as he looked her way.

"I am glad you like it. You have been a patient master."

Turning to me, she added, "Much of what I know about preparing food is thanks to Merlin."

I smiled, savoring another spoonful. "This stew is truly exceptional."

We finished our meal with light conversation, and once the table had been cleared, Merlin began steeping herbs for healing teas. Merlonius and I quietly stepped outside, fingers intertwined, and strolled to the garden. The sight of lush greenery, rows of vibrant vegetables, and fragrant herbs spoke of new growth since my last visit.

"We are going to have a bountiful garden this summer, and because of it, several good meals for when you visit."

"You and Merlin have once again outdone yourselves with this garden. I look forward to helping with the harvest."

"Arthur, would you like to see the top of the waterfall?" A breeze lifted the loose waves around her shoulders as she tugged on my sleeve, her delight radiant. "We have never been there together."

If she had asked, I would have followed her anywhere.

"Yes. Most definitely."

Hand in hand, we climbed the winding path to the summit. Cresting the hill, a breathtaking view unfurled before us. The river wound to our left, and in the distance, we could see the village with its thatched roofs. A cool wind brushed against us, and the grass beneath our feet felt soft and lush.

"The view is magnificent," I marveled, drinking in the serene landscape.

A small smile graced her lips. "Do you like it, then?"

"Indeed, I am glad you brought me to this wondrous place."

Walking along the cliff's edge, a deep tranquility settled over me. The vast expanse before us seemed to hold its breath. Beside me, Merlonius shifted, her voice taking on a distant, almost ethereal tone.

"Arthur, do you see it? There, a fortress in the distance."

I leaned closer. "A fortress?"

"A castle. There is a drawbridge… turrets, and flags." She spoke slowly, pulling her words back through the veil. "One flag bears the symbol of a dragon." Her hands trembled as she turned to me, her eyes wide. "And it is tied to your fate."

The dragon's mention stirred a deep recognition, echoing nightmares of soaring beasts. *How is my destiny part of the world of dragons?*

She swayed, her eyes closing, and I steadied her.

"What does it mean?" I whispered.

She leaned into me, her breath uneven, "I saw mounted men in armour, and others on foot with drawn swords."

I drew her closer. "Merlonius, I am here. It is Arthur."

She blinked, her focus sharpening. "My vision was for you. I do not know its meaning, but it foretells a place that is tied to you. And the image of the dragon? What does it mean? I am frightened for you. I do not know why I saw this and why now."

"We must return and speak with Merlin."

She nodded, "Yes, we should go now."

We retraced our steps, the sun sinking below the horizon, streaking the sky with fiery hues. Upon reaching the cottage, we found Merlin sitting on the stone bench outside the door, waiting for us.

"Greetings, my young friends."

His smile faded as he noted Merlonius's pallor.

"Merlonius, what troubles you? Speak to me."

While she recounted what she had seen, I squeezed her hand, offering silent reassurance.

"Merlin, the dragon I saw is tied to Arthur. What peril does it foretell?"

"Your gifts continue to grow, my dear. The Fates will, in time, show you what they wish you to see."

"Merlin, please," I pressed, "what she saw could hold the key to who my father and mother are."

"The gods reveal their secrets when they deem it right. For now, focus on what we can tend to here and now."

His calm dismissal only deepened my frustration. "Merlin, this matters. Merlonius's vision could contain the answers I have been seeking. Please tell me what you know!"

Tears welled in her eyes as she looked down. "This is my fault…"

Her hands trembled as she gripped the folds of her garment, fingers twisting the cloth tightly.

"If I could only see more clearly, maybe I could spare you this pain. My visions bring only confusion and fear."

She turned away, as if ashamed, her shoulders sagging under an invisible weight.

Merlin's hand was gentle on her shoulder. "Visions are a sacred gift. None of this lies upon your shoulders alone. Trust that all will be made clear when the gods so wish."

Overwhelmed, I retreated to the garden, collapsing onto the bench under the familiar, protective tree. The rough bark grazed my back, and I pressed against it, seeking a steadiness that eluded me. The tree's cool embrace offered little respite from the heat that clung to the day, and sweat trickled down my temples. *Why do these questions plague me still? What does my destiny have in common with this dragon?*

My fists clenched, nails biting into my palms as frustration swelled. Secrets and half-truths pressed upon me, keeping answers just beyond my grasp.

Merlonius approached and rested her hand on my arm. "Arthur, I am so sorry."

I looked up at her, tears glistening. "There is no fault of yours in this. I do not think less of you for your visions, or that you shared one this day. I am haunted by unanswered questions as to my birth father and mother and why they entrusted me to Merlin."

"In my own search for answers. I found the will to accept what the Fates presented. You are strong of will and heart, and I believe you will find the courage to uncover and embrace your truth when the time comes."

There was no denying Merlonius's fortitude as she shared her thoughts with me. I looked about, drawing in the beauty of the sky, the enduring presence of the trees, and the peace of the garden, seeking to regain control over my spirit.

Finally understanding, I said, "You and Merlin speak the truth. I must trust that the gods will reveal what they wish, when they wish."

I rose, pulling her into a reassuring embrace. Salty streaks from her tears ran down her cheeks and I wiped them away with the edge of my sleeve. It pained me to know she felt such sorrow.

"Let us return to Merlin," I said, her hand slipping into mine.

We walked slowly, our worries shadowing us. Inside, we found Merlin at his workbench, surrounded by herbs and powders. The familiar aroma of freshly prepared tinctures mingled with the sweet fragrance of blooming flowers drifting in from the open windows.

He turned as we entered. "You carry heavy burdens, my friends. The paths ahead twist and turn. Trust that the Fates weave the cloth of our journey as they must."

His words echoed in my thoughts, awakening a restless desire to glimpse what lay ahead, to understand the course the Fates had woven for me. Yet no answers came.

Seeking distraction, I filled my cup with cool water and helped myself to the leftover stew. The food was as delicious now as it was earlier in the day, and I relished every bite.

While we ate, Merlin wove stories of dragons, their majesty and might. His voice held a deep reverence and a rare warmth, especially when he spoke of Tân Wen, his beloved dragon companion. He described the shimmer of her green scales under the sunlight, her wings spanning the sky like a living storm cloud, and the wisdom in her amber eyes. Every tale revealed the strength of their bond.

Moonlight streamed through the windows, casting a silvery glow that deepened the enchantment of his stories. I was swept back to my own first encounter with Tân Wen, remembering the thrill of touching her smooth scales for the first time.

As the night deepened, Merlin set his cup down. "You both ought to retire. The morrow brings an exciting day at the tournament, and we leave at first light."

We rose from the table, clearing away the plates and cups. The dragon symbol on the flag would not leave me, a riddle just beyond my grasp, its missing pieces like fragments that might offer insight into my past. I resolved to press Merlin for answers, though I feared his reluctance would only deepen my frustration.

Merlin and I took our seats in front of the hearth as Merlonius yawned. "Rest well. I will see you both on the morrow."

"May your slumber be peaceful, my dear."

Watching her, I added, "May you find restful sleep."

We continued to sit across from each other, the hearth dark and empty. The distant chirping of crickets broke the stillness, a faint reminder of the world beyond these walls.

"Please, I need to understand," I said with insistence. "A dragon I do not recognize keeps haunting my dreams, and I feel an unfathomable pull to it. What does it mean? Why is it so significant to me?"

He regarded me with a sadness that I could not fully grasp.

"Arthur, I wish I could tell you more, but I cannot for it is not mine to share."

A sinking feeling overwhelmed me. My ties to the dragon seemed to hold the key to my past, and his reluctance to share what he knew left me feeling helpless. *Why will he not help me?*

Realizing that nothing I could say would compel him to reveal more, I attempted to guide the conversation elsewhere. "Is there anything more you can tell me about the tournament?"

"Give it your best. You have the skill and the prowess. Trust in yourself, and I know you will fare well. Now go and have a restful night's sleep."

He then turned towards the cold hearth, his composure signaling his need for solitude.

A wave of disappointment and frustration washed over me. Rising from my chair, I replied, "I shall strive to achieve success. Until the morrow."

Merlonius was waiting for me, and despite the unease stirring inside me, her presence lifted my spirits.

"Are you nervous about the tournament?" she whispered.

I took her hand, feeling its softness. "Not in the way I should be. I feel there is more to this tournament than Merlin is willing to share with us."

"I, too, sense something amiss. There is a shroud of secrecy around him. Despite this, I am confident you will prevail on the morrow."

"Your belief in me is heartening, and we shall have to wait to see how the events of the day unfold."

I removed my shoes, lay back on the bed, and extended my hand to her. She clasped it softly, her touch lingering as we drifted into sleep, comforted by each other's presence.

Merlin woke us before the sun had risen, and we quickly prepared for the day ahead. After a hasty meal of fruit and bread, we mounted our horses, which he had tethered outside the cottage door. Riding towards the outskirts of the village, we were greeted by a mist that gave the landscape an ethereal and hauntingly beautiful appearance.

Nearing the tournament grounds, the sound of the crowd swelled, their cheers mingling with the blaring trumpets that resonated across the field. I felt a thrill run through me as I realized that the events were about to begin. Merlin motioned for us to follow him, weaving through the throngs of people until we reached a grassy field at the center of the activities. In the distance, I could see a towering stone, its rough surface gleaming in the sunlight. He spoke quietly as he glanced around the field as if searching for something.

"All the victors have the chance to pull the sword from the stone. Be ready."

With that, he and Merlonius spurred their horses and galloped off to the other side of the field. I stood there, alone, feeling both anticipation and uncertainty. But then, I remembered all the training I had undertaken and the long hours of practice. I was ready, but something in Merlin's manner gave me pause. He was hiding something from me, I could feel it. My senses were alerting me to this, and I knew that I had to be careful. He had taught me to listen to my inner guidance, and now a deep warning surged through me, a silent whisper: *Beware.*

The day's competitions were a grueling test of skill, pitting me against opponents much older and larger. Yet, I emerged victorious in sword fighting, jousting, and horsemanship, besting all challengers. After hours of intense feats, only one challenge remained: pulling a sword from the stone. Standing sixth in line, I watched each man ahead of me try and fail to move the sword. A hush fell over the crowd when the last man before me stepped aside, defeated. My pulse raced, and my palms were slick with sweat. *Could I really be the one to pull the sword from the stone?*

I stepped forward, drawn by purpose, and approached the stone. At the edge of the field, Merlin and Merlonius watched me. My hands trembled as I grasped the hilt. It was icy and unyielding beneath my grip. I pulled, but sudden resistance stopped me. The blade held fast, and a wave of panic swept through me.

Then came the rustle of wind through the trees and everything else vanished.

An image formed before me, floating near the stone—a tall man with raven-dark hair and piercing eyes.

"You are my son, Arthur. Take what is your birthright. My sword is yours!"

I had stopped breathing. Drawing in a breath, I dug my feet into the earth and braced. With a final surge of strength, I pulled with all my might.

The sound of iron scraping against stone rang out across the tournament grounds. The ghostly form faded, and the crowd burst into cheers and clamor. There I stood, panting and sweating, holding the sword aloft. A force seemed to pulse from the blade through my entire being. Suddenly, Merlin appeared at my side.

He took my arm. "Arthur, it now begins. Come, we must address all who have witnessed this feat."

Flushed with the rush of victory and the ghostly encounter, I hastened to tell him, "A man appeared to me by the stone."

His grip on my shoulder tightened as he looked about the crowd.

"Patience, my boy. We shall have our time to unravel these mysteries."

Stepping towards the center of the field, I felt the weight and substance of the sword in my hand, drawing my attention back to its magnificence. With a gleaming blade and a hilt adorned with jewels, it was truly a weapon of wonder. The wind picked up, weaving through my hair, and whispers from the past seemed to brush against me, imbuing me with a sense of unity with the sword that I could not fully understand.

Merlin stood firm as he addressed the crowd, his presence alone commanding stillness. One by one, the onlookers turned to me, waiting for him to speak.

"At my side stands Arthur, son of the High King Uther Pendragon and Queen Igraine. With the pulling of Caliburn from the stone, he has proven beyond any doubt that he is the rightful heir to the throne and the next High King of Britain. In seven days, we shall return to this field, where he shall profess his vow to protect the land. All here are invited to give witness to his oath."

The crowd froze in stunned disbelief, a murmur of shock and amazement rippling through them. Then they surged forward, their footsteps churning up dust as they crossed the field. I could feel the heat of their excitement and confusion as they besieged us with questions, each noble striving to be heard. Some frowned deeply. Others clenched fists. A few blinked back tears, overwhelmed with emotion. The sound of their cries and shouts filled the space, weaving a loud clamor that seemed ready to engulf us. Nevertheless, Merlin answered each inquiry with composure, concluding the exchange with the assurance that we would meet again in seven days for the coronation ceremony.

With the last noble having departed, Sir Ector, Lady Kate, and Kay approached us. Sir Ector's brow creased with worry, sweat beading below his hairline. Lady Kate rested her hand on Sir Ector's arm, her expression solemn with pride. A hollow feeling settled in my stomach as I realized nothing would ever be the same again.

"Arthur, we never imagined you were the son of the High King Uther Pendragon and Queen Igraine," Sir Ector said, glancing at Lady Kate and Kay. "We stand with you as you take your place as High King."

Pausing briefly, Sir Ector looked down at his hands, visibly composing himself. "You shall always be our son, and our farm will always be your home."

His words settled deep within me as I grappled with my humble upbringing and my newfound royal lineage. *Can I still be the son they have known and loved, even as I become their king?*

"Father," I said, faltering, "I just do not know... I do not know how to be both your son and a king."

"Arthur, I shall always be your father, as you will be our son. You carry within you humility and strength. Those gifts will serve you well. The way forward will not always be clear, but trust in who you are; it is that same trust we have always had in you."

His reassurance found a place within me, soothing in part, yet unable to quiet the unease that lingered. I wanted to believe him, but uncertainty continued to gnaw at my heart.

"May your words hold truth," I murmured, glancing down briefly before looking back at him.

Kay stepped closer, and I saw the excitement on his face.

"Arthur, all those men who tried before you failed. You were the one to finally succeed."

"No one is better suited to be High King of Britain than you," he added with firm conviction. His hand on my shoulder sealed his pledge, a testament to the bond we shared.

"Kay, no matter what happens next, you will always be my brother. That will never change." I grasped his forearm firmly. "Remember that, always."

"We will be honoured to attend your coronation ceremony."

I nodded to Sir Ector, unable to find the words.

Merlin approached, exchanging brief greetings with Sir Ector, Lady Kate, and Kay. After they departed, we were left standing in the midst of the sun-drenched field. The sweet scent of freshly cut hay and the rustling of leaves offered a soothing contrast to my turmoil. Questions pressed at the edge of my mind, but I knew this was neither the time nor place for them.

He handed me a leather scabbard and a finely crafted belt, its clasp adorned with a small dragon emblem. "This scabbard and belt, like the sword, belonged to your father. They are now yours."

Fastening the belt around my waist, I sheathed the sword, its presence settling against my side. It was more than a physical weight; it carried the legacy and responsibilities of my father.

Everything around me moved too quickly, and I wondered if I might disappear. Merlonius's support would steady me; I needed to be with her.

"Where is Merlonius?"

"She awaits us. Come."

Taking my arm, we walked towards a towering oak tree in the distance. The sun beat down, drawing harsh lines across the dry earth. Warmth radiated from the grass, and sweat dampened my skin, a reminder of the day's oppressive heat.

Under the shade of the oak, Merlonius leaned against the trunk, shielding her eyes from the blinding light. Reaching her, I eagerly took her hands in mine.

"How do you fare, Merlonius?"

"I am well, and I bear witness to your remarkable achievement."

Words eluded me as the enormity of the day's events settled upon me. "Your presence… "

She squeezed my hand, and I knew I was not alone.

Joining us under the tree, Merlin said, "Shall we journey back to the enchanted forest, my young friends?"

We followed him around the massive tree to where our horses had been tethered. The leather reins creaked as Merlonius untied hers, and I found it a challenge to muster the strength to do the same. My limbs felt heavy, as if mired in deep mud. I longed for the comfort of the cottage and the chance to shake off the weariness clinging to me.

Mounting Madwen, I rode past the stone, and the spectral figure I had seen earlier appeared once again.

"Merlin, Merlonius, do you see him?" I shouted, pointing towards the spectral man before me.

Merlin raised his staff, and in an instant, the world around us shimmered and shifted, as if seen through a veil. An unnatural force rippled through the air, causing a chill to settle upon us.

The ghostly figure looked from me to Merlin, then to Merlonius, regarding each of us in turn. Merlin gave a solemn nod, his expression grave, his grip on the staff tightening, as if recognizing someone from his own past.

Merlonius, usually so composed, was visibly shaken by its presence. Emotions played across her features, wonder mingling with wariness. Her stance stiffened, reflecting shock and fascination.

When the ethereal figure turned towards me, a deep, unsettling awareness took hold. I felt that this otherworldly encounter contained a missing fragment vital to the unraveling of our intertwined destinies.

I stilled as he began to speak.

"My son," he said, "your destiny is written in the stars, and you shall rule honorably and righteously. Allow your inner wisdom to be your guide. Listen, and it will always ring true. You will recognize the woman who brings you light and love."

And with that, he disappeared. Merlin lowered his staff, and I glimpsed a shimmer of tears.

"Merlin, who was that man? Was that my father?"

He appeared weary, as if the encounter with the ghostly image had aged him suddenly. "We have just met the spirit of Uther Pendragon, the last High King of Britain." He faltered, and I almost thought he was finished speaking. Then, he added, "Uther Pendragon was also your father."

I looked at him, searching his face for answers. Yet, his expression remained a mystery, revealing nothing.

The truth struck hard, almost beyond bearing.

"There is much you need to know, Arthur. Let us return to the cottage where we can rest and talk."

I urged Madwen forward, still unsettled from the encounter. I sensed I stood on a precipice, ready to fall into a journey far more treacherous than I could yet imagine.

CHAPTER 10

THE RELUCTANT KING

The sun had dipped low on the horizon, casting a fiery wash of orange and pink across the sky when we reached the clearing. The steady clacking of the horses' hooves had entranced me, creating a rhythmic backdrop that added to the storm within me. The revelation that I was Uther Pendragon's son and the destined future High King of Britain pressed upon me, settling as a tightness I could not deny in my chest. Blinking back tears, I felt overwhelmed by the enormity of it all.

We guided the horses into the paddock, ensuring they were settled for the night before making our way to the cottage. A crisp night breeze carried the soothing chorus of chirping crickets as we pushed open the wooden door. The groan of the hinges blended with the welcoming creak of old wooden floorboards underfoot. At once, the rich scent of cured meats and sharp cheese enveloped us. With a wave of his hand, Merlin set the candles alight.

I unsheathed my sword with a sharp hiss, the blade gleaming as it slid free. The candlelight reflected off its surface, jolting me from a dreamlike stupor. Though I had trained with the finest swordsmen, as a mere squire I had never borne a sword beyond the practice field. A heavy sigh escaped my lips. I removed the belt from around my waist, placing the sword and its sheath side by side on the floor.

Merlonius walked to the hearth and stared at the empty space where a fire should have burned. I followed her, steadied only by the distant hoot of an owl. Her presence radiated power, and I waited in silence for her to share what she had seen.

Tears streamed down her face, tracing lines of sorrow. "Oh, Arthur, your battles shall be many, but you shall in the end be victorious. The Saxons shall be driven from Britain. But I will not be at your side."

Panic surged through me, and I reached out, gripping her arm. I could feel the heat of her skin and the slight tremble of her muscles as she sensed my fear.

"What do you mean? Tell me, what came to you?"

My questions rang hollow, even to my own ears.

She buried her face in her hands and sobbed as I wrapped my arms around her.

"Merlin, what does this mean?" I yelled, turning to him.

He glanced at me, then at Merlonius. "My dear, the visions we see of what lies ahead are often but shadows of the truth. All will reveal itself as the future unfolds."

"Merlonius, I do not understand. Pray, tell me that this will not come to pass."

"There is always more than one path to the future, Arthur. But this is the vision I saw: the one where I am not by your side."

Merlin's expression softened as he looked at us. "The future is never set in stone. It is up to us to make the choices that determine our journey."

Her weeping gradually quieted, and she looked up, her eyes meeting mine with a mixture of hope and sorrow. A deep sadness settled over me as her words stayed with me, refusing to fade. *I will not lose her*, I vowed, tightening my grip on her hand as we approached the table. Merlin sat opposite, his piercing eyes fixed intently upon us.

"Arthur, I know you have many questions," he said. "But before we begin, I must tell you something of great import. The events of this day—your victory in the tournament, your drawing of the sword from the stone, and your acceptance of your destiny—will forever alter our lives in ways we cannot yet foresee."

Misgiving took hold. "What do you mean?"

"Since the death of Uther Pendragon, many men have attempted to pull the sword from the stone and have failed. Because you have succeeded, your destiny is to become the next High King of Britain, relinquishing the life of a common man. In seven days, you will be required to take an oath to protect the land and its people."

"You expect me to change my life in a matter of hours? To make a decision based on facts that were unknown to me until now? Why did you keep this from me?" I demanded. "You know I have always trusted you and held you in high esteem. How could you, of all people, do this to me?"

His jaw tightened, his features briefly shifting, thoughtful, restrained. For a heartbeat, it seemed he would respond, but he merely drew a long breath.

"I have hopes for my life," I continued, looking to Merlonius. She shifted slightly, her hands tightening at her sides as she observed the fraught conflict between Merlin and me.

"What would you have me do? What if I do not wish to be a High King?"

Stillness settled over us, thick with expectation. The hunger for answers would not relent. He rested his hands, palms down, upon the table and finally spoke.

"Arthur, I understand this is all hard to grasp, but everything I have done was to keep you safe. On the day of your birth, there were those who would have sought your life."

"What about my mother? Did she do nothing to stop this?"

Pain shadowed his features as he spoke. "I stood at Uther's side when he informed Igraine that her baby would be given to me, someone she did not know. Her sorrow was beyond words, but Uther was High King."

"I feel betrayed. You kept all of this from me and led me to believe I was a simple squire destined for the life I had envisioned. And now you are telling me I have to relinquish those dreams."

I looked at him intently as I sought to unravel the maze of intentions behind his measured composure. A deep conviction stirred within me that there had to be another way.

"You are asking me to become the leader of a country. How can I possibly succeed?"

"The blood of warriors and kings is your heritage, my boy. I have no doubt of your success in leading with fairness and justice."

Merlin's shoulders slumped, a telltale sign of sorrow and weariness, as he recounted the events that led to my shrouded lineage. A distant look crossed his features, the past quietly reclaiming him.

"Safeguarding you was paramount, and to do so, your identity had to be hidden and shielded. I entrusted Sir Ector and his wife, Lady Kate, to care for you, and I gave you the name, Arthur.

"I spent the last fifteen years at your side to ensure your well-being and to help prepare you for the day when you would fulfil your destiny as the next High King of Britain."

"When Merlonius had the vision on the summit and saw a flag with the emblem of a dragon, was it an omen tied to my father?"

He looked from her to me, then gave a single nod, confirming my suspicion.

"The dragon is a potent symbol, intertwined with the legacy of your lineage."

Anger and confusion surged like turbulent waters, compelling me to rise and pace around the cottage's small confines.

"My recurring nightmare… it haunts me with Addaf and the dragons circling above. Tân Wen, your dragon, and mine, Proserpina and then, the third, one I cannot recognize. Did it belong to my father?" I pressed, with tears too angry to spill.

Quietly, he answered, "Yes, it is part of the legacy you were born to inherit."

I clenched my jaw, struggling to maintain control.

"What else, Merlin? What else have you hidden from me?" I shouted. "What other truths remain concealed?"

"I shall provide answers to your questions in due course. But know this, Arthur, you are still the same person. Your birth father and mother may have given you life, but I have been with you all these years, protecting and guiding you."

I shook my head, my thoughts churning with questions that refused to settle. "How did my father's sword get into the stone?"

"When your father died, no clear heir remained, and the nobles soon turned on one another. To prevent chaos, I placed Uther's sword in the stone and declared that only the one destined to lead Britain would be able to draw it forth. Year after year, the strongest among them tried and failed—until this day."

Rising from the bench, Merlin crossed to the open window with purposeful strides. Placing his hands upon the sill, he leaned forward, seeming to draw strength from the impending night.

With the full extent of his revelations about my lineage holding me captive, silence fell between us. I looked about me. It seemed the very cottage bore quiet witness, its stone walls steeped in the memory of the two it was built to protect and the path that had led me to them.

I watched Merlonius's features shift as fear, sorrow, pride, and love passed across her face, one after the other. Each expression revealed how deeply Merlin's words had moved her, just as they had me. Her struggle stirred something deep within me, awakening a fierce need to shield her even as my own uncertainty rose.

Merlin stepped away from the window and faced me. "Your nature and skills mark you as a true warrior and a natural leader. But you must understand, Arthur, that being the High King is not just a title. It carries immense responsibility and demands significant sacrifices. You will be entrusted with the protection of Britain, its lands, and its people even if it means facing grave danger."

Am I prepared for this?

"I cannot bear the thought of leaving here. This forest and this cottage have been my sanctuary, offering solace and happiness unlike any I have known. I will not embark on this path without you and Merlonius at my side."

In the dim light, Merlin's shadow merged with the encroaching darkness. He moved back and forth in uncharacteristic restlessness, the lines on his forehead revealing his concern, each furrow conveying the enormity of our changing lives.

Time stretched on until at last he halted his pacing and stood before us. "Arthur, you must be prepared for those who will oppose your coronation. There will always be individuals who seek to bring about your downfall, to seize the throne. And as for Merlonius… " His glance shifted to her. "She is the most vulnerable among us. She cannot be seen as having a place at your side, for those with malicious intentions will stop at nothing to harm her. She must remain hidden in the enchanted forest."

A fierce flame ignited, its heat threatening to engulf my very being. "Merlin, I understand the importance of Merlonius's safety. The mere notion of her coming to harm fills me with dread. Yet, must she remain forever hidden in these woods, a prisoner for my sake? What of the dreams I harbor? Are they to be forsaken, sacrificed at the shrine of duty?"

Despair consumed me as I stared at him. He moved slowly to his seat across from us, each step marked by the responsibility he carried.

"You stand at a crossroads. If you choose to accept your birthright, you must set aside personal desires. Honour will bind you to an oath of loyalty and protection, a vow to defend the realm and its people.

"And you, Merlonius, must also make your choice. Understand, our foremost duty will be to protect you.

"I do not seek your forgiveness, Arthur, but I implore you to understand my constraints. Bound by fate, I could not reveal your lineage until the sword was drawn from the stone. Yet, I hope you might find it in your heart to trust me again."

"Merlin, I want to trust you once again, but…" I hesitated, a torrent of conflicting emotions rising within me.

The scent of wildflowers clinging to Merlonius's garments drifted towards me, a poignant reminder of her bond with the enchanted forest. Her fingers brushed my skin in a tender gesture of comfort. I could not imagine a future without her.

"Arthur, I have great faith that you will fulfil your duties as king with honour and justice. Remember this: your journey is your own, and you must tread it guided by your own will and inner knowing. No one, not even destiny, can command the direction you take."

"Merlonius, so much is changing so quickly. To decide now…" I faltered, searching for words.

"Together, we shall confront whatever lies ahead."

Her words carried strength, her face determined. I took her hand in mine, holding it tightly. "I will not let this world take you from me," I said softly, barely above a whisper.

She shifted from me to Merlin. "You both are my clan. The thought of harm coming to either of you because of me is unbearable. I will heed your counsel. May we continue to attend the healing ceremonies at The Giants' Dance?"

I knew how much they meant to her, and I did not want her to miss them, but the possibility of peril cast a shadow over my spirit.

"Yes, Merlonius," Merlin agreed after a brief pause. "We will participate in the healing ceremonies, but only when I can accompany you. It is crucial for your safety that you remain close to the cottage, especially during the times I must tend to Arthur's needs elsewhere. Your protection is of utmost importance." His expression softened with a trace of sadness. "I promise to seek ways that allow you to honour the rites you hold dear while ensuring your well-being."

A glimmer of hope crossed Merlonius's face, but she did not reply, accepting Merlin's intended promise.

The revelation of my lineage to Uther Pendragon struck with a blow that unsettled every part of me. Everything I had known, from my simple life to the future I had once envisioned, was suddenly to be cast aside. I was just fifteen, now expected to rise to a throne and a life I had never foreseen. A cold dread took hold, pressing down without mercy.

"I need to step outside."

Walking towards the stream, I welcomed the night air, breathing deeply. Kneeling, I splashed water onto my face; its icy shock jolted my senses. I steadied myself, forcing my mind to clear. Images of Merlonius stirred a protective resolve within me. Then there was Merlin, whose teachings had shaped me. And my newfound kingship loomed before me, broad and uncharted.

Looking upwards at the night sky, strewn with countless stars, I was struck by its majesty, my own smallness stark in the vastness of existence. Merlonius's plea to stay true to myself, to heed the stirrings of what felt right within, filled my being.

How could I reconcile the demands of kingship with my desire to forge a life shaped by my own will? Merlin's revelations confirmed my heritage, but new doubts crept in: *Could I embrace the legacy I never knew, and would it consume the life I wish to build?*

A breeze stirred, and suddenly, the image of my father appeared before me. I stood still, captivated by his presence as I heard his words. *"Arthur, you are here because you possess the courage to wield my sword and meet the trials awaiting you. You will not be alone, this I vow."*

His form faded, and I shook my head, understanding the choice before me.

With measured steps, I reached the door and stepped inside. My breath came in shallow bursts, and my hands trembled. Merlin and Merlonius looked up, expectation mingling with weariness in their eyes.

"What have you decided, Arthur?"

I clenched my fists and looked down, my mind twisted into a knot of fear and duty.

"Arthur?"

Unable to speak, I watched as Merlin shifted his stance, his movements deliberate and measured. A subtle magic stirred around us, threading through the rafters of the cottage and into the enchanted forest beyond. It pressed lightly against my skin, like mist drifting through narrow gaps in the walls, and carried with it the scent of moss and crushed sage.

A hush settled, thick with something unspoken, as though the forest itself listened from beyond the walls.

The very air beckoned me forward, towards that which could no longer be avoided. Visions that had once haunted my sleep returned with unrelenting clarity, and I knew that fleeing from my fate was futile.

My arms fell to my sides as I surrendered to what had transpired this day. I uttered the words that would alter the course of my life. Each syllable echoed with the unshakable intent of my acceptance.

"I will embrace my heritage and accept the crown of the High King of Britain," I proclaimed, clinging to a newfound commitment, still unaware of the hardships my decision would bring.

Merlin and Merlonius watched me as I stood motionless, the events unfolding beyond me, as though I were not yet part of what was taking shape.

Merlin's voice reached me, steady and certain. "Our paths are now entwined, and our journey is now set. But hold this truth close: the bond the three of us share transcends the reach of time itself."

His words were a poignant reflection of the love that united us, reminding me of the determination we would need to meet what awaited us.

"Arthur, you shall remain with us until the day of your coronation. But for now, let us eat and rest. It has been a long day."

I drank deeply, hoping to calm the tumult in my belly. Eating or resting was out of the question; I needed a few moments alone with Merlonius to find clarity in the storm of emotion.

"Merlonius, would you like to take a walk by the stream?"

She pushed her untouched plate aside. "I would like nothing more."

We stepped into the cool, moonlit night. All that had changed pressed in on me as we followed the stream's edge. Yet even in the midst of that burden, her presence offered a quiet balm against the unrest within me.

We walked without speaking until Merlonius stopped. "Arthur, I will not turn aside from the life we share. Whatever the Fates decree, we shall face it together."

A tightness gripped my chest, and I shook my head. "But I cannot ask you to risk yourself for my sake. The dangers we must confront are too great, and I fear for your safety."

She held my gaze. "The choice is mine, and I choose to stand by you."

A sigh escaped me as I stared into the trees.

"I cannot fathom why the Fates chose to intertwine our lives, though I am grateful they did. Yet what if I fail to bring peace to the land? How can one raised far from the duties of a king be expected to rule a kingdom?"

She reached for my hand, her touch warm against the chill of the night. "I believe in you. I know the courage you carry, and you will not be alone. Merlin and I will stand by your side."

"I will miss you, Merlonius, but I promise to always find my way back to you."

"The days and the turning of each moon will seem endless, Arthur. But I am certain you will return."

We sat on the grass, the moon climbing higher, casting its pale glow over the rippling water. After a time, she inhaled deeply and turned to me.

"The shadow of my vision clouds your sight."

"Yes, if my future is one without you by my side. I do not know how I shall bear it…"

She placed her finger on my lips, silencing me. "The Fates may weave our tale, but I refuse to accept a life apart from you. We will remain united."

We rose, and I drew her close, burying my face in the familiar softness of her hair before stepping back.

"My feelings for you run deep, Merlonius. This is not the future I once imagined for us."

"Oh, Arthur…"

I took her hand in mine, guiding her towards the cottage. At the door, I paused, holding close what we had shared before crossing the threshold. Inside, Merlin welcomed us despite the weariness marking his face.

"Come, come, join me. We shall have a few days to replenish our bodies and spirits. It is my wish that you both find joy during this blessed respite the Fates have provided."

Merlonius offered a small smile, her eyes lit not with sorrow, but with a fierce calm that steadied me.

"We will, Merlin."

I met her gaze, then turned to him. "Yes, indeed, Merlin."

A breathless pause lingered, not one of peace, but of something poised to begin, as if the world itself stood at the edge of what would come.

The threat of war loomed, and the challenge of protecting our love in a world eager to divide us would demand strength neither of us had yet been called to summon.

Though disquiet pressed at the edges of my mind, I looked at Merlonius. The bond between us steadied me, even as the weight of the crown and all it might demand loomed before me.

I had spoken the words, claimed my heritage, and there could be no turning back. Merlonius was the light I would carry into the unknown, and with her courage joined to mine, I would meet whatever trials awaited my rule.

CHAPTER 11

BINDING HEARTS

The days leading up to my coronation were filled with joyous freedom, untouched by the burdens that loomed beyond the forest's edge. In the company of Merlin and Merlonius, I immersed myself in the magic of their world, where the ordinary blurred into the extraordinary. Candles lit with a mere gesture, and food and water appeared and vanished just as effortlessly. With such wonders at hand, I savored each fleeting breath of this life, each one precious, as if the woodland realm itself had granted me a final gift before I was called away.

On the sixth day, Merlonius and I retreated to the garden, a haven of serene beauty where time seemed to slow. I was captivated by the joy she found in the smallest of things, turning even the simplest tasks into experiences filled with wonder. More often than not, she left me smiling. On that day, as I knelt beside her in the garden's stillness, I felt a spark of excitement course through me.

"Shall we embark on an adventure?"

My question brimmed with anticipation. My desires, my dreams took hold, and within the forest's embrace, I would share them with Merlonius.

"Of course. Where shall we go?"

"Let us follow the stream and see where it leads us."

She jumped up, clasping my hand in hers. "Lead the way!"

We ran through the grass, our laughter rising to the sky like carefree birds on the wing. The stream wound through the woods, and we followed its meandering path, pausing now and then to admire a particularly beautiful flower or to listen to the melodies carried on the breeze.

Eventually, we came upon a small, tranquil pond, encircled by lush grass and vibrant plants. Ducks paddled lazily across the glassy surface, and sparrows flitted between the branches, their songs weaving seamlessly with the rustling leaves. We settled on the soft ground by the water's edge.

Sitting beside her, I plucked delicate blades of grass from the earth, twisting them into small circles. A determination grew within me, kindling my commitment to carry out the plan forming in my mind. The simplicity of weaving the grass calmed me, guiding my thoughts to what was to come.

Taking her hand in mine, I said, "Merlonius, I want to make a pledge to you."

"A pledge?"

"Yes, for with these rings," I continued, holding up two grass circles I had made, "I wish to pledge our hearts to one another." I slid one of the rings onto her finger. "You are my dearest friend, and my feelings for you run deeper than any words could ever convey."

"And I pledge my heart to you, Arthur," she replied, accepting the other grass ring from me. "With this ring, I promise to be your enduring companion and your support as we journey forward."

With a smile, I extended my hand, and she took it, sliding the grass ring onto my finger.

I entwined our fingers and said softly, "We shall face the challenges of the future together." Wrapping my arm around her, I pressed a kiss to her forehead.

"Arthur, these past days with you have brought me such joy. I know our destinies are intertwined, but as you leave to fulfil your duties as High King, I will miss our laughter, our talks, and the time we have spent together."

I tightened my embrace. "Merlonius, being with you has brought completeness to my life that I had never thought possible. I desire more than you can know, to have the freedom to remain by your side always."

We watched as the daylight dimmed with the setting sun, holding tightly to the fulfillment we shared, reluctant to let it slip away.

Hand in hand, we began our walk back to the cottage. The rustling of leaves accompanied our steps, and the distant song of a nightingale wove its melody through the shaded wood. A deep contentment filled us, knowing we were now promised to each other.

Merlin greeted us. "Welcome back, my friends. The meal is nearly ready. Why not enjoy some bread and cheese while we wait?"

Seated at the table, his sharp eyes studied us intently. "What is this I see? Do you have good tidings to share?"

Merlonius beamed, and Merlin's smile broadened as I announced, "We pledged our hearts to one another by a serene pond we discovered this day."

"Then let us toast," he said, raising his goblet. "To the hearts of Merlonius and Arthur!"

We lifted our cups, and a gentle joy settled around us. I relished the cool, clear water and the warm loaf of barley bread, its crisp crust crackling at the slightest touch. Tearing off a piece, I added a crumble of sheep's cheese, enjoying the simple yet satisfying flavors.

"What gives this bread such flavor?"

"Ah, my boy, it is the skill of the baker, the choice of the finest barley, and perhaps just a hint of magic."

Merlin served us bowls of lamb stew, each spoonful brimming with tender meat and fragrant herbs. The rich flavors captivated my senses, far surpassing my expectations. Yet as we ate, I found myself cherishing not only the food but also the fleeting solace we shared.

"Merlin," I exclaimed, taking another bite, "you have truly created a feast for us."

Merlonius echoed my enthusiasm. "This meal is an unexpected delight. Will you teach me how to make this?"

"But of course, my dear. We shall plan on doing so."

Throughout the eve, our laughter and conversation wove themselves into memories we would hold dear for years to come. A tranquility settled over us, unbroken until the distant hoot of an owl reminded us that the hour was growing late.

Merlonius sighed, "I fear weariness has overtaken me. Good rest to you both."

"Sleep well, Merlonius," we replied in unison, rising from the table.

"Magic will serve its purpose this night," Merlin announced, sweeping his hand gracefully across the table, whereupon the remnants of our meal vanished as if it had never been.

"Let us discuss the morrow," he continued, guiding us to the chairs before the unlit hearth, which had lost its purpose with the mild approach of summer.

I settled into the chair, and a heaviness descended, a wordless herald of the impending conversation. Disquiet wrapped around me like an unwelcome shroud. I braced myself for what was to come, each breath a deliberate attempt to still the unrest stirring within me.

"Arthur, my boy," he began, "I recognize your enduring virtue and honour. Yet, I sense your doubts about the path fate has woven for you. Understand that our lives are threads in a tapestry, often beyond our unravelling."

I longed to cling to these last moments of serenity before the morrow, but I knew I must respond.

"Merlin, I have not spoken of what the coming days may hold, hoping to immerse myself in the world you and Merlonius have nurtured within this enchanted forest." My words faltered, emotions constricting my throat.

After a brief pause, I regained control. "I cannot forsake who I am, nor will I sacrifice it. Do you understand my resolve?"

"Yes, I understand. And I promise you, Merlonius and I will always be a part of your life, both as Arthur and as the High King of Britain."

I searched his face, seeking any sign of deception, but found only sincerity.

"Your word on this?"

"My word."

"Merlin, let us speak no more of it."

"As you wish, Arthur. Until the morrow."

I rose and walked to my bed, my thoughts held fast to all that waited beyond this stillness. The scent of evergreens wafted in through the open windows, evoking memories of the lush forest that had once soothed me. Glancing over, I saw Merlonius watching me, her expression tender, and a pang of guilt struck me for burdening her with my worries.

She sat up in her bed and swung her legs to the side, facing me. "I have been waiting for you," she said, placing a tender hand on my arm. Her touch was light and soothing. "I know you shall be a great king, Arthur."

Fear and uncertainty filled me. "Do you truly believe I can do this?"

She squeezed my arm. "Yes, with all certainty. I know the courage you possess, and you shall guide the people of Britain to victory."

I leaned over and pressed a kiss on her cheek. "Your belief in me steadies my heart. Rest well until the morn."

"Rest peacefully, Arthur."

I lay on my back, staring at the rafters, haunted by the realization that I still had much to learn before I could become worthy of the crown. The question that had haunted me since the day I drew the sword remained. *Could I truly unite the kingdom and bring our people to victory?* I would need more than courage. Wisdom, sacrifice, and an enduring will would be demanded of me. What I did not yet realize was that what was to come would test not only my fortitude but the very unity of our kingdom.

CHAPTER 12

THE CROWNING OF THE HIGH KING

First light broke across the fading night sky as Merlin's call echoed through the cottage, heralding the arrival of a new day.

I quickly washed and made my way to the paddock to tend to our loyal companions. Whinnies from Madwen, Frey, Tuft, and Sweetness greeted me as I entered. The earthy scent of hay mingled with the aroma of horses, and as I stroked their velvety noses, a feeling of serenity and belonging washed over me. Their warm breath touched my skin, and the rhythmic sound of their chewing reminded me that here, in the enchanted forest, surrounded by these magnificent creatures, I was more at home than anywhere else.

The yearning to become the master of my own horse farm with Merlonius as my wife returned to me. I kept this dream close, unsure whether it would remain forever out of reach. I had carefully planned how events would unfold: the purchase of a small plot of land, the home and stable we would build together. I would, of course, ask her to wed before all of this, and together we would choose the stallion and mares. In time, we would breed a strong line of horses and leave behind a legacy for our children.

Picking up the pitchfork leaning against the shelter, I carefully cleaned the stalls, waiting for the horses to finish feeding. Once they seemed content, I began saddling them for the day's journey, letting Tuft graze within the paddock since Merlin had arrived on Frey from Sir Ector's farm.

I stroked Tuft's neck. "Tuft, my good boy, you are still needed here. But today, Merlin rides Frey."

Tuft seemed to understand, nudging my chest as if to offer his reassurance.

Leading the horses from the paddock to the rail, I secured their reins and readied them for departure. The crisp morn air was bracing as I headed back. Though my inevitable destiny had settled deep within me, a part of me still longed to defy its call.

Inside, a quick meal of berries, cheese, bread, and water awaited us. Seated at the table, we ate quietly, savoring the simple nourishment that would sustain us through the journey ahead. Between us lay an unspoken pause, each of us adrift in thought as we ate.

When we finished, I rose slowly, taking in the familiar space one last time. Every detail stood out more clearly than ever: the stone-framed hearth, the inviting chairs, the worn wooden bench, and Merlonius's loom. These walls held echoes of laughter, stories, and joy from days gone by, memories I longed to carry with me always.

Merlin came to stand by me. "We must depart, Arthur."

Reluctantly, I nodded, unsettled by the uncertainty of what lay ahead. Soon, this place, this life, might exist only in memory. I led the way to our tethered horses, casting one final look back at the cottage, bidding farewell to a life I cherished.

With Merlin and Merlonius at my side, we retraced our path through the forest, riding back to the very spot where destiny had woven my future with the sword in the stone. The clearing teemed with excitement as villagers and members of the nobility had assembled, drawn by the historic meaning of my impending coronation. Merlin led us away from the bustling crowd, finding a secluded spot.

After securing our horses to sturdy branches, I turned towards Merlonius and, with tenderness, pressed a kiss to her cheek. Our eyes met, and in that instant, we understood each other completely. No words were needed to convey the fears we both carried, nor the promises of love and loyalty that passed between us.

"All shall be well, Arthur," she whispered.

The burden of my fate bore heavily on me, but in that fleeting exchange, I drew strength from her presence.

Merlin's words reached us. "Arthur, we must proceed."

He turned, his staff tapping the ground.

Shaking off the last remnants of indecision, I braced myself for what lay ahead and advanced. With Caliburn at my side, Merlin and I strode purposefully towards the heart of the field, where vibrant banners fluttered in the breeze, their colors catching the sunlight like shimmering jewels.

Merlin lifted his staff, casting a brilliant light that enveloped us both as I knelt before him. A reverent silence fell over the crowd, their attention fixed on us.

"Arthur, son of Uther Pendragon and rightful heir to the throne, do you solemnly swear as High King to honour and protect the land?"

Drawing in a measured breath, I released it slowly and affirmed, "I solemnly swear as High King to honour and protect the land."

Merlin extended his hands before me, and summoned by an unseen force, my father's crown appeared in his grasp, cradled with great care and reverence. Its design balanced simplicity and grandeur, golden arcs elegantly encircling its form, like the graceful antlers of a stag in the light of early morn. Each curve and contour spoke of tales long past, rich with history and mystery. This was no mere relic, but a symbol of the authority and responsibility now mine. A deep sense of honour and humility surged through me, binding me to the path forged by my ancestors.

As he stepped closer, I realized that this ancient symbol of kingship, shimmering in his hands, would soon grace my head, forever sealing my destiny as the High King. With deliberate grace, he carefully placed it atop my head. This was not just an emblem of rule, but a silent vow to the people I would serve.

"I crown you the next High King of Britain," he pronounced with great dignity.

With a wave of his right hand, he conjured a goblet into his left, its contents gleaming with rich amber hues.

"Arthur, drink from this sacred cup of honey mead." The liquid shimmered as he extended the goblet, his eyes reflecting his pride. "In doing so, you bind yourself to the land, entering into a sacred union. The honey mead carries the nourishment and sweetness that the land bestows upon its people. By partaking in it, you pledge your devotion to safeguard and cherish them."

Lifting the cup from his hand, I pressed it to my lips. The liquid brought with it the scents of wildflowers and fertile earth, mingling as I drank. I tasted the sweetness of the honey along with flavors of wild berries and oak.

Merlin took the cup from my hands, and with a swift motion, it vanished, leaving only the the faint taste of honey on my tongue. He clasped my arm, approval shining in his eyes.

"Well done, my king, well done."

A thunderous roar swelled around me as I rose to my feet. Standing beside Merlin, I took in the sea of faces, some reflecting loyalty, while others held a wary curiosity, cautiously weighing what lay before them. It was as though I had been swept into a rushing river, carried swiftly towards an unseen fate. My heart beat in time with the coursing current, and I could almost feel the spray of the imagined waters on my face and hear its mighty roar echoing in my ears.

I shook my head, attempting to cast off the feelings that swirled within me. My oath was humbling and daunting in equal measure. A deep stillness settled within me, at odds with the rising voices of celebration that swirled around.

Merlin rested his hand on my shoulder, steady and firm, as the warm breeze stirred the air with the promise of change. The resounding fanfare of trumpets heralded the dawning of a new era. Surrounding us, noble figures assembled. Among them, Sir Ector stood, his expression unmistakably proud. Lady Kate's expression mixed delight with a touch of wistfulness, likely reminiscing about my journey to this day. Kay, meanwhile, bore a broad grin, his bearing easy, clearly pleased at his brother's ascent.

"Kay," I called out across the crowd, "will you join my band of warriors and stand beside me in defence of our land and people?"

"Arthur, my king, my brother, it would be my honour to do so."

Merlin looked at Kay. "Your loyalty and valour are renowned, Kay. In a fortnight, meet us at the base of the north mountain. There, we shall forge our paths and confront the challenges that lie ahead."

"I will be there, Merlin. Ready to serve and fight alongside our king."

"Indeed, Kay. We shall see you at the appointed time."

My mother was watching me, elation and concern evident on her face as she witnessed one son stepping into his destiny and the other vowing his allegiance. Her look, shining with love and pride, offered encouragement. With a deep ache, I realized how much I would miss her gentle strength.

I met her eyes one last time, then turned back to the field. Just as those who had assembled began to take their leave, a composed young man stepped forward.

"My lords, I am Bedwyr." He bowed. "On this momentous day, I pledge my allegiance to you. Though I offer little more than my skill with the lance and my bond with horses, my loyalty is as constant as the mountains. I shall stand as your stalwart ally in all your quests."

He stood tall before me, a glint of adventure in his dark brown eyes, while the sunlight wove through his hair, hinting at a life shaped by the wilds of the forest. As we looked at each other, a recognition of shared ideals and mutual respect became instantly clear. In that brief exchange, I sensed the depth of his dedication, a truth beyond words, already known to us both.

"Bedwyr, I am delighted to welcome you into the ranks of my trusted warriors."

Merlin briefly held his look before speaking. "Welcome, Bedwyr. Meet us at the base of the north mountain in a fortnight. It is there that we shall embark on our journeys and face the trials that await us."

"It would be my greatest honour."

After he bid farewell and left the field, we stood alone. A restless stir passed through me as I searched for Merlonius, but of her, there was no sign.

"Merlin, where is Merlonius? Is she safe?"

"All is well, and she is protected," he assured me. "Shall we find her and make our way back home?"

We set off towards the edge of the field, our horses waiting in the distance. Relief washed over me when I saw her standing calmly, waiting. I quickened my steps to reach her.

"Arthur," she said, clasping my hands, "I witnessed the ceremony and heard your oath. You will be a great king, of that I have no doubt."

Our fingers intertwined, her grip tightening as Merlin approached, his eyes sharp despite the day's demands.

"A long day indeed, Arthur," he said. "The sun sets on the birth of a new morn. Let us return home and find the peace this eve promises."

We rode through the enchanted forest, vibrant green hues blurring past, while the wind played with my hair. The rhythmic hoofbeats of our horses moved in time with the thoughts circling in my mind, shaped by all that had unfolded. Uther Pendragon, my father and a former high king, cast a long shadow over my lineage. At just fifteen years of age, the full force of my heritage pressed upon me, and with it came a rush of fear.

The setting sun cast its final light across the horizon, streaking the sky with deep orange and gold as we neared the paddock. Merlin left us to prepare a meal while Merlonius and I began settling the horses for the night. They responded with nuzzles and whinnies, their presence a balm after the emotions of the day.

In the fading light, we rubbed down their glossy coats, their soft nickers and contented snorts mingling with the sweet scent of hay. A mild breeze carried the freshness of damp soil and wildflowers as the last traces of daylight softened into twilight.

We walked from the paddock, securing the gate behind us. The dusty road had left us parched, and we eagerly anticipated reaching the cottage. Merlin had prepared a delectable assortment of fare, with warm bread and fresh cheese, accompanied by large goblets of water. We settled onto the wooden benches, drinking deeply and savoring each bite of the meal, finding a brief respite from the burdens of the day.

As the dimming light settled over us, I approached Merlonius. "Would you like to walk to the waterfall with me?"

She smiled. "Of course, Arthur."

Together, we made our way to the pond and sat on one of the stone benches. I reached for her hand, and she wove her fingers through mine. Her touch brought solace, easing the turmoil I could not yet name.

"Merlonius," I began, "pulling the sword from the stone has forever changed the course of our lives. I do not know what lies ahead, but one thing is certain: you are not just a part of my life—you are woven into my very being. Pledging myself to you was only the beginning."

I took a slow, steadying breath. "I love you, Merlonius. With all that I am, I will always cherish you."

She met my eyes, her voice a breath of certainty. "I love you, Arthur. No one else will ever claim my devotion but you."

Our lips met in a tender embrace, the longing between us deepening with the kiss. When I pulled back, I took in the delicate contours of her face, and I knew there was something else I needed to share.

"I wish to remain in this enchanted forest with you, Merlonius," I murmured, feeling my strength fade. "I could live a thousand lives in this forest and never tire of its magic."

Her fingers moved through my hair with slow, deliberate care, and the unrest within me began to ease.

"Oh, Arthur, if only our wishes could bend the will of destiny." She sighed. "But the Fates have deemed otherwise."

A deep weariness settled over me, and I leaned into her for support.

"You are tired."

I kissed her once more.

"Yes, we should rest."

We rose to our feet, and I held her close, cherishing the feel of her body against mine. I brushed a stray lock of hair behind her ear, and the scent of it surrounded me, igniting a fire in my heart. I knew I never wanted to let her go.

Our steps were slow as we made our way back to the cottage. Pushing open the door, we stepped inside and found Merlin seated by the hearth. I pressed my fingers to my lips, signaling Merlonius to remain quiet, for we could see he was fixed on the fire's heart, his gaze turned towards a world hidden from our own.

We waited by the door until he turned, his eyes adjusting to our presence.

"Arthur. Merlonius…"

"Greetings, Merlin," Merlonius responded wearily. "It has been a long day, and now I bid you peaceful sleep."

"Of course, my dear. Sleep well."

Once Merlonius retired to her bed, I settled into a chair opposite him. The distant call of an owl echoed softly, filling the stillness between us.

"Merlin," I said, keeping my voice low, mindful not to wake Merlonius, "every part of my being resists this royal destiny that has been thrust upon me. I do not want this. Do my feelings carry no meaning for you?"

"Arthur, to claim I fully understand what it is to bear the life of a High King would be misleading, but I do know what it is like to be set upon a path without a clear choice."

"You say you understand what it means to be pushed towards an unwanted future, and I want to know what you mean," I pressed. "Can you not understand that I refuse to lose what I have found here with you and Merlonius? I love her, Merlin, and I know you are fully aware of this."

He sighed as the lines on his forehead deepened, "Arthur, my life, my fate are tales for another time. And, yes, as you have surmised, I know full well the depth of your feelings for each other. I have seen the threads of your futures interwoven, though perhaps not in the way you might expect."

"What do you see? You must explain, not as I would expect. Does Merlonius's vision, where she did not see herself at my side, have anything to do with this?

"Merlin, you must tell me!"

He hesitated. My stomach tightened, frustration clashing with helplessness. But he remained silent, unwilling to give voice to what I longed to know. Instead, he looked away, leaving me with only silence where I had begged for answers.

Realizing that no more would be revealed this night, I exhaled, my chest tight with lingering unrest. A memory stirred—years past, when he and Sir Ector had told me I was not blood kin to the man I had called father. I had stood before them, demanding answers, the urgency in my words mirroring the desperation I felt now: *Do you hold the key? Do you know?* But then, as now, silence was his answer. The outcome was the same. So I relented.

"May you find peaceful rest, Merlin."

"Good rest to you, Arthur."

With solemn steps, I made my way to my bed. Merlonius was already asleep, her breathing soft and even. I quietly slipped into my own bed, but sleep eluded me. I lay awake, grappling with the looming uncertainties and mysteries of our future.

The next morn, sunlight streamed in, stirring me from sleep. I made my way to the other side, where I poured a goblet of water. Seeking out Merlin and Merlonius, I found them near the garden, seated on the bench under the majestic oak tree.

"Good morrow," I greeted as I approached them.

Merlonius welcomed me with a smile, though a trace of sadness shadowed her expression at Merlin's words.

"We must leave the enchanted forest now that you are High King and assume your responsibilities. Our first stop will be to return Frey to Sir Ector's farm."

My hopes of further solitude with Merlonius were shattered, and I glanced at her, seeing our shared disappointment.

"When do you wish to depart?"

"Within the hour."

Though I longed to protest, I refrained, not wanting to further upset Merlonius.

"If that is what you wish. And when do we journey back?"

"We will return," Merlin assured, his expression distant, as he peered into the mists of time. "But I cannot say when."

A hollow feeling took hold as I turned to Merlonius. "Will you walk with me?"

"Yes, Arthur."

We followed the path past the pond, then turned right, ascending towards the summit. The uncertainty of when I would see her again gnawed at me, sharpening the ache of our parting. When we reached the center of the grassy clearing, we sat down side by side, and I grasped her hand.

"Merlonius, I do not know what lies ahead for me as king. I dread what awaits me, but even more, I fear leaving you behind."

Tears welled in her eyes, yet her voice did not waver. "Arthur, you know I stand by you. I believe in you. And I will wait for you, no matter how long the path. But my concerns for you are great. There will be many challenges as you fight the Saxons, and there will be those who oppose your reign."

I tightened my grip on her hand. "I know. I wish I could assure you that all will be well. But I can promise you this: no matter what may come, I will return to you. Always."

"I believe you, Arthur."

As we held each other, the comfort of her arms eased my racing thoughts, even as uncertainty loomed ahead. Our lips met in a gentle kiss, her touch offering a fleeting escape from the burdens I carried. The forest around us seemed to still, its sounds fading until only the steady beat of my heart and my vow to return to her remained.

We stayed on the summit, her head resting against my chest, my arm wrapped around her shoulder. *If only we could remain here, safe from what awaited us.* With a deep sigh, she pulled away, finding the strength I could not.

"Arthur, we must go now, as you must depart with Merlin."

I knew she was right. Taking her hand, we began our descent. With each step, the sorrow deepened.

At the cottage door, my fingers traced her cheek before our lips met in a kiss both tender and full of longing.

I pulled her close, whispering in her ear, "I love you, Merlonius."

"And I love you, Arthur."

Inside, Merlin patiently awaited our return.

"Are you ready?"

Facing him, I stood firm. "Yes, Merlin. I am."

He went to Merlonius and placed his hand on her shoulder. "You are safe here. Remain near the cottage and the pond, and no harm will come to you. I shall return when Arthur is settled as king."

She nodded, holding back her tears. "I shall be well, and I will miss you. But please, return to me only after Arthur stands strong on his own."

He looked at her, and though neither spoke, their parting was felt deeply. He gently touched her cheek.

I secured the scabbard and sword around my waist and picked up my leather bag, mindful of the crown inside, a symbol of the daunting responsibilities awaiting me.

"It is time, Arthur. Shall we go?"

Together, we made our way to the paddock, where Tuft and Madwen stood saddled. Frey wore only a halter and reins, as he would accompany us as far as Sir Ector's farm.

Merlonius whispered, "Be safe, Arthur," as we mounted our steeds.

My voice failed me. I could only nod.

Guiding our horses through the enchanted forest, I took one last glance at Merlonius, standing at the edge of the clearing with her hand raised in farewell. I lifted my own, knowing the love we shared would face trials, yet endure.

"We shall return, Arthur. You have my word."

"We must, Merlin, we must."

With clear purpose, we rode into the unknown, fallen leaves scattering beneath our horses' steps as the forest watched in silence. I wondered what lay ahead and how much I was leaving behind. I held tight to my bond with Merlonius as I crossed the threshold from squire to king.

CHAPTER 13

MY LINEAGE

Merlin and I rode across the countryside, rallying support and assembling a formidable warband. With each passing day, our mission to defend the land from the encroaching Saxons began to take shape. The thick scent of damp earth and leaves clung to the woods around us. We rode through the dense growth, the rustling foliage whispering alongside us as we pressed on. Drawing upon his vast knowledge, Merlin became my most trusted guide, leading me along the treacherous path of kingship.

Two moons had passed since my coronation. As I moved through the wilderness, the forest's solitude brought clarity, allowing a fierce determination to take hold. I knew without doubt that what I had devised would help us drive the invaders from our land.

"Introducing war horses into our battle plans against the Saxons will catch them unawares."

Merlin walked beside me, his cloak trailing, silent as he pondered my words.

"You speak wisely, Arthur. I know of skilled horse traders who can lend their support to our cause."

Merlin stopped abruptly, and I narrowly avoided running into him as he turned to face me. "Arthur, the blood of your lineage flows through you. The spirit of warriors and kings lend their might. They watch over you still. With their strength, victory may yet be won."

I studied him, drawn not just to his words but to the ever-present mystery that shrouded him. His bearing and the way he spoke of forebears and ancestry held me fast. It was as though the veils of the past had lifted, offering a glimpse into a realm of ancient truths and hidden lines of kin. I felt compelled to understand my own role in this story and to interlace the threads of legend and my own fate.

"Merlin, I must know the truth of my origins."

With deliberate care he stroked his beard, a familiar gesture that always heralded moments of great import. He paced to the right, then turned sharply and retraced his steps. When he halted before me, his bearing was both commanding and reassuring.

"Yes, it is your right to have your ancestral ties unveiled."

From his lips, a chronicle unfolded, an account of eras past and destinies entwined. His words flowed, each syllable revealing the birthright entrusted to me. Through his telling, I came to know of my forebears, their ordeals, their victories and their sacrifices.

"You know that your father, Uther, was the younger son of your forefather Constantine," he began. "But you may not know that your kinsman, Aurelius Ambrosius, was Constantine's eldest son and Uther's brother."

He paused, his expression pensive as he delved into the past, unveiling both knowledge and sorrow.

"At the moment of Ambrosius's death, a comet blazed across the night sky, its fiery form like that of a dragon. It heralded the dawn of a new era. I stood beneath that celestial spectacle and foresaw Uther's ascent to the High Kingship. From that time on, your father became known as Uther Pendragon.

"This emblem is woven into your very being, Arthur. Its meaning will endure beyond time itself."

The image of the dragon-shaped comet remained with me, a symbol of hope and a harbinger of destiny. In the years following the revelation that I was not Sir Ector's son by birth, I often wondered about my true origins. Learning of this lineage felt beyond belief, for I was once a simple squire.

Merlin motioned for us to sit on massive tree trunks strewn across the forest floor. Once we had settled, he rested his staff across his lap, the smooth surface of the wood imbued with an otherworldly quality.

"Arthur, I understand that learning of this is daunting. Your ancestors were known to me, and I walked beside them as the Fates willed it. Their devotion and fortitude were unwavering; I can attest to that. But now, we must speak of your mother."

He regarded me in silence, something ancient stirring behind his eyes. With a solemn nod, he revealed a truth long held in trust.

"Her name was Igraine.

"The tale of your father and mother is a complicated one. Your father met Igraine when she was the wife of Gorlois, the Duke of Cornwall, who was a staunch supporter of your father's cause. Fate, it seems, had a hand in this, for Gorlois introduced her to the High King at court."

He hesitated, lost in the echoes of the past. Slowly, he returned to the present, a deep sigh escaping his lips.

"At first sight, Uther fell hopelessly in love with Igraine, and Gorlois, ever vigilant, sensed his growing affection. In response, Gorlois took her away to Tintagel Castle, a near-impenetrable stronghold perched upon cliffs that overlooked the tempestuous sea, placing an unbreachable distance between them.

"Desperate to be with the woman who had captivated him, your father sought my aid. I agreed to help, but under one condition: that the child conceived that very night would be given to me. Your father, driven by his love for Igraine, swore to my terms.

"I used my magic to transform your father into the very image of Gorlois. Uther, wearing Gorlois's form, came to her, and that night unfolded in both longing and deceit. Meanwhile, the real Gorlois and his men clashed against Uther's forces, and tragically, he met his untimely end before the dawn."

Seeking more answers, I pressed, "How did it come to pass that I was entrusted to your care?"

His focus shifted, ensnared by distant memories. He began quietly, "I knew the exact hour of your birth and arrived at the castle precisely on that fateful day. True to his word, your father, a man of honour, entrusted you to me. Your birth was a constant reminder of the night you were conceived, and Gorlois's death weighed heavily upon him.

"Igraine, unaware of the agreement between your father and me, initially reacted with sorrow and resistance upon learning that her newborn child would be placed in the care of a stranger. Yet, as Uther was the High King, she had no choice but to submit. Despite her own sadness, she eventually grew to love your father. They ruled as king and queen, their bond a source of happiness and stability, although no further children were born from their union. She stood by your father's side as queen until he died."

He grew still, as if sifting through the fragments of a life long gone. I sat beside him in thoughtful silence, eagerly awaiting the continuation of his narrative.

"Arthur, my visions revealed the perils that awaited you and the kingdom should your lineage be known too soon. I concealed your birthright to protect you, ensuring that you would reach manhood, inherit the throne, and bring healing to our land. That is why I entrusted your upbringing to Sir Ector and his wife, Lady Kate. I bestowed upon you the name Arthur and bade them raise you as their own, unaware of your true origins. By doing so, I kept you safe from those who would have sought to destroy you and the legacy you were destined to fulfil."

"Do you regret what transpired?"

His expression tightened, as pain crossed his features. "I could not alter the course the Fates had already laid before us. Your father, determined in his pursuit of Igraine, remained unswayed. Once I understood this, I foresaw that the child conceived that night held the key to the healing of our land. That child, Arthur, is you."

"What became of my father?"

"The relentless battles against the Saxons took a toll on your father, and he fell gravely ill. We had grown distant by then, and during one particularly fierce encounter with the Saxons, spies infiltrated his encampment, poisoning his drinking water. His death was swift, the work of fate's bitter hand."

A chill swept through me as I listened to the tragic tale of my father's demise, a stark reminder of life's frailty and my own mortality.

Recognizing my unease, Merlin offered a reassuring smile amidst the tumultuous revelations.

"Arthur, take heart. The Fates have set your path in motion, but how you walk it is yours to decide. You have the power to forge your own way and lead our people to a brighter future."

I inhaled deeply. "After pulling the sword from the stone, pledging my oath to the land, and striving to be a fair and just king, I cannot help but wonder. What shall become of me? Will I become the man I hope to be?"

He rested his hand on my shoulder. "The choices you make will shape the man you become. You already carry the heart of a just king, and with each trial, that truth will be revealed. Trust in yourself as I trust in you."

"May your belief in me prove true."

"Now, my boy, consider your heritage. The russet hues interwoven in your brown hair are a gift from your mother's kin. Your father's dark eyes reflect his legacy, and in time, his might and stature will be yours as well. Your mind is shaped by a lineage of wisdom far older than your forefather's time."

Merlin and I rose. Standing beside him, I watched as he gestured with a sweep of his arm. Wisps of light swirled into an ethereal circle before us, where the forms of a man and woman took shape.

"Behold, the High King Uther Pendragon and Queen Igraine, your father and mother."

My mother's beauty captivated me, while my father's regal bearing reflected the resolve and wisdom of a warrior long tested by time. Seeing him again, now beside her, stirred a deep yearning within me. It was a longing for the kin I had never known.

The images shimmered in the light, their presence rekindling memories of the spectral figure I had encountered by the stone. Yet, as swiftly as they had appeared, the ghostly forms faded, leaving behind a celestial afterglow.

"Merlin, your magic exceeds even my most daring imaginings. To see them together, my father and mother, even for a fleeting instant, is a blessing beyond words. The bond that ties me to them is a treasure I will hold close always."

His gaze remained forward as if he could still see them. Slowly he turned to face me. "Your father and mother were noble people, united by duty and sacrifice. You must believe me when I tell you that your birth was written in the stars, and entrusting you to me was for your protection. This vision is but a glimpse of the love that forever ties you to them. They watch over you still, guiding your steps as you bear the crown."

His words stirred something deep within me. I thought of my father, a warrior king bound to duty. And yet, love had found him. *Would the same be true for me? Could I claim both duty and love?*

"I must confess that my mind has often strayed from preparing for war against the Saxons. My love for Merlonius has only deepened, and I am determined to build a future with her by my side, as my queen."

Resting against a tree, Merlin gave a slight nod, his brow furrowing as he considered my words.

"Arthur, our foremost duty lies in ensuring the realm's safety. Matters of the heart, though deeply important, must be secondary until we drive the Saxons from our land."

His measured response did little to ease the longing within me. A veil of secrecy seemed to shroud his answer, leaving me unsettled and searching for deeper answers.

"How fares Merlonius? Is all well?"

"She is thriving, wholly dedicated to her calling."

I sensed something more, but before I could press him further, he turned the course of our conversation towards another revelation.

"You have two half-sisters. The elder, Morgause, is wed to King Lot of Orkney. They have been blessed with five sons: Gawain, Gaheris, Agravain, Gareth, and Medrawt. Your other half-sister, known as Morgan le Fay, walks a more shadowed course."

His words wove a complex tapestry of my ancestry, giving meaning to each name and its place in my heritage. I leaned forward with curiosity and uncertainty, eager to learn every detail about these newfound kin.

"Morgan le Fay did not choose her path willingly. Uther, frustrated by her defiant nature, sent her to the Isle of Avalon, where she honed her mastery over herbs, medicine, and the hidden arts. She has become a sorceress of great power. Yet tread carefully, Arthur. Beneath her formidable abilities lies a deep-seated envy towards you, rooted in the fate of her father and Uther's union with Igraine."

"Envy?" I repeated, the word settling heavily in my mind. "How could she envy me for my father's actions or even for my birth?"

Merlin's expression darkened. "It is not envy of what you have done, but of what you represent. To her, you are the child of betrayal, the heir to a throne built on the ashes of her family's honour. That pain shaped her path, and her ambition burns—not for rulership, but for vengeance."

I stood in silence as Merlin's final word, "vengeance," drifted into the night, dissolving into the hush of the forest. His grip on his staff tightened, as if weighing the burden of what lay ahead.

"We shall face her darkness together, Arthur. Come, let us return to our men."

Without another word, we walked back to the encampment, the crunch of our boots on the forest floor the only sound. Ahead, the faint glow of firelight filtered through the trees, and the low murmur of voices reached us as we neared.

Several of the men sat gathered around the fire. Some polished weapons, while others shared laughter over bowls of stew. A squire approached, offering steaming bowls to us with a respectful nod. I accepted mine with murmured thanks, and Merlin did the same, his movements slow, burdened by his reflections. He settled onto an empty log near the fire, and I chose a seat beside him, the fire's heat a welcome contrast to the coolness of the night air.

The camaraderie of the men should have brought comfort, but my mind was far from their cheerful chatter. The flames crackled and danced, yet in their shifting light, I saw only the story Merlin had shared, shadows of Morgan's envy and the challenges that lay ahead.

The night deepened around the fire, and the tale of Morgan le Fay haunted my thoughts. Though I appeared composed, a storm churned within me as I pondered the darkness surrounding her. It was a stark reminder of the vigilance needed to navigate the tangled paths of kingship and destiny.

CHAPTER 14

RETURNING HOME

A year into my reign, I found solace beneath the wide-reaching branches of a mighty oak. The canopy overhead sheltered me while I perused a manuscript, its sheets filled with the latest strategies for battle. The rustling leaves and distant clatter of training lent the illusion of serenity, masking the ever-elusive nature of true peace.

The sound of deliberate footsteps drew my attention as Merlin approached, his robes brushing the forest floor in time with his steady pace.

"Arthur, a king must have a home."

Setting the manuscript aside, I looked up and met the firm look in his eyes.

"What weighs on your thoughts, Merlin?"

He stood before me, his staff planted firmly in the earth.

"The time has come for you to reside in a fortress befitting a High King—a symbol of power and unity for the people. With your consent, I will begin the construction of a castle."

His plan to build a structure of such magnitude amidst the kingdom's unrest seemed daunting, but then it was Merlin.

"If you deem it necessary, then proceed. But ensure there is a place for you and Merlonius."

"Once the stronghold stands tall, I shall call you to return home."

As he withdrew into the embrace of the woodland, I was left to consider all that awaited me. One responsibility of my reign was to travel extensively across the kingdom. This I did with those who had sworn allegiance to me. Together, we ventured forth to forge bonds with the people, seeking to understand their plight and fortify the lands under my care.

We had travelled far from our home encampment when, before the full harvest moon, a dream visited me. It carried me to the edge of a mist-covered lake, surrounded by ancient trees whose gnarled branches reached towards the heavens. A gentle breeze stirred through the foliage, bringing with it the sweet scent of wildflowers and the distant song of birds. I heard Merlin speak to me.

"Arthur, return to the cottage in the forest."

The dream held me captive, weaving its tendrils through my senses. Slowly emerging from its depths, a yearning filled me. Its remnants clung to me, the forest's essence and Merlin's message remaining.

At first light, I roused my men. "Prepare yourselves. This day, we journey back to our encampment."

My men blinked away the last vestiges of sleep, their faces shifting with confusion and suspicion. Our site lay only a mile from the edge of the enchanted forest, and they were well aware of its bewitching charm, harboring a lingering fear of its magic. This was a realm where the ordinary intertwined with the otherworldly, where time held a different sway, and where mythical creatures roamed in unseen depths. Even ten miles from its edge, their unease would linger, haunted by tales of the lost and the forest's unseen perils.

"Fear not," I said, needing to ease their concerns. "We shall encamp at a safe distance from the forest's edge, guarding against its potent magic. We will remain vigilant, and our journey shall be swift. Trust in our purpose and the force of our brotherhood, for we carry the light of honour and destiny on our path, and no sorcery shall sway us from it."

At my words, the men straightened, exchanging nods as they gathered their belongings. The sound of swords being sheathed and supplies packed filled the air, their movements steady and purposeful as they readied themselves for the journey ahead. For several days, we travelled through familiar paths, the land leading us steadily towards our woodland haven. On the seventh day, with the sun sinking behind the distant hills, we finally arrived.

With nightfall approaching, the men worked in unison, their skilled hands fashioning humble shelters from woven cloth and animal skins. These makeshift lean-tos offered modest yet sturdy protection against the harsh winds and cold. The encampment took shape, the shelters seamlessly blending into the natural surroundings.

At its center, a crackling fire cast an inviting glow, its dancing flames warding off the encroaching darkness. I motioned for Bedwyr to join me at a secluded spot, away from prying ears, where we could speak in private.

"Arthur, is everything well?"

"Merlin has summoned me home in a dream. I shall be absent for the night and will return on the morrow. Ensure the men find ample rest and provisions, my friend."

"Consider it done. Stay safe."

I mounted my steed and ventured into the woods. The rhythm of hooves upon the forest floor merged with my thoughts. *Had it been four moons? Five? No, nearly seven turns of the moon had passed since I last inhaled the sweet scent of these trees, since I last saw Merlonius's radiant smile.*

Upon reaching the paddock, I swiftly dismounted, relishing the cool night air as melodies from flutes and lyres, played by welcoming wood nymphs, drifted through the trees. After ensuring my horse was settled, I approached the cottage.

At the weathered wooden door, I rested my hand on the rough-hewn planks, their solid feel a reassuring reminder of this familiar place. This sanctuary, where I could shed my kingly mantle and simply be a man, welcomed me once more. With a knock, the door creaked open to reveal Merlonius, warmth lighting her features in the dimness.

"Arthur, welcome home. You have been missed."

Joy surged within me. "You are so beautiful," I murmured, pulling her into my embrace. Her lips were soft against mine, her scent as familiar as the forest itself.

Merlin's resonant voice called from within. "Arthur, my boy, greetings!"

"It feels good to be home."

"We are delighted to have you back with us. Let us share a meal and celebrate."

He approached the table and, with a sweep of his arm, it was suddenly laden with an array of foods. Merlonius and I took our places side by side, facing Merlin. I reached for her hand, finding solace and familiarity in her touch.

"Arthur, how have you fared during the recent moons as king?"

Her eyes, the same deep green I had always known, danced with the light. Lost in their depths, I felt a surge of contentment.

"Well enough. Discovering what the people value most has been enlightening. Yet, I have missed this place and both of you. So, Merlonius, what have you and Merlin been working on during my absence?"

I sensed her eagerness, a hint of something she wanted to share with me. "We have been cultivating more medicinal plants in the garden," she began, "and Merlin has been teaching me the art of making tinctures and salves for skin ailments. But I have a surprise for you."

She rose from the table and walked to where her loom stood. When she returned, she held a grey-blue cloth. The color, a bold blend of woad and natural wool, was exquisite, a testament to her skill.

"You made this for me?"

"Yes, I did. It is my gift to you."

"This tunic is truly stunning." Running my fingers over the fine texture, I added, "Your work is remarkable."

Merlin cleared his throat, drawing my focus. "Your castle, Camelot, stands ready, Arthur, and we would like to take you to see your new home at dawn on the morrow."

So this is why Merlin called me back in my dream. "The castle is completed? Your magic never ceases to amaze. Let us indeed visit it on the morrow."

I hesitated briefly before adding, "Camelot, Merlin. Pray, why have you named it thus?"

"Camelot is more than stone and mortar, Arthur. Its name came to me in a vision, whispered by the Fates themselves. They revealed a place destined to be the heart of this land, a beacon of unity, power, and hope."

He murmured, "Camelot."

Rising, he walked to the window and looked out, his expression distant, his gaze touching the boundaries between worlds. Turning back to me, he continued, "Its name echoes the old ways, drawn from the spirit of the land itself. It harks back to Camulos, the ancient god of war and guardianship, whose strength once shielded these isles. But it is not war that shall define Camelot. It shall be peace, justice, and the promise of a better future."

I felt the depth of his words. "A dwelling born of visions and the spirit of the land. It shall be a great responsibility to lead from there, though my heart will always belong to this place."

Merlin inclined his head, a quiet calm settling over his features. "Camelot may not hold your heart, Arthur, but it will stand as the center of your reign and a symbol of hope for your people. It is yours to guide and uphold."

Turning to meet Merlonius's gaze, I saw the reflection of change beginning to stir. An unspoken understanding passed between us.

"Arthur, could you stay this eve?"

Her words stirred a shared longing for times past.

Merlin's brow furrowed slightly, then eased as he nodded, "It is settled then."

Facing Merlonius, I took her hand in mine. "Yes, I will stay," I said. "My men are encamped a mile from the edge of the forest, and Bedwyr is aware of my journey here. I will need to return to them on the morrow."

Her expression softened with affection as she squeezed my hand.

I looked about the cottage, a place steeped in shared history. Against the far wall rested the workbench, marked by food preparations and tinctures and potions. The unassuming wooden chairs before the hearth stirred memories of winter nights spent captivated by Merlin's tales of magic and dragons. The scents of dried herbs and fragrant potions mingled with the sound of the crackling fire, drifting about us.

Breathing deeply, I reminded myself that within these walls, the burdens of the realm dissolved. Here, I was simply Arthur. The eve unfolded in laughter and heartfelt conversation. The night wore on, with the sounds of the forest reminding us of the late hour.

Standing, Merlin said, "I will step outside and enjoy the stars. Until the morrow my young friends."

"Rest well, Merlin," Merlonius replied.

"And may you have a peaceful sleep," I offered.

When the door closed behind him, we moved to our beds. Merlonius had become the center of all I cherished, and I longed simply to remain by her side.

"Merlonius, I have missed you through each moon we have been apart."

She reached out, her touch cool against my skin, "Arthur, I too have longed for you. It brings me such joy to have you here again."

I raised her hand to my lips and kissed it.

"To be with you once more heals my spirit. Tell me, have you any adventures to share?"

"Oh, yes, Arthur! When Merlin and I were last at The Giants' Dance, a warrior approached, badly hurt from battle. Merlin urged me to place my hands on the wound. Touching his arm, I felt the healing power flow from my hands. Slowly, the skin drew together, and his pain gave way to relief. I was amazed."

"Your courage in walking the path laid before you strengthens me. I draw from it as I face my own destiny."

Leaning closer, I felt her warm breath against my cheek, inviting and comforting. Our lips met in a tender kiss.

"Arthur, our time apart has been long, and each eve I would lie here wondering how you fared."

"Yes, far too long. Each night, as I looked up at the stars, I thought of you. Know this: my heart is always with you, no matter the distance."

With these words, we settled into our beds, turning to face each other. Slowly we slipped into restful sleep. Yet, beyond the safety of this cottage, the world and all its trials waited for us. Dreams of the life we might have lived, free from the burdens of my crown, drifted through the darkness, stirring a longing for what could have been.

CHAPTER 15

CAMELOT

I woke slowly, my senses stirring from the depths of sleep. Echoes of dreams lingered, slipping away like whispers on the wind. I blinked away the last traces of slumber, greeted by the familiar crackle of the hearth and the pale light of morn filtering through the window.

A faint sound roused me fully from sleep. "Good morrow."

"Good morrow to you as well, Merlonius," I replied, a smile unfolding as I stretched, easing the last vestiges of sleep from my limbs.

She moved gracefully behind the curtain to change. Reaching for the tunic she had woven, I admired its rich cloth. Its perfect fit surprised me as I dressed. Joining them by the hearth, I caught Merlin's amused glance.

"Arthur, that color suits you well."

"It does, does it not?" I replied with a grin.

Merlonius added, "It fits you perfectly, and the color truly becomes you."

Merlin motioned towards the table now laden with the morn's fare. "Come, let us break our fast. The day beckons, and with it, the promise of new sights."

I took my seat next to Merlonius, with wooden cups and plates before us filled with the rustic bounty of the forest: fresh berries, slices of soft cheese, and bread still warm from the hearth.

"These berries are from our garden," Merlonius said, passing me a bowl.

"They are indeed sweet," I responded, savoring one. "And Merlin, your bread surpasses itself with each baking."

He smiled, tearing into another piece with evident satisfaction.

After we finished our meal, the anticipation for the day's journey deepened. We rose from the table; Merlonius cleared away the remnants of our meal to the workbench at the back, while Merlin carefully doused the hearth, ensuring no embers remained.

I secured my scabbard around my waist, the familiar weight of the sword now a reassuring comfort. Outside, the crisp air of morn greeted us, our horses saddled and impatient for departure.

"Merlin, my thanks for tending to the horses," I said as we approached.

"No trouble at all, my boy," he replied, mounting his steed with ease.

He took the lead, guiding us along a previously untraveled path through the enchanted forest. We continued beneath the whispering leaves and shimmering shadows until suddenly, Merlonius gasped.

In the distance, a majestic castle rose against the horizon, its gleaming stone walls crowned by six slender turrets reaching skyward like the fingers of a giant. Flags of red, blue, and purple danced in the breeze, each hue representing the unity of Britain's diverse realms under a single crown. Among them, a crimson dragon banner rose above the others, bold and unyielding, the symbol of my father, Uther Pendragon, and now mine as his rightful heir, the High King of Britain.

We stopped to take in the breathtaking view, awe lingering in the air as Camelot loomed like a vision from a dream.

"Merlin," Merlonius said, "this is the very castle I saw in my vision, before Arthur pulled the sword from the stone."

"Yes, my dear, the gods granted you foresight of this day. But it was not for me to share that knowledge until the future became the present. And now it has."

"I remember it vividly," I recalled. "Not just the castle, but the flag bearing the image of a dragon. Your insights and your gifts are deserving of the highest respect."

"Indeed they are," Merlin affirmed. "Come, let us proceed."

We rode in silence, each of us drawn forward by the force of change.

The castle rose before us as we crossed the drawbridge, its timbers creaking beneath our horses' hooves. Passing under the archway, we dismounted onto the cool stone.

Merlin raised his staff, the crystal at its tip glowing faintly. With a groan, the great oak doors swung open, revealing a vast space beyond. Simple benches and tables stood unadorned, offering a humble welcome to weary travelers seeking rest.

Merlonius and I traced the smooth grain of the tables, our hands still entwined. The pieces, crafted from rough-hewn oak, glistened in the torchlight. They seemed rooted in place, as if the stone had grown to cradle them.

Deeper inside, the scent of burning wood enveloped us, rising from fire pits blazing in the center. Openings in the roof allowed the smoke to rise and drift beyond the castle's walls.

Her grip tightened in mine as we ascended the broad stair. At the midpoint, it split into two directions. Merlin led us to the right.

"Arthur, let us continue to your quarters."

We entered a dimly lit passage lined with thick stone blocks. The torches cast their light, unsettling the darkness clinging to the walls. Looming ahead, a large wall marked the end of the passage, with two heavy wooden doors nestled in the corner. With a wave of his staff, they slowly swung open, unveiling a spacious chamber.

"This shall be your sanctuary. A place for you to retreat, away from the sounds of the castle."

A large four-poster bed, adorned with soft woolen blankets and rich velvet coverings, commanded the space, while the hearth bathed it in a welcoming glow. Two wooden chairs of weathered oak stood before the flames, their grain and knots adding rustic charm. Beside each chair, small wooden tables waited, ready to hold goblets and trenchers.

In the middle, a substantial square table stood, its simple design favoring utility over decoration. Four wooden chairs with straight backs and solid seats encircled the table, each crafted for practical use.

Merlonius and I approached the two tall windows on the opposite wall. Though narrow, they offered a magnificent view of the surrounding forest. Light pierced through the narrow openings subtly brightening the chamber. A faint breeze carried the earthy aroma of soil and foliage; a simple reminder of nature's enduring beauty.

"Merlonius," I said, gesturing towards the horizon, "the enchanted forest lies in that direction."

She gave a slight squeeze of my hand, her gaze lingering on the forest beyond, as if sensing all that lay between us. *This place was so different from our cottage; there, the forest felt alive with guardian spirits, their murmurs carried on the breeze, rustling softly through the leaves and calling to my soul.*

"Arthur, you need not be here always. Whenever possible, return home to the forest, to me."

The feel of her hand in mine steadied me amidst the tide of emotions stirring within. She understood the depth of what I felt, and her knowing brought me comfort.

This was to be my dwelling, a haven in some ways, but also a gilded cage, its splendor a reminder of the burdens I must carry. This pressed upon me, but I did not speak of it, unwilling to diminish the pride Merlin had showed in presenting his achievement.

"Merlin, I am grateful for all of this."

"Ah, but our tour of the castle is far from over."

We proceeded down the hall, moving away from the stair and turning right into a dimly lit passage. The coolness of the stones offered a welcome contrast to the warmth of the flames, their light dancing along the path ahead. When it curved to the left, we came upon a new chamber.

He gestured towards a large door. "Here is where Bedwyr shall reside."

We stopped before the door, and I found myself wondering why Merlin had arranged for Bedwyr to dwell so close.

"Merlin, why have you placed Bedwyr so near?"

"You will always need those who can be trusted to remain close," he replied. "Bedwyr is a loyal friend, and he has shown unwavering resolve to stand by you, no matter the challenge. Your safety is strengthened daily by his presence.

"Now, let us explore more of the wonders of this castle."

I caught the gleam of amusement in his eyes as we followed him. He walked with purpose, then paused before a door slightly set apart from the others

"These quarters are for a very special friend."

I glanced at Merlonius, a faint flush spreading across her cheeks. The thought of her staying in the castle stirred long-buried yearnings.

"Merlonius," I whispered.

She looked at me, and I raised my hand to gently caress her cheek.

"This indeed will bring me joy, Merlin," I said, turning to him.

I longed to ask when she would join me, but he was already motioning for us to follow. At the end of the hall, he reached up and pulled a sconce downward, setting a hidden enchantment into motion. The wall slid open without a sound, revealing a secret passage. Even for us, long accustomed to his magic, the smooth, silent motion and the light shimmering along the seam left us momentarily spellbound—a quiet reminder that wonder lived at the heart of all he did.

"This passage leads directly to our cottage in the enchanted forest. Your movements will be cloaked, while the way will light with my magic."

He pushed the sconce upward, and the wall closed with a soft whisper, merging as if it had never parted.

"Come," he urged, leading us back to the broad stair we had ascended earlier.

He guided us down the steps to the center platform, then up the other side to another part of the castle. At the top, he paused, gazing down the hall, his expression momentarily distant.

"Those who will play significant roles in your reign as king shall reside along this hall."

Merlonius and I exchanged a glance, well aware that Merlin's foresight often hinted at deeper truths. Whatever lay ahead, Merlin seemed unwilling to dwell on it. He straightened, as if setting aside whatever doubts lingered.

"Now, I must disclose something of great importance," he said, turning to lead us back down the stair.

Upon reaching the bottom, we turned right and proceeded down a passage leading to a vast chamber. At its center stood a large round wooden table, its surface smoothed to perfection, glinting faintly in the torchlight.

"Arthur, here all are equal."

The table, crafted from thick, dark wood, held a commanding strength, its presence solemn and sure. I approached, drawn by a pull that felt both ancient and destined. Resting my hand on its surface, I traced the finely worked grain. I saw my knights gathered around it, each one bound by their solemn vow.

This was no mere table; it would stand as a symbol of unity, the foundation of the code we would uphold. It would be the heart of our fellowship, a place where honour and duty would guide our every decision.

"This table will serve me and the land well," I affirmed. "Soon, I will call my men to gather here, and we shall speak as one, united in our cause."

"Excellent, my boy, excellent, as it should be," Merlin said.

"Now, come. There is more to see," he added, beckoning for us to follow him.

He guided us through the cooking rooms at the far rear of the castle. The stone hearths stood cold and empty, awaiting the fires that would one day prepare feasts for those who would dwell here. Iron pots and kettles, hanging from hooks above, reflected the shifting glow of the few torches mounted on the walls. Long wooden tables stretched across the space, their surfaces unmarred, waiting for the hands that would chop, knead, and prepare meals.

We then stepped outside, making our way to the stables. Built in an L-shape, the stone structure boasted many stalls crafted from oak and adorned with ironwork. Here, the valiant warhorses destined to carry my knights into battle would find shelter.

Merlin pointed to the stalls with his staff. "Arthur, these stables shall serve as shelter for your horses, especially those ridden by your foremost warriors. We shall build more dwellings as our number grows."

"Indeed, for we shall claim victory with each knight riding into battle."

From the stables, we approached a structure, its thick stone walls rising, strong and unyielding. Within, spacious chambers had been crafted to shelter my knights, simple yet sturdy, offering a place of rest and fellowship.

As we moved through the structure, Merlin explained, "These quarters will provide a retreat for your men, Arthur, after long days of training. It will be a place where they may find solace and renewal before riding into battle."

"They will need such a place. Every knight deserves a sanctuary to restore his vigour."

Following him back outside, he smiled, "Shall we now explore the grounds and gardens?"

The verdant expanse stretched before us, an oasis amidst the imposing stone walls. Neatly arranged rows of herbs and flowers bordered the pathways, their vibrant hues softening the fortress's stern character. Birds sang in the distance, their melody weaving through the stillness. Merlonius walked beside me, captivated by the carefully cultivated blooms.

"These grounds reflect Camelot's spirit," Merlin said thoughtfully. "They offer solace and remind us of the harmony we must preserve."

We strolled along the garden, the castle walls rising protectively around this serene haven. Beyond the neatly tended beds lay an orchard, where apple and pear trees stood in tidy rows, their young branches swaying gently in the breeze.

"Well, Arthur, do you find the grounds appealing?"

I looked around, my heart straying to the enchanted forest where simplicity and freedom shaped our days. That life seemed far removed from Camelot's grandeur. Yet, I understood these gardens as a symbol of sanctuary and renewal, a reflection of the balance we sought to preserve. Merlin's thoughtfulness was evident, and I would not diminish his gift. I chose my words carefully.

"These gardens and the orchard will be a welcome retreat from the castle's walls, a place to gather one's thoughts and find clarity."

At the front gate, a question surfaced. "Merlin, where are your quarters? I have not seen them in our walk."

"Arthur, my home has always been in the woods, in my cave, and now with Merlonius, in our cottage amidst the trees. Yet, rest assured, I shall always be near."

He glanced towards the horizon, his expression reflective. "My heart belongs to the wilderness, but my devotion to Britain and to you remains unwavering. Wherever you go, whatever path you tread, I will be there in spirit, watching over and guiding you. Our bond transcends the walls of any dwelling."

A heaviness settled over me as I realized he would not be joining me in Camelot. His counsel had been a wellspring of clarity and quiet determination, a steady support through every trial. Amid Camelot's towering walls, I found myself yearning for his companionship, for the comfort of a trusted friend's presence.

"Arthur, it is time to bring your men to their new home," Merlin urged with pride, drawing me back from my reverie to the responsibilities that awaited.

No words seemed worthy of the gratitude I held. "Merlin, your wisdom and enduring support have been my pillar throughout this journey. I am forever grateful."

Meeting my eyes, he nodded solemnly, stirring something deep within me. I continued, "Though you may not reside within the walls of Camelot, your teachings will endure within these halls forever. You have shaped the leader I am becoming, and your guidance will always be with me."

A subtle shift in his stance revealed a fleeting hint of emotion before he regained his composure and motioned for us to mount our horses. We rode back through the gate and over the drawbridge, the rustling leaves and chill wind at the fork in the road signaling our parting.

"Merlonius and I will return home now."

She drew herself up with a slow inhale, her bearing composed. A shared sorrow rested between us, pressing upon me like an unseen tether, pulling me in the direction of the sheltering forest they were bound for. But the unyielding call of duty held me back, reaffirming the separate paths we must now take.

"I will see you both again soon."

Straightening in his saddle, Merlin's expression held its usual calm resolve. "Take care, and remember, what you seek already lives within you."

With a final exchange of looks, they began their journey into the enchanted forest, leaving a solemn stillness in their wake. Their departure bore down upon me, and I felt the solitude that came with wearing the mantle of high king.

"*The paths we choose are never easy, Arthur,*" Merlin's voice echoed in my mind as they faded from sight. "*But they are yours to walk, as king and guardian of this land.*"

I turned my horse back to the encampment where my loyal men awaited. Doubts about ruling fairly and justly flitted through my mind like restless thoughts at twilight, but with a firm shake of my head, I dispelled them. I needed to be a beacon of stability for my men, for my kingdom.

With renewed purpose, I urged my horse forward. The path before me held uncertainty and sacrifice, yet I accepted what must come to safeguard my people and honour the legacy entrusted to me. Even so, one truth burned brighter than all others: I would not let the burdens of the crown sever what bound my soul to Merlonius.

As the first stars emerged above the treetops, I whispered my vow to the heavens: "I will return to her. Whatever trials await, she and I shall shape a life beyond the reach of duty alone."

CHAPTER 16

VISIONS OF THE HEART

We faced the Saxons again on the battlefield in the third year of my reign, another chapter in a war that refused to end. As the sun began its descent over the open field west of Camelot, its fading light cast a solemn hue across the ravaged field, bearing silent witness to the toll of our latest campaign. The wounded lay scattered across the blood-stained ground, anguished cries mingling with the whispers of those lost. Each fallen knight stood as a testament to the cost of this relentless conflict, their sacrifices woven into the very tapestry of our struggle.

"Tell the men to retreat! Return to Camelot now!" I bellowed across the field, my command carrying the strain of our collective exhaustion and unyielding will.

Bedwyr rode off to fulfil my orders and the battered remnants of our forces turned their steeds, retreating from the grim scene. My horse, Thor, bore me away, the iron hauberk heavy on my shoulders, a tangible burden of battle. But the mantle of High King weighed heavier still, laden with the memory of all those lost under my rule.

Riding back to the castle, the rhythmic drumming of hooves intensified my fervent desire to devise a plan. *How could we triumph over these relentless adversaries?* Their cunning strategies had claimed too many of our men, leaving me with a growing uncertainty. I clenched the reins, knuckles turning pale, as I grappled with failure and a burning need for a course of action that would lead us to victory.

Inside the castle walls, the worried stances of knights and the furrowed brows of attendants mirrored my own unrest. Their silent questions did not escape me, and they only deepened my resolve to overcome our current challenges.

Kay approached, his jaw set and his eyes shadowed with determination. "Arthur, I shall return to the battlefield with Gareth, Tristan and Bors. We will gather those who have fallen and light the funeral pyres."

I placed my hand upon his shoulder, holding it firmly. "My brother, your willingness to take on this duty does not go unnoticed. Be safe."

Gareth stepped forward, the lines of grief evident across his features. "Their sacrifices will not be forgotten. We will see them honoured."

Tristan, always quiet but fierce in his loyalty, nodded. "They shall receive the respect they earned."

Bors, his voice gruff yet steady, added, "You have my word, Arthur. It will be done."

"My valiant knights, the honour you bear and the love you carry for the fallen will see you through this sorrowful task."

With a final nod to them, I made my way to my chambers, shedding the chainmail that had been my shield through the trials of the day. The resounding clatter as it hit the floor marked a tangible release from the responsibilities I carried. Exhaustion washed over me, and while a hot meal, some ale, and a night's rest would comfort my men, I knew I needed something more.

After dining with my knights, I requested Bedwyr's company in my quarters. We settled into the wooden chairs before the hearth, where the crackling fire burned low and the scent of wood smoke clung to the stones. Its heat pressed gently against the chill that seeped through the castle walls, though it could not reach the deeper cold within me.

My mind turned to my duties as king, the well-being of my knights, and the ever-present threat of the Saxons. Memories of battles past and looming challenges churned within me, a storm I struggled to calm.

Thoughts of a course of action consumed me as I wrestled with how to defeat our relentless adversaries and rekindle hope among our people. Yet, as I looked into the fire, another need surfaced, one I had kept buried deep.

"Bedwyr," I began, the familiarity of our bond steadying me, "the brotherhood of the Round Table, along with your loyalty, friendship, and unmatched skill, hold immeasurable value to me." I hesitated, pushing aside images of the battlefield to broach a deeply personal matter. "There is something of utmost importance that I must discuss with you."

He leaned forward, clasping his hands.

"You have my trust, Arthur."

"Before that fateful day when I pulled the sword from the stone and discovered my royal lineage, before I ascended to the throne and took up the burdens of a kingdom, I lived in obscurity. I roamed the forests with Merlin and cherished the freedom and simplicity of those days. And then, I met Merlonius."

Recognition sparked in his eyes. In a hushed breath, he said, "The healer. Tales of her skills and kindness have reached even my ears."

A fond smile graced my lips. "Indeed, she is a gifted healer, and more. She holds my heart. Merlin, wise and ever watchful, has cautioned us to conceal our feelings, warning that our enemies might use her against me as a weakness."

Bedwyr's brows drew together as he carefully considered his words. "I must agree with Merlin. Your enemies, and those who covet the throne, might use your affection for Merlonius against you. It is wise to keep your feelings hidden. You have my solemn word to protect you both."

I rose and walked towards the tall windows that framed a view of the castle grounds. I sensed the distant echo of Merlonius's voice in the rustling leaves and the wind's whisper, though it felt as faint as a memory. My yearning to be with her, to feel the calmness she could weave into my restlessness, was an unquenchable fire.

I turned from the window and returned to the hearth, its warmth failing to chase the chill of longing. I met Bedwyr's eyes.

"Your loyalty to both Merlonius and me is of immeasurable worth. I trust you above all others with this knowledge. She remains under Merlin's watchful care deep in the enchanted forest, a realm accessible to only a select few. It has been far too long since I last saw her, and this night, I intend to visit her. In my absence, I entrust you to oversee the affairs of the court. I will return within two days."

"Arthur, I vow to guard the secret of your love for Merlonius with all I have. It shall never be spoken."

"Words fall short of the weight this carries in my heart. This is no mere charge, Bedwyr. It is a sacred trust. And in keeping it, we protect what remains most dear to me."

After he left my quarters, I gathered my belongings and reached for the grey-blue tunic Merlonius had woven for me. Though it no longer fit, as my frame had grown since the day she gifted it to me, the recollection still brought a smile to my lips. Carefully, I placed it back on the shelf and chose another. Then, with my sword secured in its scabbard, I made my way to the stables, my footsteps light against the fading sounds of the day.

I approached Thor while a stable boy readied a horse that had not seen the recent battle. "My trusty companion, your great courage this day shall be remembered. You are weary, as we all are. Rest now."

He lowered his head lightly on the gate, his eyes meeting mine with familiar knowing. Letting out a nicker, a sound full of reassurance, he pressed his warm breath against my hand as I offered him an affectionate rub. His coat was soft under my touch, and the familiar scent of the stables surrounded us.

I stayed with him until Aled, my riding horse, was ready. After thanking the young lad for his assistance, I glanced back at Thor.

"I go now to find my own rest. Worry not, for I shall return."

Beyond the stalls, I swiftly mounted and secured my bag. The saddle, worn but reliable, fit comfortably beneath me as Aled's hooves echoed with purpose across the courtyard. We crossed the drawbridge and began our journey towards the enchanted forest.

Pale beams of the moon threaded through the trees, casting delicate shadows on the road ahead. The journey was peaceful, the rhythm of our passage melding with the stillness of the night. As the edge of the forest drew nearer, joy welled up within me, stirred by the eager anticipation of seeing Merlonius again.

Venturing through the trees, the cottage came into view. I dismounted Aled and led him into the paddock, quickly removing his saddle and bridle. With a pat to his flank, I left him to rest.

At the threshold, I tapped lightly on the weathered door. It swung open, revealing Merlin.

"Welcome, Arthur. Please come in," he said, stepping aside to let me enter.

The fire burned steadily within, and the scent of oak and simmering herbs swirled about me, a reminder that I was finally home.

Merlonius approached with serene grace, the firelight softening her features.

"I am overjoyed to see you once more, Arthur!"

I stepped forward, drawn irresistibly to her. Our hands met, and just as I leaned in to kiss her, Merlin called us to join him by the hearth.

"Come, both of you, take your seats," he invited, gesturing towards the chairs arranged around the hearth.

Once we were settled by the fire, I looked at Merlin, grateful for his familiar presence. There was a comfort in being by his side again, a sense of ease that only he could bring.

"Merlin, how have you fared since I last saw you?"

"I am well, and it eases my heart to see you safe. I have seen the remnants of your recent encounter with the Saxons through the veil. You struggle, do you not?"

A deep sigh escaped my lips. "I am weary. It feels as if, despite our best efforts, we are not making any gains."

"You will overcome these challenges, my boy. Do not lose hope."

His words brought some solace, yet doubt persisted. "I want to believe it shall be so."

Merlonius placed her hand lightly on my arm. "Arthur, you seem in need of rest. Perhaps retiring for the night would do you well. We will speak more on the morrow."

Grateful for her understanding, I nodded and stood. "Yes, I am weary. I shall bid you both good sleep."

I looked into Merlonius's eyes and caressed her cheek before turning towards the sleeping quarters. After pulling off my boots, I slipped beneath the thick blanket and allowed sleep to claim me. In my dreams, I sat beside the pond with Merlonius, basking in the sunlight. The serenity of the dream gently stirred me awake. With the morn's stillness surrounding me, I dressed in a fresh tunic, drank from a goblet of water, and made my way to the stream.

The water's murmur flowed over smooth rocks, mingling with the soothing melodies of birds above. Together, they wove a tranquil sanctuary under the open sky. Pixies flitted, their smiles enchanting and familiar, reviving recollections of laughter that had brightened my days since childhood. Sitting by the stream, looking out over the vast expanse of the sky, I let recollections of my youthful days unfold before me. I recalled those carefree years when I roamed the woods, free from the burdens that would later shape my path. A longing for those simpler times began to unfurl, softening the hard lines of the present.

Lost in my thoughts, I was startled by the sound of footsteps approaching from the direction of the waterfall. Merlin and Merlonius came into view, their voices blending in low conversation. A glance at the sun, now high in the sky, revealed that several hours had slipped by since I first sat by the stream.

"Well, you are finally awake. How are you faring, my boy?"

"Rested."

"Merlonius and I spent our morn by the waterfall. It is a perfect spot for lessons."

"The waterfall and pond are indeed one of my favorite havens."

Merlonius stepped closer. "Arthur, would you like some food?"

"I am a bit hungry, yes."

"Well, then, let us head back," Merlin said with a twinkle in his eye.

Once inside, he paused, as if considering something, before lifting his hand in a subtle gesture. With a graceful sweep, an array of food appeared.

Merlonius and I exchanged a knowing glance.

"Merlin," Merlonius said, "you always know how to brighten a day."

"You are kind to say so, my dear," he said, his tone light and amused. "Now, shall we enjoy this meal and each other's company?"

Once we had settled in our customary places, Merlin on one side of the table and Merlonius and I on the other, we ate, talked, and laughed through the day. As the sun began its descent, its light bathed the table in a golden hue, and we lingered there, at ease in one another's presence.

Merlin rose and stepped to the hearth, taking two logs from the stack and placing them onto the fire. Flames curled around the fresh wood, their glow dancing across his thoughtful expression.

Merlonius and I sat in silence, sensing his deep contemplation as he stared into the flame, lost in a vision. We waited.

At last, he turned to us, a certainty in his bearing.

"My young friends, this eve I leave you to enjoy each other's company and will see you both on the morrow."

Merlonius and I joined him as he prepared to depart. Before stepping outside, he added, "Oh, and Arthur, I will tend to your horse."

We watched him disappear into the paddock, then closed the door behind us. I looked at Merlonius, and the yearning for time lost could not be hidden in my eyes. She reached up and lightly touched my face. I took her hand in mine and we crossed the room, making our way to the sleeping quarters at the back.

There, we paused. The two smaller beds were gone. In their place stood a larger four-poster bed, its carved posts and soft coverings unmistakably touched by Merlin's magic, a quiet gift from him.

Desire stirred within me as my gaze shifted to Merlonius. Drawn to her, I leaned in, and our lips met in a gentle kiss. She responded, deepening the moment. A rising warmth unfolded, wrapping us in longing.

I guided her down onto the bed, wonder and joy sweeping over me. Here, in this enchanted place, we were two hearts united. Fingers interlaced, breath quickened, we surrendered to the rhythm between us, our forms pressed together.

The caress of our hands, the softness of skin, and the slow blooming of yearning built steadily, rising on whispers and sighs. She guided me, and I followed, our bodies moving as one. Together, we crested in the fullness of our union. The very air seemed to pulse with the force of our love, as though each breath carried its rhythm. We lingered in each other's arms, basking in the aftermath of our closeness.

The night passed in a haze of passion. As dawn painted the sky, we remained entwined, unwilling to break the spell of what we had shared. For a time, we lay unmoving, as though the world beyond the cottage had slipped away.

Reluctantly, we rose and dressed before stepping outside, hand in hand. Settling on the stone bench in front of the cottage, we treasured the morn together.

"Last eve stirred something deep within me. That time with you, I will hold close, always."

"And I shall keep its memory as long as my heart remembers," she whispered.

A hush fell between us, filled with reverence and the trace of the night's wonder.

We sealed our words with a tender kiss, a silent vow that held us fast. The forest around us faded into a distant murmur as we clung to each other, lost in the embrace of our passion.

She rested her head upon my chest, her breath rising and falling with mine. The stillness was broken by Merlin's greeting as he stepped from the woods.

"Well, my young friends, another fine day!"

I reached for Merlonius's hand. "Merlin, your kindness touches us deeply, recognizing as you do the love we share."

"I know full well your hearts."

With a knowing glance, he nodded towards the door.

"Shall we enter?"

Magic danced from his staff as we stepped inside, and we watched as a humble feast unfolded before us: soft cheese, ripe berries, and wooden cups brimming with water. The hearth's crackling fire added to the soothing sense that this place was truly home for us.

Time passed in contentment, with laughter woven between thoughtful exchanges.

"Merlonius has become quite skilled at riding Sweetness in your absence, Arthur. On our last ride together, they took off in a run, and Tuft gave me a look I shall not soon forget," Merlin said, a hearty chuckle escaping him at the memory.

Merlonius's shoulders lifted in a small shrug as a mischievous smile played upon her lips.

I could not help but laugh, easily envisioning her galloping ahead while Merlin struggled to keep her in sight.

While Merlonius straightened the plates and cups on the back workbench, I approached her. "Would you accompany me for a walk?"

Merlin joined us as we stepped outside and, with a subtle nod, headed towards the garden, his words lingering in the air: "A day as bright as the future before you."

Merlonius and I took the path leading to the pond, and as we walked, my heart drifted to dreams of a life with her, to wed, have children, and raise the finest horses together. Against the soft glow of the sky, her profile stirred a deep yearning within me, and I simply watched her, lost in the vision of a future that could not be.

Her voice drew me back. "Arthur, let us climb to the summit."

Agreeing, we ascended the gradual slope. At the top, the familiar beauty of the landscape unfolded, the river winding to the left and Camelot's turrets to the right. The sight served as a solemn reminder of my kingship, dimming the splendor before me.

We settled beneath the towering tree, and as I took in the expanse of the sky above, a thread of doubt wove through me. Sensing my unrest, Merlonius tightened her grip on my hand.

"Arthur, no matter the twists of fate, our bond endures."

A heavy sigh escaped me, torn between the crown I bore and the life I yearned to share with her. "Ascending to High King brought forth challenges I never expected. All I desire is to be by your side, always."

"And I with you."

I pulled her towards me and pressed my lips to hers. In that kiss, the burdens of duty fell away, replaced by the truth of what we could not speak aloud. For that fleeting instant, we belonged only to each other.

"I endure a constant struggle," I confessed, "caught between the king I must be and the man I long to be with you."

"Arthur, I know this to be true. You carry more than most, yet our love remains, despite the crown."

Merlonius shifted and pulled away, leaning back against the tree. Then her breath quickened, a prelude to what she saw beyond this world.

She stared into the unseen as her words reached me. "Our love will be tested, Arthur. I foresee another in your life, a woman with shadows in her hair, entwined with your destiny as king, not tied to your heart."

Tears streamed down her cheeks as she returned to me. Her eyes, brimming with sorrow and fear, sought mine.

Between sobs, she said, "Oh, Arthur."

I reached out, cradling her face in my hands, brushing away the tears. "Merlonius, listen to me," I implored. "There is no future, no foretelling, where another stands by my side. It is you and only you that I cherish."

Her turmoil eased, and she reached up, her fingers tracing my features, drawing me into a kiss that deepened with the ache we bore. Beneath the ancient tree, we surrendered to the pull of our love, our bodies joining in a union both tender and fervent. Every whispered sigh became a pledge woven in touch.

In the stillness that followed, our hearts beat in rhythm, our breaths mingling softly. I knew no one else would ever hold my love. Though our bodies remained entwined, I felt her slipping into a place of knowing I could not yet reach, a sorrowful awareness of what had not yet come to pass and which I would fight from becoming. I drew her closer, sensing her quiet withdrawal, already mourning a future she feared the Fates had begun to weave.

She lifted her eyes to meet mine. "We should seek Merlin's counsel about my vision. Do you think he will share its truth?"

Her words stirred a deep concern. I caressed her arm, offering comfort, though doubt still shadowed my thoughts. Merlin had been far from clear with other visions. Would he reveal the truth now?

Not wishing to trouble her further, I answered, "Yes, let us speak with him."

Reluctantly, we disentangled from our embrace, the earth's cool touch a stark contrast to the passion we had found in each other. Our steps, hesitant yet inevitable, carried us from our secluded haven back to the cottage, each movement away from the tree heavy with the portent of what lay ahead.

Merlin greeted us as we returned. "You have arrived just as the stew is ready."

Seated at the table, Merlonius stared at her untouched bowl.

"Merlin, there is something I must tell you…"

He was cutting a piece of bread when his hand stilled. "What burdens you, my dear?"

She steadied herself, voice low as she shared what had come to her beyond the veil. Merlin listened intently, his expression unreadable.

"Merlin, is this woman destined to be at Arthur's side in my stead?"

Fear and defiance flashed in her eyes as she sought the truth, her look shifting between hope and dread.

I reached for her hand. "Merlonius, whatever came to you…"

Merlin stayed my words.

"The glimpses the Fates allow us beyond the veil carry more riddles than revelations. It is essential we root ourselves in the present and confront the challenges that lie directly before us. While matters of the heart are pressing, they also allow for patience."

His glance met mine, and I sensed there was more he was not saying, a deeper truth concealed behind his eyes.

I laced my fingers through hers. "Merlonius, you stand unfaltering by my side. Together, we have faced challenges, and it is our unity that will bear us through whatever shadows lie ahead. Let us not be swayed by the specter of possible futures."

She gathered herself with quiet resolve, though a tempest of emotions churned within her. Turning back to the stew, she stirred in silence, the spoon moving in slow, thoughtful circles.

During our meal, our conversation shifted from the concerns of a clan to the affairs of a kingdom. Personal desires and the duties of kingship pressed upon me with equal force.

"Arthur," Merlin began, setting his cup down with deliberate care. His eyes narrowed, the usual lightness gone. "With the winter moons approaching and the clamor of war fading, we must consider our next actions. Have you thought about the timing for the next campaign against the Saxons?"

"Bedwyr and I have been working tirelessly, conferring with trustworthy scouts. We are considering an early offensive, possibly when the seedlings moon rises. But tell me, Merlin, how do you see the potential success of this course?"

His eyes darkened as he delved into realms beyond our mortal grasp, his bearing distant as he drew upon the power of his sight.

"It could work," he replied with measured hope. "Nevertheless, we must not misjudge the Saxons. They are cunning foes who will likely foresee your every move and prepare accordingly."

Concern and self-doubt gripped me, the thought that we might have overlooked the Saxons' vigilance weighing heavily on my mind. I strove to remain calm despite all that remained unclear.

"Merlin, the risks are known to us, but our people's future compels us onward."

"Yes, Arthur," he replied, his tone grave, "how I know this to be true."

He withdrew to a world we could not see. We waited in silence until he returned to us.

"Launching an attack as the moon completes its fourth turn of the year, as you have planned, may catch the Saxons unprepared. Proceed with caution; the outcome is not yet set, but you hold the power to shape it."

I nodded, the truth of his words settling within me, steadying my resolve.

When our discussion neared its end, Merlonius rose and went to her loom, returning with a cloth the color of the deep woods.

"Arthur, I wove this for you. It will serve you well in the battle to come," she said, placing it in my hands.

Holding the cloth, images of lush forest canopies flooded my mind. A magic, undeniable and ancient, awakened within me as I traced its woven threads.

"Keep it close to you. Its weave is bound to a fate yet to unfold."

"Merlonius, your counsel will not be forsaken."

She moved back to her place beside me at the table, her words lingering.

Lifting my goblet, I swirled the rich ruby wine, its deep hue holding my gaze, yet my thoughts refused to still. The vision Merlonius had shared haunted me, a woman at my side, her presence foreign yet certain. Shaking the image from my mind, I resolved: *I will not lose Merlonius. I shall not.*

A slow breath escaped me, the pressing demands of my kingly duties intertwining with the longing to remain. The thought of a life free from these intricate struggles pulled at me, an unattainable dream.

"I must ride now to Camelot. Merlin, do not be a stranger to the castle."

"The winter moons bring more chances to gather supporters," Merlin replied. "Rest assured, I will be at your side. Expect me within a fortnight."

We rose from the table with a solemn understanding. I tucked the cloth beneath my tunic, and at its touch, I felt Merlonius's essence—her sorceress's touch.

Stepping outside, the chill of night pressed against us as we walked to the paddock. I looked at them both, committing the moment to memory before duty carried me away.

"I will carry this time with me."

I grasped Merlonius's hands, their warmth pushing back the eve's biting cold. A kiss to her forehead carried my promise: *I will return.*

"Be safe, Arthur. I will miss you dearly but I know we shall be together once more."

Mounting Aled, emotion tightened my throat. A piece of me lingered behind, leaving a hollowness I could not dispel. Each hoofbeat carried me farther from what I held dear, and sorrow gathered around me, heavy and unrelenting.

The woods grew still, the faint rustle of leaves brushing the silence with a haunting presence. Yet deep within me, a spark of hope remained, kindled by Merlonius's enduring affection. It promised to guide me through the impending darkness, a constant beacon until our paths merged once more.

CHAPTER 17

LONGING AND DUTY

Winter settled over the land soon after I left the enchanted forest, its icy grip covering all in snow. Howling winds swept across the fields and through the forests, rendering everything still and serene. Daylight grew scarce, as the sun emerged late and retreated early.

Mindful of the importance of Merlin's counsel, I knew I must secure the loyalty of my followers during the moons of the long dark. Within Camelot's great hall, I received guests from near and far, offering each the courtesy their station required and striving to fulfil my role as a gracious host. Skilled musicians caressed the strings of lutes and harps, while dancers twirled and swayed to the rhythm, their movements weaving beauty through the air.

Meats roasted over the fires, and tables groaned under the abundance of pies, sweets, and other delights, inviting all to partake in the merriment. Laughter echoed as guests delighted in the cheer and abundance.

Yet amid the revelry and feasting, thoughts of Merlonius held fast within me, and the longing to be with her pressed down on my spirit. Even as I carried out my duties as king, her absence shadowed each passing day. Night after night, I joined the gatherings, often with Merlin at my side, until the point of the darkest night marked his departure.

As the frost lay heavy upon the land, a restlessness stirred within me. On one such eve, I beckoned Merlin to join me in the solitude of my chambers. We ascended the stair, the dimly lit hall guiding our way. Upon entering my quarters, we were greeted by the scent of burning wood and the fire's steady crackle.

We stood in silence by the hearth. At last, I turned to Merlin.

"How fares Merlonius?"

Still looking into the fire, Merlin answered me, his tone touched with strain. "She misses you. But she is deepening her learning and refining her craft, eagerly awaiting your return to the forest."

"Would you convey my message to her?"

He looked at me, his features softening, though a shadow of sadness lingered. "What do you wish me to say?"

"She is ever present with me, and my love for her is unwavering. Once I can leave Camelot without notice, I will journey to her."

"Consider it done."

We stood facing one another, two men bound by destiny, both weighed by the demands of duty and their shared love for Merlonius.

"You have my thanks, Merlin," I said sincerely, resting a hand on his shoulder.

He returned the gesture. "I will see you on the morrow, Arthur."

With his departure, a chill settled in the air, leaving me yearning for the reassurance only Merlonius could provide. I clung to the memory of our days together, unwilling to let them slip away.

I sought relief in the chair near the fire, for sleep continued to elude me. Merlonius completed me; this I knew to be true. As moonlight streamed through my windows, I stared into the flames, seeing us walking, laughing, riding our horses through sunlit fields. In my mind's eye, we were once again entwined in love's embrace.

Yet the dawn approached, bringing light to the challenges of the day, and memories gave way to the pressing needs of the kingdom. With duty upon us, Bedwyr and I devoted ourselves to rigorous training alongside the Knights of the Round Table. We honed our swordsmanship and devised strategies to counter the Saxons.

Maps of the land became our constant companions, aiding us in studying the strengths and weaknesses of our adversaries while charting our campaign to reclaim the lands seized by the Saxons. At the same time, I enlisted the realm's most skilled blacksmiths to craft fresh weapons and armour, including chainmail and reinforced leather protections for my knights, ensuring that each piece was painstakingly fashioned with the utmost care and precision.

After weeks of relentless preparation, the time had come to decide our course. Based on reports gathered by our scouts, we concluded that the next waning moon, just a fortnight away, would be the most opportune time for our offensive. Nevertheless, before engaging in battle, there was someone I needed to see.

"Bedwyr, I must leave the castle for a few hours to visit Merlonius. I will return after the darkest hour of the night. Can you ensure my absence goes unnoticed?"

"Of course, Arthur. The hour has grown late. When do you wish to depart? I can instruct the stable lads to prepare your horse for you."

"I shall leave the castle without being noticed, through another route. Come, let me show you."

I gestured for him to follow me, leading him through the labyrinth of halls until we reached a solid stone barrier.

"There is more here than appears," I said, lowering the sconce. The wall to our right slid inward, revealing the opening to the secret tunnel.

"Merlin crafted this passage with enchantments. Once entered, it glows and winds its way underground, eventually emerging within a tree in the enchanted forest."

I pushed the sconce upward, sealing the way. Bedwyr's eyes widened as he took in the wonder of the hidden passage.

"This is an extraordinary marvel of magic. With this, you can pass undetected. I suggest you go now," he added urgently. "I will ensure no one enters this part of the castle while you are gone."

"Agreed. Your readiness to stand guard during my absence is valued. Allow me to retrieve my cloak and sword from my quarters."

We returned to my chambers, where I swiftly secured my sword to my waist and donned my woolen cloak.

"My thanks to you. I shall return soon."

"May the gods watch over you, Arthur."

Together, we left my chambers, and he took his post at the stair leading to our part of the castle. My need to see her quickened my steps through the castle's winding halls until I reached the hidden door. After stepping through, I pushed the sconce upward, sealing the opening behind me, and set off at a brisk run. The faint whispers of my footsteps echoed against the walls, while a soft silver light glowed from the stones, guiding my path.

At last, I reached the door in the tree and pushed it outward, stepping into the enchanted forest. The cottage's lights shone brightly through the trees, guiding me towards it.

As I neared, the door swung open, and Merlin greeted me at the threshold. "Arthur, you made it. So glad to see you. Come in."

I removed my cloak and unfastened my scabbard, resting them upon a nearby bench.

Merlonius rushed into my arms. Our reunion was long-awaited and much-needed.

"I have missed you."

"As I have you."

"We were just about to sit down to eat. Would you like to join us?" Merlin asked.

"Indeed, I would be delighted."

Gathering around the table, the inviting aroma of stew filled the space, and the crackling fire warmed our spirits. Sitting beside Merlonius, her hand in mine, the challenges of the day seemed lighter, and I found comfort in her company.

As the night wore on, the flames dwindled and the chill crept in. Merlin stirred the fire to life once more.

We sat without speaking, content in the closeness, until Merlonius looked at me. "Arthur, when must you return to Camelot?"

"I must depart soon. Bedwyr is keeping watch at the castle, ensuring my absence remains unnoticed. There is still much to prepare as we plan another offensive against the Saxons with the waning moon."

"The path before you is arduous, but know this, Arthur: you shall fulfil your purpose and return to me."

Her fingertips brushed my cheek, a gesture that dispelled the shadows of doubt. A strength, steady and sure, stirred within me, kindling a spark of hope for the battles ahead.

Merlin, observing our exchange, offered his reassurance. "Arthur, we are with you even when unseen. We continually send our protection to you and to your knights."

"Your support is crucial for our success in the battles to come. I rely on both of you to be my side to secure victory."

Though I longed to stay, duty beckoned me back to Camelot. We rose from the table and prepared to depart. Wrapping my cloak tightly around me, we stepped into the moonless night. Merlin held his staff upright, its crystal tip casting a bright light to guide our path.

When we reached the door in the tree, I took Merlonius's face in my hands and kissed her lips.

"I shall forever love thee."

A quiver touched her lips as she returned my whisper, "As I shall forever love thee, Arthur."

I glanced at Merlin, "I leave a part of me here with you both. Take care."

A shadow of sorrow remained with me as I entered the passageway and closed the door behind me. Leaving her was never easy, but with time, it was becoming harder still. At the castle, I stepped into the hall, ensuring the door was sealed once again. A fleeting thought of turning back crossed my mind, but I continued towards my chambers, my resolve firm despite the ache within.

I found Bedwyr waiting, vigilant as ever.

"How goes it?"

"All is well."

"This is good news."

We walked down the passage, our footsteps echoing softly. Reaching my quarters, I placed a hand on his shoulder.

"Rest well, my friend."

"You also, Arthur."

He departed for his chambers, and I entered mine. Standing by the table near my bed, I removed my sword and looked about. A void filled the space, pressing upon me with unbearable heaviness. I walked to the window, drawn northward, pondering how different my life might have been had I not been bound to this path. With a deep sigh, I turned from the window and let thoughts of the impending battle settle over me, pushing aside what my heart longed to keep close.

CHAPTER 18

THE BATTLE'S TOLL

The clash of iron resonated throughout the battlefield, a chaotic uproar echoing in the cold dawn. With unrelenting strides, my knights and I charged ahead, our horses' hooves pounding the churned, rain-slicked earth. The flat expanse south of Camelot had become our stage, with the Saxons as our fierce adversaries. They wielded the sax, a brutal knife designed for swift and lethal strikes, and were skilled in the use of spears, shields, and battle axes.

I drew Caliburn from its sheath, the blade catching the pale light, casting an unearthly shimmer. My heart pounded with a fierce rhythm, torn between the thrill of anticipation and the shadow of fear. With a resounding war cry, I spurred Thor onward, leading the charge straight into the thick of the battle.

Amid the chaos, my brave knights hurled themselves upon the Saxons. The enemies' braided hair and beards lent them a wild appearance, adding to their fierce visage. Driven by anger and tenacity, they engaged in a tireless dance of swords and axes, displaying resolute valour. The air hung heavy with the iron tang of blood, mingling with the anguished cries of fallen warriors. Yet, through the carnage, the battlefield bore witness to the Saxons' staunch refusal to surrender, even in the face of mounting adversity.

I became a fury of motion, my blade driven by instinct and forged skill. Each swing carried the rhythm of survival, striking down one enemy after another. My strength surged, heightening my senses and sharpening my focus.

On the battlefield, my commands rang out, directing my knights in strategic maneuvers. "Lancelot, Kay, circle to the left! Bors, hold the right flank!"

With each calculated move, I evaded a swinging axe and seized the opening to drive Caliburn deep into the chest of a Saxon warrior. The enemy fell to my blade, yet their relentless advance continued, testing our fortitude and endurance. For every adversary struck down, another rose in their place. The fighting raged on, brutal and unyielding, and the strain of battle began to wear upon us. Slowly, their numbers began to thin, and amidst the chaos, a glimmer of hope emerged.

I searched for Bedwyr and found him surrounded by Saxons advancing with swords and battle-axes. Everything else blurred as I focused on his plight. He and his horse, Awen, were vastly outnumbered, encircled by enemies. Fallen horses, victims of Saxon axes and spears, littered the ground around them, and I knew he would do anything to protect his stallion.

Dismounting and abandoning his spear for his sword, he swiftly killed two Saxon warriors advancing on him. A shout rang out from him, "Awen, go, go quickly!" as he urged the horse away with a slap to its hindquarters.

Amidst the chaos of dust and clashing swords, I drove Thor towards Bedwyr's perilous position, determined to reach him in time. A towering figure, a giant among warriors, stepped forward with a fierce battle cry, brandishing a massive battle-axe. I met the giant's charge, our weapons colliding with a shower of sparks. In a brutal duel, I drove my sword into the giant's chest.

Pressing forward, I witnessed Bedwyr locked in mortal combat with several Saxons. Movement became painfully deliberate, each motion stretched in the thick of battle, when one of the Saxons raised his sword and severed his left hand. His agony pierced the tumult as he fell to his knees, his lifeblood flowing freely. Defenseless, he became the target of the Saxons, who relished their anticipated victory.

Raising Caliburn high, I cleaved through the enemy with deadly precision cutting down anyone who dared stand in my way. Upon reaching him, I knelt beside him and swiftly retrieved Merlonius's forest green cloth from the pouch attached to my chainmail. Acting swiftly, I tied it tightly around his arm to stop the bleeding. Then, securing my grip around him, I lifted him to his feet and helped him onto my horse.

I looked back to the battlefield. The tide had begun to turn, and the enemy wavered before retreating. With a resounding shout, I rallied my men.

"Forward, men! After them!" I called out over the clamor of battle. The knights around me charged with renewed vigour, pushing the enemy back.

Leading Thor across the field, I was joined by my half-sister Morgause's sons, Gawain and Agravain, who rushed to our aid, swiftly dispatching any enemies that approached. Reaching the woods where Bedwyr's horse awaited, they secured him with a rope to Thor, while I mounted Awen.

Holding onto Thor's reins, I shifted in the saddle. "Gawain, Agravain, I take Bedwyr now to The Giants' Dance. Once the Saxons have fully retreated, make your way to Camelot. I will join you there when I am able."

Concern creased their brows.

Gawain's expression darkened as he bowed his head in understanding.

"May the gods and goddesses be with you, kinsman."

"Protect Camelot in my absence."

I guided Bedwyr north through the dense forest, the severity of his wounds weighing heavily on my mind. The cloth, woven by Merlonius, stood as a stark reminder of the fragile line between life and death. Each step carried the grim rhythm of uncertainty as I sought to preserve his well-being. Yet, even in the dimness of these woods, I felt the mystical presence of Merlin and Merlonius, their unseen sorcerous vigilance guiding us like a beacon through the darkness, offering powerful reassurance amid dire trials.

With dusk approaching and the ancient stones of the circle looming ahead, a silent plea formed on my lips: *Bedwyr, hold on. We are almost there. Do not leave me now.* He was once so full of life and vitality, but now lay senseless, overwhelmed by pain and blood loss. His breaths, shallow and strained, seemed to resist the deepening stillness of the coming night.

When we reached the solemn embrace of the stone circle, I leapt off Awen, my movements driven by dread and fierce intent. Merlin and Merlonius appeared, emerging from the trees with the silent grace of the forest itself, their faces shadowed with concern, their purpose clear in their bearing.

"Bedwyr has lost his hand, and his breaths are faint. We must act swiftly to save him!" I shouted, as the bond of brotherhood, the desperate need to save him, and the fear of loss converged, threatening to overwhelm even the iron will of a king.

They joined me without hesitation, their actions quick yet measured. With Merlin's help, we carried him to the stone platform, his body ghost-pale and still as if caught between worlds. Swiftly, yet with great care, we began to remove his chainmail. Merlonius then stepped forward, her hands skillfully poised above his severed hand. With a delicate motion of her fingers, the forest seemed to reflect her intent, the scent of pine intensifying and the wind rising in unison with his pained groans.

When she raised her arms, a lightning bolt streaked across the sky, casting a brilliant light over us. She then delicately began to unwind the makeshift bandage, her touch as light as a whisper. Beneath her attentive care, something magical unfolded. New skin began to weave itself over the gaping wound, as if guided by her will.

This act of healing seemed to be more than just the mending of flesh. It was as if Merlonius was stitching the very essence of his life back together. Her movements, though purposeful, flowed with a natural grace, creating a pure harmony between her magic and the ancient powers that surrounded us.

The power of her chant intensified, resonating around us like a tangible force. She swayed to the rhythm of her incantation, her hands delicately poised above his chest. I watched, entranced, as his breath began to align with the rhythm of her spell, growing steadier and stronger. Yet, he lay unmoving in a soundless slumber, oblivious to our desperate efforts.

When her chanting ceased, tears glistened on her cheeks, a silent reflection of the battle waged within her. She turned and faced Merlin, speaking with a gravity that belied the gentleness of her tone.

"Merlin, we must take Bedwyr to our dwelling in the enchanted forest. Only there can he truly heal. His hand is beyond my reach, but his life is not. He is our friend, a knight as valiant as any. We cannot fail him now."

His eyes, usually so full of wisdom and certainty, shimmered with a rare glimpse of vulnerability.

With a heavy sigh, he finally spoke. "Yes, we must act quickly. Let us go, then."

We moved with urgency, yet with reverent precision, lifting him from the cold stone. Merlin, with a whispered incantation, conjured a makeshift wooden frame, adorned with the softest furs to cradle our fallen companion.

With sure hands, we laid him upon it, his form barely stirring. The furs wrapped around him, offering a small comfort in his fragile state. I secured the frame to my steed, my movements deliberate, trying to keep the tremor from my hands and prevent the sorrow from overwhelming me.

Mounting Thor, a wave of worry for Bedwyr engulfed me, clouded with images of his suffering. Merlin led Awen forward, his steps measured, one hand resting gently on the horse's neck, offering reassurance with every motion. Merlonius followed, her expression tender, her pace sure despite the sorrow shadowing her features. Her presence calmed me and I knew I could not face what lay ahead without her near.

Together, we ventured into the dense forest, the whispering leaves and the earthy scent of the woods accompanying our solemn march.

At the cottage, we eased Bedwyr onto Merlonius's bed with great care. Stripping off my chainmail and sword, I dragged a chair to his bedside, keeping watch over him. A faint stir drew my focus as his eyes fluttered open, revealing a glimmer of awareness. His parched lips parted, but only a weak sound escaped. Merlonius draped a soft blanket over him as Merlin appeared with a steaming cup of healing brew in hand.

"Bedwyr, this is Merlin," he said softly. "Drink a little of this tea; it will aid in your healing."

I assisted him in sitting up, and he drank from the cup, managing to express his gratitude. "I am indebted to you for your kindness," he murmured before his eyes closed once more, and we gently guided him back down onto the thick pillow.

Merlin began preparing healing salves, and Merlonius quickly gathered more blankets to cover him, as a fever had taken hold. The familiar scent of the healing tea swirled around us, bolstering my hope for his recovery.

Throughout the long night, we took turns placing cool cloths, steeped in a healing tincture, upon his forehead, hoping to alleviate his fever, while Merlin diligently applied salves to his wound. The air carried the scent of comfrey, yarrow, and meadowsweet, a faint reminder of our efforts.

With sunrise approaching, I remained faithfully beside Bedwyr when Merlonius came to my side.

"Arthur, please sit by the fire and rest. I will watch over him."

I took her hand in mine and gave it a gentle squeeze. "Merlonius…"

"I will not leave his side. Rest now."

I made my way towards the hearth, offering my thanks to the gods and goddesses for their divine aid. Collapsing into a chair, I was overwhelmed by the exhaustion that had accompanied the sleepless night preceding the battle with the Saxons.

Merlin kindly brought me a hot cup of tea. "Drink this," he said, "you need to regain your vigour."

The warm liquid, infused with honey and lavender, brought relief as I handed the cup back to him. "My heartfelt thanks to you, for without your help and Merlonius's gift of healing, Bedwyr would have surely perished."

"As Merlonius reminded me, he is our friend. We will care for him."

Sleep overtook me at last, heavy and unbroken. When I awoke to the setting sun, I hastened to Bedwyr where I found Merlin and Merlonius sitting nearby. His pale complexion and sweaty forehead told of his struggle, but the weak rise and fall of his chest reassured me.

"How does he fare?" My voice was barely above a breath.

"His fever broke about an hour ago," Merlin said, his words hushed.

"He will recover?"

"Yes," Merlonius reassured me. "He is on the path to wellness."

Relief unfolded within me, like sunlight piercing through clouds, easing the strain in my shoulders and unwinding the tightness around my heart.

"That is truly heartening news. May I bring either of you some food or drink?"

Merlonius met my gaze. "A cup of water would be most welcome."

I poured three cups of water, one for myself, and the remaining two I carried to them. Returning, I brought over a chair and placed it near the bed.

"I will sit with him now, if you wish to step outside."

"Let us go," Merlin replied. "The fresh air may serve us well."

I found myself reflecting on Bedwyr, feeling truly privileged to have him not only as a loyal supporter of the throne but also as a dear friend. From our first meeting, his formidable character was apparent, his physical might matched by his keen mind. He quickly became one of my most trusted knights. Our bond felt immediate, as if destined by fate, evidenced by an unspoken unity that guided our actions and motives. It was to him that I entrusted what I cherished most.

His breathing shifted, and he stirred, gradually blinking a few times to adjust to his surroundings. I spoke quietly and deliberately, careful not to startle him.

"Bedwyr, it is Arthur. You are safe in Merlin and Merlonius's cottage in the enchanted forest."

He turned his head, his eyes searching mine for reassurance.

"Arthur, are we alive? The battle was fierce, and I believed I had met my end. My hand… " His eyes fell to his left arm, now concealed beneath layers of cloth.

I could feel his despair as tears welled up, his anguish profound. "So, it is true. I have lost my hand?"

"Sadly, yes. But not your life, my friend."

Gently, I laid my hand on his right arm. "You remain one of my most valiant knights."

The severity of his injury was evident in every line of his body, each mark speaking to his inner struggle.

"Rest now, for you are not alone. I shall stay by your side."

He nodded, gradually overcome by weariness as he surrendered to the embrace of slumber.

Watching him sleep, I whispered, "Gods and goddesses, I call upon you. Grant my friend Bedwyr healing, not only in body but in spirit."

The creak of the door announced Merlin and Merlonius's return. Their presence brought with it purpose, pulling me from my vigil. Rising to join them on the other side of the cottage, I felt the mantle of duty settle once more upon my shoulders.

"I must journey to Camelot to ensure the well-being of my fellow knights. I shall leave now and return before the point of darkest night. Bedwyr briefly woke, and I let him know that he is in your care. Alas, he is aware of the loss of his hand. If he awakens during my absence, pray tell him I have gone to meet with the other knights and will return."

"Arthur, we will take good care of him. Be safe, and we shall await your arrival," Merlin assured.

I held Merlonius close, and our lips met in a kiss that deepened with longing. The closeness of her touch filled me with an overwhelming yearning to never leave her, though I knew I must.

"He will recover," she said with certainty, her hand pressing briefly against mine.

I released her, allowing a touch of my fingertips against her cheek. With a heavy heart, I turned and made my way to the paddock, my chainmail draped over one arm, Caliburn resting at my hip.

Entering the enclosure, I found Merlin had attended to our horses. Thor waited, flanks twitching, the last light of day glinting off his coat. With skillful hands, I saddled him, ensuring all the straps and fastenings were properly secured for our journey. He was lively and eager to run, sensing the impending adventure.

We swiftly reached the great doors of the castle. Dismounting, I instructed the stable hands who greeted me to prepare Thor for departure within the hour. I pushed open the large wooden doors and hurried through the halls towards the feasting hall.

The somber mood was evident in the hushed air, the torches casting unsteady light that deepened both the solemnity and the surrounding shadows. A few of my knights were finishing their meal, but upon seeing me, their conversations faltered. They rose and gathered around.

Gareth, with his grizzled beard, spoke first: "What news, Arthur?"

Lancelot, unfailing in his loyalty, gave a nod of silent assurance.

Gawain, his brow furrowed with worry, stepped forward. "How fares Bedwyr?"

"He has lost his left hand," I began. "But with the intervention of the Fates, Merlin, and the healer Merlonius, he will recover."

Breunor, usually a beacon of enthusiasm, sat subdued, his usual spark noticeably absent. His fingers tapped a rhythm on the table, betraying his pensive state. Beside him, Percival's mouth hung open, his ever-present curiosity shadowed by bewilderment. He blinked slowly, as if each blink were an effort to understand what he had just heard.

Lancelot moved to stand before the men and surveyed those gathered before him.

"The physical pain Bedwyr endures, though great, is nothing compared to the anguish of losing his hand. We all know him as a formidable warrior, renowned for his mastery of the spear. Despite his injury, his courage and perseverance will drive him to continue fighting. I speak for all when I say his sacrifice was not in vain. I vow to fight even harder to defeat the Saxons and protect our land. Let us pay tribute to his bravery by standing united as Knights of the Round Table, this day and always."

He held the attention of every man present, his bearing conveying the gravity of what lay ahead.

Their response was immediate and unified. A resounding "Aye" filled with conviction rang out around us. I looked upon these warriors, these men of valour, and as their voices filled the hall, I felt only gratitude and pride.

My thoughts turned to the battle. "What of our gains and losses?"

Kay came forward. "Arthur, we drove them back, but the ground gained was slight. We mourn the loss of five knights, brave warriors who fought with unswerving resolve. Another twenty bear wounds, but they are receiving care, and many shall yet return to strength.

"The Saxons suffered a heavier toll. We counted at least twenty-five slain on the battlefield, and another fifteen to twenty were wounded and carried away. Our decision to mount the offensive on horseback proved favorable, helping secure our hard-fought victory."

Sorrow settled over us as we mourned our fallen, their absence pressing on our spirits like stone. Yet, amid our mourning, a spark of hope stirred, for I noted the heavy blow we had dealt to the Saxons. I placed my hand on Kay's shoulder, then turned to address the gathered knights.

"In confronting this formidable challenge, let us continue to uphold the principles of the Round Table: valour, honour, and unity," I declared. "We preserve the memory of our fallen, sharing in the heartbreak of their kin. Their sacrifices shall not be forgotten. Armed with renewed determination, we shall regroup, forge new strategies, and reclaim our land from the Saxons. Let us now call upon the gods and goddesses to aid our wounded, that they may be restored in body and spirit."

My devotion to my men ran deep; each had forsaken his previous life to stand courageously by my side for our land and its people. The absence of any one of them pressed heavily upon me.

The knights responded in unison, "For our king, for the swift recovery of Bedwyr, and for the protection of Camelot."

Their solemn pledge bore the emptiness left by our fallen brothers' absence, and as I looked to the empty chairs, each was a wordless tribute to the valiant lives we had lost.

"I bid thee, hold fast to our oath, for I must journey once more to the enchanted forest to remain with Bedwyr. We shall return as soon as Merlin deems him strong enough for the journey."

"May the gods and goddesses ensure your safe return."

Leaving the hall, I ascended the stair to my chambers. Setting my chainmail beside the bed, its presence served as a solemn reminder of all that had been endured: lives lost, the wounded, and most of all, Bedwyr's severed hand. Slipping into a fresh tunic, the crispness of the linen offered a subtle yet welcome respite from the day's burdens. I reached for a clean outer tunic, its weave thicker against the evening chill. While readying myself for the return to the cottage, thoughts of Bedwyr's recovery and how this injury might have changed him filled my mind.

Thor awaited me at the great doors. I mounted my loyal steed, the powerful strike of his hooves resounding through the courtyard. Galloping along the dirt road towards the enchanted forest, the wind howled around me, driving us forward towards the path that led to the clearing. Swiftly dismounting, I secured the reins to the paddock fence and hastened to the door, giving it a firm knock.

Merlin swung it open.

"How does he fare?" I asked, crossing the threshold.

Exhaling slowly, the corners of his lips lifted ever so slightly, though exhaustion dulled his eyes. He blinked slowly, as if trying to shake off the weariness that clung to him.

"Bedwyr is still asleep," he murmured. "And Merlonius is keeping a vigilant watch."

We moved quietly towards the hearth, where Merlin added, "Let us replenish our strength. I will prepare some food while you go to them."

Placing my scabbard and sword near the hearth, I moved to the bed and sat down beside Merlonius. Gently holding her hand, I noted the slow rhythm of her movements, and the shadows beneath her eyes from her relentless vigil over Bedwyr.

"Merlonius, you must rest."

Her response, imbued with fortitude yet not diminished by tiredness, was firm. "I will when I know that he is awake and getting stronger."

Understanding her unshakeable spirit and her natural compassion, I simply said, "Ah, Merlonius."

"He was so close to death when you reached The Giants' Dance. I was unsure if I could pull him back from the doors of the Otherworld."

At the mere thought of losing my closest friend, a chill of fear seeped into my bones. My determination to do all in my power for his survival rose above all else. Merlonius, with her serene resolve, had steadied me from the moment we met. Now, pouring all her care into Bedwyr's recovery, my admiration for her only deepened.

As we kept watch over his peaceful slumber, the early morn's light crept across the floor. All was still, save for the crackling of the flames and the creak of the wooden planks as Merlin drew near. We followed his gesture and quietly walked to the table, where a steaming tureen of soup awaited us.

"Arthur, I have taken care of your horse; he is settled in the paddock. Now, we must nourish ourselves."

He ladled the rich broth into our bowls, its savory aroma swirling around us, drawing us to the meal.

"My thanks for the excellent care you have given to Thor, and for this delicious meal."

"You and Merlonius must rest now. I have prepared a bed for you in the front. Please make use of it and allow yourselves the much-needed respite. I will be watchful and wake you as soon as he stirs."

Before Merlonius could share her objections, he added, "I insist, for both your sakes. Rest is essential in these trying times."

We nodded, weariness pressing heavily upon us. With slow, weary movements, Merlonius settled into the bed's comforting embrace. I joined her, drawing her close, our bodies finding solace in each other.

Lying together in tranquil stillness, the day's worries quickly faded. The steady rhythm of our breathing soon lulled us into a deep, peaceful sleep.

I was roused by the urgent sound of my name.

"Arthur, Arthur, wake up."

Quickly sitting upright, I shook off the remnants of drowsiness and glanced around for Merlonius, only to find her absent. As clarity returned, I recognized Merlin standing before me.

"Merlonius is with Bedwyr. He is sitting up and asking for you. He has shown remarkable improvement."

I hastened to join them.

"Good morrow, Bedwyr."

"Arthur… seeing you again lifts my spirit."

"How are you faring, my friend?"

"I am feeling stronger. My gratitude for saving my life knows no bounds."

"You would have done the same for me. We are truly glad to see you on the path to recovery."

Merlin approached, and Bedwyr looked to him. "Merlonius told me it was by your blessing I was brought here. I am deeply grateful."

"You are a member of this clan, Bedwyr. It is both our duty and our honour to tend to one another."

Merlin's words lingered long after they were spoken, weaving through my heart with unwavering resolve. The bond between us was not merely born of duty, but shaped by loyalty, forged through hardship, and bound by love. I knew then that whatever trials lay ahead, it was this enduring tie between us that would steady us and carry us forward.

CHAPTER 19

MENDING IN THE ENCHANTED WOODS

Each day that followed, I left the cottage mid-morn to return to Camelot, ensuring there were no pressing concerns. Yet comfort accompanied me, for I knew Bedwyr rested in the capable hands of Merlin and Merlonius. By the time the sun began its descent, Thor and I would retreat to the serenity of the enchanted forest. It was in these moments with Merlin, Merlonius, and Bedwyr, that a strong feeling of home and belonging unfolded around me, as natural and comforting as the forest's embrace.

By the fifth day, he had regained enough strength to rise from his bed and join us at the table, taking a seat next to Merlin. I took my usual place as Merlin brought forward a large tureen of venison stew, setting it before us. Merlonius followed, carrying a pitcher of cool water and a basket of bread, its crust warm from the hearth.

Our bowls brimmed with the hearty stew, filled with tender venison and crisp vegetables that melded well together. Water filled our cups, and the bread, crusty on the outside and soft within, invited us to savor each bite.

"Merlin," Bedwyr exclaimed with enthusiasm, "this is one of the finest venison stews I have ever savored! It is truly delicious, and with each spoonful, I feel myself growing stronger."

"I am pleased, my lad. Magic lends its aid, but never underestimate the healing power of a well-prepared meal."

While we ate, Merlin wove tales of Britain's history, the enchanted forest, and his own adventures. His stories flowed as richly as the stew, holding me spellbound. I found myself journeying through the passages of time, each tale unfolding in bold strokes, spun from the threads of the past.

"The Fates smiled upon me when Merlonius entered my life six years past and I have never encountered a more brilliant apprentice," he said, casting a fond look towards her.

"Merlin, it is I who am grateful. You have provided not just a home and a purpose but a haven where I belong, enriching my life immeasurably."

Looking to Bedwyr, she inquired, "Arthur has told me that you have been with him since the beginning of his reign. Where is your village?"

He looked from Merlonius, to me, then to Merlin, and back to Merlonius. "Ah, Merlonius, those days feel like a distant past. Arthur and I were but fifteen when we first met. I had spent the previous year alone in the forest; my home was in the northwest, on beautiful farmland where my father, mother, and I lived. My father taught me much, not just the arts and the study of numbers, but swordsmanship and fighting as well."

Sorrow and longing for days gone by shadowed his features. "Sadly, when I was coming into my own, both my father and mother fell ill. Though the folk of the village tried to help, none possessed the healing skills that you, Merlonius, now wield. They passed swiftly, leaving me adrift without purpose or direction."

His trembling hand betrayed the pain he felt as he recounted his past. "I wandered the woods for nearly a year. Then, drawn by an unexplained urge, I moved closer to the village and arrived on a morn charged with excitement. News had spread that the sword had been pulled from the stone, and a new High King would be crowned. I was in the crowd when Arthur swore his oath to the land and drank from the cup of mead. Without hesitation, I knew I must pledge him my allegiance."

Merlonius reached out to touch his hand. "Bedwyr, I am sorry for your loss, but know that you are now a vital part of our clan," she said, her glance briefly meeting mine. "And remember, with Arthur as High King, he needs one he can trust by his side, a friend upon whom he can rely. You, Bedwyr, are that person."

My eyes met Bedwyr's, and I nodded, offering silent support. We resumed our meal, the unspoken understanding between us a testament to the trust we had built.

In the days that followed, Merlin kept a vigilant watch over Bedwyr as he tended to the wound. With meticulous care, he unwrapped the cloths and applied a balm, crafted beneath the moonlight and infused with ancient magics. Bedwyr's vigour returned steadily, a clear reflection of Merlin's profound healing arts.

With the passing of the days, we recognized the import of returning to Camelot. Merlin, ever the guardian, insisted on accompanying us, determined to oversee Bedwyr's full recovery within the protective walls of the castle.

Merlonius met our worries with serene assurance. "Do not fear for my solitude. This cottage and the forest—this is my home. Sweetness will be my companion, and we shall ride often. When each day draws to its close, I will deepen my studies from all you have taught me, Merlin."

A softness came to his features as he listened to her words. He nodded slowly, the corners of his eyes crinkling with a smile that spoke of affection and pride. Reaching out, he placed a reassuring hand on her shoulder, conveying his trust in her abilities and his enduring support.

"I will return as soon as I am assured of Bedwyr's recovery."

With our departure drawing near, I approached Merlonius, sadness beginning to take hold at the thought of our impending separation.

"Would you join me in the garden?"

We held hands as we walked towards the stone bench beneath the ancient tree at the garden's edge, its branches offering shelter and sanctuary.

"Merlonius, losing Bedwyr would have left a void in my life."

"Through you, Arthur, he has become my friend, and I too would have felt his absence. I gladly share my gift with him."

Uncertainty gripped me as I continued, "I cannot say when I will return, but know that my love for you endures."

Our arms wrapped around each other, and as our lips met in a tender and passionate kiss, the world fell away, leaving only us.

With longing and affection, she breathed, "I will miss you dearly and will await your safe return."

We shared one final kiss, slow and tender. The taste lingered, a promise that would carry me forward until we were reunited.

Rejoining Merlin and Bedwyr, we made ready to embark on our journey back to Camelot. Before leaving, Bedwyr stepped towards Merlonius.

"M'lady, I marvel at your gifts and am thankful for your kindness and for saving my life," he said earnestly. "Should you ever have need of my sword, know that it is ever ready to protect you, and I will give my life to do so."

Merlonius pressed her fingers briefly to her lips, her expression softening as she met his gaze. The corners of her mouth lifted slightly, a reflection of both gratitude and understanding that passed between them.

"Your words touch me deeply, Bedwyr. Be well, my friend, and carry my gratitude with you."

We bid our final farewell to Merlonius and mounted our horses. Reaching the path that led to the road, we slowed and turned for one last look at her standing near the cottage. We raised our hands, and she returned the gesture. I held the image of her in my mind as we turned away.

We urged our steeds forward, emerging from the forest onto the road. The journey back to Camelot passed in thoughtful quiet, broken only by the rustling of leaves and the distant calls of the wild.

When the turrets and flags came into view, I glanced at Bedwyr and saw the weariness settling in his features. We crossed the drawbridge without delay and handed our horses to the waiting stable boys. Then we entered the castle through its broad doors.

"Come, let us go to the feasting hall," I suggested, aware that food and rest would be welcome after our journey.

Upon entering, we found the knights finishing their eve's meal. Catching sight of Bedwyr at my side, they erupted in joyous cheers and surged forward to greet him.

"Bedwyr, you are a welcome sight! Merlin, we owe you a debt of gratitude for bringing him back to us!"

Though still recovering, Bedwyr moved among them, his resilient spirit evident beneath every wince and half-smile. He endured hearty slaps on the back and playful shoulder jostles from his fellow knights.

I motioned for Merlin and Bedwyr to sit before turning to address my men.

"We are gladdened beyond measure to have Bedwyr among us once again. Please continue your meal and we shall gather on the morrow."

After the knights bid us peace, we ascended the stair and made our way down the familiar hall to his chambers.

Concern lingered, knowing the path ahead would be long and arduous for a knight whose mastery of the spear had once defined him. He would need to adapt, mastering the art of battle with just one hand while striving to maintain his precision in hurling his spear with his right.

Bedwyr stood in the center of his quarters, bathed in the glow of the hearth's flames. His eyes fixed on the wall where his spears were displayed, their tips gleaming in the faint light.

I placed my hand upon his shoulder. "Bedwyr, if anyone can ride and fight with one hand, it is you. I have no doubt—you shall remain a formidable warrior."

His eyes met mine, glistening with unshed tears. "Arthur… I truly aspire for that to be true." In his hushed tone, both determination and vulnerability were clear, revealing the full extent of his struggle and strength of will.

Merlin placed his bag of herbs on the table near the hearth, and his presence brought ease as Bedwyr and I stood in wordless understanding.

"This chair by the fire, Bedwyr, shall provide me with a restful night's sleep, and I shall be within reach should you require any assistance."

Once he was settled, Bedwyr reached out and touched his arm.

"Merlin, your kindness truly means more than I can say."

"We shall overcome this challenge together, my lad," he reassured, his hand resting over Bedwyr's.

Observing the weariness on both their faces, I asked, "Do either of you have any needs?"

"I think we have all that is required for this eve. Why not return to your quarters, Arthur, and try to rest?"

"Very well, may you both find peaceful slumber," I replied, closing the door behind me.

With measured steps, I made my way back to my quarters, troubled by Merlonius's absence. Upon entering, I placed my scabbard and sword on the table and approached the windows. The moon cast its silvery glow over Camelot's courtyard below yet my mind wandered northward, to the place I yearned to be.

Under the starry sky, concern for Merlonius tugged at me with undeniable force. Alone in the forest, she had no way to call upon me if needed, a truth that weighed heavily on my heart. I sighed deeply, the sound merging with the night's stillness as I murmured a wish into the breeze, "Sleep well, my love."

The echo of my own voice faded into the stillness. I paced, haunted by an unrelenting question: *How many more battles must the Fellowship of the Round Table endure to rid Britain of the Saxons?*

Once our land was free from its tormentors, I would ask her to be my bride. Together, we would reign as King and Queen, ending our painful separation. Drawn to the shelf by my bed, I picked up the quartz from Merlin's cave, still resonating with her essence. Holding it against my chest, her image formed within me, stirring a longing I could not quiet.

The solitude of my quarters felt oppressive. Loneliness, once a familiar companion, now felt like a fierce adversary. I sat before the flickering fire, yearning for the night to pass and eager for the sunrise to herald a new day.

Watching the dance of the red and orange glow, my thoughts shifted to Bedwyr, his near loss and remarkable recovery. We had fought countless battles together; his prowess with a spear and a sword matched only by his loyalty. The last battle had taken his hand, leaving a wound deeper than any blade could cut. Yet I knew he would never accept defeat, and for that, I would remain beside him.

Sleep eluded me as my mind would not settle. I rose and walked about my chambers until the first rays of dawn painted the sky in hues of gold and amber. Standing near the casement, I caught the scent of dew, and as the distant stirrings of Camelot marked the day's renewal, I dressed in fresh garments. Making my way to Bedwyr's chambers, each step carried me towards fulfilling the vows I made to the people of Britain and to those I hold dear. *This day, like all days to come, we rebuild, we heal, and we rise.*

Bedwyr had given more than I could ever ask of any man, his courage and loyalty unwavering even when fate struck cruelly. I hoped my presence might bring him a measure of strength, just as his resilience had so often steadied me in my darkest hours.

Outside his chamber, I paused, then, drawing a deep breath, I knocked on the door.

CHAPTER 20

THE LADY OF THE LAKE

During the early years of my reign, the Saxons intensified their relentless assault upon our lands. Yet Camelot stood resolute, its towers reaching skyward, a beacon of strength and hope.

The clamor of valour rang through its halls, heralding an era of unmatched growth. Noble families from across the kingdom sent their sons to join our Round Table, eager to see them shaped into knights of honour and chivalry.

Even as Camelot's glory rose, a lesser king dared to challenge its might. His arrogance defied the values we held sacred. He took shelter in the woods near the castle, jeering at our knights as they passed and delighting in hollow triumphs.

His insolence endured, but my patience waned. Moved by righteous fury, I rode forth alone upon Thor, Caliburn firm in my grasp. My resolve hardened. I would end his defiance and restore order.

As I approached the wooded clearing, he emerged to meet me—a lone figure clad in mail and leather. Menace marked his every motion. Without pause, he hurled taunts, his sneering expression twisted with contempt.

"So, the great High King Arthur finally comes to meet his match."

"Your games with my knights amuse only you. We settle this now."

We secured our helms and spurred our steeds onward. The rival king met my charge with force, his blade fierce and unrelenting. The clash of iron on iron rang out as the fury of our combat grew. My pulse raced, for I knew that justice demanded I prevail.

With swords poised to advance, he pressed forward, and we were both thrown from our horses. The shock of striking the ground was sharp, but we rose swiftly to our feet. The fight continued, fierce and close, our swords sweeping through the shadowed glade.

His ferocity soon overwhelmed me, my sword hand straining and trembling under his relentless assaults. A crushing blow landed on my shoulder, forcing me back. I swung again, but as Caliburn met his blade, my father's sword gave way, splintering before falling to the earth, like echoes of lost battles.

I grabbed the king's sword arm, pushing the blade away, but could not avoid the brutal strike from his other hand. The world spun around me, and a sharp pain throbbed at my temple as darkness claimed me. Awareness slipped away, leaving my fate uncertain. I drifted beyond reach, surrendered to the void's embrace. Yet even then, from deep within the Otherworld, Merlin's foresight stirred. His vision reached across time, following the threads of destiny, perceiving what had not yet come to pass.

This rival king prepared to deliver the final, devastating thrust when Merlin emerged from behind an imposing oak tree. As he murmured incantations, a mighty gust of wind swirled around the king, lulling him into a deep slumber. He then cast a veil of invisibility over him, ensuring the king would remain hidden until his return.

With utmost care and remarkable might, Merlin lifted me onto my steed. He guided us through the trees, the surroundings blurring into a faint mist. Dimness clung to me, my thoughts scattered like embers in the wind. Only the movement of the horse tethered me to this world, and beyond that, all else slipped away.

The forest closed in around us as we made our way to the cottage. There, I slept deeply, untouched by the world, until the first light of dawn crept in. I stirred at the sound of Merlin's voice.

"Arthur, we are here with you."

A haze clung to my vision as I fought to clear it. Blinking away the remnants of sleep, I found Merlin and Merlonius beside me, their watchful eyes filled with concern.

Anguish and disappointment took hold, pressing heavily upon me. "I have lost Caliburn."

"We are aware," Merlin answered. "But do not despair. When you are fully recovered, we will speak of the path to your next blade."

"My father's sword… What different course could I have taken to avoid this outcome? I believed I was fighting for the honour of Camelot. How could it have come to this?" I shook my head, my frustration and self-doubt threatening to overtake me.

Merlin leaned closer. "Even the strongest of us falter. Caliburn is lost, yes, but it does not define your strength or your purpose. You are far greater than the weapon you wield."

His words settled over me like a balm, momentarily quieting my inner storm. He gave my shoulder a reassuring squeeze.

Merlonius asked softly, "Arthur, can you sit up?"

"I believe so."

With their support, I eased upright, the effort slow but not beyond my will. She offered a cup of healing tea, the warmth rising from it wrapped in the scent of crushed herbs and honey.

"Please, drink this," she encouraged.

Taking a careful taste, I felt its calming heat easing into my limbs. Memories of the battle with the king and the loss of Caliburn surged, unsettling me. Yet, Merlonius's touch against my skin stilled them. I reached for her hand, seeking solace. She held onto mine, her presence steady as I struggled to keep my heavy eyelids open.

I fell into a dreamless slumber and awoke as the sun dipped below the horizon. As my eyes adjusted to the dimming light, I found Merlonius still by my side.

"Arthur, how do you fare?"

"Much better, but my vitality has not yet returned."

"With rest, nourishment, and time, you will be strong again. Would you like some food?"

"I could do with something to eat."

"Well, then, let us see if we can get you to your feet."

With her help, I rose, my body yet bearing the strain of battle. Together, we walked towards the table, where the aroma of a prepared meal greeted us. Merlin turned to us as we approached.

"You are up, a welcome sight indeed. Come, you must eat."

I watched them, their movements effortless, flowing in rhythm like a minstrel's melody. With practiced ease, they set a steaming tureen of hare stew upon the table, accompanied by freshly baked bread and a pitcher of cool water. Each bite of the hearty stew and sip of fresh water eased the weariness still clinging to me, my vigour gradually returning. Yet, despite the physical renewal, I found myself drawn back to the clash with the king who had come so close to ending my life.

"Merlin, the king who nearly killed me—what has become of him? Has he recovered?"

"He is still in a deep slumber and will have no recollection of your encounter. I have also taken measures to ensure he relinquishes his games with your knights. You need not worry about him any longer."

A slow breath steadied me. "It is no small mercy that our fight did not end in my death. Nevertheless, I am grateful his treacherous schemes have come to an end. Once again, I am indebted to you. Without your intercession, I might not be seated here now." A pause settled between us before I continued, voicing the questions gnawing at my mind. "But, Merlin, how could this have happened? How could I lose Caliburn?"

"We are all presented with lessons in our lives."

"But why me?" The words slipped out, seeking clarity.

"Why do you think?"

I held his eyes as memory carried me back to the battlefield, to the reckless boldness that had driven me to face the rival king alone. Slowly, the answer formed. It was not a sudden revelation but something I had known all along, buried beneath layers of stubbornness.

"My pride," I confessed at last.

Merlin inclined his head, his expression holding neither judgment nor reproach.

"Yes, misguided certainty has been the downfall of many great men who walked the journey before you. Every loss, Arthur, is a reflection of our greatest flaws. Though rashness led you here, wisdom will guide you forward."

I let his words settle, their truth undeniable. My own folly had clouded my judgment and nearly cost me my life. It would not happen again.

Staring into the fire, I made a silent vow to remain ever watchful, to temper my resolve with humility, and to wield my power not as a weapon of vain glory but as a shield for those I swore to protect.

"I will remain vigilant," I said at last, "ever watchful for the fiery specter of ego that may rise again."

Merlin gave a small nod. The firelight caught the worn lines of his face, his expression calm and unreadable. Then his eyes met mine, steady and clear, with a glint of unspoken approval, as though he had long awaited this moment of understanding.

"Then you have taken the first step to master not only your sword, but the strength within yourself."

Merlonius reached for my arm. I placed my hand over hers, taking comfort in her presence.

"Now," Merlin said, "as your vitality returns, the three of us will embark on a journey to the Land of Lakes, a realm two days' journey from here, to seek a worthy successor to Caliburn. There, ancient forces will aid us, but how you command what is given will be in your hands.

"I shall inform Bedwyr of recent events and assure him of your continued recovery. He will oversee affairs at court and ensure that your absence does not raise any concerns."

"It means much that you make the journey to Camelot and place these matters in Bedwyr's care. I hold firm in my trust of his loyalty and ability to lead in my absence."

"You grace me with this charge. Bedwyr has proven himself to us time and again."

"I recognize that my choices are not always wise, though my intentions are true. But know, Merlin, that I am always grateful for your guidance and support."

Merlin rose and stepped to my side, resting a firm hand on my shoulder.

"Arthur, it is both my duty and my honour."

Fatigue crept over me, and Merlonius, ever watchful, asked, "Shall we return to bed, Arthur?"

"Yes, that would be wise."

With her help, I eased back into bed. Once settled, I looked at her.

"Merlonius, I love you."

She offered a tender smile and brushed a stray lock of hair from my forehead. "I also love you. Now, please try to rest."

I nodded, a sense of peace settling over me. As sleep claimed me, I found solace knowing I was not alone.

When the first rays of sunlight pierced through the window, I awoke to find her seated by my side, her hand holding mine. I made an effort to rise, but she gently pressed me back down.

"Have you not slept?"

"I found some rest, but I wanted to be here when you woke. Tell me, how do you fare?"

"Stronger, much stronger. I would like to don fresh garments."

She helped me wash and change into a clean tunic. Slowly, we made our way to the table. After ensuring I was comfortable, she set down fresh water, cheese, and bread before me. While we savored our meal, the door creaked open, and Merlin entered, staff in hand, joining us at the table.

"I see you are up and about, Arthur. How are you faring?"

"Much improved."

"Good, very good. I spoke with Bedwyr earlier this day, and he will handle the affairs at court in your absence. "

"My thanks, once again, Merlin."

"Indeed, and now you must rest and heal."

Over the next two days, we devoted ourselves to my recovery and to making final preparations for our journey. I felt my vigour returning, and with each sunrise, my anticipation grew.

By the third morn, as dawn's radiant glow bathed the land in light, Merlin declared me fit to travel, satisfied with my recovery.

We gathered around the table, breaking our fast. Merlin leaned forward, a slight, eager smile playing at the corners of his mouth. "Shall we begin our journey to the Land of Lakes, my young friends? Caliburn's replacement awaits you, Arthur."

"I stand ready, Merlin."

Excitement stirred within us as we readied for departure. The crisp, earthy scent of the forest surrounded us, and a breeze carried the promise of adventure. The day passed swiftly as we travelled through uncharted lands with Merlin's magic guiding our way.

As twilight blanketed the forest, Merlin led us to a small clearing off the path.

"This seems a good place to spend the night, would you not agree?" he remarked, surveying the area.

He raised his staff towards the darkening sky, and with a whispered incantation, a surge of unseen power stirred around us. Flames leapt up from the ground, casting light over the clearing. Nearby, a woven basket brimmed with succulent meats, crusty bread, tangy cheeses, and goblets of rich, spiced wine and cool, clear water. The savory scents invited us to partake, and the crackling fire cast dancing shades of red, orange, and yellow across the surroundings.

"Your magic never ceases to amaze, Merlin. This feast is beyond anything I could have imagined."

Merlonius nodded. "Even for me, who has witnessed your countless wonders, this eve is a delightful surprise."

"Much gratitude to you, both. Now, let us finish our meal and settle in for rest."

After clearing away the remnants of our feast, we gathered around the fire. Overhead, stars shimmered in the vast night sky as the distant hoot of an owl echoed through the trees. Wrapping my arms around Merlonius, she rested her head against my chest. I pressed a kiss to her forehead and whispered, "I love you." She nestled closer, releasing a blissful sigh.

We surrendered to slumber, comforted by the protective veil of Merlin's magic, ensuring our safety through the night.

By the time the sun began its slow ascent, its touch eased us from sleep. Still holding Merlonius close, I murmured, "We are being called to rise."

Her eyes opened, their gaze meeting mine, and the love I saw there pulled at my heart. I leaned in and we kissed, a silent promise passed between us.

After tending to our horses and breaking our fast with cups of fresh water, cheese, and berries, Merlin waved his staff to dispel the dwindling fire. We mounted our steeds and continued on our way.

As the sun climbed higher, the trees grew taller and more robust, their ancient limbs stretching skyward. The air felt heavy, like the moments before a storm, while a crisp breeze bore the unfamiliar scents of blooming wildflowers and evergreens, fragrances distinct from those we had known before.

Merlin raised his right hand, signaling for us to stop. "We have entered the Land of Lakes."

After tethering our horses, we followed Merlin onto a trail veiled in moss that wound through the weathered forest. A sweet fragrance of pine and damp earth wafted around us, hinting at the age-old secrets hidden beneath the forest canopy. We halted in a wide glade where the trees parted, revealing the clear sky and a vast body of water.

A mist rose over the lake, blurring the edges of the trees on the opposite shore. The cool dampness wrapped around us, and a faint haze clung to the world as though holding its breath. Gradually, the veil lifted, and we stood in awe of the beauty before us.

The ethereal strains of pan flutes filled the glade, unseen wood nymphs weaving their melodies through the trees. From the depths, an arm broke the surface, brandishing a gleaming sword. I stared at the spectral vision before me, its purpose uncertain, its presence otherworldly. It felt like a dream made real.

Merlin stood at my side. "Arthur, behold the sword that shall replace Caliburn."

The water bubbled and churned as a figure rose from its depths, at once graceful and majestic. Clad in a delicate white garment, she held the sword in one hand and a scabbard in the other. With effortless grace, she floated above the water's surface, her movements not of this realm.

"Merlin, who is this damsel?"

"She is the Lady of the Lake presenting you with her sword and scabbard. The sword was forged in the Otherworld and holds enduring might, while the scabbard bears magical powers. With it in your possession, no mortal wound shall befall you."

As the Lady of the Lake stood before us, the flutes fell silent, as though heeding an unspoken command.

"Arthur, within you lies the enduring might to restore peace to the land. It is for this reason that I bestow upon you my most precious gifts—Excalibur, my sword, and my scabbard that shall protect you from harm. When you wield this sword, others will be inspired to follow you, and my blessing shall be upon you. Accept them now and understand that you have been chosen for a great destiny."

At Merlin's beckoning, I stepped into the water, an unseen force guiding me forward, pushing me onward. The water rose to my chest, and an irresistible urge compelled me to raise my right arm. Her sword soared towards me and settled into my waiting hand. In turn, my left arm lifted, and the scabbard flew to meet my grasp. Upon accepting these gifts, the water began to swirl about us in a mesmerizing dance.

Stepping back onto the shore, I found myself entranced by the Lady's majestic bearing. Reverence overcame me as I cradled the sword and scabbard in my hands. An unshakable certainty took root within me. These sacred gifts held the key to bringing lasting harmony and justice to our realm.

Standing alongside Merlin and Merlonius, I watched as the Lady's attention shifted towards Merlonius, motionless and transfixed. A silent recognition passed between them, needing no words. Merlonius stood firm, her courage unflinching.

"My dear Sorceress and Merlin's most talented apprentice," the Lady's voice carried over the water, "we hold your spirit and the remarkable gifts you bring to this king and his land in the highest regard. May your courage and boundless love guide you unwaveringly on your path."

The Lady of the Lake next looked to Merlin. "Merlin, my friend, I stand united with you in the effort to restore this land. May wisdom and protection be your companions, and may your influence bring healing where there is division. We shall meet again."

With graceful poise, the Lady vanished beneath the water, leaving behind the echo of her message.

Merlonius remained fixed on the place where the Lady had vanished, her form rigid, as if still caught in the web of the Lady's enchantment.

I rested a hand on her shoulder, breaking the spell that held her.

She looked at me, her cheeks glistening with tears, her expression reflecting a tumult of emotions.

"Arthur," her words but a breath, "to receive such a gift from the Lady of the Lake is indeed a great honour."

My brows furrowed, sensing there was more to her encounter. "Merlonius, did the Lady of the Lake have aught else to share with you beyond what we heard?"

Her eyes met mine briefly, hesitation passing within them. Looking away, she seemed burdened by her distress.

"You carry sorrow. Pray, tell me."

Merlin stepped near. "Come, let us return now to our world, but first, it would be wise to dry your garments." He pointed his staff at me, the crystal at its tip glowing. In an instant, they were dry.

Feeling the surging might of the sword coursing through my being, I held Excalibur upright, marveling at the intricate carvings of two gilded serpents adorning each side. They coiled and twined, their scales shimmering like burnished gold, a symbol of wisdom and change. In the glowing light, the age-old inscriptions seemed to come alive, whispering truths of the past and prophecies for the future.

I fastened the scabbard to my waist and inserted Excalibur, the weight settling comfortably at my side. Mounted once again, we set forth, leaving the glistening lake behind, a place now fixed in my memory as a sanctuary of countless secrets and mysteries. I remained watchful of Merlonius, who rode beside me, her expression distant and contemplative. Unease stirred within me. *What message had the Lady given her, unspoken in our presence?*

With the fall of darkness, Merlin signaled for us to halt. In a small forest clearing, we dismounted, the crunch of dried leaves beneath our boots breaking the stillness of the eve. We secured the horses to branches, their breath visible in the coolness of night.

Merlonius and I moved with practiced care, checking their hooves and loosening the saddles. From the sacks prepared for the journey, I took out grain, pouring it into my palm and offering it to them. With a sweep of Merlin's staff, buckets of fresh water appeared beside them, the surface rippling as if drawn from a clear spring.

Once fed and settled, Merlonius approached Sweetness, running her fingers through the mare's mane as she whispered, "You have my gratitude for carrying me this day. One more day, and we shall be home."

Sweetness flicked her tail, as though she understood the promise. Moving to Tuft, Merlonius stroked his neck. "You too, my friend. You have done well. Rest now."

I rubbed the sweet spot between Thor's eyes, murmuring, "You have served me well once again, my friend. For all that you provide, I am grateful." The steady warmth of his breath brushed my arm, and he pressed his head against my chest.

Glancing at Merlonius, I said, "We lean on them far beyond what we speak of. Their endurance carries burdens greater than our own."

"Aye. Their loyalty is silent, but it speaks to the heart."

A short distance away, Merlin rested his hand upon his staff, the faint glimmer of moonlight bringing light to the worn wood as he watched us in thoughtful silence. Then, he turned and approached a hollow in the ground. Circling his staff around the edge, its crystal began to glow, beckoning a smoky cloud to swirl inside it. A sudden burst of light followed, and flames leapt forth, pushing back the night.

Merlonius and I joined him as the fire caught and held, casting its warmth into the eve. A gentle breeze stirred the branches above, rustling the leaves in a soothing rhythm. In the distance, the murmur of a stream wove through the forest, filling the night with a tranquil lull.

After he conjured a hearty stew, its scent mingling with the woodsmoke, we gathered around the fire. The embers glowed softly as we sat, each of us lost in thought. It was then I noticed Merlin, his expression distant, as he wandered through a vision far beyond our reach. Slowly, he returned, his eyes meeting mine.

"Arthur, your destiny is woven in the stars. With Excalibur at your side, believe unshakably in the victory that awaits you. The land will heal. Britain shall rise free once more, liberated from the clutches of invaders."

"Merlin, you gift us with promise and hope. With the Lady's blessing and Excalibur in my hand, I feel an uncompromising purpose surge through me. I am confident in our power to vanquish the Saxons and protect our land. Yet amidst this certainty, a sadness remains. Do you sense it as well? I implore you, share with me the nature of this sorrow we must confront."

Merlonius lowered her head slightly, her breath unsteady. Firelight caught the sheen of tears tracing silent paths down her cheeks. "Arthur, remember the vision I had when we returned to the cottage after you drew the sword from the stone? Do you recall it?"

A rush of dread churned within me, the memory surging back with unsettling clarity. "No, that cannot be our fate. You will remain by my side, I vow it." My determination was clear, yet a subtle tremor in my voice betrayed my fear.

"My dear boy, let us not dwell on what has not yet come to pass," Merlin urged. "The future holds many paths, fraught with challenges, sacrifices, and losses. Yet you possess the fortitude to overcome these trials, and I will guide you, steadfast by your side."

Merlonius and Merlin exchanged a glance that carried an understanding beyond words. It was as if their spirits were entwined by an invisible thread, sharing what could not be seen or spoken. Overcome with emotion, she gasped and sobbed, her hands trembling. It was unbearable seeing her thus, and I quickly enfolded her in my arms.

"I will never leave you. My heart yearns only for you, and together, we will overcome all that the Fates lay before us."

Seeking clarity, I entreated Merlin, "What have you foreseen?"

He did not answer, his focus seemingly lost in the wavering flames, as they whispered truths only he could hear.

As the storm within her began to calm, her sobs quieted. She pulled away from my arms, straightening as she looked into my eyes.

"Being with you, Arthur, brings a completeness to my soul. Your devotion fortifies me, enabling me to confront the unknown. My love for you is boundless, alive in these woods, the enchanted forest, and Camelot. From the day we pledged to each other, my love has only deepened."

Emotion surged within me. "No force, not even the Fates, can diminish my love for you." I sealed my words with a tender kiss.

Merlin let out a slow sigh, releasing his hold from beyond the veil. A sorrow touched his face as he looked to Merlonius and me.

"Arthur, I do not see all ends, nor do I have power to bend fate to my will. Yet know this—love, true love, is not so easily severed. Though the path ahead may be veiled, I sense that your bond with Merlonius is interwoven with forces greater than you or I. Hold fast to her, to each other, and do not let fear dictate your steps. What is meant to be shall unfold in its own time."

I held his stare, absorbing the depth of his words. "Your magic is great, Merlin, and our love is true. I will hold fast to it, as you have counseled."

I took Merlonius's hand, our fingers intertwining. For some time, we sat together, watching the flames dance, savoring the solace found in each other's presence.

As weariness settled over us, we stretched out by the fire. I held her close, feeling her breath rise and fall in time with mine. My gaze drifted to the vast expanse above, where countless stars shimmered against the darkened sky.

I appealed to the gods and goddesses, *Please, allow our paths to remain as one. Do not take her from me. Grant us the fortitude to overcome the struggles ahead.*

With that silent prayer carried into the night, we drifted into peaceful slumber, braced for whatever hardships the new day would bring.

At dawn, the first light stretched across the land, soft and pale. The dying fire crackled, its faint smoky trace curling into the breeze of the morn as we prepared to leave.

After tending to our horses, their coats glistening beneath the early light, we securely fastened their saddles, the leather creaking softly with each adjustment. Before setting forth, we ate a handful of berries from our provisions and drank from our waterskins, quenching our thirst after the night's rest.

At last, we set out on our homeward journey, the rhythmic clip-clop of hooves echoing along winding paths, where the softness of the morn still held sway. We pressed onward through the day until we reached the familiar, well-trodden path, shaped by countless travelers and marked by the imprints of many footsteps and hoofprints.

When Camelot drew nearer, the road split before us, and we slowed our steeds, bringing them to a halt.

Merlonius guided Sweetness ahead and looked at me. "Arthur, I shall miss you."

"And I shall miss you, Merlonius." The urge to go with her was strong. "Take this truth with you: your light and love brighten even the darkest of my days."

She held my gaze, time seeming to still. Then, with a solemn nod from Merlin, she urged her horse onward towards the edge of the enchanted forest. When the trees had taken her from sight, Merlin and I set our steeds upon the path leading to the castle.

As Camelot rose before us, my hand brushed the hilt of Excalibur, the blade humming with a quiet enchantment that seemed to pulse through the leather at my side. The Lady's prophecy lingered like a shadow just outside my grasp, a foretelling far more unsettling than the gleam of the sword or the power bound within its scabbard. For all the might she had placed in my keeping, none weighed as heavily as the thought that Merlonius might not remain at my side in the years to come.

A wistful ache tugged at my spirit, widening the vast expanse that now lay between us. Yet, I clung to the lasting strength of what we shared, as steadfast as the ancient stone pillars that defy the ravages of time.

Though the journey ahead was a lonely one, the memory of Merlonius and the love we shared sustained me. Riding forth on my destined path, guided by the enchanted allure of Excalibur and driven by unwavering determination, I carried her presence within me, a wellspring of solace against all I must yet endure.

CHAPTER 21

THE TWELFTH BATTLE

Eadgar and Ceolwulf were brothers, born and raised in the rolling hills and dense woods of the countryside. Their childhood was steeped in the ways of the land, their days spent tracking deer and boar through the thick undergrowth of the ancient forests. The rustle of leaves, the calls of birds, and the rich scent of moss-laden earth wove through their world, binding them to the wilds that had shaped them.

Eadgar, the elder, bore the hardened frame of a warrior, his years of wielding spear and bow evident in every muscle. Ceolwulf, quieter but no less formidable, possessed the keen eyes of a hunter, his blade as sharp as his sight for hidden prey.

It was after one of our earliest clashes with the Saxons that, weary and battle-worn, Merlin, my men, and I sought refuge in the forest. Beneath the towering pines and venerable oaks, we rested, our spirits seeking solace in the glow of the fire. There, I first beheld the two men.

Out from the trees, they emerged, slipping through the underbrush like part of the forest itself. Clad in rough-spun garments of green and brown, they blended seamlessly with the woodland around them. Their bronzed skin bore the mark of countless days beneath the open sky. They approached with ease.

I unsheathed my sword in a swift motion, prepared to defend against any who might mean harm. Yet the pair merely stood, their features revealing little.

Merlin stayed my hand with a single motion. "Hold! These are friends, not foes."

Eadgar stepped forward with sure, deliberate strides, his spear gripped in a hand long accustomed to its weight. His shoulders were squared, his eyes steady, a man tempered by hardship yet unbowed. When he spoke, it was with the certainty of one who had accepted his fate.

"We come to offer our services to Arthur, High King of Britain."

I moved a step closer, meeting the steadiness in his stance. "I am Arthur. Speak your purpose."

Ceolwulf, the younger brother, answered in a calm but equally determined manner. He carried a bow crafted from yew wood, strung with sinew, and a quiver of arrows, with a knife sheathed at his waist.

"We have lost our clan to a Saxon raid and wish to offer our services to you and this kingdom. The forest is our home. With our deep knowledge of the land, we can gather vital insight about the Saxons' numbers, weapons, plan of attack, and movements."

I observed them closely, sensing both the burn of vengeance and fierce dedication to serve this kingdom.

"Merlin, what say you to accepting their offer?"

"The wind whispers of your deeds, young warriors," he began, his focused scrutiny delving beyond what mere men could see. "And within its essence, I discern the weaving of your fate with that of Britain's. Do you swear allegiance to the king?"

They responded in unison and without hesitation, "We do, sire."

Merlin faced me. "Behold your scouts, Arthur."

Eadgar and Ceolwulf, unflinchingly loyal and steadfast in their mission to rid Britain of the Saxons, risked their lives battle after battle, employing their skill in scouting and stealth. Despite our relentless efforts to drive the Saxons south and out of Britain, their advance persisted—until the sixth year of my reign.

At dawn, the day after the full moon when meadows first flourish, the brothers arrived at the castle. A low mist clung to the grassy fields, veiling the land in a hushed stillness. Bedwyr and I welcomed them into the chamber where the Round Table stood, and soon Merlin joined us.

"Eadgar, Ceolwulf," I greeted, noting their weariness. "What news do you bring at this break of day?"

Stepping forward, Eadgar tightened his grip on the hilt of his knife before conveying his message urgently. "My king," he began, "we slipped into the enemy's encampment undetected a fortnight ago. They are plotting an offensive seven days hence, south of Camelot at Mount Badon."

Merlin remarked, "A brave move, my valiant young men."

Eadgar gave a brief, respectful nod. "It was necessary. Yet, more enemy forces have made landfall upon our shores. We believe our knights face a grave challenge, as the Saxons outnumber us at least three to one."

Ceolwulf's furrowed brow and the tight set of his mouth revealed his inner turmoil as he continued to provide additional details.

"Our foes wield spearheads, round shields, and battle-axes, forging a heavily armed force. Ruthless and savage, they are formidable adversaries."

With Ceolwulf's words settling over us, silence deepened, dread taking hold. Merlin stepped forward, his composed presence easing the fear that had gripped us.

"I have foreseen the profound struggles upon this fated field," he began. Looking to me, he continued, "Arthur Pendragon, with your unyielding spirit and the dauntless valour of your devoted warriors, you shall forge a path to victory."

"Merlin, your visions have never wavered. You have led us to triumph before, and I have no doubt your wisdom shall do so again."

I beckoned Eadgar and Ceolwulf. "Come, join us in the feasting hall. You have served faithfully, and your presence is valued."

Our steps carried us forward, my thoughts consumed with the looming conflict drawing near. *This would mark our twelfth clash against the relentless Saxons. For six long years, we have bled to safeguard our sacred land from their invasions. But this battle, I vowed, would be more than mere defence; it would bring a resounding triumph.*

After Eadgar and Ceolwulf returned to the shelter of the forest, we assembled the knights on the training grounds.

"My brave men," I began. "Our scouts have carried news to us that the Saxons plan to attack Britain at Mount Badon, to the south. We shall meet them with might and valour on the seventh dawn."

A chorus of voices rose from my men. "We stand ready!" they shouted, their hands gripping their swords and spears with renewed vigour. "For Camelot and for Britain!" Their loyalty never faltered, and as one, they prepared to meet the battle that awaited.

With each dawn, the warriors of Camelot trained with a fierce determination, their chainmail catching the sunlight's gleam. Bedwyr and I joined them, our blades meeting theirs in swift exchanges as we refined our skills. We stood tall and undaunted, the clinking of the iron rings marking the rhythm of practice as we readied ourselves for what we hoped would be the final battle against the Saxons. Swords clashed, and the thunderous impact of shields echoed the force of our efforts.

Each man prepared for what lay ahead in his own way. When the stars shone in the night sky, some knelt in solemn contemplation, seeking guidance from the gods and goddesses, while others gathered in small clusters, exchanging tales of past victories and considering strategies for the battle to come.

The scent of freshly sharpened iron hung in the air, mingling with the raw earth churned beneath their feet. When the day's preparations yielded to the stillness of our final eve, the knights dispersed into their own musings.

From where I lingered, watching my brave, loyal men, both pride and sorrow swelled within me. Each had found his place in the long rhythm of war, shoulders squared and spirits lifted. But I could not join them in rest.

I stood apart, knowing what the dawn would ask of us. The plans were set, the swords sharpened, the prayers offered, yet a hollow still echoed in my chest. If this was to be my final eve, I needed more than iron and oath to face it.

I rode from Camelot along the narrow road that led to the enchanted forest. The day had cooled, and a stillness lay upon the trees.

Thor moved with certainty beneath me, knowing the way. When we reached the familiar place where the woods deepened and the ancient path turned from the road, he slowed without command. I guided him through the trees until the clearing opened ahead.

I dismounted and led him to the paddock, tying the reins as I had done many times before. I walked the few paces to the stone cottage and knocked once.

Merlonius opened the door.

"Arthur."

She stepped into my arms, and I held her close, drawing her in as our heartbeats moved as one.

Her head rested against my chest. For a time, we stood unmoving, the forest wrapping around us, the only sound the gentle rhythm of her breath.

She looked up, and I kissed her. There was no need for words.

Still in the circle of my arms, she turned slightly and guided me inside. The familiar scent of herbs greeted us, and the warmth of the hearth carried the faint trace of burning wood.

Merlonius moved to the hearth and took up a small clay vessel, its surface marked with symbols older than time. She returned to me and led me to the bench by the wall. Sitting beside me, she took my hand and dipped her fingers into the vessel.

She touched my left palm and began to trace three lines: slow, deliberate, and sure. The Rune of Tiwaz (↑).

The deepening color of her eyes, as she imparted the wisdom of Tiwaz, reflected a knowledge beyond mortal understanding. The ancient sorcery between us bound us not only as king and sorceress, but as two souls joined by fate.

"It is the Rune of courage and dedication," she murmured. "He who carries the strength of the gods, earned through righteous and honorable deeds, shall receive the blessings of the Fates in all battles to come. Keep Tiwaz close, my love, and it shall become one with your being."

I looked down at the mark she had left on my skin, her touch still warm. "You are my courage. But there is something I have never spoken aloud."

She waited, her eyes unwavering.

"In my first battle against the Saxons, I was but a young man. They called me High King, but I had not yet earned the right. In the chaos of the field, I struck down a man older than I, a warrior fierce in his charge."

The memory rose with sharp clarity—his eyes wide in the instant before death, the sound of his fall.

"I felt no triumph. Only a sickness in my heart. Not from fear, but from the knowing that I had ended a life. I began to wonder what I might become. Whether I would grow hard, forsake the man I wished to be, forget the value of what I swore to protect."

She reached for my other hand and enclosed both within hers.

"But I held to my oath, to defend this land and its people. That vow has guided me through every battle since. Still, I have never forgotten the mark that first death left upon me."

"Nor should you. You remember because your soul remains whole."

I looked once more at the rune drawn on my palm. "Tiwaz is not only courage."

"No, it is sacrifice. Truth. Love offered freely, even when the cost is great."

I raised my eyes to hers. "Then I will carry it into battle, not only as king, but as the man you have known and loved. Should I fall, let it be said that I stayed true to myself."

She looked to my waist, her brow furrowing slightly.

"And you wear the scabbard still?"

"I do. It has spared me more than once. But magic cannot shield the soul, Merlonius. And it cannot promise I will return unchanged."

Her grip on my hands tightened. "Then return with your spirit whole, even if your body bears the cost.

"I have seen your return to me, Arthur. Not as a dream or a wish, but as truth. You must carry that with you."

I searched her face, drawn into the calm certainty in her words. Her gift had never failed to reveal what lay hidden beneath the surface of the world.

I bowed my head, pressing her hands to my lips. "Then I will trust in what you have seen."

She rested her head once more against my chest. I wrapped my arms around her, holding her close.

When I knew I must leave, as the hour had come, I pressed a final kiss to her brow, then her lips, holding to that moment as long as I dared.

"You will return," she whispered. "The gods have not yet finished weaving our tale."

I looked into her eyes and caressed her cheek before turning and making my way back to the paddock. Thor waited, his breath rising in puffs as I untied the reins. With a last glance towards the door, Merlonius raised her hand in farewell. I nodded my head, and mounted.

As we passed beneath the trees, the trace of her magic lingered on my palm, and the memory of her embrace stayed with me. I rode through the forest and back to Camelot, each step carrying me nearer to the battle that awaited.

That eve, I sat alone in my chambers, the hearth casting flickering light upon stone. I stared into the flames, recalling how Merlonius's fingers moved with her magic as she traced three lines upon my left palm—the Rune of Tiwaz (↑). That mark remained, now a part of me, as were her words, steady and unshaken by fear. In a world ruled by iron and storm, her vision became my light. So long as I drew breath, I would find my way back to her.

The night stretched into its darkest hour when a loud knock at my door pulled me from my reverie. Merlin entered, his cloak brushing against the doorframe, bringing a comforting yet solemn presence. He eased into the chair opposite me.

"I was with Merlonius this day," I confided, extending my hand to reveal the symbol of Tiwaz (↑) carved upon my palm. "She bestowed this gift upon me, saying it carries the power and blessing of the Fates."

He examined the symbol closely, the corners of his mouth lifting slightly in a faint smile. "Arthur, with Excalibur's might and Tiwaz at your side, victory shall be assured. Envision your success," he urged with conviction.

I immersed myself in the vision of our triumph over the Saxons, each detail crystallizing vividly before me. As the scene unfolded, Merlin raised his staff high and a brilliant light burst forth. This overwhelming surge of magic ushered me into a deep slumber, the powerful images remaining with me.

When the first light of day broke over the horizon, Merlin roused me.

"My boy, the hour has come. Rise, and ride to victory."

I secured the final clasp of my chainmail, and destiny's grip closed around me. The finely woven mesh clinked with each motion, a testament to the royal armorer's craft. A richly adorned belt, bearing the emblems of past kings, fastened the hauberk, a mark of my lineage.

We left my quarters and walked the vast passageways of the castle, our footsteps echoing against the stone. I cast one last glance behind me, knowing I would be marked by whatever this day would demand of me.

Beyond the towering castle doors, knights awaited on horseback, their banners rippling in the morn's breeze. They stood like sentinels of devotion and might, each rider prepared for the trials ahead.

Merlin's hand settled on my shoulder. I looked to him. His expression was resolute, his eyes steady, the lines of his face shaped by years of wisdom and unyielding purpose.

"Arthur, you are not just the King of Britain by title," he said, his breath warm against my ear. "You are the king by virtue of your actions, your courage. This day, let your valour shine as brightly as Excalibur's blade."

I met Merlin's eyes and offered a firm nod, the resolve in my heart needing no words.

Approaching Thor, I adjusted my helmet and set it upon my head. With this final piece secured, the mantle of both protection and duty was complete.

Determination coursed through me, strengthened by Merlin's guidance. I mounted Thor and secured my shield by its strap, the solid weight of it reassuring as it hung ready at my side. Riding forward, my thoughts turned to Merlonius: the love in her eyes, her touch that seemed to fortify my very spirit. Prepared for the impending battle with Tiwaz and Excalibur, I faced destiny, filled with a fervent hope that victory was indeed at hand.

Near the hillside, the strategic advantage of the Saxons, poised atop Mount Badon, became starkly evident. Their figures formed a menacing line against the sky. With a resounding shout, we charged, the din of clashing swords and battle cries breaking the stillness of daybreak. Our sudden and aggressive assault caught the Saxons off guard, their lines wavering under our onslaught.

Advancing further, their ranks faltered in the dawn's light, our blades gleaming with renewed might.

The air grew thick with the mingled scents of blood and sweat, a grim shadow settling over the battlefield. Flashes of past battles haunted me, fueling a dread swiftly met with a strong purpose to protect Camelot and my knights, ensuring that their sacrifices were not in vain.

For three relentless days, the battle raged, far exceeding our expectations. The knights of Camelot displayed valour unmatched, facing overwhelming Saxon forces. The casualty toll climbed, with the outcome hanging in perilous balance.

On the fourth day, crows wheeled above, their dark wings a grim omen of defeat, while the dust of trampled earth mingled with the iron tang of blood. The shadow of loss pressed hard upon me, yet through the din, a sudden vision of Merlin and Merlonius broke through like a rallying cry. Their message was clear and resonant:

"Arthur, we stand by your side. Focus on Tiwaz and seize the hill."

Their presence felt tangible, and their words rekindled the fire within me. I raised Excalibur aloft, invoking the might of Tiwaz and the ancient powers of the land:

"In the name of righteousness and honour, grant us victory!"

Spurring Thor forward, I led a renewed charge up the hill, my knights rallying behind me. The Saxons, though unyielding, could not withstand our driven advance. The brutality of the battle intensified, the stench of death ever-present, yet we pressed on, driven by a surge of valour and the indomitable will to prevail.

When the sun reached its peak, the very earth beneath us seemed to stir with a hidden power, as if a chorus rose from its depths. I recalled Merlin's teachings about the silent guardians of this land. With the burden of our losses heavy on my heart, I called out:

"Spirits of the land, guardians of truth, lend us your light in our darkest hour!"

At my summons, the air around us seemed to stir with an ageless presence. The blades of our knights, weathered from the relentless battle, began to shimmer with an ethereal glow, casting shafts of radiance across the battlefield. The Saxons, startled by the sudden brilliance, faltered, momentarily blinded by the glow shining from our swords. The spirits themselves had imbued our weapons with the luminance of the sun, shifting the battle in our favor.

With victory in sight, I shouted, "The Saxons are in retreat, men! Summon your might and claim our triumph!"

As our foes fled, the battlefield, now brightened by our fortified spirits and radiant blades, bore witness to the turning tide. The Saxons' retreat marked not just a physical victory but a testament to the union of human valour and ancient powers safeguarding this sacred land.

With the Saxons driven back towards the shore, we reclaimed the battlefield, now littered with the wounded, the dead, and the dying. The harsh cost of victory was painfully clear, marked by immense casualties on both sides and a heavy toll on our kingdom. In the aftermath, I vowed to use my authority to prevent such devastation in the future, dedicating my reign to restoring peace and prosperity.

Turning my attention to the wounded knights, I guided my horse to those nearest, dismounting with urgency and calling for aid and litters. Men hurried forward, lifting the wounded with great care and transporting them to our stronghold to dress their wounds.

For hours, I traversed the field among those mortally wounded and those who might yet be saved, ensuring that each received the care they desperately needed. By late day, most of the fallen had been solemnly placed on one side of the encampment. Surveying the scene, Bedwyr approached, and I clasped his arm, comforted to find him unharmed. Gratitude passed between us, a silent understanding of our survival through the grievous battle.

With the sun setting, casting a somber light over the battlefield, Bedwyr stood at my side. The haunting moans of the wounded rose around us, a veil of sorrow and pain enveloping the scarred land.

"Arthur," Bedwyr's voice was low, his words heavy with sorrow, "you must give the order to set fire to the bodies of those we have lost."

I looked out over the vast expanse. "It must be done. We cannot let pestilence spread among the living."

As the flames rose to consume the fallen, their shapes twisted in the firelight, dancing briefly against the twilight before vanishing into smoke. My thoughts turned to the wounded still among us, their cries drifting across the field, sorrowful as wind through broken branches.

With unwavering determination, I declared to my knights, "We shall carry our brethren to The Giants' Dance upon the great plain."

Gawain's brow furrowed as my message took hold. With a hesitant nod, he said, "But, my lord, the journey ahead is long and treacherous."

I met his eyes, sensing the reflection of my own doubts in his concerns. The dangers ahead and the care of our wounded were undeniable, yet my decision remained firm.

"I understand, Gawain. But we cannot abandon our wounded to suffer and perish in this grim aftermath."

He rubbed the back of his neck, deep in thought, before looking at me with renewed conviction.

"You speak true, my lord."

The knights stepped forward, their allegiance to the Fellowship of the Round Table driving them as they helped the injured warriors onto their horses. Each movement betrayed their weariness, yet they pressed on, the weight of their chainmail and the burden of their duty carried without hesitation. Litters secured to the horses cradled the severely wounded, their stark pallor and pained expressions revealing the depth of their suffering. The journey was heavy with fatigue and the uncertainty of what was to come as we rode through the night.

With the first light of dawn cresting the horizon, solemn relief washed over us as we reached the sacred expanse of The Giants' Dance. Slowly, the wounded were placed within the protective embrace of the circle.

"Here, we will heal, and we will honour our fallen," I declared firmly.

"Indeed, Arthur," Bedwyr affirmed.

While we awaited the arrival of Merlin and Merlonius, the haunting screams of my fallen men echoed in my mind. Though the battle was won, the weight of their loss pressed upon my weary spirit.

As daylight began to spread through the forest, they emerged, moving like shadows becoming form. Merlin, his grey robes billowing like a wraith, led with a determined pace.

"We must hasten," he called out as he approached through the clearing, his urgency clear in the swift strides that brought him closer. "The wounded are in dire need of our aid."

Entering the sacred expanse of The Giants' Dance, Merlonius moved with purpose among the injured. Her touch was delicate, imbued with a mystical force, as she pressed her palms upon their foreheads. While she worked, Merlin watched her every move. He held his staff tightly in his left hand, the crystal at the tip glowing with a pale, ethereal light. With each whispered incantation, a wave of soothing power radiated from her fingertips, the circle stones humming with the potency of her healing magic. The very clouds seemed to descend closer to earth, as if drawn by the spellbinding quality she wielded. Slowly, the wounded stirred, their injuries visibly mending under her care.

"Rest now," she whispered.

One by one, the warriors succumbed to a deep, healing slumber under her vigilant care. With measured steps, she came to where Bedwyr and I stood.

"Arthur, Bedwyr, are you injured?"

Bedwyr answered with a weary smile. "I am unharmed, but am in need of rest, m'lady."

"My scabbard shielded me from the worst," I offered, "yet the blows I endured weigh heavily upon me," my fingers drifting to my aching side.

Her gaze met mine, unwavering, knowing. In that instant, I remembered her words. *I have seen your return to me.* Her vision, once spoken in faith, now stood fulfilled before us both.

Merlonius laid her hands atop my head, and her healing essence flowed into me, soothing my bruises and rekindling my strength.

I clasped her hand. "Merlonius, my gratitude for helping my knights is beyond words."

"To know you are well brings me great comfort."

She attended to Bedwyr next, her movements graceful and practiced. Each touch lifted the veil of fatigue that had settled over him, softening his features into repose and ease.

"My thanks for your healing, m'lady."

"Be well, my friend."

She approached Merlin, who stood nearby. "Merlin, Arthur must rest at the cottage. He is worn from more than just the battle. I trust Bedwyr will remain with me. Together, we can care for the others."

Returning to me, she touched my cheek tenderly, angling her body to shield the gesture from any watching eyes. She spoke softly. "Please, Arthur, go with Merlin. I will join you once the healing is no longer needed. Have no concerns; Bedwyr will oversee the knights' return to Camelot."

"Merlonius, I do not wish to leave you here among so many wounded."

"All shall be well, have no concerns. I shall be with you before long." She looked to Bedwyr, "Will you walk with me among those who still need my help?"

"As you wish, m'lady."

Merlin came to my side, his touch steady on my arm. "Let us depart, Arthur."

He helped me mount my horse, exhaustion clinging to me. Glancing back, I saw her tending to my men, with Bedwyr standing watchful at her side. The battle had ended, but the echoes of its fury had not yet faded. I turned forward as Merlin led me through the trees.

Upon reaching the cottage, I dismounted with his help, my body aching and my legs trembling from the exertions of battle. I shed my chainmail, sword, and heavy leather boots, and collapsed onto the bed. Merlin, ever attentive, left to tend to Thor, ensuring all was well.

Sleep began to take a firm grip of me, when the door opened, and his footsteps approached.

"Arthur, drink this before sleep claims you fully. It will aid your healing," he said, gently shaking my shoulder.

He handed me a vessel of spiced drink, its heat still rising in curls. I drank deeply, then returned the cup.

"Many thanks, Merlin, for all you do," I murmured, my voice weak even to my own ears.

I settled back, the soft bed a sanctuary from the harsh world outside. He brushed back my hair.

"Rest now, my king. Heal, my son."

My mind began to wander and I could almost see Merlonius walking among the wounded, and later, I would learn that she and Bedwyr had remained vigilant. For even now, within the sacred circle of The Giants' Dance, Bedwyr directed the remaining knights to prepare for their journey to Camelot. He helped move those still in slumber to the litters and stood by the edge of the circle as the final knight mounted his horse. Merlonius stood at his side, her eyes following each one as they disappeared into the distance.

Bedwyr watched the fading silhouettes of the knights before turning to her. "M'lady, I will walk with you to the boundary of the trees."

Together they made their way to the forest's edge, the towering stones of The Giants' Dance slowly receding behind them. At the first tall oak, he paused and looked into the dim forest beyond.

"I must bid you farewell here. My thanks for aiding my fellow knights. I trust you to care for Arthur."

She smiled, touching his arm. "Fear not; I will see to our friend. Your courage is admirable, Bedwyr."

He gave a brief nod, a silent exchange of gratitude passing between them.

With that, she vanished into the forest, her form fading into the twilight beneath the trees.

Drifting into sleep, the faint scent of lavender, so distinctly hers, stayed with me, woven with the whispers of the wind. Memories of laughter and hand-holding on a hillside filled my thoughts.

"Do you recall those days?" I murmured in my half-waking state.

Her words floated through the stillness. "Of course, my love. A simpler time, forever cherished in my heart."

Descending into dreams, the violence and bloodshed of the battlefield gradually faded away. In that tranquil realm, I was no longer the High King of Britain, but simply Arthur, a man cherishing a life filled with love, beside Merlonius—the one who completed me in ways no crown ever could.

CHAPTER 22

A HEART SPLIT IN TWO

I awoke as light streamed through the window, the warmth caressing my face and offering a gentle contrast to the remnants of a restless slumber.

Rising, I made my way towards the hearth where I found Merlin and Merlonius seated at the wooden table. Their whispers barely disturbed the tranquil morn, yet beneath their hushed tones, I sensed a thread pulled tight with strain.

As I neared, the familiar cadence of Merlonius's voice swept away the last traces of sleep.

"Arthur, you are about. How are you faring?"

"Better, much better."

Even so, I felt an unsettledness beneath the measured calm.

"I am sincerely thankful to you both for your care."

I paused. "How are my knights faring, Merlin?"

"You have led your knights with courage and skill. Your valiant efforts have driven the Saxons from our shores, and for that, I commend you," he said with respect. Yet, his eyes held a gravity that belied his encouraging words. "Most are healed, and others are on their way to recovery."

A wave of relief moved through me, mingled with pride, but it was tempered by a somber truth.

"Many good men perished in this battle. To know others will live out their days brings comfort."

Yet, Merlin's concern did not escape me.

"What troubles you, my friend?"

"Let us walk," he said, gesturing towards the door, his tone carrying a new urgency.

I looked to Merlonius and saw that she, too, sensed something was amiss.

We made our way to the pond, our steps brisk yet shadowed by unease. Upon reaching the water's edge, where the early light touched the surface, I was poised to inquire about the issue at hand. But before I could speak, without pause, he began.

"Arthur, I understand the depth of your love for Merlonius, and I know how profoundly she shares that love. Nevertheless, it is not ordained for her to become your queen."

His eyes, veiled with sadness, settled on some distant point across the pond. I waited, my breath quickening, for him to continue.

"Another is destined to assume that position in history, and her name is Gwenhwyfar, daughter of King Leodegan. You are aware of Leodegan's loyalty since you ascended the throne."

Merlin's revelation struck like a blow, leaving me momentarily speechless, my chest tightening as my heart pounded fiercely. Restlessness drove me to pace, my boots pressing into the grass, barely aware of the mist from the nearby waterfall. Anguish and disbelief clashed within me, spilling out in a furious outburst.

"No, this cannot be!"

The realization that Merlonius's long-ago visions held true pierced me like a dagger. Turning to him, my fury was as sharp as the pain his words inflicted.

"And you have known this all along, have you not? Why did you keep this from me all this time?"

His jaw tightened, sorrow shimmering briefly in his composed expression. His shoulders sagged slightly, and his gaze fell, revealing the unspoken burden he had carried alone for years.

"I did not withhold this knowledge to deceive you. I knew it would bring pain, not just to you, but to Merlonius as well. I delayed as long as I could, hoping that perhaps what the Fates had decreed might change... but some paths cannot be altered."

He hesitated before speaking again, his tone low but measured. "You have driven the Saxons from our shores and united the land under your banner. I feared sharing this earlier would cloud your mind, distract you from the battles you needed to win and the kingdom you sought to secure. I wanted to shield you both, for as long as possible.

"But the time has come. With your recent victory on the battlefield, you were ready to take Merlonius as your queen. I could no longer keep this from you."

My anger swelled beyond restraint. "And do you expect me to accept this now? What cruel twist of destiny would bring the woman I love into my life, only to deny me the happiness of union?

"I cannot abide it. My heart belongs wholly to Merlonius. She is not only a beloved companion, she is also woven into the very cloth of who I am. My deepest desire is for her to stand beside me, ruling as my queen."

I poured out my frustration and anguish until my breath alone was left, the words having taken all they could from me. Merlin, as unyielding as the stones at The Giants' Dance, stood firm, saying nothing. The silence stretched between us. At last, he spoke again.

"Arthur, the people will never embrace Merlonius as your queen. While they welcome her as a sorceress and healer, they will never see her crowned beside you. Even my magic, as much as I wish it could, cannot change this."

His words carried undeniable truth. Losing her was unthinkable, and the urgency to find a solution consumed me.

We made our way back, the sun high above us. Upon entering, Merlonius rose and stood before us. Looking at her, my love for her only deepened. *Surely the gods had not brought us this far only to part us now.*

"Would you walk with me?"

I extended my hand, and she placed hers in mine.

"Of course."

Approaching the door, the anguish on Merlin's face was evident, but I said nothing further to him, unwilling to let my anger take hold. Merlonius and I stepped outside, walking hand in hand towards the waterfall.

Beside the pond, I pulled her close, holding her as if to shield her from the cruel fate before us. She touched my face, stirring a flood of emotions within me. I felt her love, as strong and deep as my own for her.

"I love you, Merlonius. I want to spend the rest of my life with you as my wife, my queen, but Merlin has just revealed our destined paths, and every part of me pushes against what awaits us."

Her foresight had already given her a glimpse of what was to come. She lowered her hand, a single tear tracing the curve of her cheek in silent surrender.

I let out a sigh and drew in another breath. The mere thought of Gwenhwyfar's name left a bitter taste.

"Merlin tells me I must take another as my queen. Her name is Gwenhwyfar, daughter of King Leodegan, who has shown loyalty to me since my coronation."

I could feel the heaviness of her sorrow as she spoke. "So, Merlin's revelation gives truth to my past visions and the message from the Lady of the Lake." Shaking her head slowly, as though the burden were too much to bear, she continued. "You are to wed… this woman named Gwenhwyfar?" Tears welled in her eyes before spilling over. "How am I to endure this fate, Arthur?"

"Merlin has said that the people who hold you in high esteem as a sorceress and healer will never accept you as queen. This angers me deeply. How can I be king and yet be denied the one I wish to have by my side? This is not what I want, nor what I ever desired. The very thought of being without you tears at me."

I clenched my fists, struggling to contain my frustration. "I cannot imagine ruling without you, Merlonius. You are not only my love, but the presence that keeps me whole. How can I exist in a world where you are not by my side as my queen?"

"When is this to happen?"

"I do not know. But I swear this to you—our hearts will always be joined. My life is yours, now and forever. I cannot let you go."

She lifted her eyes to mine, her fingers closing around my hand, trembling yet resolute. "Swear as you must, Arthur. Our spirits are twined beyond the reach of crowns. Though fate may sever our paths, my soul will still seek yours, in this life and beyond."

Her words cleft me open; for a moment I knew only the torment of losing her and the cold truth of my duty.

We clasped hands tightly, whispering hurried plans. Would the loyalty of some ally bend to our cause? Could Merlin contrive a charm? Might I lay down my crown and flee with her into hiding? One idea followed another like stones laid across a stream, yet each, upon closer thought, dissolved. Allies owed oaths of their own; enchantments asked prices I was not certain I could pay; to lay down my crown would leave Britain unguarded.

The melody of the waterfall, its cascading waters blending with the rustling breeze, stood in stark contrast to the turmoil stirred by Merlin's foretelling. Seated beside her on the stone bench, my heart ached with the desire to be with her beyond the confines of this life. Time slipped away, each breath a search for a way to defy the decree of the Fates.

The sun moved steadily across the sky towards dusk, casting softened light upon the pond. As it sank lower and the heavens signaled the day's end, another kind of light emerged, dim and ethereal, touched with mystery. The pond, previously a mirror of daylight's clarity, now reflected the softer, mysterious radiance of twilight.

Our exchange stretched on, seeking a glimmer of hope amid rising doubt. As the stars emerged one by one, silent witnesses to all that had been spoken, Merlonius and I shared a look of mutual understanding, marked by her calm acceptance.

"Arthur, we cannot defy the Fates' decrees. They have woven our lives in a way we cannot undo," she said with resignation.

"Merlonius," I murmured, "our love is boundless and enduring. It transcends the limitations of time, and though we may confront an uncertain future, our spirits shall remain joined as one."

I took her hand and led her to a small, secluded grove by the pond. Beneath the shimmer of the stars, we sought reassurance in each other's arms. Our love burned through the night, fierce and unrelenting, offering fleeting solace from the sorrow we could not escape.

With the first light of dawn breaking across the sky, I awoke with my arms still wrapped around her. Brushing a wisp of hair from her face, I kissed her tenderly.

"Merlonius, I swear to you that my pledge will be honoured: not only to Britain as High King, but also to what we share. Rest I shall not, nor shall I falter, until the day comes when I may call you my wife. Our future is woven with the threads of our devotion, and I will protect it with all that I am."

"Arthur, I shall wait for you here in the enchanted forest, for as long as the stars shine in the heavens."

I tightened my embrace, unwilling to release her, unable to imagine a life without her. A mantle of kingship had been thrust upon me that I had never sought. Because of this, the woman who completed me was hidden away, our love shrouded in secrecy. Every path leading to our union seemed obstructed, yet I clung to an unshakable certainty: our love would endure every trial. Together, we would forge not just a future but a life worthy of the gods' notice.

CHAPTER 23

THE INTRODUCTION

Though still a young king, I had led Britain to victory, driving the Saxon invaders from our land. In the year since the Battle of Mount Badon, I endeavored to meet the pressing demands of my crown while seeking frequent escapes to the enchanted forest. There, the solace I found with Merlonius provided the respite I needed from my regal duties. With each stolen breath of time, our trust and commitment deepened, binding us ever closer.

Yet this day, I paced restlessly in my quarters, tormented by a path laid before me that I could not willingly tread. The scent of parchment and age-old scrolls was ever present, a constant reminder of the long hours spent at the table. There, Bedwyr and I worked late into the night, poring over decrees and treaties that shaped the kingdom.

The struggle between my duty and my desire to be with Merlonius tugged at me relentlessly. My responsibilities—governing wisely, defending the realm, and forging alliances among the lords—bore down on me, and I knew that choosing love over duty could have dire consequences.

The rustle of robes signaled Merlin's arrival. "Arthur, we must prepare to leave. This day King Leodegan has arranged for you to meet his daughter, Gwenhwyfar."

A surge of anger rose within me. "I have no interest in meeting her," the words escaping more sharply than intended.

His expression hardened. "We have already spoken of the need to secure the support of the lower lords. Taking Gwenhwyfar as your queen will give you this. The Fates have deemed it so."

I drew in a long breath, trying to restrain my frustration. The absence of Merlonius cast a profound emptiness within me, leaving a void that seemed impossible to fill.

Could the Fates truly be so cruel? After all I have endured, after every battle fought and every sacrifice made, is my greatest struggle not to be waged with sword and shield, but within my own heart?

My love for Merlonius is unshakable, yet the weight of Britain rests upon me. I have sworn to protect this land and its people. A king's duty demands sacrifice.

Steeling myself, I forced the words from my lips. "I am ready."

We left my quarters and made our way to the waiting horses. In place of my trusted steed, which had carried me into countless battles, a more subdued mare awaited. As I neared, she nuzzled me, providing a fleeting comfort. With reluctance, I mounted her.

We set off, crossing the drawbridge and riding towards Cameliard. The journey ahead would span several hours, during which I had no desire to discuss its purpose or the sorrow that clung to me.

The quiet stretched between us, the steady rhythm of hooves the only sound until Merlin's voice broke through my reverie. "Arthur, you are well aware of King Leodegan's proven loyalty to your late father, Uther Pendragon. He is also one of the kings who has accepted you as his overlord."

I said nothing, fully aware of Leodegan's allegiance, yet this knowledge did little to ease the decision before me. A union with his daughter strayed far from the life I had once envisioned. I longed for a simpler existence, one where I could share my days closely with Merlonius. We would live on a small farm, breeding horses, surrounded by the laughter of our children, exploring this land together. This dream, unyielding and sharply drawn, had always stayed with me.

Here I was, shackled by royal obligations, a relentless reminder of my ties to the land and the people of Britain, unforeseen when, at fifteen, I unwittingly accepted the title and burdens of the crown. Had I known that claiming my lineage would demand I forsake the one I truly loved, I would have refused the mantle of High King. Anger and resentment threatened to surface, but I consciously pushed them aside, as had become my custom. Seeking distraction, I turned my attention to the world around me. The dirt road wound like a pale ribbon through the trees, the heavy scent of damp leaves clinging to the air. My thoughts, restless and bitter, stirred with every bend of the path.

At long last, we arrived at King Leodegan's castle. Dismounting from our horses, we were ushered into a magnificent hall with fluttering banners, their vibrant colours suspended from the towering walls. A grand feast awaited us, a long table laden with lavish fare.

As we waited, King Leodegan entered. His sharp eyes gleamed with piercing cleverness.

"Greetings, my friends, let us sit and discuss the matter at hand!" King Leodegan's words were measured and precise, more aligned with tradition than genuine enthusiasm. He directed us to one side of the table, taking a seat opposite.

"Pray, enjoy the meal and good wine. Gwenhwyfar will join us soon."

Though I had no hunger, my throat was parched from the journey, so I tasted the wine.

"King Leodegan," Merlin began, "we greatly value your willingness to arrange this introduction between King Arthur and Gwenhwyfar, and we hope it will lead to a mutually beneficial alliance. If it pleases you, we would like to meet Gwenhwyfar."

"We are honoured that you, King Arthur, would consider my daughter suitable to be your queen. Though there is a great difference in age between us, I offer you the same respect and support I gave to your father, Uther Pendragon," Leodegan lifted his goblet and took a drink. "When I first met Gwenhwyfar's mother, I did not know what to expect, but with each encounter, I found myself more at ease in her company."

I gave King Leodegan a slight nod. He had spoken of duty, not love, and left their hearts unmentioned. Merlin cleared his throat, pulling me from my musings.

Leodegan gestured to his servant, who promptly left us. Within minutes, Gwenhwyfar entered the hall. Her delicate beauty, with skin as pale as moonlight and hair flowing in straight, silken tresses of rich chestnut, was striking. She was stunning, each step measured with practiced grace. Yet something about her presence felt distant, as if she stood behind an invisible veil.

Whereas Merlonius, with her wild curls, rosy cheeks, and infectious smile, always brought light to my spirit. I could picture her now, walking barefoot through the woods, her laughter like music on the breeze.

Merlin's hand on my shoulder pulled me from my thoughts of Merlonius. I closed my eyes briefly, clearing my mind as Gwenhwyfar stood before us.

King Leodegan rose from his seat. "King Arthur, I present my daughter, Gwenhwyfar, also known as Guenevere."

I stood and bowed to her. Gwenhwyfar curtsied, and I noticed the absence of a smile or a blush on her cheeks.

Merlin glanced between us. "Arthur, perhaps you and Gwenhwyfar might take a stroll in the garden while King Leodegan and I attend to other matters."

I looked at Gwenhwyfar. "My lady."

She led us from the hall towards the rear of the castle and into a small garden, lush and vibrant with flowers of every hue. Birds chirped melodically, but not even the beauty could lift the heaviness between us. We followed the winding path as sunlight danced through the foliage, sketching ever-changing shapes across the ground. The rustle of leaves kept pace with our hesitant steps, and a faint chill stayed with us, reflected in Gwenhwyfar's unyielding, detached expression.

Upon reaching a secluded bench beneath a canopy of blooming roses, I gestured for her to sit. She did so, holding herself with rigid reserve. The fragrance of roses surrounded us, their blooms arching close, untouched by all that was not right between us.

"Gwenhwyfar," I began cautiously, "how do you truly feel about all of this? About joining your life with a man you do not know?"

She turned towards me, pausing thoughtfully. "My lord, what do you mean?"

"I mean, how do you feel about the possibility of our union? Do you have any doubts, any desires of your own?"

Her brow furrowed slightly, "Who would not want to be your queen?"

Her words made it clear; she saw the crown, not the man.

I exhaled a resigned sigh. "Very well, it has been my pleasure to meet you. Shall we return to join your father and Merlin?"

She nodded, her features briefly revealing a hint of relief. We retraced our steps as the unspoken strain of obligation and hollow formality settled over us, as heavy as the armour I once wore in battle.

Upon entering, Merlin and Leodegan's voices drifted towards us.

"I agree, Merlin," Leodegan was saying. "Six moons will provide the perfect span to prepare for the ceremony, and the harvest moon is an ideal time of year for the festivities."

Gwenhwyfar's poised smile was measured, revealing nothing but intent. Her words and actions spoke not of love, nor of care, but only of ambition. The idea of our union felt hollow, a formality driven by position and power rather than genuine affection.

My mind drifted to Merlonius, in whose presence I found a haven of serenity and love. The contrast between the two was stark, and thinking of what lay ahead settled over me like a gathering storm I longed to escape.

We drew closer, and their conversation faded into silence. Merlin's sharp eyes flicked towards my clenched fists, then shifted to the tautness in my jaw. With a knowing glance, he spoke to Leodegan.

"Our thanks for the gracious welcome you have given us, my lord. We will speak again." He then offered Gwenhwyfar a respectful nod. "It was an honour to meet you, my lady."

She responded with a nod.

Looking to Leodegan, I said, "Farewell, my lord."

Then, addressing Gwenhwyfar, I said respectfully, "It has been my pleasure to meet you."

A shadowed understanding passed between us, hinting at the mutual guardedness. With a small bow, I left the hall. The encounter weighed on me as Merlin and I made our way to the great doors of the castle.

Stepping outside, the fresh air and open sky were a welcome reprieve from the stifling affair we had just left behind. Yet the heaviness settled in my chest, a sharp reminder of the union I was bound to, devoid of love. Our horses stood ready, and I thanked the stable boy before swinging into the saddle.

"Shall we make for Camelot?"

I hoped the familiar landscape would calm the unrest in my mind.

With practiced ease, Merlin mounted his steed. "Indeed, Arthur."

I urged my horse forward, leading us towards Camelot. We rode in silence, the closeness of the forest pressing around us, broken only by the occasional creak of leather and the sighing of the wind.

Gwenhwyfar's cold bearing and the ambition in her eyes stayed with me. This was not the future I had envisioned with Merlonius, whose love had been my solace through every trial. Together, we had weathered storms and celebrated victories, bound by something far deeper than titles. The idea of being with someone other than Merlonius, even a queen, stirred a bitterness within me. *How could anyone understand the depth of our affection or the emptiness her absence would leave behind?*

We rode without speaking until the castle came into view, the stillness between us unbroken. Merlin's sudden remark startled me.

"Gwenhwyfar is a fine woman, is she not, Arthur?"

My hands tightened around the reins, the leather biting into my palms as I pulled my horse to a stop. Beside me, he did the same. A surge of raw and unrestrained emotion tore through me, and I shifted in my saddle to face him.

"How dare you speak to me of her!" I shouted, fury spilling forth. "You, who have been the most important person in my life for as long as I can remember, care nothing for what I desire most. How can you defend this arrangement? You are asking me to wed a woman I do not love! You know who brings me joy, who I love. How can you condemn me to a life of misery? Do you not want me to be happy?"

His voice rose to meet my anger. "My feelings for you run deep, and you know that. But they are eclipsed by my love for the land, for Britain itself! Merlonius would not survive the court, and the people will not accept her as your queen."

I said nothing and spurred my horse, galloping fiercely towards Camelot. Nearing the drawbridge, I slowed, and he caught up, guiding his horse beside mine.

"I will send word to King Leodegan that the union will be held after the final harvest," he declared with resignation.

Without sparing him a glance, I raced towards the castle, desperate to reach Merlonius before Merlin's plans could unfold. Handing the reins to the stable boy, I made haste up the stair, my footsteps echoing through the deserted halls. Careful to avoid detection, I sought out the hidden passageway, my breath quickening as I moved forward.

Upon reaching it, I pulled down on the sconce, and the door swung open. I stepped through and secured it behind me before turning and running. Every stride brought me closer to the one I loved, and with each step, I weighed the risks I was willing to take for the only happiness I had ever known. *Could I balance them with my oath to the land?*

CHAPTER 24

BETRAYAL

The door, concealed in the ancient trunk at the heart of the enchanted forest, beckoned to me. With a forceful push, it swung open. I hastened through, the towering trees cloaked in deep brown, their gnarled limbs twisting across the path ahead.

When the cottage came into view, my dread deepened. Standing before the door, the familiar scents of drying herbs and the earthy coolness of stone greeted me, as did the sound of crying. Without hesitation, I rushed inside.

Merlin and Merlonius sat opposite each other. Her tears flowed freely. I rushed to her side, overcome by the harsh truth of my betrayal—wounds too deep for words. Stumbling forward, my breaths came in ragged gasps.

I struggled to find my voice. "Merlonius," I whispered, my throat tight with sorrow. But she refused to look at me.

"Please, Merlonius," I pleaded, reaching out to grasp her hands, my fingers trembling. "Do not push me away. You know I never wanted this. I love only you."

She covered her face with her hands, her shoulders quaking from the force of her sobs. I wrapped my arms around her, drawing her close. With her head against my chest, I tenderly stroked her hair.

Merlin leaned forward, his expression softening. "Merlonius, we are bound as one clan, and that will never change. You and I spoke of this matter after the Battle of Mount Badon. Now that Arthur has driven the Saxons from our land, he needs a queen the kingdom will accept. You would face intense scrutiny, not only from the people, but also from those in his court. I know you care for him deeply, and you want him to succeed as king, do you not?"

She pulled away from me, wiping her tears with shaking hands. "I want Arthur to be happy, to be a successful king," she said, her faltering tone betraying her efforts to maintain composure. "Yes, we have spoken of this matter, but during this year, I have prayed for the Fates to smile upon us. I want nothing more than to remain with him. Now you share that another shall stand at his side. Why, Merlin, did you bring him into our lives? You possess the gift of sight and foresaw these events. Why did you watch as I fell in love with him, only to have my heart broken?"

Her pain seemed to strike him deeply. He turned his head slightly, his jaw tightening, restraining words he dared not speak. The silence between us deepened, broken only by the crackling of the hearth. In that stillness, I could see the strain in his bearing, the unrelenting conflict he carried yet could not voice.

"Merlonius," I whispered, "our love is and will always be sacred. I promise to find a way to fulfil my obligations as king while cherishing and honouring you. I cannot bear the thought of losing you, for you are woven into the very essence of my spirit."

She looked at me, her expression tender, filled with a deep love. She kissed me and without another word, rose and walked out the door. It closed behind her, and I felt the sharp despair of losing her. I started to follow her, but Merlin stopped me.

"Wait, Arthur."

My steps faltered. I knew he was right. Restlessly, I paced in front of the hearth, while he sat at the wooden table, his eyes unmoving from the door, as if willing her to return. The silence stretched, heavy and unyielding, yet my thoughts strayed only to Merlonius. I could not bear the thought of her alone in sorrow, beyond my reach.

I could wait no longer. I pushed open the door and stepped into the cool night. The sky held only a delicate sliver of moon, casting faint whispers of light that barely touched the treetops. I hastened down the path towards the waterfall, our cherished haven, where countless memories lived.

When I reached the pond, I found her seated on one of the stone benches, staring at the tranquil surface.

I love her, and cannot lose her. The thought gripped me as I called in a low voice, "Merlonius."

She offered no response. I settled beside her, taking her hand, waiting, sensing the ache that hung between us.

A slow inhale lifted her shoulders before she turned slightly to face me. "Arthur, what is it that binds your soul to mine?"

The weight of her question stirred something deep within me, something I feared to name. If I failed to make her understand how much she meant to me —how inseparable she was from my very existence—I risked losing her forever.

"It is not just your beauty that draws me. What captivates me most is the brilliance of your spirit, the sharpness of your mind, and the kindness that defines you. You are the other half of me; you make me whole." The tightness in her fingers eased as I spoke, and the furrow in her brow was no longer visible.

"And what is it that pulls you towards me?"

She stared at me, her very essence entwined with mine. "I feel we are joined by something greater than ourselves. I am drawn to your wisdom, your kindness, and your courage. With you, I am complete."

Overwhelmed by the love between us, I drew her close, and we kissed, the fire between us stirring every whispered promise. Each touch rekindled dreams we had long buried, our embrace tightening, drawing us deeper into each other. Our slow caresses intensified the bond that both consumed and fulfilled us.

With a final burning kiss, we sat side by side at the pond's edge in silence, the rippling water a soothing rhythm to our racing thoughts. Our hands remained clasped, the last echoes of our desire fading into the night.

Merlonius shifted ever so slightly turning towards me. She idly traced lines on the stone bench as she spoke in a hushed tone. "I pushed aside my visions and the message from the Lady of the Lake, not wanting to believe that another would stand at your side. I dreamed of our union, Arthur, and the children that would come from our love. And now, sorrow clings to me like a shadow."

Her breath shuddered as she fought the turmoil within her. "Even so, I could never find happiness with another, for my heart belongs to you."

I grasped for words that might ease our sorrow, but the uncertainty of our future settled heavily upon me. *What kind of man was I to make promises that might not be in my power to keep?*

Fate had already carved a course I could not ignore, one that could tear us apart. And yet, the thought of losing her, of allowing duty to sever the bond that had shaped my very soul, was unbearable. *My love for her was as undeniable as the forces pulling us apart,* and I stood between the demands of a king and the desires of a man.

"Merlonius," I said at last, "no one, no matter what unfolds, shall ever take your place, for my love belongs only to you. I, too, have desired a life with you, of raising our children together."

Even as I spoke, a whisper of doubt stirred within me, warning that this life I envisioned might be nothing more than a dream. But I could not voice that fear, not now, not while her heart was already so burdened.

She shook her head as tears streamed down her cheeks. I squeezed her hand and brushed them away, wishing I could wipe away her sorrow just as easily.

"Oh, Arthur, if only the Fates had allowed us to preserve the happiness we found here in the enchanted forest." She looked towards the waterfall, as though seeking answers hidden beneath its cascading flow. At last, she looked at me, the joy I used to see replaced with sorrow. "But alas, that is not to be. We must face our destiny. Let us now speak with Merlin for I know he awaits our return."

We made our way down the winding path. The rustling leaves whispered of escape, luring us into the embrace of the woods, away from all of this. If only we could.

Reaching the cottage, I pulled her into my arms, lifting her chin before pressing a kiss to her lips, laden with all I could not say. I wanted to stop time, to remain in this embrace, to hold her firm against the tide of fate. *Should we defy what has been set before us?* The thought surged within me, but duty held fast.

We stepped inside to find Merlin still seated at the table. We took our usual places opposite him. The strain showed in the shadows beneath his eyes, yet he waited in silence, letting us speak first.

Merlonius turned to me, and I felt the first stirrings of her power. I reached for her hand as she faced Merlin, a silent reassurance between us. Her strength was undeniable.

"Merlin, as I have shared with Arthur, I did not wish for my visions or the message from the Lady of the Lake to bear truth. Since the day my father and mother cast me aside, and you became my mentor, my guiding father, I have found comfort and love. Because of you, I have come to accept my true nature as a sorceress, a gift I once feared and rejected."

Though her voice wavered slightly, it soon steadied as she pressed on. "I dreamed of standing by Arthur's side, of raising our children together, and of living a life rich with purpose, filled with light and meaning. I held tightly to that hope, believing it was the path meant for us. But now, I am left to mourn the dream that will never come to be."

She brushed the edge of the table, as if seeking something solid in a world shifting beneath her. "It is not merely the loss of the life I envisioned that weighs upon me. It is the cruel irony that the Fates, who bestowed this power upon me, have also decreed the cost. I would change it all if I could—undo the visions, defy the Fates, forge another path. But I see no other way but to accept what lies before me."

Regret or perhaps his own ache, crossed Merlin's features. Her words bore down on him, and his silence was a poignant reminder that even he could not alter what the Fates had set in motion.

Drawing upon her fortitude, she continued, "Merlin, you and Arthur are my only clan, for my blood ties were severed long ago. Though I long to alter what has been set in motion, I know I cannot. But I must understand: why was the secret passageway between Camelot and the enchanted forest created? What purpose does it truly serve?"

Merlin's expression softened, the sadness in his eyes tempered by affection. His usual composure wavered for but a moment, and he took a slow, steadying breath before speaking.

"I built the passage so that, no matter what the Fates decreed, you and Arthur would always have a way to be together."

She bowed her head briefly, the truth of his words settling upon her. Her determination hardened as she made her choice.

"So be it. I shall await Arthur's return here, in the enchanted forest, within these walls, and at The Giants' Dance. For, as you told me when he drew the sword from the stone, I must also choose my path. I do so willingly now, for no other shall have my heart, save for Arthur."

When her gaze met mine, love was all I could see reflected in her eyes.

Facing Merlin again, she said, "I see now that you glimpsed this future and labored to ensure we would not be torn apart. I cannot exist without both of you in my life. Without either of you, I would have no purpose, no reason to rise each day."

"My dear, never did I wish sorrow upon either of you. The gods can be harsh in their dealings, but I will do all within my power to ensure your happiness."

She offered him a solemn nod. "As I know you, Merlin, I know you speak the truth."

She turned to me once more. "Will you stay the night, Arthur?"

The depth of her love was undeniable, pulling me towards her with a force beyond reason.

"If you would have me, my lady, then yes."

We rose from the table, and a subtle shimmer in the air hinted that Merlin's magic was at work once again. He met my eyes briefly, understanding all that remained unspoken between us. With a final, knowing glance towards Merlonius, he offered a quiet nod and slipped out through the door.

When we stepped into the sleeping quarters at the back of the cottage, I saw that her modest bed had been transformed, no longer just a place for rest, but a sanctuary prepared for the joining of two hearts.

I clasped Merlonius's hand. The dreams we shared shone in her eyes, mirroring my own longing.

With a fiery kiss, our embrace deepened, passion and tenderness entwining as one. Her skin was soft beneath my touch, her breath a gentle whisper against my chest. Our love filled the space around us, and we clung to each other as if letting go would make the other disappear.

We traced each other's faces, our lips meeting in a dance of urgent yearning and delicate tenderness, as we sought to express our boundless love for one another. With her, the world beyond us faded, leaving only the promise we had made to one another.

The first light of day crept in, pale and steady, stretching across the bed. I held Merlonius close, our breathing slowing in unison as sleep overtook us. The memory of this night would endure, and whatever trials awaited, we would face them together.

CHAPTER 25

THE NEXT SIX MOONS

After the battle at Mount Badon, my life began a profound transition from warrior to steward. The victory heralded a turning point, compelling me to reconstruct Britain, stone by stone, decree by decree. Under the sage guidance of Merlin and with the unwavering support of Merlonius, we strove to continue the restoration efforts initiated by my forebears, Ambrosius and Uther.

Merlin's hand on my shoulder steadied me against the heavy responsibilities. "We stand at the threshold of a bold venture, Arthur. With your fair leadership, our kingdom will flourish anew."

Guided by Bedwyr's invaluable counsel, whose strategic foresight was crucial, we shaped new laws and restored order across the land. He further proposed we reach out to distant realms to build new alliances.

"Let us honour their traditions and the legacies they aim to preserve," Bedwyr urged. "We will demonstrate how an alliance with Camelot offers benefits and enduring peace."

Reflecting on his words, the task before us appeared almost beyond our measure, yet it stirred a resolute determination within me. Embarking on this endeavour alongside Bedwyr, Bors, Gawain, and Kay strengthened my resolve. The arduous journeys deepened our vision of a unified Britain. Each return to Camelot, though laden with royal duties, inevitably drew me back to the enchanted forest where Merlonius awaited.

One night, as I neared the cottage nestled amidst towering trees, I was welcomed by the sounds of crickets and the hooting of owls. There, under the shimmering stars, Merlonius sat, captivated by the night sky.

She stood to greet me. "Arthur, you are here. How I have missed you."

Our embrace was a refuge from my kingly duties. Her scent, earthy and sweet, rekindled a deep-seated yearning. Holding her, a flood of emotions washed over me: gratitude, love, longing.

Once inside, the soothing familiarity enveloped us. She moved towards the table where a pitcher stood filled. "Would you care for some water?"

"Yes, I am indeed thirsty." I took a seat beside her, feeling at home once again.

"And how have you withstood the realm's demands?"

"Each day brings its challenges, yet they are not beyond my endurance." I reached over to take her hand, caressing her skin. "And how have you fared?"

"I am well, though I have longed for your closeness."

Our eyes met, and emotions surged. "My yearning for your company has never waned. From our early days together until now, my love for you has only deepened. The tie between us remains as strong as ever."

She squeezed my hand, her touch soothing my weary spirit. "Our love endures, a testament to our combined fortitude."

Looking at her, I reflected on all she had come to mean in my life. We had grown from youths of thirteen and fourteen to the fullness of our years, our love blossoming as we did. I now stood tall, well over six feet, my form shaped by relentless training in swordsmanship and numerous battles. Unlike my kinsmen, my hair, deep brown with specks of red, was kept short, matching the close-trimmed beard that framed my jaw. Merlonius, tall and poised, stood so that when I embraced her, her head rested comfortably against my chest. Her eyes, reflecting the verdant depths of the forest we cherished, looked up into mine. Her skin bore the glow of sunlit days spent in the garden, her beauty deepened by its light, and with it, my longing to never part from her.

Seated side by side, a glimpse of a future together stirred within me, one that held the dream of having children with her. The idea moved deep within me as I imagined our child's eyes reflecting both my deep brown and her vibrant green. Yet, I quickly turned my mind from those thoughts, for such dreams brought a melancholy for a life that might never be. Instead, I resolved to cherish the time we had together.

Merlonius's touch on my cheek drew me back into the moment.

I looked at her. "Being here with you again fills me with joy."

"I, too, am glad we are together again. But tell me, how went your journey to the remote provinces?"

"It was long and wearying, but necessary," I began, eager to share the strides we had made. "The territories are still recovering from the aftermath of Mount Badon, yet I am hopeful that our new laws will foster healing and unity."

"I have no doubt that they will."

"We have secured agreements from the local leaders to maintain order and uphold honour, even in my absence."

"That is a remarkable achievement! You are truly evolving from a warrior into a High King."

Her words washed over me, easing the self-doubt that occasionally clouded my spirit.

Inhaling deeply, I confessed, "This is not a life I would have chosen willingly."

"Arthur, I understand your struggles and share your dreams. You possess a fortitude that surpasses that of ordinary men."

My love for her felt boundless, transcending the constraints of our shared hardships. I longed for nothing more than time alone with her, beneath the expanse of stars, just the two of us.

"Shall we take a walk?"

Her face brightened with a smile. "I would like that very much, Arthur."

We made our way towards our secluded sanctuary by the cascading waterfall. Seated on one of the worn stone benches, we looked out over the serene pond before us. The murmur of the water and the cool breath of night enveloped us. With my arm wrapped around her shoulder, I felt a welcome release from my life as king.

We rose and continued our walk, following the winding path that hugged the water's edge. Along the way, we encountered two mallard ducks, floating serenely, their bodies nestled together in slumber.

Observing the peaceful pair, I remarked, "Have you ever noticed that ducks mate for life? They remain bonded to each other, much in the same way that you and I have traversed our destinies."

I paused, admiring the feathered companions.

"So, are you implying that we should compare ourselves to ducks now?" she asked, amusement and affection clear in her tone.

"Not as ducks, but in their unwavering commitment to each other, just as you will always hold a special place in my heart." I leaned in with a tender kiss, feeling the brush of her lips against mine.

The serenity of the forest stayed with us as we returned to the cottage. Once inside, I tended the fire, and after the flames were well kindled, we made our way to the sleeping area. To our surprise, where Merlonius's smaller bed once stood, there now was a four-poster bed, a thoughtful gift from Merlin. This gesture of respect for our love held immense value for us.

"Merlonius," I began, unable to push away my unease, "in the days to come, I shall embark on another journey throughout the kingdom. And when I return—"

She placed her finger on my lips. "I know what awaits us. But for now, let us surrender to the love we share."

That night, as we lay together, sleep eluded us. Our passion rekindled like embers fanned into flame. We clung to each other, unwilling to let go, our breaths and heartbeats falling into a shared rhythm. Some time after the darkest point, our longing eased, and we drifted into a peaceful slumber, entwined in each other's arms.

With the first light of morn, we wakened to the songs of birds. Rising, I joined Merlonius in preparing a light meal of cheese, bread, and honey. As we sat at the table, we spoke with ease until a knock sounded at the door.

"Merlin."

"Yes," she answered as she greeted him.

He appeared more weary than I had ever known him to be. A sorrow surrounded him, unlike any I had sensed before.

"Merlin, good morrow. Come join us," I invited.

He took a seat opposite us. "It is good to see you. How were your travels to the outer regions?"

"Better than I anticipated," I replied, taking a bite of the warm bread.

"That is good," he said, though his words bore the mark of distraction. "Arthur, we should return to the castle. Most of the details have been worked out with Leodegan, but you should have a say, as it is also your day."

At his words, a chill settled over my spirit. My jaw clenched as anger stirred within me. *This was to be a day unburdened by duty, not one stirred by reminders of a union I never chose willingly.*

Merlonius rose abruptly, her hurt unmistakeable. Without a word, she left, the door slamming shut behind her.

"Why now, Merlin? Why this day, of all days?" My frustration was evident as I stood and followed her outside.

I found her by the stream, her garment stirred softly by the breeze as she sat on the grass, staring at the flowing water. I settled beside her, reaching for her hand.

"Merlonius," I said, hoping to bridge the distance between us, my voice barely a murmur against the rustling leaves.

She turned slightly, as if weaving her thoughts into something whole. A tremble touched her lips, a glimpse of the tempest within, but she quickly cloaked it in resolve.

"Arthur, you were born to be king, and you will be a wise and good one." Her eyes followed the stream's meandering path before returning to mine. "I will wait for you, and I will miss you, but know this: my love for you will endure. Go with Merlin now. Your destiny calls."

I searched her face for reassurance, but all I saw was pain. Guilt filled me. Leaving her behind, forcing her to bear our separation again, only deepened the conflict inside me. Had my choices wounded her beyond healing?

A fierce ache spread through the center of my being. Each decision tightened like a cold iron chain around my heart, every link a bitter reminder of the life I had chosen without knowing the price it would demand. Driven by longing and sorrow, I leaned in, and our lips met in a tender, desperate kiss. I wanted to lose myself in the comfort of her embrace, to forget the mantle of kingship. The thought of sharing the throne with any woman but Merlonius was unthinkable. *Why must the crown demand I turn from the one who held my heart?*

I caressed her face, then, with a deep inhale, rose to my feet and left her side. With each step, the divide between the king I must be and the man I longed to be grew wider.

At the stream's edge, I watched the morn's light ripple across the water. Though I longed to remain with Merlonius, the demands of rule pressed upon me, steady and ceaseless. The Fates loomed large, their will unyielding.

Making my way back to the cottage, emptiness echoed within me. I clung to Merlonius's promise to await my return, even as uncertainty clouded the road ahead. *How had the reins of my life slipped so far from my grasp?*

Lost in that haze of doubt, I shook my head and pushed open the door.

Inside, Merlin sat at the table, a constant reminder of the intricate web of fate and choices that bound us both. I paused by the doorway, observing him before stepping inside.

"Are you ready to return to the castle?"

I hesitated, my eyes fixed on Merlin, silently pleading for another answer, for if I could, I would never leave this place. *There must be a way, some magic that can change this outcome.*

"Merlin, I entreat you, please, you must alter this course. Your magic is strong. I cannot exist without Merlonius."

A deep melancholy shadowed his eyes. "Arthur, if but I could…" His voice, usually so sure, wavered under the burden of what he could not change.

I nodded, sorrow pressing close as the truth settled between us. Without another word, we stepped outside. Mounting our horses, we left the shelter of the enchanted forest and began the journey towards Camelot.

My entire being resisted the impending union with Gwenhwyfar. The memory of drawing the sword from the stone flashed vividly before me, the day my father's spirit appeared, imparting a message that had remained with me.

"My son," he had said, "your destiny is written in the stars, and you shall rule honorably and righteously. Allow your inner wisdom to be your guide.

Listen, and it will always ring true. You will recognize the woman who brings you light and love."

Merlonius was that light, the woman I cherished. *Why then did the Fates decree Gwenhwyfar to be my queen?*

If only I could ask my father how to change this outcome.

As we rode, Merlonius's words and the memory of her touch clung to me, bittersweet and enduring, like a vow carried on the wind. The legacy of my lineage lay upon my shoulders, and with it, the ache of being parted from the one I loved. The path ahead would ask more than fortitude; it would ask for the part of me I had left behind beside the stream, in the place where love and duty parted ways.

CHAPTER 26

THE PREPARATIONS

There had been nearly six turnings of the full moon since I first met Gwenhwyfar, King Leodegan's daughter. I had not seen or spoken to her since that brief encounter. The days leading up to our ceremony were consumed by ceaseless preparations. Merlin, ever watchful, kept me occupied with guests and tasks, his efforts to keep me away from Merlonius seeming both deliberate and relentless. The closeness we once shared had become strained, and we rarely spoke of matters of importance.

Two days before I would take Gwenhwyfar as my queen, I wandered through the garden, deep in thought. My steps carried me to Merlin, seated on a stone bench among the earthy hues of fallen leaves and the subdued shades of late-blooming flowers. The briskness of the waning year filled my lungs, carrying the faint scent of damp soil and the sharpness of approaching frost.

"Merlin, I have seen to everything you required for the ceremony. Is there anything more you need of me, or have I finally fulfilled your every demand?"

I did not attempt to hide my disdain for all that was transpiring; it was plain upon my face.

He looked up and, heedless of my bearing, motioned for me to join him. "Sit with me, Arthur," he said, his eyes lingering on the garden. "These days of harvest remind me how the land whispers of endings and beginnings."

I hesitated but took the seat beside him. Silence stretched between us, broken only by the whisper of the breeze and the distant caw of a lone crow.

"Our journey together has been long," he began, his words carrying a heaviness I had rarely heard from him. "I regret that my loyalty to Britain must come before all else, including the bonds I hold most dear."

I looked at the ground, unwilling to meet his eyes.

"When I was a young boy, I was brought before Vortigern, the usurper. They intended to spill the blood of a fatherless child to steady his crumbling fortress. But the gods, or fate, had other plans. My gifts revealed themselves that day, and I escaped what was meant to be my end. That moment set my feet upon the path that leads to you now."

I said nothing, uncertain whether to offer comfort or condemnation, for both felt beyond my grasp.

Merlin's trembling hand reached for mine as he steadied himself. "Merlonius was presented to me by her father and mother. If I had not accepted her as my apprentice, they would have killed her. The same would have been your fate had I not taken you from your father and mother. I foresaw the danger and intervened to protect you both."

He drew in a sharp breath. "In all my years walking this earth, I have allowed only two people into my heart: you and Merlonius. I love her as my daughter, and I love you as my son. You have my word, you will always have each other."

I struggled to speak, the gravity of his confession pressing upon me. At last, I managed. "Your word?"

His hand tightened around mine, his promise strong. "Yes, my word."

Hope stirred within me, faint yet undeniable. A weight lifted, unshackling burdens I had carried alone for too long. Rising to my feet, I looked at him.

"I am glad you remain by my side, Merlin."

Our eyes met and I saw the shadow of sorrow before he shared. "I am equally joyful to stand with you, Arthur. Go now. I will ensure your time remains undisturbed."

"You have my thanks, Merlin." With a final nod, I turned and walked from the garden. The path ahead felt clearer, my purpose renewed.

Climbing the central stair, I found Bedwyr awaiting me.

"Arthur, may I have a word?"

"Of course."

Together, we continued to my quarters, where the warmth from the crackling fire was a welcome relief from the cold. We settled into the chairs across from each other. Bedwyr's fingers tugged on the hem of his cloak, betraying his inner struggle. He finally raised his eyes to meet mine, taking a deep, steady breath before he spoke.

"Arthur, the challenges we have faced together have only strengthened our kinship. Governing the northern territories on your behalf, striving for balance and prosperity, my duty has been clear," he leaned forward, his earnestness evident in the intense set of his jaw and the strength in his regard. "Now, returning to Camelot to witness your union with Lady Gwenhwyfar, I find myself compelled to ask, what of Merlonius? I have witnessed the love you share with her, and she with you. The thought of you taking another troubles me deeply."

He gripped the arms of his chair as if to steady himself. "To part from her…" His voice broke, and he looked away, as if searching for answers in the flames. The lines upon his face deepened, each one marking the distress he carried.

Feeling the strain of my own decisions, I revealed the extent of our difficulties. "Bedwyr," I began, pausing as he turned in his chair to face me, "the Battle of Mount Badon now seems minor, merely a small clash compared to the towering challenges that loom before us. Merlin has extended his counsel, advice I cannot overlook. The grip of fear and resistance to change tightly binds our people. Merlonius, gifted by the Fates as a sorceress and healer, provides invaluable aid to those who accept her gifts. Yet, he has foreseen she will not find acceptance as my queen."

Bedwyr shook his head in resignation. "Arthur," he began, but his emotions overwhelmed him, and he could not continue.

Bound by the duty of the crown, I pressed on, "As High King, my choices extend well beyond mere personal desires. Merlin has advised me that Gwenhwyfar, King Leodegan's daughter, is the key, he says, to securing the kingdom's unity."

His clenched fists did not go unnoticed, a clear sign that loyalty alone could not make the heart accept what duty now demanded.

"He considers this alliance not merely beneficial but essential for securing lasting peace and forging crucial ties. He assures me this union will bind the lesser lords and other kings together, strengthening our rule as one Britain."

"And Merlonius?"

At his question, the ache in my heart grew sharper, a solemn proof of the sacrifices required by my kingly duties. The thought of joining with Gwenhwyfar tormented me, a betrayal of all that I held of value. My love for Merlonius was profound, resonating with a depth that no duty could overshadow. For no one could ever take her place.

"The kingdom demands much from me, yet it is the deep love and tested loyalty I share with Merlonius that truly define who I am. Understand this: I cannot—will not—abandon her, for she gives meaning and purpose to my existence.

"That is why I implore you to stand with me, to protect her should danger loom. Though ensnared by these challenges, I am resolved to forge our path forward.

"I will not forsake her."

Bedwyr rose, his movements deliberate, each step purposeful as he approached the casement windows. His form stood stark against the twilight, looking out at the courtyard below, where distant voices murmured. Moments passed as he pondered my words, before he turned back and faced me again.

"Arthur, many years ago, I swore to protect you and Merlonius with my very last breath, and that promise remains as resolute as ever. The pain of being apart from one we love is a burden familiar to me," he admitted, a trace of concealed sorrow shadowing in his eyes. "But remember, my presence at your side transcends the duty of a knight to his king; it is the pledge of a friend devoted to your cause."

"Bedwyr, since the day of my coronation, through every battle and hardship, you have stood steadfastly by my side. You are more than a friend; you are a brother to me."

Memories of the day Merlin unveiled the great halls of Camelot, and his thoughtful choice to place Bedwyr's quarters near mine, rose swiftly in my mind. It was a testament to his deep understanding of our brotherhood, laying a foundation for the many challenges we would confront together.

"And even without your left hand," I added with a smile, "you can still strike fear into the heart of our enemies with your spear."

He drew a breath, meeting my look briefly, thoughtful curiosity evident in his eyes.

"Arthur, is the empty chamber in this part of the castle intended for Merlonius?"

Hearing his question, I thought once more of the life I longed to share with Merlonius, filled with laughter, serene moments, and the certainty of love. These were not mere reveries, but my hope for our future together.

"Yes."

"Then I shall ensure that no one else learns of it," he vowed, his pledge of protection unmistakable.

I joined him as he prepared to leave. We clasped hands in a solemn farewell at the threshold.

"Good rest, Arthur."

"And to you, my brother."

As the door closed behind him, I looked about my chambers, the formidable walls standing firm, silent guardians of all within. Beyond the windows, the night stretched vast and unbound, whispering of freedom. Drawn to the casements, I welcomed the coolness against my skin. I held fast to Merlin's hopeful promise: that Merlonius and I would always have each other.

Once the castle's bustling sounds faded to hushed murmurs, I left my chambers, moving quietly through the dimly lit halls. My strides were measured yet purposeful as I made my way to the concealed passage. Sealing the hidden way behind me, I pressed forward, urgency growing with each brisk step.

At last, I reached the door hidden within the old tree. Pushing it open, I stepped into the forest, where the ancient magic stirred around me. The need to see Merlonius, to ensure her safety, and to be near her once more deepened within me.

The trees, bathed in silver moonlight, stood watch over the landscape. The cottage was empty, and the garden still. *Where could she be?* Following the stream's winding course and ascending a slight incline, I found her.

Seated on a blanket, her gaze fixed on the valley below, Merlonius seemed a part of the tranquil surroundings. Strands of her hair danced in the wind, each movement capturing the twilight's embrace. The sight stilled my breath.

"Merlonius," I murmured. She rose, her smile an embrace before her arms reached me. I drew her to me, savoring our kiss. With her I was a free man.

We settled back onto the blanket, and I wrapped my arm around her shoulder. "I have missed you deeply these past days, but sadly, I cannot stay the night. The halls of Camelot are filled with many visitors, and my absence would surely be noticed."

She looked at me, her hand warm against my cheek. "My longing for you deepens with each day we are apart. Let us enjoy the time we do have."

I twirled one of her curls around my finger. "How have you been spending your days? How are you faring?"

"I am well, though your absence has weighed heavily on me. Merlin continues to deepen my knowledge of his craft, teaching me spells that draw upon the moon's power. My healing gift strengthens with each passing day. And you, Arthur, I know you have been preparing for…"

I placed my finger on her lips, stopping her words with a slight shake of my head. "This night, let us not speak of that. I have longed only to see your beautiful face. To know that you thrive brings me joy."

She leaned her head against my chest. Beneath the vast expanse of the starlit sky, time itself seemed to pause. Contentment filled me, yet the moon's steady journey across the heavens reminded me that our time together was fleeting. I knew I must return to Camelot.

We rose together, hands clasped, and walked slowly towards the cottage, each step deliberate, as though this might prolong the inevitable. The heaviness of all that was left unspoken settled between us, its presence undeniable. Once there, I held her by the shoulders and looked into her eyes.

"Merlonius, I am sorry for all of this—for our forced separation, for the pain it has caused you. I cannot say when, but I give you my solemn vow to return. Please, believe me when I say that my love belongs only to you."

"I do believe you, and I will always love you," she whispered, tears shimmering as she spoke.

We shared one last kiss, and as I reluctantly pulled away, I felt her sadness merge with the ache within me. With a heavy heart, I forced myself to turn away and retraced my steps from earlier that night.

Each step through the secret passage resisted my will, a bitter measure of the distance from all I cherished. Emerging from the passageway, I entered the familiar halls of the castle, where the burden of my upcoming duties pressed down on me. Approaching my chambers, I noticed Bedwyr standing vigilant by the stair, his hand on the hilt of his sword.

"How goes it, Bedwyr?"

"I am keeping watch to ensure no one wanders into this part of the castle."

Wearied by the emotions tied to my forthcoming union with Gwenhwyfar, I could only reply, "You have my gratitude. I shall see you on the morrow."

We walked back to my chambers, the sound of our heavy footfalls echoing in the dimly lit hall. I made no attempt to hide my sorrow, and Bedwyr, sensing my distress, placed his hand firmly on my shoulder.

"Arthur, these duties weigh heavily upon you. We have faced much together, and should you wish to unburden your thoughts, I am here."

I looked at him and nodded, my voice lost to the sorrow pressing within me.

"Rest well, Arthur," he said softly.

With a final clasp on my shoulder, he took his leave, leaving me to reflect on all that consumed me.

At the shelf near my bed, I retrieved the quartz crystal that Merlin had bestowed upon me from his crystal cave when I was a young squire. It had been a talisman of hope in times of darkness before, and now, I sought its solace once more. Cradling it in my hands, I offered a silent plea to the gods for respite from the torment of my sorrow and the strife churning inside me.

Yet, as I lay in bed, the pull of duty and honour continued to eclipse my own desires. Even Merlin's potent magic could not alter the path laid before me. I shook my head, resigned to what the morrow would bring. But for now, all I yearned for was rest.

CHAPTER 27

UNWANTED UNION

I stood before the casement windows of my chamber, looking out upon the rolling hills and verdant forests beyond. The magic of a new day lent the horizon a shimmering radiance, offering fleeting respite from the dread stirring within me. As dawn broke, the night's dark tapestry gave way to the tender flush of dawn, and with it came a brief calm that softened my troubled thoughts.

Yet, this beauty could not fully ease the tightness in my stomach, the constant reminder of the day fast approaching when Gwenhwyfar would be declared my queen. The strain of the crown seemed to grow more oppressive with each passing breath, casting its presence over the enchantment of the morn's light.

Just then, the doors opened, and Merlin entered, a solemn reminder of the duty I could not evade.

"Arthur, the day before you are to wed has arrived, and Gwenhwyfar, along with her ladies, will be arriving with the first light. Her father, King Leodegan, and her mother will also be joining them. Are you prepared to greet them?"

Facing him, I allowed my frustration and torment to surface. "Do you think me so weak that I would forsake my obligations for what I desire most?"

"I have known you since you were born, and I know your fortitude. Yet, I am all too aware of the burden that kingship places on one's spirit. Tell me, how do you fare?"

My vision blurred as the words poured from me. "Knowing that I shall leave Merlonius for another is unfathomable to me, a truth that pulls at my heart and very being."

Merlin studied me intently, the usual light in his eyes dimmed. A faint crease lined his brow as he exhaled slowly.

"How does she fare?"

My tears fell freely as my anguish took hold, spilling out in unguarded honesty. "Am I truly strong, when her courage outshines mine? She bears this sorrow with grace, while I falter beneath its weight. I know I have brought her such pain, and yet she gives me only love in return. How can I deserve such devotion when I am the source of her suffering?"

Sadness crossed his features, reflected in his eyes. He placed a steadying hand on my shoulder, his touch firm yet gentle. Silence stretched between us, heavy with words left unsaid.

Shaking his head slightly, he murmured, "The time has come. They await us below."

I might as well be walking to the gallows, I thought. I cast him a final glance and, with a wordless nod, we left my chambers.

We reached the great doors just as the sun crested the horizon, bathing the front hall in mellow light. Merlin and I had little time to speak before Gwenhwyfar and her mother entered in splendid array, adorned in the finest silks and richly dyed cloths, their hair crowned with delicate flowers and glistening gems. King Leodegan and his retinue followed close behind, the king's raiment clearly reflecting the significance of the coming ceremony.

I greeted them with a courteous smile. "Welcome to your new home."

Gwenhwyfar curtsied gracefully, while her mother answered, "Our thanks, my lord."

Turning to one of the waiting servants, I instructed, "See the ladies to their chambers."

He bowed and addressed them, "If you would kindly follow me."

They proceeded up the stair, and I watched as they were led to the left, away from my own chambers. Across the hall, Merlin was busy welcoming other guests and overseeing preparations for the day's festivities.

Though Gwenhwyfar had arrived, I felt no desire to seek her company. We were strangers still, tied not by affection, but by decree.

The bustle of preparations surrounded me, stirring my unrest. Seeking solace, I was drawn to the stables. The rich scent of horses and hay enveloped me, the rhythmic creaking of leather saddles filling the space. I joined Kay in brushing one of the mares. We worked without a word, our tie as brothers easing my thoughts.

"Arthur, the morrow heralds great change for you," he said quietly, his fingers idly brushing over the horse's coat.

I could not find the strength to answer him.

Kay's brush moved in slow, deliberate strokes. More than once, he glanced towards me, weighing whether to speak. In the end, he held his peace, choosing instead to revisit the carefree days of our youth.

"Do you remember, Arthur, how we would escape to the forest, to that tranquil pond? You loved the water, basking in the rays of the sun on your skin."

"Yes, those were truly joyful times."

His expression matched mine, but the slight furrow of his brow and the faint absence in his smile revealed a truth born of shared memory. We knew those days would not return.

After spending several hours tending to the horses, at ease in one another's company, the pull of my charge grew too heavy to ignore. I knew I needed to return to the castle.

"Well, my brother, I must see to my obligations."

"Take care, and remember, I am here if you ever need my aid."

"Kay, I know, and your loyalty means more to me than I can ever fully say."

With a parting nod, I turned back towards the castle, duty pressing in like a cage, each bar forged from burdens I could not escape.

The feasting hall was astir with servants and courtiers, each attending to their task in preparation for the night's festivities. The sweet scent of fresh flowers mingled with the savory aroma of roasting meat, drifting through the chamber. Banners adorned the walls, adding vibrant splashes of color.

I slipped away unnoticed to my quarters, remaining there through the day and into the first hours of the night. I stood at the window, gazing towards the enchanted forest, lost in contemplation. Images of Merlonius haunted me, and I wondered whether her love for me still lived amidst the storms we had endured. An overwhelming fear gnawed at me that her broken heart might never mend, even with Merlin's protective magic.

As the stars twinkled in the sky, Merlin appeared at my door. "Arthur, you must don your garments and join the feast. Gwenhwyfar and her father and mother have been waiting for over an hour, and questions have begun to arise about your absence."

"I shall join you anon."

He hesitated, sensing my distress, but did not reply. He left without uttering a word.

I dressed as if drifting through a dream, feeling detached from my own body. Walking down the hall, my thoughts consumed me. *How could this be happening? I love Merlonius with every part of my being and have since we first met. Why can I not stop this madness?*

The sounds of merriment grew louder with each step, yet they seemed distant, like whispers from another world.

Descending the stair and entering the feasting hall, I moved as an outsider amidst the laughter and merriment. My knights sat at various tables, immersed in feasting and revelry. I took my place at the head table, flanked by Gwenhwyfar to my right and Leodegan to my left.

"Greetings, King Leodegan. I hope you are enjoying the meal?"

"King Arthur, it is all of the finest."

I turned to Gwenhwyfar, seeking to engage her in conversation. "And you, my lady, are your quarters to your liking? Are you content?"

She looked away, responding curtly, "Yes."

Throughout the night, a strain lingered between us, refusing to fade. Despite my attempts at casual conversation, Gwenhwyfar remained distant. Once the meal concluded, I decided to retire to my chambers.

"I shall see you at the church on the morrow."

She tilted her head slightly, her silence heavy in the space between us, a stark reminder of the challenges ahead.

"Good rest, King Leodegan." I bade him farewell and left the hall.

Standing at the bottom of the stair, I looked up and found myself unable to breathe. Turning away, I stepped through the side door and into the night.

Drawn by the solace the stables offered, I walked towards them once more and made my way to Glenda, the magnificent mare I had groomed earlier. She stood regally in her stall, her coat glistening in the moonlight filtering through the high windows.

"Hey there, girl. Remember me?" I whispered, careful not to startle her. She nuzzled against my chest, and I ran my hand along her sleek neck.

"You truly are a beauty," I murmured. "Tell me, how am I to endure the ache in my heart?" Resting my forehead against her neck, I let out a shaky breath.

I considered saddling her and riding towards the enchanted forest to seek Merlonius, but quickly dismissed the reckless notion.

After a while, she stepped back and lowered her head to drink from the water bucket.

I left the stillness of the stables and stepped outside. A chill pressed against my skin, and above me, the heavens stretched vast and endless, scattered with stars. Memories of Merlonius, her laughter ringing out, swept over me.

A movement in the shadows caught my eye. Merlin emerged, his form distinct in the moonlight, his approach measured.

"Arthur," he called.

Facing him, I made no effort to mask my displeasure. "Yes, Merlin, what brings you here now?"

Unmoved, he beckoned me forward. "Walk with me."

We ventured into the field behind the stables, the tall grass brushing against our legs as we moved farther from the castle.

"I visited Merlonius this day. She bade me carry a message to you."

The usual sternness in his bearing eased, his hands loosening from their tightly clasped hold.

"This eve, she will be looking up at the night sky, following the very stars that once united you both. She wanted you to know that you continue to hold a cherished place in her heart, now and forever."

She carried such strength, to still love me after all of this.

"How does she fare?"

"Resolute, yet her heart still longs for your company. She devotes herself to mastering her craft, determined to tread the course that lies ahead."

I swear I shall return to her, for not even the Fates shall stop me.

"Merlin," I murmured, "please tell her I wish she were by my side, and that my love for her remains as strong as ever."

He gave a solemn nod. "I will, Arthur. And remember, you have my vow— no matter where your paths may lead, you shall always have each other."

"While your promise carries an undeniable truth, and I value your support, the road ahead is fraught with sacrifices neither of us can escape."

"I know, Arthur…"

Even with the ceremony to wed Gwenhwyfar looming, I knew our bond could not be dimmed by challenges or duty. It was a force unto itself, destined to endure despite the hardships that awaited us.

Walking back to the castle, memories of Merlonius and all we had shared clung to me. I felt adrift as I ascended the stair to my chambers.

Once inside, I stood still, the stone floor cold beneath my feet, the walls pressing in with a silence I could not escape. Recalling that fateful night when I agreed to accept my heritage, one thought haunted me:

What have I done?

"Merlonius," I whispered into the stillness, her absence pressing heavily upon me. "I miss you and carry the blame for the sorrow this separation has caused. My love belongs only to you."

I imagined my words as delicate fireflies drifting through the starry sky, searching for her to deliver my message. Exhaling a sigh, I made my way towards my favorite chair by the crackling hearth. Resigned to another sleepless night, I sat still, staring into the emptiness.

Night gave way to dawn, the first light reaching through the window. Splashing water on my face, I relished its coolness, hoping to clear my mind.

The simplicity of my coronation as High King surfaced in my thoughts. I remembered the day nobility encircled me, and even now, the sweetness of the honey mead I drank after professing my oath lingered in my memory. Merlin proclaimed my destiny that day, sealing my fate for this life.

Yet now, under the growing influence of the church, a dimming had begun over the old ways, fading like the leaves at harvest time. The fairies, the enchantments, and our deep tie to the earth were giving ground to the laws and doctrines of men. The coming ceremony, held within their walls and led by their priest, marked a significant departure from the traditional rites I once knew.

A firm knock at the door pulled me from my reflection.

The hinges creaked as I opened it, revealing Bedwyr standing in the hall.

"Arthur, I came by to see if I can be of assistance to you."

I looked at him, briefly considering asking for his help, confessing my desire to escape the impending union with Gwenhwyfar. I shook my head, forcing the thought aside. My oath to the land could not be broken. The ruin it would bring would destroy all that I cherished.

"Please come in," I said, gesturing towards the crackling fire.

"Have you heard from Merlonius? How does she fare?"

He settled into a chair near the hearth, the firelight casting shifting shadows across his face.

"Merlin came to me last night. She entrusted him with a message, assuring me that our love endures in her heart."

Pain crossed his features; he struggled to find the words to ease this suffering for us.

"We both recognize her steadfastness and her love for you, Arthur. You were destined to be the High King, and she understands the oath you took to protect the land."

There was no more to be said. I simply nodded, quickly finished dressing, and together we descended the stair to the front hall where Merlin awaited us.

Sunlight poured through the tall windows, tracing soft lines across the floor and lighting the edges of his flowing grey beard as it draped over his dark, somber robes. His eyes held the sorrow of what awaited me, a fate I could not escape.

"Shall we proceed?"

"Yes, let us make our way to the church."

The horses nickered and snorted, eager to set off, as we swung into the saddle. The short journey unfolded in silence, broken only by the rhythmic sound of hooves and harnesses. Upon our arrival, we handed the reins to the stable boys and entered the church through a side door. Inside, a solemn chant echoed through the space. Merlin gestured for me to follow him through another door.

I stepped through and found myself at an altar, where a man in ceremonial robes stood waiting. Smoke from burning herbs swirled about us, heavy with the scent of sandalwood.

Gwenhwyfar appeared as a vision in white, her slender figure revealed by the close-fitting gown. Her fair skin gleamed in the dim light of the church, and her long, dark hair cascaded down her back.

The chanting ceased, and the priest began to speak.

"This day, we gather to celebrate the union of King Arthur and Lady Gwenhwyfar," he announced. "King Arthur, do you vow to protect and ensure Lady Gwenhwyfar's safety?"

This union was an arrangement, not one of the heart. As such, I could protect her while remaining true to my love for Merlonius. With measured conviction, I replied, "I will safeguard her, as I ensure the safety of all who dwell in the realm entrusted to me."

The priest looked to Gwenhwyfar. "Lady Gwenhwyfar, do you vow to serve as a devoted queen, in loyalty and respect?"

With poise and grace, Gwenhwyfar responded, "I accept the duties of my role as queen and will serve with honour to the throne."

After the priest declared us wed, we stepped out of the church into a waiting horse-drawn carriage, greeted by the joyous cheers of the villagers. No kiss was exchanged, no show of emotion required, and for that, I was grateful. Upon our arrival back at the castle, we found the feasting hall already filled with lively celebrations. Goblets lifted in toasts, the scent of roasted meats thick in the air. Minstrels strummed their lutes, their melodies weaving through the revelry.

Gwenhwyfar moved effortlessly through the crowd, laughing and dancing with the guests, her grace and charm captivating everyone. Yet, as I observed her with Lancelot, the pull between them became undeniable, drawing him apart from the others. When she returned to my side, the hollowness between us deepened, and no rite could close the divide.

The torches lining the walls burned brightly as I sought out Bedwyr, hoping to find solace in his company. Our conversation drifted through discussions of the ongoing festivities, until the words between us faltered, yielding to a sorrow we both understood yet dared not voice. Gwenhwyfar may have become my queen, but it was Merlonius who held my soul.

"Arthur, I bid you good rest and will see you in the stables on the morrow."

"Yes," I murmured, managing a faint smile. "I will be there."

Returning to Gwenhwyfar, I offered a brief bow. "Rest well."

A faint flush rose to her cheeks, but she gave no reply. Her emotions, like elusive shapes in the moonless night, remained beyond my reach.

As I turned away, the low growl of distant thunder reached my ears. Outside, clouds massed, their dark weight pressing close upon the castle walls. With each step I took up the stair, the storm swelled, the air thickening as if the very stones absorbed its power. A storm rose within me as well, gathering strength until I reached my chambers.

I looked down at the table where I studied parchments and understood I no longer belonged to any of it. Defiance surged through me. My hands curled into fists, and I brought them down hard upon the worn wood. Thunder cracked overhead, lightning split the sky, and the fury beyond the walls answered the one rising within me.

"Fates, gods and goddesses, hear me now! I am still Arthur, the man who loves Merlonius. Though I have taken a queen to fulfil my duty, Gwenhwyfar will never be my true wife, nor I her rightful lord. Merlonius alone holds the key to my heart."

I stood, chest heaving, resistance fading into a hollow ache.

That night, and for many more that followed, I did not seek out Gwenhwyfar's chambers. Our conversations, though courteous, were distant, revealing only a shared understanding of our roles, nothing more, nothing less. The knights and people accepted her as their queen, and as Merlin had foretold, the local rulers were appeased.

But as I watched her walk through the gardens with Lancelot, the truth settled upon me. She seemed to glow in his company, while he hung on her every word.

Watching their growing affection eased the guilt I carried, for it was evident they might find something together that I could never give her. I had to let them explore what was unfolding between them, as I held tight to the love I shared with Merlonius.

CHAPTER 28

DEFIANCE AND PROPHECY

S tepping out of the castle gates, my boots sank into the cool, damp earth. Four moons had passed since I took Gwenhwyfar as my queen, and in all that time, I had not seen Merlonius or felt the comfort of her touch. Despite my efforts to escape the confining walls of Camelot, a feeling of being trapped persisted. An emptiness settled within me, a constant reminder of her absence that I could not ignore.

The winter winds had started to lose their bite, offering some relief from the cold. Seeking solace, I mounted my horse and rode towards the cliffs as the sun set. The rolling land blurred as my steed galloped, and I looked to where The Giants' Dance stood in solemn stillness. Many a night, I stood atop that height, asking the gods and goddesses for a glimpse of her at the altar. Though my desire was often not granted, on fortunate nights, I beheld the sight of her and Merlin entering this sacred space. Even from afar, the wind carried their exchange to me as she continued to share her magic for all who needed it.

"My lady, I beseech your aid," implored a knight, approaching Merlonius with his left arm hanging limp at his side. She extended her hands, and with a guiding touch, summoned healing into his body. Grateful, he turned and walked away, his movements steadier than before. Then came mothers cradling ailing infants and leading unwell children by the hand, and she tended to them with boundless devotion. For everyone who sought her aid, I knew her gifts grew stronger with each act of mercy, even from this distance.

"I must see her," I whispered, yearning to join her in that sacred place. But the duties that bound me to Camelot called, and reluctantly, I guided my steed back towards the castle, each step away from her tearing at my heart. Long after I had departed, her image remained with me, surrounded by those she ministered to, a vision I could not release.

The moons passed, each marking time's unceasing march. A strong pull led me beyond the castle's walls, into the embrace of the open countryside. To oversee the affairs of the realm, I travelled among the nobles near Camelot. Our reach gradually extended to the more distant realms, with Bors, Bedwyr, Gawain, and Kay accompanying me. Often, we encamped near rivers and streams, spending many nights away from Camelot. During these deliberate absences, I ensured Lancelot stayed at Camelot, allowing his tie with Gwenhwyfar to flourish.

On our return from one of these journeys, as we neared the edge of the enchanted forest, my longing to see Merlonius grew stronger. I knew that if I proposed an encampment here, Bedwyr would understand, and the men would welcome another night under the stars.

I pulled up on my reins, and Bedwyr did the same.

"Let us remain here for the night."

"As you wish, Arthur."

We settled in a small clearing, the forest looming to our right. While the men set about building a fire, preparing food, and making ready for the night, I kept my distance. Before long, a subtle nod from Bedwyr let me know it was safe to venture into the woods.

The trees stood tall and imposing, their branches creaking and groaning in the night breeze, mingling with the faint rustle of leaves and the distant hoot of an owl. A soft light glowed ahead, guiding my steps as I neared the familiar doorway. My pulse quickened as I paused at the threshold, eager to see Merlonius once again.

I knocked, and soon footsteps approached. The door creaked open to reveal Merlonius, her face streaked with tears, her cheeks flushed, and sorrow still visible in her eyes.

"May I come in?"

She flew into my arms. Her shoulders trembled as she struggled to steady her breath.

"Arthur, is it truly you?" she gasped between sobs.

I held her closer, pressing my cheek to her hair. "Yes… Yes, I am here."

We entered and settled at the table, our hands clasped. Firelight danced across her face, tracing the delicate curves of her cheekbones and lips.

With each word exchanged, the strain and sadness in her features gradually eased. Sitting beside her, I felt a deep tranquility settle within me, a balm to my spirit.

"I have missed you so very much," I murmured, kissing her forehead. "I am so very sorry for the suffering I have caused you."

She shook her head. "Please, do not blame yourself for my tears. I have longed for you dearly. But tell me, can you stay?"

"I wish I could, but my men are encamped just at the edge of the forest. I can only linger for a short while."

"Seeing you now, eases the ache of our separation."

"Merlonius, I cannot bear being apart from you, nor the silence where your voice should be. If you will have me, I will come to you as often as I find the freedom to do so."

"You are always welcome, my love."

I touched the curve of her cheek, letting my hand remember her.

"Tell me, how are you faring?"

"Now that I can see you once again, touch you, kiss you…"

Our lips met in a sweet reunion.

"Are you well, Arthur?"

As I had done so many times before, I revealed my world to her again. "I am distancing myself from the affairs at court and focusing on rebuilding Britain. It may be a laborious undertaking after years of battle, but I am driven by a passion to breathe new life back into the land and its people."

I continued, recounting the struggles and tribulations experienced in the distant territories, and she listened, absorbing each detail. We deliberately avoided discussing Gwenhwyfar.

"Arthur, your devotion to restoring Britain is a testament to your determination. I see it in your eyes, in every word you speak. It has never left you."

I met her gaze, moved by the certainty in her voice. No title, no crown, no sword had ever offered me such reassurance. My fingers curled gently around hers, holding fast to the truth she had given me.

"When you are beside me, I am not the king the world demands, but Arthur, the man who loves you, and shall love you until my last breath, no matter the pull of the crown."

"You remain the man who holds my heart, yet the crown, too, is part of you. Arthur, when the trials ahead press hard upon you," she said softly, "guard your well-being as you would guard the realm. Promise me you will not let the burdens you bear extinguish your spirit."

"What will diminish me is never being with you again, my love. You fill me with strength and hope. Without you, I am left with only emptiness."

I drew her close. The press of her skin against mine kindled our passion, deep and enduring. Enfolded in my arms, our bodies moved in perfect harmony. I felt an intense unity, as if nothing else existed beyond this moment.

The hearth's fire wavered and waned and a solemn realization settled upon me for the hour to depart had come. Rising, I took her hand in mine, our fingers interlocking as we approached the door.

She wrapped her arms around my neck, whispering, "I love you."

Pulling away, I bore the sorrow of our imminent parting. "I will cherish you until my final days."

Our lips met in a tender kiss. I gave her one last look and whispered, "I shall return to you soon," willing every word to reach her heart.

Her reply was soft, yet it carried the weight of a silent plea. "Stay safe."

Returning to my men, her lingering fragrance clung to my skin, a trace of our time together that remained with me. My longing and love for Merlonius stirred restlessly within me, urging me to hasten back to her side.

Upon reaching the encampment, Bedwyr stood watchful.

"I ask you to rest for the night, for I shall keep vigil now," I whispered to him. He met my eyes, a knowing passing between us.

He gave a slight nod. "Very well, until the morrow."

Bedwyr settled in for the night, his outline bathed in the dancing firelight. I stood watch, the responsibilities of the crown bearing down upon me, just as strongly as my yearning to be by Merlonius's side. Yet, honour compelled me to stand firm, committed to my duties as Britain's leader.

The moon's luminous glow bathed the land, its light reflecting the contrasts within my spirit. *In professing my oath to the people and this land, what of the sacrifices borne by those dearest to me?* The vow I had made bound me to a future I had not entirely chosen, and yet I carried it as my own.

The night held its secrets, as if it alone understood the depths of my turmoil, leaving me restless and consumed by an insatiable longing. I closed my eyes, recalling the comfort of her arms, the fierce tenderness in her gaze, and the love that had never wavered. Even the stars above seemed to mourn our parting, their cold shimmer a distant mirror to the ache within my heart.

By dawn, a dense canopy of clouds unfurled from the east. My men awoke to a sky heavy with the promise of rain. If we made haste, we could reach the castle gate before the storm began. After swiftly dividing the last of our berries and smothering the fire, we made ready for the journey back to Camelot.

We mounted our horses, the sound of hooves drumming against the firm earth. The air grew cooler, the rhythm of our pace steady and familiar. Soon, the stables came into view beyond the trees. Upon arrival, we dismounted and handed our reins to the awaiting stable lads.

Nearing the castle doors, I found Merlin standing in my path. His appearance was unchanged by time, with his hair shimmering in a silver hue much like moonlight, his wiry frame bearing no sign of age. A neatly trimmed long beard, interspersed with silvery tufts, lent him a presence of wise dignity.

"Arthur, how did your journey fare? Was it worthwhile?"

Sensing another meaning, I remained guarded in my response. "The outskirts have indeed found respite."

"Come with me into the woods, where no other ears can hear."

At his words, the dark sky parted, releasing a gathering rain that began with a few drops before quickening.

"Merlin, let us converse inside the castle," I countered.

His response was sharp. "Nay, Arthur. What must be said cannot be risked within stone halls. And what of a little rain, eh?"

"As you wish."

In the unceasing rain, we followed a winding path through a thicket of trees, their branches forming a cover above us. He raised his arm, signaling for us to halt. I realized we were standing in a small clearing, our footfalls finally hushed.

He faced me, posture firm and unwavering. "The people are questioning when you will produce an heir. This matter cannot be overlooked; it holds great importance."

I drew in a long breath, attempting to quell my surging fury. *How could he question the choices I have made?* My anger simmered, hot and fierce, while the cool, relentless downpour continued. I felt myself drawn into the storm's embrace, almost welcoming the distant roll of thunder.

"Merlin," I retorted sharply, "you befriend dragons, command fire, and chart the tides of destiny. Surely, you understand the path I have chosen."

Our eyes locked. "There will be no heir to the throne," I declared with cold detachment. Rain cascaded down, soaking me, leaving my hair limp and my vision blurred.

He began to speak about my oath, but my rage surged forth before he could finish. With fists clenched, I advanced a step.

"My oath goes beyond mere duty; it is interwoven with the very essence of my being," I shouted, the fire burning within me matching the fervor of my proclamation.

"Through this vow, I took a queen as you instructed. Yet, I will not bow to the shackles of tradition. I am a man, not some stallion to be bred for the sake of an heir! I will choose the one who holds my heart!" With each word, I struck my chest with a clenched fist, my will unyielding as I declared my truth.

Merlin stood motionless, his expression unreadable. Parting his lips to speak, he hesitated, weighing the force of my words. A rare glimmer of conflict passed over his face before he looked skyward, seeking counsel from forces unseen.

When he finally spoke, his voice was measured but firm. "I understand your position on this matter. You have given much to this land, and I accept that no successor shall come from your queen. But caution must guide us. You are High King of Britain, and your actions shape not only the people's fate but the future of the realm itself. Lancelot and Gwenhwyfar's love must remain veiled. If exposed, they risk death under the new faith, and you would be powerless to stop it. I will shield them, preserving your reign."

I studied him, searching for doubt, but found none.

"I, too, will ensure their safety. Can I entrust you to protect Merlonius from danger?"

His hand settled upon my shoulder. "Though my emotions may seem absent, know that I care for you both deeply. You have my promise to safeguard Merlonius."

Through the rain, we made our way back to the castle. In my quarters, a lively fire danced in the hearth. With a wave of his magic, the chill of the rain vanished, our garments drying as if they had never been wet.

When the fury of the storm waned, Merlin approached the casement, his focus drawn beyond the tangible realm. I stood by, waiting for his return. At length, he turned from the window, moving purposefully towards the hearth, a mystical air surrounding him.

"Our challenges extend beyond rebuilding Britain. The Fellowship of the Round Table, once bound by unshakable unity, now teeters on the brink of dissolution. Though Mount Badon was a great victory, it has left our knights adrift, their purpose lost among the remnants of past glory."

"What do you propose? Perhaps campaigns in France to occupy them?"

"Such pursuits may offer momentary distraction, true fulfillment will not be found, neither for them nor for you. I have foreseen a cycle of discord, a tide of weariness destined to reach its end."

He continued, "The gods and goddesses shall send a vessel of enchanted power to float above the Round Table. Bathed in radiant light, it shall beckon all who see it. Our knights, noble and true, will embark on a voluntary quest, their hearts and purpose rekindled as they seek to unravel the mysteries of the Grail."

"Does this mark the end of the Fellowship of the Round Table?"

His expression turned distant, as he peered through time itself. When he finally spoke, his voice carried the burden of inevitability.

"Indeed, that is the destiny that looms. But before that final saga, those who have sworn their allegiance will embark on a journey, a year and a day, or longer if the Fates decree it. This quest shall breathe new life into the Fellowship, as each knight sets forth in search of the Grail."

"This is not my path, is it?"

I knew the answer even before I asked the question.

He stared at the dancing flames before answering me, "No, my boy, it is not."

I walked to the window, looking northward to the enchanted forest.

"When is this to begin?"

"That has not been given, but signs will soon appear."

He crossed the room to stand by my side. "Arthur, you are a great king and an equally good man. Merlonius and I have more years of joy still to share with you, but change is on the horizon."

The sky was dark, cloaked in persistent clouds that mirrored my deepening reflections. Merlonius gave my life profound meaning and purpose. Even with the tumultuous changes foretold by Merlin, I believed that with her by my side, all could be endured. Yet, it pained me to accept that everything we had built together was now veiled in uncertainty, a realization that settled over my spirit.

I exhaled slowly, pushing past the burden pressing on my spirit. "Come, Merlin. Let us take a meal together."

He placed a steadying hand on my shoulder. "A fine thought, my boy."

Together, we left my chambers, and as we entered the feasting hall, the familiar brotherhood of the Round Table surrounded us. Whatever trials awaited, I knew this truth: with Merlin's wisdom and Merlonius's enduring strength, I was not alone. Though the Fates had carved the road ahead, it was mine to walk. And with Excalibur in hand, I would meet it with courage, wherever it led.

CHAPTER 29

GWENHWYFAR

I had taken Gwenhwyfar as my queen to unite the overlords and secure lasting peace, but the rule of my heart held firm—a promise to honour and cherish Merlonius. Gwenhwyfar was never my wife in any true sense. Our arrangement, forged by necessity of alliance, was a bond in name alone, devoid of warmth or understanding, a carefully maintained illusion for the sake of appearances.

Yet beneath her delicate beauty, Gwenhwyfar carried struggles of her own, a tempest of unspoken sadness as she endured a loveless union and yearned for a man she could never claim.

As the day waned, marking the close of courtly affairs, we parted with little more than a nod, each retreating to our separate chambers. An invisible divide stretched between us. *How deeply did she mourn a love she could not openly cherish?* Though the answer was a mystery, one truth was certain: she bore the burden of our arrangement with endurance.

The wheel of the Fates turned as it must, testing us beyond the bounds of daily existence. During one May Day celebration, a fleeting reprieve from the tedium of courtly life, events unfolded that set the balance trembling, drawing us to the brink of war.

Beneath a bright sky, Gwenhwyfar and her handmaidens reveled in the festivities of May Day. Though now condemned by the new church, the celebrations still brought a wild joy to those who honoured them. Donned in verdant garments adorned with daisies and herbs, the maidens twirled like enchanting spirits. Their laughter, a harmonious choir, carried through the woods, mingling with the rustling of leaves.

Amidst the joy of May Day, Melwas, the ruler of the Summer Land, a fertile realm southwest of Camelot, plotted his deceit. With hair like ripened wheat and eyes the sharp green of forest light through dew, he was undeniably handsome, wielding a charm that easily obscured his ruthless ambitions. Driven by a relentless thirst for power and dominion over the neighboring lords, Melwas carefully planned each move with cold precision.

Unbeknownst to Gwenhwyfar and her retinue, Melwas lay in ambush. His forces closed in, surrounding her and a handful of lightly armed knights. He offered Gwenhwyfar a grim choice: the lives of her ladies and the knights would be spared if she went willingly with him. Gwenhwyfar made the difficult decision to surrender, burdened by the knowledge that her loyal protectors were outnumbered and no match for the enemy's might.

I had scarcely finished my last bite in the feasting hall when Kay appeared abruptly before me, his every movement edged with urgency. His steps were quick and purposeful as he beckoned me to the great doors.

"Arthur, you must come at once," he insisted, his brow furrowed.

Just beyond the threshold, the handmaidens were huddled together. Gawain, Geraint, and Hector stood close by, their stances rigid. Hector stepped forward to relay the grim news.

"My lord, we found ourselves outmatched and surrounded by Melwas and his men. They threatened our lives unless the Queen surrendered. We protested, but she insisted. Melwas has sent word that he has taken Queen Gwenhwyfar to Glastonbury Tor in Somerset."

Hector's message sent a tremor through the ladies, their dread unmistakable.

Despite the tidings shared with me, I knew that composure and immediate action were needed. "I am relieved to find you all unharmed. Ladies, please seek rest in your chambers."

Turning to Kay, I issued my command. "Find Lancelot and bid him to meet me in my quarters."

In the refuge of my chambers, I awaited his arrival. A knock sounded at the door, and upon opening it, I found Lancelot du Lac standing there. Renowned for unmatched skill and valour, Lancelot bore a heart ruled by passion and a loyalty deeply entwined with Gwenhwyfar.

Stepping aside, I gestured for him to enter, then bade him take the seat across from mine as I took my place at the table.

"Melwas has taken Gwenhwyfar captive at Glastonbury Tor. This act of treachery is but one of many threats looming over our kingdom. He seeks to claim the throne through such vile means."

Lancelot's expression shifted, the careful reserve giving way to raw concern.

"My lord, I understand the seriousness of what has occurred. When do we depart?"

"We leave at dawn on the morrow. Gather the knights. We ride to bring Gwenhwyfar back to Camelot."

Lancelot rose and made his way to the door.

If Melwas succeeded, even for a day, doubt would spread through the realm, weakening the loyalty of allies and emboldening our foes.

Once he was gone, I released a measured breath, fortifying my resolve for the battle ahead.

With the sun rising over the horizon, our band of knights assembled, their weapons and chainmail catching the first light of dawn. I mounted my steed, with Lancelot at my side, leading fifty valiant riders across the drawbridge. A steady wind met us as we crossed, carrying with it the scent of damp earth and the hush of anticipation. Though I kept my bearing, within me stirred a storm of thoughts—of duty, of the woman we sought to reclaim, and of the uncertain cost this journey might demand.

The distant clamor of war drums could be heard as we approached the treacherous land of Somerset. Glastonbury Tor, mystical as it emerged from the undulating hills, displayed its weathered stones bearing the marks of time. Perched atop the steep-sided hill stood a wooden fortress, encircled by an impenetrable forest. At its base, the springs and streams murmured, home to the Fae, where those elusive spirits were said to dwell.

Before swords could be unsheathed, Gildas, the monk of Glastonbury Abbey, intervened. Through his steadfast composure and calm authority, he secured a parley between myself and Melwas. By the grace of that tense exchange, Gwenhwyfar was released, and bloodshed narrowly averted.

When she descended the hill, escorted by her captors, Lancelot could no longer contain himself. He swiftly rode to her side, dismounted, and enveloped her in his protective arms. Tears of release streamed down her face. Honouring their need for privacy, I turned away and rode back to our assembled knights.

Our journey back to Camelot was filled with silent reflection, Lancelot and Gwenhwyfar riding side by side behind me. Upon crossing the drawbridge and dismounting before the broad doors, Gwenhwyfar approached me.

"Arthur, my thanks for rescuing and returning me to Camelot."

"I am relieved that you have emerged unharmed. Now, go with Lancelot to the feasting hall for nourishment and drink, as I intend to retire early this night. I embark on a hunting trip on the morrow and will be absent for several days."

"As you wish, my lord," she replied, glancing at Lancelot.

We parted ways, and in the solitude of my chambers, the mystical allure of the enchanted forest and my yearning to see Merlonius consumed me. The demands of court and kingdom had kept me distanced for far too long. After the tumultuous events of the day and witnessing the heartfelt scene between Lancelot and Gwenhwyfar, my resolve to visit her grew even stronger.

After finishing a light meal brought to my chambers, I prepared for the impending journey. A small gift, a stone I had found in the garden just beyond the orchard, along with a few garments, was carefully packed in my bag. Waiting until the castle had settled into the profound stillness of the darkest hour, I left my quarters.

The winding halls lay still, their emptiness echoing the sound of my deliberate footsteps. With Bedwyr in the northern territories, I cautiously approached the secret passageway. Entering, the sounds of the castle faded behind me, replaced by a stillness.

With each step, the path shimmered and glowed, Merlin's enchantments lighting my way, guiding me swiftly towards the door concealed within the gnarled tree. I pushed on the rough bark of the door, feeling its coolness against my palm, and it opened. Crossing the threshold, the familiar fragrance of pine trees mingled with the wondrous scents of the forest.

Nearing the cottage, light spilled from its windows, and faint laughter drifted through the night. I knocked lightly on the door, and it swung open to reveal Merlin, his face lighting up with a smile.

"Arthur, what a welcome sight you are, my boy. Come, join us."

"It gladdens me to see you again, Merlin," I replied, stepping inside and setting my bag near the door. The strain of my duties eased as the comfort and familiarity of the surroundings welcomed me.

Merlonius, seated at the wooden table, rose and hurried towards me, the light in her gaze holding all the affection I had longed for.

"Arthur, welcome!" she exclaimed, holding me tightly.

"Merlonius, I have missed you."

We settled down at the table, taking our accustomed places across from Merlin, the three of us united once again.

"So a war was averted this day," he remarked, a note of seriousness threading through his otherwise joyful tone.

"Yes, thankfully it was," I replied, briefly meeting Merlonius's look, where relief mingled with the day's fading strain.

"How have you fared, my love?"

She studied every line and curve of my face, as if preserving them in her thoughts.

"I am well, and you?"

"Much better now that I am here, and I am able to stay for a time."

She hugged me tightly once more, whispering, "Yes, yes, yes."

I looked to Merlin. "How have you been faring? It has been quite some time since we last saw each other."

"I have been well. Merlonius and I have been deeply engaged in expanding her studies of the ancient arts. Forgive my absence, but I trusted that all was well in your hands."

"I would not claim that all is well with so many people around me."

His piercing, dark eyes met mine. "We will catch up on the morrow. But for now, I must bid you farewell," he said as he rose.

Merlonius and I accompanied him to the door.

"Return soon," I urged.

"I will return with the day's light," he promised, vanishing just as he had when I was a young boy.

The door closed, leaving behind a faint trace of doubt. I suspected there was more to Merlin's absence, but that was a discussion for another time.

I reached for Merlonius's hand. "Would you like to sit under the stars?"

Her smile was like a burst of light in the dim twilight. "Arthur, nothing would make me happier."

We settled on a stone bench in front of the cottage, under the vast expanse of the night sky, our fingers intertwined.

"Arthur, Merlin told me about Gwenhwyfar's capture and her safe return."

"Yes, I am grateful she was unharmed. I swore to protect her, and now that she is back at Camelot, she will be safe."

I wrapped my arm around her shoulder, finding serenity in the touch. We fell into a comfortable silence, both of us avoiding any further conversation pertaining to Camelot and Gwenhwyfar.

"Do you remember when we first met? Our tie formed in an instant and has endured ever since. Your constant support has not only fortified me, but has also imbued my life with purpose."

"I have never forgotten that long ago time when we were so young. I heard Merlin calling my name and came from the garden to find you standing beside him. I felt drawn to you from the first I saw you," she touched my cheek. "Arthur, to know of your wellbeing, to share in your life, holds immeasurable value for me, for you are woven into my very being," she sighed before continuing. "I often revisit our early memories, especially that day we walked towards the waterfall and truly began to understand each other."

I smiled, a wave of joy washing over me. "And who could forget our first kiss by the pond, as all of nature stilled in anticipation?"

She leaned closer. "Arthur, the passion I felt then has never waned, even with the passing of years."

I drew her close, overwhelmed with gratitude. Our love had endured through the years, stronger than ever. "We are indeed two kindred spirits, bound together as one."

She rose to stand before me, then leaned forward, placing her hands on my shoulders as she kissed my forehead, eyes, nose, and cheeks. She savored each touch until her lips finally met mine. She inhaled deeply, as though trying to capture the very essence of our love.

"Arthur, my love for you is so deeply a part of me that I can scarcely tell where I end and you begin," she spoke earnestly. "This love will sustain us in this life and beyond, even into the Otherworld."

"Your words uplift my spirit, reassuring me that regardless of this existence's outcome, we shall be united once again."

She tilted her head, a playful glimmer in her eyes. "Shall we go inside?"

Holding hands, we made our way to the sleeping quarters only to be greeted by Merlin's thoughtful magic once again. Merlonius's usual modest bed had been replaced with a larger one. After what felt like an eternity apart, we found ourselves wrapped in each other's arms once again, our hearts beating in unison as we held each other tightly, relishing our long-awaited reunion.

Pulling away slightly, our eyes met with tenderness, brimming with love and fiery passion. Leaning in, our lips joined in a kiss that spoke of yearning and devotion. Our bodies pressed close, lost in the fervent exchange, our hands exploring each other's forms, seeking to reclaim the moments we had lost. All else faded into oblivion. Our love for one another became the very center of our existence.

"I love you, Merlonius," I said, with the certainty of a thousand lifetimes.

Curled in my arms, she sighed contently, "I shall always love you, Arthur."

We knew with absolute certainty that no matter the challenges ahead, our devotion would remain strong and enduring. Sleep came quickly as we sought comfort in each other's arms, ushering us into a peaceful slumber.

CHAPTER 30

MORGAN LE FAY

After but a few hours of sleep, we drifted awake, still wrapped in the warmth of our shared closeness. While Merlonius prepared a light meal, I stepped outside, yearning to momentarily shed the burdens of kingship. The cool forest breeze eased my thoughts, and the air, alive with the scents of wet soil and fresh blossoms, lifted my heart.

Stretching leisurely, I watched as the sunrise unfurled across the sky in fiery reds, warm oranges, and honeyed hues. Amid this serene backdrop, nature's steady rhythm restored my weary spirit.

I ventured to the far side of the cottage, drawn to the sanctuary of the vegetable garden. The soil's richness mingled with the faint sweetness of new growth. A rustle to my right announced Merlin's arrival from the forest, his robes billowing with each stride.

"Good morrow, Arthur."

"Greetings, Merlin. Come, break your fast with us."

"Yes, of course, but first we must discuss a matter of utmost importance."

It had been many moons since he had spoken with such gravity, and unease took root within me before he said another word.

"What distresses you?"

I guided him to the bench beneath the towering tree at the garden's edge. We sat, and he gripped his staff with both hands.

"As you know, Arthur, we are bound to shield and protect Merlonius from those who seek to harm her. Among them is your half-sister, Morgan le Fay, who poses a grave threat and will stop at nothing to challenge you."

"What has transpired?"

"I recently discovered that Morgan has been closely observing your movements—whom you speak with and where you go. She has even uncovered the hidden feelings between Lancelot and Gwenhwyfar."

He inhaled sharply, then continued. "Several days past, I found Morgan lurking at the edge of the enchanted forest. She cast a shadow over the protective boundaries I had created. Though her magic holds no power within my realm, her nearness to Merlonius was deeply troubling.

"I cast a spell, placing her in a deep slumber, and with the help of my apprentices, brought her back to her quarters in Camelot. When she awoke, she believed it was only a dream."

Morgan's cunning was legendary, and I knew she would not yield easily.

"Does she have any knowledge of Merlonius or my feelings for her?"

"No, Arthur, she does not. Rest assured, she currently lacks the means to penetrate our protections and uncover the truth. Nevertheless, we must not underestimate her persistence. To further safeguard Merlonius and our sanctuary, I have strengthened the spells that shield the entire enchanted forest. It will remain accessible only to the three of us."

The specter of my half-sister's malevolent determination haunted my thoughts.

"Should any harm befall Merlonius…"

"Arthur, she remains under my vigilant watch. I vow to keep her safe."

"Morgan's relentless hostility towards me, Uther Pendragon's son and heir, is most troubling. Despite her influence and gifts, she clings to an insatiable need to provoke me. I fear she will stop at nothing to gain what she craves most, my fall from the throne."

Merlin nodded, "I know, Arthur. Her seething resentment goes far back."

I pondered my half-sister's wicked intent, the enormity of the danger pressing upon me. Strengthening our defenses for all we held dear had never felt more urgent.

"I often wonder whether I should exile her from Camelot and our realm," I mused, my frustration evident. "I have granted her an undeserved status due to our clan ties. Only with her departure could we truly be liberated from her dark influence."

"We must proceed with caution, Arthur. It is often wiser to keep our enemies within reach, where we can anticipate their moves."

"Does Merlonius know of these recent events?" I pressed, leaning forward, fixed on him.

"No, I believe it is best to shield her for now."

"I am of the same mind."

"It is for this reason I have remained in the enchanted forest with her. Not only to protect her, but to ease the void left in your absence. We must also address the matter of Lancelot and Gwenhwyfar's bond. Morgan is relentless in her pursuit to expose them, scheming to manipulate you into making a decision as king that could trouble you for years to come."

"Morgan's plotting never ceases. She will twist whatever truths she uncovers to serve her own ends. I must be prepared for whatever treachery she sets in motion."

Before I could say more, Merlonius stepped into view.

"Welcome back, Merlin! Join us for a light meal," she called out, her voice a cheerful contrast to the gravity of our earlier discussion.

"Hale, Merlonius. Some food would serve me well now. Let us go," Merlin replied as he rose from the bench.

Upon entering, I unfastened my bag and withdrew the stone I had found.

I placed it on the table beside Merlonius. "On one of my walks through the garden, just beyond where it meets the orchard, this caught my eye. I deemed it worthy of your notice. Perhaps you or Merlin can reveal its secrets."

She picked it up, turning it over in her hands, admiring its rich, earthen tones, veined with fiery red.

"It is quite lovely," she remarked, passing it to Merlin.

Taking the stone, he rose from the bench and moved to the window, lifting it into a beam of sunlight. The light struck its surface, kindling its rich depths, like smoldering embers stirred to life. A hidden radiance glowed within, its inner fire stirred by the light of morn.

Merlin studied it closely before speaking. "This is a rare piece of amber, known not only for its beauty but also for its protective qualities to combat fear."

He returned it to Merlonius. She held it once more in the palm of her hands, cradling it as she had the crystal from Merlin's cave. Her gaze lifted to mine.

"Arthur, your gift will bring me comfort on the nights I spend alone, and you have my thanks."

She rose and carried it into the sleeping quarters. Though I could not see her, I knew she would place it on the small table by the wall, nestling it among a cluster of crystals and treasured keepsakes.

Her words lingered. She had never before spoken of the loneliness that crept in during my absences. Longing stirred within me as I thought of the nights I would be far from her, unable to offer her comfort or the warmth she found in me.

When she returned, she sat beside me and took my hand.

"This amber is a treasure, Arthur, for it carries your care with it."

"If it were in my power," I said, "I would see to all your heart's desires."

She placed her hand on my arm, her smile tender with affection.

"Ah, Arthur… My only wish is to share my days and nights with you."

"Indeed, I yearn for the same, and fortune grants me leave to stay until the morrow. What would delight you most during our time together?"

Her smile broadened. "Until the morrow! Such a gift. A journey to the summit would delight us all! What say you, Merlin?"

"A splendid idea indeed!"

"I shall prepare a basket, and we shall be ready to set forth soon. But let us break our fast first."

We helped ourselves to the berries, bread, and water Merlonius had carefully laid out on the table. Then, while she prepared what was needed for our visit to the summit, Merlin and I wandered alongside the stream. The rush of water over stone soothed my mind.

"Another plot is brewing," he began, his brow furrowed as if navigating the murky currents of fate. "Morgan, along with your kinsman Medrawt, conspires to seize your throne. Each harbors plans unbeknownst to the other, both aiming for the same treacherous end." He sighed deeply, his gaze drifting to the horizon as though weighing the course ahead.

"Rumors in Camelot grow troubling regarding Lancelot and Gwenhwyfar, yet no tangible proof of their affection has surfaced. They have been cautious. Still, we must remain vigilant on all fronts."

"Is there immediate urgency?"

"No, the time has not yet come. But we must be ready to act."

"Indeed, we must keep a watchful eye on their every move, ready to defend what we cherish most."

We both turned at the sound of Merlonius approaching, a basket of food cradled in her arms. A breeze tousled her hair, framing her face with delicate wisps. She stepped towards us, radiant with quiet grace. At the sight of her, a stillness settled over me, deeper than thought or breath.

"I am ready, if you both are," she said, casting an eager look between us.

"I am prepared. And you, Merlin?"

"Indeed, Arthur, let us go."

"Then let us embark on this worthy venture."

We ascended the incline, and at the pinnacle, the tree that had long stood as our refuge beckoned, its branches reaching towards the boundless sky.

From that height, I beheld the distant turrets of Camelot, proud and unyielding, their banners dancing in the breeze. Merlonius came to my side, and I drew her close, feeling the lasting strength that had bound us together.

"Merlonius," I murmured, "I thank the Fates each day for bringing you into my life."

"As do I. The light you have woven into my days knows no bounds."

I kissed her gently, then pressed my forehead to hers before burying my face in her hair, breathing in the familiar scent that never failed to calm me.

Merlin called to us, "Come, let us rest here and lose ourselves in the tales of my adventures."

We joined him beneath the large oak, where he wove captivating accounts of battles won and spells cast, conjuring vivid visions of a world before

Camelot. The midday sun bathed us in a mellow warmth, easing what chill lingered from the early morn.

Time seemed to vanish as Merlin carried us away with his stories, until at last, he looked at Merlonius with a playful glint in his eye. "My dear, shall we see what you have brought?"

With quiet delight, she opened the woven basket, spreading a blanket across the soft grass. A feast followed: crusty bread, creamy cheese, ripe berries, and crisp apples. At last, she poured ruby-red wine into three cups, the sunlight catching the liquid's gleam.

"Food fit for kings and sorcerers alike," Merlin declared, settling back against the tree with a contented sigh.

The slight breeze stirred around us, lulling Merlonius into slumber, her head resting in my lap. I met Merlin's steady regard.

"Rest yourself, my boy, I shall keep watch."

I closed my eyes, surrendering to the drift of the afternoon. Sleep soon followed.

With the sun's descent, painting the sky with hues of pink, purple, and red, we stirred from our rest.

"Well my young friends, now that you have refreshed yourselves, shall we return to the cottage and our eve's repast?"

Merlonius and I swiftly gathered what remained of our meal, tucking the goblets and blanket back into the basket. With appetites renewed, we descended the incline and followed the winding path.

As we neared the clearing, Merlin raised his staff. A sudden flash of light burst forth, illuminating the path before us.

"Ah, come now, my friends, the hearth bids us return!"

Upon entering, the rich aroma of bean pottage and freshly baked bread mingled with the comforting scent of crackling wood.

Merlin's bean soup, as rich and hearty as his tales, along with the bread, satisfied our hunger. With the table cleared, we immersed ourselves in our favorite game. Laughter rose around us as we rolled the casting stones, their lively clatter against wood mingling with the low hiss and snap of burning logs.

The fire cast a welcoming light, holding the night at bay. In this cherished time together, our bonds of friendship shone as brightly as the flames.

When our laughter faded and and the fire's crackle became the only sound that lingered, Merlin stretched, his movements slow and deliberate.

"Well, the hour for rest has come," he said, glancing around at the quieting scene. "Arthur, would you stay with us another day?"

"I will, but I must bid farewell by midday on the morrow. I eagerly await our next encounter in Camelot."

"Of course, my boy. Until then, stay true to your path, and may fortune favor you."

Turning to Merlonius. "My dear, I shall visit soon."

"Please return before long, Merlin."

For a breath, he looked at her, as if wanting to say more, but he did not. Instead, he opened the door and stepped outside.

After it closed behind him, she crossed the room to me, her steps unhurried. She settled at my side, and I reached for her hand, squeezing it gently.

"Merlonius, being with you has brought me immeasurable happiness. Seeing you again… I do not wish to leave, neither you, nor this home."

She clasped my hand a little tighter, her eyes searching mine, reflecting the sorrow I felt.

"I know, Arthur, for our parting weighs just as heavily on me. Come, let us cherish the precious hours we have left together."

We linked fingers and walked towards our bed. I cradled her face in my hands, looking deeply into her eyes. Leaning forward, our lips met in a fiery kiss, our profound yearning entwining us in a union beyond the physical. We lost ourselves in that instant, merging in a celebration of love that defied all constraints. Our bodies pressed close, each touch tracing the contours of devotion and memory, a map of all we had endured and become.

The burning glow of passion gradually softened into the tenderness of our closeness. I held her in my arms, her head resting upon my chest.

"Merlonius, the thought of you carries me through the darkest of days. It is the knowing that I shall return to your arms that gives me the strength to endure."

"My love, I too find solace in the memories of our times together. We are forever bound."

With a deep kiss, we surrendered to sleep, holding on to each other and to the peace of dreams.

With dawn's light streaming through the windows, we stirred. Merlonius caressed my face, rekindling our ardor. Still held in the solace of our union, we yielded once more to the pull between us, rising together to that familiar place where love and desire meet.

Breathless, we remained in the peace that followed, the sun's slow arc across the sky reminding me that midday neared, and with it, the moment I would have to part from her.

As I gathered my belongings, Merlonius stayed close. Clasping our hands a little longer, we both hesitated to part. Our lips met in a tender kiss, rich with longing and affection.

"I will visit again as soon as I am able," I whispered.

"I know you will." Her thumb lingered upon the back of my hand.

We walked outside together, and as I turned away, I battled the urge to look back. Each step towards the castle carried thoughts of Merlonius. The halls lay hushed as I emerged from the passage and returned to my chambers. At the casement, an emptiness gripped me, deepening as I stared northward.

My heart was bound to our love. Merlonius completed me, and the void of her absence felt unending. I shook my head, a fierce need rising within me to break free of these unyielding walls. Yearning for more than fleeting visits and brief encounters, I swore with single-minded purpose to find a way to bind our hearts, defying the destiny laid out by the Fates. The answer, I believed, might lie hidden in the murmur of the wind or the rustle of the leaves. The promise of reuniting with Merlonius called to me, whispering of a destiny yet to unfold.

Though the world lay bathed in sunlight, it could not rival the light she had kindled within my soul. Her presence lingered, woven into every breath I drew, and though distance parted us, I felt her spirit near. I closed my eyes, surrendering to the certainty that love such as ours would not be denied, neither by kings nor by the Fates themselves.

I hastened from my quarters to the vast chamber of the Round Table. Though I knew the nobles awaiting me would demand much, nothing could diminish the strength I carried within me, knowing she waited for me—now and always.

CHAPTER 31

STRATEGIES AND ALLIANCES

Merlin's message, laden with the ominous threats of Morgan and Medrawt, echoed ceaselessly in my mind. The danger could no longer be dismissed, calling for careful and discreet preparations. With his insight now more crucial than ever, I grew increasingly restless in his absence.

Three days after my return to Camelot, Merlin finally appeared. In the main hall, flanked by knights, I watched him approach.

"Arthur, we must speak in private."

Ascending the stair to my chambers, I noted the lines of weariness on his face and the fatigue evident in his every step. Once inside, he paced, hands clasped tightly behind him. I remained still, pondering the menace he had unveiled. Abruptly, he halted, concern passing between us.

"Morgan continues to search for her lost memory of attempting to enter the enchanted forest," he began. "She believes it holds the key to unlocking a secret that could unravel the very spells protecting the kingdom and undermine your rule."

His words revealed Morgan as a danger beyond mere ambition for power. No longer guided by dominance alone, she now pursued something far more perilous.

"Please, go on."

A shadow crossed his expression. "Medrawt seeks your crown, driven by personal vengeance and a ruthless thirst for supreme authority. He plans to exploit Lancelot and Gwenhwyfar's secret love, hoping to fracture the unity within Camelot.

"The Christian faith's stance on the queen's fidelity places us on a precarious edge. An exposed indiscretion would not only lead to severe consequences but could also threaten the very foundation of our kingdom."

The weight of his warning bore down on me. My challenge was no longer leadership alone, but the preservation of the realm's harmony, the safeguarding of its future, and the protection of the innocents who depended on us.

"What do your visions reveal about their likelihood of success?"

"They work independently, their ambitions hidden from one another. With careful stewardship, their threat could remain distant."

His wisdom once again proved to be a guiding force. While immediate action might not be necessary, the need for constant vigilance and a measured response was clear. Defending against Morgan and Medrawt required a thoughtful, sustained approach to ensure our readiness never faltered.

"Merlin, what if we were to assign Medrawt the stewardship of a region near Camelot? This would enable us to keep a close watch over his every move."

Reflecting briefly, he nodded. "A wise course, and one that must be undertaken without delay."

I paused, then continued. "I have been considering spending more time away from Camelot."

Crossing the chamber, I rested my hand on the casement ledge and looked out over the trees towards the enchanted forest. The view stirred thoughts of what might unfold in my absence, and I began to see the good that could come of it.

"This would grant Lancelot and Gwenhwyfar the privacy they require, within the sanctuary of her chambers. And truthfully, I yearn for more time with Merlonius."

"Yes, Arthur, that will serve all parties involved. I will watch over Morgan and Medrawt's movements closely, and you should do the same."

"Agreed. Does Merlonius remain unaware of these plots?"

"Yes, I have ensured she has no knowledge of them."

"I do not want her to bear this worry."

"We are of the same mind."

"Merlin, walk with me through Camelot. The knights must see us side by side once more."

"My boy, excellent. Let us proceed."

We emerged from my quarters and walked through the halls, exploring the many chambers and admiring the flourishing grounds. The trust between us guided our every step. Merlin's fame as a formidable wizard preceded him, while my reign had long proved my worth to the people.

Later, he joined me in the feasting hall for the eve's repast, giving the knights a chance to converse with us. When we entered, I noticed Gwenhwyfar nearing the end of her meal. After a cordial exchange of greetings, she excused herself and departed. Shortly thereafter, Lancelot quietly left the hall. Merlin nodded subtly, conveying his understanding as he caught my brief, knowing glance. With a deft touch, he redirected everyone's attention elsewhere, infusing the mood with his lively humor that brought laughter and ease to the room.

When the meal concluded and we exchanged wishes for a peaceful night, Merlin and I made our way back to my quarters.

Standing near the square working table, Merlin looked at me with deep intent.

"Arthur, I have noticed Medrawt distancing himself from the other knights, and their wariness of him is growing."

"Without the support of the knights, it will be difficult for him to mount a full rebellion. Would you not agree?"

"It will indeed be much harder. But I am concerned that he may still find ways to garner support from our enemies."

"You do not imply that he would dare approach the Saxons?"

"Sadly, yes."

His hand on my shoulder steadied me as I felt the profound impact of his words. "We will weather this storm together, and do not forget, Merlonius's sight is also expanding. She might see events that I do not."

"Yes, thank the gods for her."

"She is the echo of our ancestors' wisdom, Arthur. Her path entwined with ours long before we knew it.

"Well, Arthur, the morrow marks the beginning of our strategic endeavors. Let us meet again soon at the cottage."

"The dawn shall find us ready. I will travel to you after I speak with Medrawt. Be safe, Merlin," I added as he left, whispering a silent prayer to the gods for his protection.

Stepping to the casement windows, I looked northward, my thoughts reaching for the enchanted forest. The longing for Merlonius burned ever brighter, undimmed by time or distance. The morrow was the day when my dreams would take form, reclaiming my true happiness.

At the morn's first light, I rose early and joined the others in the feasting hall. After breaking the fast and speaking with a few of my knights, I left and encountered Kay.

"Good morrow, Kay. Would you find Medrawt and ask him to join me in the great hall?"

"Good morrow to you as well, Arthur. I will bring him to you without delay."

At the heart of Camelot's keep, the High King's throne stood, the cornerstone of our kingdom's sovereignty. Though wrought of plain wood, its high back and sturdy arms gave it a commanding presence, a seat meant not for comfort but for judgment. Beyond the throne, the hall itself bore the marks of majesty.

Around me, the lofty beams and richly adorned walls exuded a solemn grandeur. The faint scent of beeswax lingered on the stone floors, while shafts of sunlight pierced through narrow windows, casting slender rays that danced across the chamber.

I settled into the seat of power, the wood smooth and cool against my fingertips. Bound to this throne by the crown I wore, a profound sense of responsibility pressed upon me. With a measured breath, I prepared for my conversation with Medrawt.

The kingdom yearned for a worthy successor, yet my loveless and duty-bound arrangement with Gwenhwyfar offered no hope of such. If only Merlonius stood by my side as queen; to raise children with her would complete my heart and carry forward a legacy born of love.

Without an heir, I was driven to secure my kin's rightful place on the throne. Yet the recent plots by Morgan and Medrawt were a sharp reminder of the dangers that lurked within such ambitions, threatening both the kingdom and the future I so desired.

My reflections were abruptly interrupted as the doors swung open. Kay entered, followed by Medrawt, who commanded attention with his imperious bearing. His eyes gleamed with a calculating glint, a stark contrast to the honour and integrity of his brothers, esteemed Knights of the Round Table. Unlike them, Medrawt's haughtiness was of an entirely different nature.

I gave him a nod. "Medrawt."

In response, he offered me a tilt of his head, his face a mask of stoic restraint. I detected a subtle curl of his lip, betraying an underlying arrogance that simmered just beneath his composed exterior.

"Kay has informed me that you wish to speak with me." His words carried a thread of disdain, carefully veiled yet unmistakable.

"Indeed. I require your formidable skills in the southeastern lands. Reports have reached us of marauders terrorizing the farmers there. You will be joined by Sir Geraint and Sir Agravain. Together, you must put an end to this menace and ensure the safety of our people."

A smug smile tugged at the corner of his mouth as he grasped the task. "Consider it done. We shall depart on the morrow and restore order to the lands."

"Very well. Your loyalty to the throne is commendable. May success accompany your efforts."

With a shallow bow, he turned sharply, his cape billowing as he departed. Though outwardly loyal, his conceit was impossible to ignore, and I now recognized the deception hidden beneath his well-crafted bearing. I held my poise, though bitterness stirred within. *How had one born of our blood grown so bent on discord?*

Stepping down from my throne, I approached Kay. His brow creased slightly, his expression suggesting he sensed something amiss.

"Arthur, do you need any further assistance?"

Our youthful days, when we shared confidences and carefree explorations in the forests, surged back to me. Those times had since faded into the past, transformed into cherished memories that spurred both longing and gratitude for what once was.

"Your support means a great deal to me, but for now, I believe I can handle matters on my own."

"As you wish, Arthur. Know that I am your brother and stand by you, always."

Our eyes met briefly, and with a final nod, Kay departed. Now alone, a fervor burned within me, spurring me forward to reach for my dream. Guided by a firmness of purpose, I made my way to the gardens, each step a stride towards the destiny that awaited realization.

Arriving at the sheltered nook within the gardens, I found Lancelot and Gwenhwyfar, their heads bent close in earnest discussion. Seated together, wrapped in a world apart, they only became aware of me when I stepped into the light, clearing my throat.

"Good morrow, Lancelot, Gwenhwyfar."

They turned, their faces shifting quickly to masks of formality. Lancelot rose, his back straight, offering a nod that mixed respect with ease.

"Good morrow, Arthur."

Gwenhwyfar followed, her movements deliberate, her smile measured, reflecting his gesture of respect.

"Good morrow, Arthur."

"I will be leaving Camelot for several days as I venture south to survey our lands. Lancelot, the Queen's safety rests in your hands during my absence."

Watching him, I caught the brief hardening of his stance, and a shadow crossed his face, betraying the struggle beneath his composed bearing.

"I am duty-bound to fulfil this charge, my lord."

His assurance was marked by a subtle tightening of his grip on his sword's hilt, a gesture that hinted at the unrest he sought to master.

Gwenhwyfar's lips parted slightly, then closed before she spoke.

"Travel safe, Arthur."

Her glance towards Lancelot was fleeting yet heavy with meaning, hinting at deeper currents.

"Lancelot, your steadfastness is an honour to us."

To Gwenhwyfar, I offered a bow.

"You grace me with your kind words, Gwenhwyfar. Until my return, then."

Our exchange was a careful dance of courtly grace, each step taken with precision upon the intricate tapestry of our intertwined fates.

Intent on embarking upon my plans, I walked from the gardens to the stables. Quickening my pace, I inhaled the familiar scents that so often brought me solace. At the farthest stall, where Bedwyr attended to his horse, the contrast was clear: here was a place of straightforwardness and loyalty, far removed from the tangled web of royal intrigues.

"Good morrow, Bedwyr."

Startled, he looked up from his task. "Good morrow, Arthur."

"Would you walk with me?"

Without hesitation, he carefully placed his shovel aside and secured the stall gate with a resounding click. He held my look slightly longer than usual, clearly intrigued by my appearance and request.

"Where shall we go?"

"Come, let us walk in the woods, where no ears may overhear us."

We followed a winding path deeper into the trees. The rustle of unseen creatures stirred the underbrush, and the soft murmur of a distant brook could be heard.

Reaching a sunlit clearing, we found our secluded haven. Here, we stood close, alert to any intrusion. The trees stood watchful, as if nature itself conspired to safeguard our exchange.

"Bedwyr, a decade has passed since I reluctantly wed a woman who held no claim upon my heart—a woman I did not even know." I paused, letting the gravity of my declaration settle between us before I spoke again.

"In that time of vulnerability, I entrusted you with my resolve to ceaselessly seek a way for Merlonius, the true love of my life, to remain forever by my side. This day, the Fates appear to favor my cause."

"How do you intend, Arthur?"

"My request comes from the depth of my heart. You are my unswerving and trusted friend, and I humbly implore your support at The Giants' Dance on the morrow. It is there, under the full moon and amidst our ancestors' revered magic, that I intend to exchange vows with Merlonius. While I have yet to seek Merlin's blessing or her consent, I ask that you stand with me in this."

He stood motionless, his jaw tightening as he absorbed the gravity of my words. A furrow formed between his brows before he slowly turned away, his boots stirring the scattered leaves. Wordless, he weighed the truth I had set before him. Finally, he stopped before me, his stance no longer rigid, his features shifting from deep contemplation to a firm resolve.

"Arthur, it is a great honour to be asked to be a part of this momentous ritual, but how can this be? Gwenhwyfar is your queen, bound to you by the ceremony of the new church."

"She holds the title as queen per the new religion's dictates, yet ours is a union of duty and necessity, devoid of love and affection. My vow to protect her remains intact. Yet it is Merlonius who has captured my heart. It is with her I wish to unite, embracing the age-old enchantments and ways of our forebears."

Bedwyr exhaled slowly, his eyes searching mine, weighing the enormity of my decision. Then, at last, he stepped forward, placing a steadying hand on my shoulder.

"It will be my honour to witness your union with Merlonius. Though the path you tread is not without its challenges, I shall be at your side at The Giants' Dance. May the Fates smile upon you both."

Emotions swelled within me as I clasped his forearm. "Bedwyr, your support means a great deal. Now, I must ride to the enchanted forest to speak with her. And gods willing, we shall make ready for the ceremony. Until the morrow."

With a final nod, we parted ways. I watched as he walked back along the woodland path, his figure gradually disappearing into the dappled light. I felt truly fortunate to have such a stalwart and loyal friend.

Memories surfaced of our encounter eighteen years ago when I professed my oath to protect the land and its people. He stood before Merlin and me, offering his service. Through the years that followed, we fought side by side in countless trials, among them the battle that claimed his hand. Fear held me that day, thinking it might rob him of the life and purpose he had so fiercely embraced. Yet Bedwyr endured—his spirit unbroken, his loyalty unshaken. His place in my life was a gift beyond measure, one I vowed never to take for granted. Whispers of thanks escaped my lips, carrying my heartfelt prayers to the benevolent Fates who had woven our paths together.

CHAPTER 32

THE PROPOSAL

Excitement and certainty surged within me as I made my way to my chambers. The time for action had arrived, and I knew this as surely as the sun rose in the east. Swiftly, I gathered the necessary garments, each choice carefully considered, hoping they would befit the days ahead. A bowl of apples on the table caught my eye and drew a smile. I selected a few, tucking them into my bag, knowing the simple pleasure they would bring my trusted steed, Odin. Though Thor, my loyal companion for many years, had died, his successor had proven himself worthy, carrying me with the same steadiness and loyalty. A flood of hope and desire carried me forward, lending sharp purpose to my preparations.

With my scabbard securely fastened around my waist and Excalibur by my side, I ventured to the stables. There, my magnificent black stallion, his coat as dark as night, eagerly pranced before me. The rhythmic sound of his hooves echoed in the stables as I hoisted myself up onto his back, feeling his taut muscles beneath me.

Crossing the drawbridge, I could feel Morgan le Fay lurking nearby, her watchful eyes haunting us like the cold grip of a vengeful ghost. Yet, my determination spurred me onward, and I urged my horse into a full gallop. Relinquishing the reins, I let him stretch his mighty legs, and with a thrilling burst of speed, we left the reach of Morgan's scrutiny far behind. The wind whipped through my hair, carrying the tangible freedom and escape it promised.

At the edge of the enchanted forest, I reined in Odin, his breath heavy from the rousing ride. The mist wove through the trees, a spectral veil casting an eerie light upon the gnarled branches, reaching skyward like the fingers of spirits.

We followed the dirt path to the clearing, the stream's flowing song a soothing backdrop. As I dismounted beside the paddock, the supple leather reins slipped through my fingers.

Patting Odin's neck, I whispered as I removed his bit, "Well done, my trusted companion. You have earned a reward."

Retrieving my knife, I reached into my bag and withdrew an apple. With practiced movements, I cut it into quarters and offered them to him. He whinnied with pleasure, savoring each piece.

After securing his reins to the post and ensuring he was comfortably settled, I left him to rest and made my way towards the familiar thatched cottage. Upon arriving, I knocked but received no answer. Just then, Merlin emerged from the garden, his robes stirred by the breeze.

"Arthur, it is good to see you. How did Medrawt react to his new assignment?"

"Surprisingly well, given his arrogance. He continually challenges the honour of our clan."

"That is ever his way. He must be watched closely; his intentions remain focused on removing you from the throne. I shall continue to keep a vigilant eye on him. Now, can you stay a while?"

"Yes, most definitely. Where is Merlonius?"

"She is at the waterfall. Shall we surprise her there? I am certain she will be overjoyed to see you."

He stood before me, leaning slightly on his gnarled wooden staff.

"Yes, but first, there is something I must discuss with you. Let us walk to the stream," I gestured for him to follow.

"Of course."

Reaching the water's edge, he faced me. "What stirs your thoughts?"

"Merlin, I seek to wed Merlonius. I would be honoured if you would officiate our union at The Giants' Dance under the guiding light of the moon on the morrow. Bedwyr will stand as our witness.

"Gwenhwyfar may hold the title of my queen, but as you know, our union exists in name only. I long to tie myself to Merlonius through the ancient rites of the gods and goddesses, hoping to seal our love with your magic blessing, should she agree."

His face conveyed no trace of emotion before he turned away, his attention captured by the flowing stream. I held still, anxiously awaiting his response. His approval—or his blessing—felt as necessary as breath itself. I hoped my words had adequately conveyed my intentions.

"Arthur, it would be my utmost honour to officiate your handfasting ceremony with Merlonius," he finally declared.

His hand briefly pressed to his chest before he smiled. "Go now, find her and pose your question. I will ensure your steed is comfortably settled with the other horses."

Relieved and overcome with gladness, I laughed. "Merlin, your support means a great deal to me. And many thanks for taking care of Odin!" With that, I set off to find her.

Excitement and nervous expectation coursed through me. *What if she does not wish to wed?* I forcefully pushed the thought aside. Reaching the waterfall, I saw her, gracefully seated on one of the stone benches, captivated by the serene waters of the pond.

"Merlonius," I whispered.

A radiant smile spread across her face, and she stood, hurrying towards me.

"Arthur, you are here," she breathed, nestling into my arms.

Our lips met in a tender kiss, a promise rekindled in the closeness between us. When we parted, the light in her eyes reached into me, steady and sure, like the glow of a hearth on a winter's night.

"I have missed you," she said. "How long can you stay?"

"Several days." Taking her hand, I lead her back to the bench.

"Several days! This is such good news. Tell me, how have you fared?"

"I am well. And you, my love?

"My heart is lighter for seeing you."

She leaned in again, and this time, our kiss was filled with all we had missed, the warmth of reunion mingling with the ache of days spent apart. It deepened, carrying both solace and longing.

"Merlonius," I began softly, "I wish to speak with you about a matter of great import."

"Yes, what is it?"

"We have known each other close to twenty years and during this time, my love for you has grown ever stronger." I moved a wisp of her hair from her forehead. "I would ask if you would become my wife on the morrow, in a ceremony at The Giants' Dance beneath the full moon's light. Merlin has agreed to conduct the handfasting ceremony, with Bedwyr bearing witness."

She listened, tears welling up. Tenderly, she lifted her hand to my cheek.

"Nothing would bring me greater joy than to be your wife, Arthur, but what of your queen…"

I lightly pressed my finger to her lips. "Gwenhwyfar is my queen, it is true, but only in title. Though we have never spoken of this, I have never been with her as a true lord, for you have always held my love. The ceremony that made Gwenhwyfar my queen was performed by a religion I do not follow, and the vows I made to her were to protect and keep her safe, which I have done to the best of my power. Long ago, I told you that I would find a way to honour and respect you, and I have kept that promise. Now, I ask you to join in union with me, Arthur the man, not Arthur the king."

I paused, searching her face. "Merlonius, will you take me as the one bound to you in love?"

"Yes, yes, yes! You are a part of me, Arthur, and nothing would make me happier."

"Let us find Merlin." I drew her close, unable to hide my joy.

"Then we shall tell him at once!"

Crossing the threshold of the cottage, we found Merlin at the back, busy with his tinctures and salves. Merlonius hastened to his side.

"Merlin, Arthur has asked me to wed, and I have gladly accepted. He has told me you will preside over the ceremony, and Bedwyr shall bear witness to our vows."

His smile softened as he clasped her hands. "My dear, to see such joy in you is a blessing to my spirit. I am deeply honoured to take part in this sacred union."

"Merlonius, the day is still before us. What say you to a walk to the summit?"

"Oh, yes, Arthur—unless Merlin has need of me?"

Merlin gave a brief wave. "Go, my dear. Enjoy the day."

Hand in hand, we closed the door behind us and set off along the path to the incline. As she often did, Merlonius marveled at the sky, the birds, and the flowers along our way, her delight bringing life to all that surrounded us.

Reaching the top, she turned to me with playful mischief in her eyes. "Race with me, Arthur!" she called, twirling before dashing to the great oak.

A breathless laugh escaped me as I gave chase, the wind rushing past us. When I reached her, I swept her into my arms, lifting her effortlessly. Carrying her, I bore her to the shelter of the tree, where I held her close. Desire flared, drawing us swiftly into the depths of our passion.

She traced her fingers along my jaw, her touch featherlight. I pressed a kiss to her lips, slow and reverent.

Guiding her down onto the cool earth, I worshiped every part of her—the curve of her shoulders, the rise and fall of her breasts, the way her body welcomed me with undeniable longing. Beneath the vast expanse of sky, we surrendered to love's sacred embrace, moving in harmony, bound by a love that defied time itself.

As the world grew still around us, I held her close, my heart steady against hers. "Merlonius," I murmured, brushing my lips over her brow. "My heart dwells with you, now and always."

She sighed, her fingers tracing idle patterns along my arm. "Your heart is part of my being, Arthur, for we are one."

Reluctantly, we untangled from each other and sat side by side, our backs resting against the trunk of the tree.

Merlonius turned to me, a thoughtful crease forming as she pondered. "I wonder, Arthur, why my visions did not reveal this day. My heart stirs at the thought of the ceremony that awaits us, yet I did not see it."

I considered her words, looking to the horizon where the sky kissed the rolling hills. "Perhaps it is because I set this path into motion only this day," I mused. "The Fates could not weave what had not yet been decided."

She studied me, then her lips curved in a warm smile. "Or perhaps, some things are meant to be discovered only when the time is upon us."

I took her hand in mine, pressing a kiss to her palm. "Then let us cherish every moment we are given."

With a gaze that held both love and certainty, she reached up, her fingers threading through my hair with tender reverence. I closed my eyes briefly, savoring the feel of her touch, the way it sent a shiver through me as though she traced the very contours of my soul.

Our lips met, a soft caress at first, but as our longing rose, the kiss deepened, igniting a fire that neither of us wished to quell. She sighed against me, her breath mingling with mine, a wordless plea that mirrored my own. With aching slowness, we settled beneath the tree, the world beyond this sacred haven fading, leaving only the two of us.

In every touch, a promise; in every whisper, the echo of a love bound beyond time. I worshiped her with my hands, my lips, with every fiber of my being. She welcomed me wholly, drawing me deeper into the bond that united us, not by fate, but by choice, by devotion, by the sheer certainty that we were two souls made one.

In the embrace of the ancient oak, we surrendered once more to the passion that held us, undiminished by the passage of days or duty.

A silence settled between us as we lay entwined, the warmth of our bodies lingering as the dappled sunlight played over us through the sheltering branches. The grove held its peace, broken only by the slow rhythm of our breathing and the occasional chirp of birds nestled among the boughs. Merlonius rested her head against my chest, her fingers drifting lazily over my arm. I cradled her close, running my fingers through the silken strands of her hair, relishing all that we shared.

For a time, we spoke little, content in the stillness. As the afternoon waned, the shifting light signaled the sun's slow descent towards the horizon.

Merlonius stirred. "We should see to the horses." Her reluctance to move mirrored my own.

I pressed a kiss to her brow, a silent token of all we had just shared. We rose, brushing stray blades of grass from our garments. With our hands clasped, we made our way down the incline, the distant paddock coming into view. Odin lifted his head at our approach, ears pricked forward in greeting. I ran my hand along his flank, offering words of gratitude, while Merlonius saw to the others, ensuring their water trough remained full.

Satisfied that all was well, we returned to the cottage as the eve settled upon the land. The sky, painted in hues of amber and rose, cast a golden end-of-day light over the fields and hills. Reaching the door, I paused, gathering her gently into my arms.

"Another day draws to its end," I murmured.

Her eyes reflected the contentment that filled my own. "And we have woven memories that shall remain."

Merlin greeted us as we entered, the rich scents of stew bubbling over the hearth and bread baking near the flames swirling about us.

"Hail, my young friends. The food is ready to enjoy."

With that, we gathered around the table. The stew warmed us with each savory spoonful, while the crust of the freshly baked bread offered a satisfying crunch with every bite. Conversation turned lighthearted as we ate, a sense of contentment settled around us.

"Arthur, do you recall the time you and Merlonius attempted to make pottage?" Merlin's eyes sparkled with a playful gleam. "You were so eager to impress that you forgot two of the vegetables."

Merlonius laughed. "I remember too well. We praised it mightily, yet we were barely able to swallow it."

"So, the truth comes out now?" I teased. "Is that why, in all these years, you have never required my help in preparing a meal again?"

"I am afraid so, my boy," Merlin said, his mirth blending with ours.

The easy banter of close friends wove through the merriment. Stories and good cheer flowed as freely as the wine, each tale drawing us closer together.

As the night unfolded, our worldly cares slipped away, leaving space for friendship and dreams. In that small, fire-warmed shelter, we found a haven of happiness, filled with anticipation for what was to come. Our bonds deepened, binding our futures together with threads of love and promise.

An owl hooted in the distance, a reminder of the late hour. Merlin rose from his seat with a low groan, rubbing his neck. "I must rest. I will return in the morn to prepare for the joyful occasion."

We stood with him, following to the door.

"We are most grateful for your guidance and for the meal you have prepared. This night has given us memories we shall treasure always."

"Indeed, Merlin, we shall hold this eve close to our hearts," Merlonius added.

"You are both most welcome. May your sleep be filled with peace and dreams of a beautiful future." With that, he stepped out, softly closing the door behind him.

We lingered, the glow of the fire dancing across the walls, and a stillness settled around us, the depth of our emotions resting softly upon my heart. I reached for Merlonius's hand, threading my fingers through hers, letting their touch convey all I felt.

She leaned into me, resting her head against my chest, and I pressed a kiss into the silken strands of her hair, breathing in the scent of wildflowers that clung to her. There was no urgency, only the unshakable certainty of the love we shared.

Lifting my hand, she placed a kiss upon my palm before guiding it to rest over her heart. "This has always belonged to you," she whispered.

Emotion tightened my throat, and I cradled her face, my thumb tracing the softness of her cheek. "And mine to you."

At length, we withdrew to our bed. I held her close, attuned to the rhythm of her breath, the soft rise and fall of her body beneath my touch.

There was no crown, no kingdom, no burdens of duty, only the woman I loved, the life we were about to forge, and the certainty that I would choose her in every life to come.

Sleep wove its spell upon us, and as my eyes drifted shut, I saw her as she had been on the day we first met, her hair wind-tossed, a smudge of dirt upon her cheek, her laughter ringing out like the song of the earth itself.

Tomorrow, our hands would be bound beneath moonlight, our hearts joined in the ancient way.

And with that thought, I drifted into dreams of all that awaited us.

CHAPTER 33

THE HANDFASTING CEREMONY

With the first brushstrokes of dawn stretching across the horizon, painting the sky with breathtaking colors, sunlight caressed the cottage, heralding the day. Built of stone with a thatched roof, it truly felt like home. Within its walls, the crackling hearth spread warmth, releasing a comforting aroma of sweet smoke that subtly perfumed the space. I pressed a tender kiss to Merlonius's forehead as I held her close. Her eyes sparkled, aglow with the love and happiness that graced this auspicious day.

"Shall we break the fast by the stream?"

"That is a marvelous idea. May I be of help?" I offered, eager to share in the preparations.

We rose and dressed, then I retrieved a woven basket from beside the hearth. Together, we filled it with food and a container of water.

"Now, we are ready." She picked up a woolen blanket dyed in shades of green and blue.

With the basket and blanket in hand, we ventured outside to the stream, where the day welcomed us with glorious splendor. The sun shone brightly, while only a few clouds dotted the expansive blue sky. We carefully spread the blanket upon the thick grass.

I took in the tranquil scene, taking pleasure in the serene beauty that surrounded us. Beside me, she radiated a calm that deepened my gratitude for her presence. Our love, having endured many challenges, now flourished anew, promising a future rich with aspirations and enduring commitment.

Opening the basket, we unveiled our simple yet delightful fare. The crusty bread beckoned us to taste its hearty grain, accompanied by creamy cheese and succulent berries. A clay container of water completed the meal, a modest repast beneath the endless sky.

As we shared our meal in quiet joy, I turned to her. "Merlonius, as we celebrate this eve, is there anything I can offer you?"

"I desire nothing more than your love, which you generously bestow upon me, and your happiness."

Moved by her words, I cradled the back of her head, drawing her close for a kiss.

Tracing the curve of her chin with my fingers, I whispered, "My love for you knows no bounds."

"Arthur, without you, my life would lack meaning. The depth of my love for you is immeasurable, and it always will be."

A rustle of robes and the soft tread of footsteps announced Merlin's approach.

"Join us, Merlin."

"What fare have you?"

"Cheese, bread, berries, and water. Please, sit with us."

Settling onto the blanket, he wasted no time, his words flowing with the quick certainty of a mind always in motion.

"We need to speak of this night's ceremony. Both of you must prepare your vows to recite under the stars. It would be fitting to bring the finest wine we have, along with our best goblets. Because of the enchantment of protection, Bedwyr will not be able to join us at the cottage. We shall celebrate near The Giants' Dance after the ceremony."

With a nod of finality, he reached for a chunk of bread and a handful of juicy berries.

Merlonius looked to me.

"Arthur, we need a period of solitude to prepare our vows. Do you agree?"

"Yes, most definitely."

A shared smile passed between us, full of excitement for what the day would bring. The murmur of the stream and the warmth of the breeze surrounded us as we stayed a while longer, sharing laughter and conversation. We passed the hour enjoying this time together as the sun rose above us. With a final look of understanding, we packed the remaining food into the woven basket and folded the blanket. Our steps were light with anticipation as we made our way inside.

I helped Merlonius empty our basket before asking, "Where do you wish to work on your vows? I would prefer the garden under the oak tree."

She looked towards Merlin, then smiled. "By the waterfall."

"Well then," Merlin added, "shall we meet back here when you are finished?"

We answered in unison, "Agreed."

He handed each of us parchment, ink, and quills. "May your hearts guide your words."

Merlonius and I lingered in a quiet moment, our love enduring still, and soon, through our vows, we would be bound forever.

As she walked towards the path leading to the pond, I paused to watch her, her steps light with purpose. A smile rose unbidden as I made my way to the stone bench beneath the towering oak tree near the vegetable garden. Settling there with parchment and quill in hand, I prepared to write my vows. The rustling leaves offered a soothing harmony, stirring cherished memories I had long held for my life with Merlonius.

I thought back to the days before I pulled the sword from the stone, when I had dared to dream of asking her to be my wife. I could still picture the home I once imagined for us, set among quiet hills, with stables nearby for the horses we would carefully select for breeding. With a sigh, I released those youthful visions, offering my thanks to the Fates for the union that would take place this night.

Returning to the parchment, my words flowed, each stroke of the quill a declaration of love. At last, after all these years, she was to become my wife, my partner before the Fates.

Having finished my words, I walked back towards the stream. Moments later, as if summoned by my longing, Merlonius appeared on the path from the waterfall, her presence answering the call of my heart. I gathered her into my arms, and our lips met in a tender unity.

The door creaked open, and Merlin stepped out. With measured steps, he made his way towards us, his wizard's staff rhythmically tapping the earth like a magical heartbeat.

"Arthur, we must prepare The Giants' Dance for this eve's joining. Will you accompany me?"

"Of course, Merlin."

A gleam of affectionate amusement lit his eyes as he looked at Merlonius. "My dear, I have left a surprise for you on the bed. Try it on and see if it fits."

Gasping with delight, she cast me a quick, grateful glance before disappearing inside.

"She will be the fairest of them all," I remarked.

His expression softened. "This night is of great import for all of us. I want her to feel like the queen she is."

"Your thoughtfulness will ensure that she feels truly honoured, though she has always been a queen to me."

"I know she has, my boy. Come let us be on our way."

We walked through the dense woods, the ground beneath our feet soft and spongy, covered in fallen leaves, while the fresh, natural fragrance of the forest filled my senses. Leaves rustled, birds chirped, and fleeting movements in the underbrush hinted at the curiosity of unseen observers.

With each step towards The Giants' Dance, a deepening chill enfolded us, and the forest sounds withdrew into silence. This was a sacred place, protected by magic. Merlin and I worked in accord to create a smaller circle within the larger one, using small rocks gathered from the surrounding area. This would be the hallowed ground where Merlonius and I would speak our eternal vows and solemn oaths to each other.

When the circle was complete, Merlin raised his staff high. "And now, Arthur, let us call upon the gods of the sky and the wind to protect this space from all and any intruders, both of men and of spirit."

The circle shimmered with a crackling magical force, the stones responding to his call as if awakened to life.

The sun passed beyond the horizon, setting the forest aglow with amber light. A calm descended, as if the world itself paused to mark the close of day. We retraced our steps, and when we arrived at the cottage, Merlonius greeted us.

"I have prepared a light meal."

"How welcome," Merlin replied. "Come, Arthur, let us take our places at the table."

We sat down to share a light meal of cold hare, flatbread, and soft savory cheese, though excitement surged through each of us. Our minds, so consumed by the imminent ceremony, left the food nearly untouched. Yet, the fresh, cool water and wine were a much-needed refreshment after our journey through the dense forest.

At last, Merlin rose to his feet and announced, "Let us proceed to The Giants' Dance!"

Without hesitation, we began to ready ourselves. While she dressed behind the curtain, I laid out my cream-colored tunic, its gold stitching catching the light, and my cloak the color of forest leaves. My hands moved steadily, though my heart beat with quiet purpose. After one last glance at my vows, confident I carried them with me, I stepped out to join Merlin.

I was captivated by his stunning dark purple robe.

"Merlin, the colour becomes you as though it were born of your spirit."

A faint smile touched his lips. "Do you think so? I must say, your own garments are equally fitting for this momentous event."

His footsteps created a rhythmic sound on the wooden floor as he paced. Around his neck, I noticed a leather cord from which hung a crystal pendant that caught the candlelight, casting a mystical radiance. The scent of wine, rich with oak, drifted from a nearby basket holding four goblets.

Quietly observing Merlin's purposeful movements, I positioned myself by the hearth, where the crackling fire added comforting warmth and the faint aroma of burning wood drifted around us.

My attention shifted to Merlonius as she approached with calm grace. She was adorned in a flowing ivory garment with gold embellishments on the sleeves, collar, and hem. Gossamer-like cloth cascaded from her arms, creating an enchanting effect. Her hair, meticulously braided and interwoven with delicate flowers, crowned her head, while waves flowed down her back. She drew near, radiant with delight, her eyes sparkling in the firelight.

Merlin's eyes softened. "My dear, you are a vision."

I nodded, unable to contain my admiration. "Merlonius, you are beyond compare."

A faint flush touched her cheeks as she glanced at Merlin. "I am grateful for this beautiful garment, Merlin." Her eyes shifted to me, soft with affection. "And to both of you, I hold deep gratitude for your kind words."

She reached for my hand, and for a breath, we stood together in silence, content in our shared joy.

We turned to leave, the door closing softly behind us. The woods were alive with the soothing sounds of crickets and distant owl hoots. The moon, large and luminous, cast its silver light upon the forest floor, painting the trees in ethereal shades of grey. Each step we took was softened by a thick carpet of fallen leaves, and we soon arrived at the revered and magical place.

Emerging from the cover of the trees, we were greeted by Bedwyr at the edge of the enchanted circle. He was dressed in a regal blue linen tunic with intricate designs along the hem, a flowing mantle draped over his shoulders. His shoulder-length hair was neatly arranged, and at his side hung a gleaming sword, a symbol of his readiness and valour.

I approached him, placing a hand on his shoulder. "You came. My thanks, my friend."

Bedwyr clasped my forearm in return, his grip firm, unwavering. "I consider it a privilege to stand with you both on this blessed night."

Merlonius drew near. "Bedwyr, having you here means much to us."

"Welcome, Bedwyr," Merlin added. "Your company enriches this celebration."

He bowed as Merlin proclaimed, "Now, my dear friends, let us step into the hallowed center of The Giants' Dance to witness the binding of these two great souls."

We crossed the threshold into the ring of stones as they glowed with a light deepened by the moon's touch. The scent of meadowsweet and sage lingered in the air, an offering from the natural world that heightened the enchantment of the night.

Bedwyr stood to Merlin's right as we took our place before them. A stillness surrounded us as Merlin raised his staff, the crystal at its tip gathering a mist-like radiance. Slowly, he lowered it and, looking at both of us, he began.

"Arthur and Merlonius, you stand here, bound by a love that transcends time and the mortal world. The promise you make this night, under the gaze of the heavens and witnessed by us, shall unite you forever, never to be parted."

I turned to her, and as our fingers entwined, the words rose from a place deeper than thought.

"I, Arthur, take you, my dearest Merlonius, to be my wife. You are the one with whom I dream and share my love. From this moment forward, I promise to cherish you always, not only in this lifetime but throughout the countless lifetimes we will have together. We will walk hand in hand, guided by the boundless steadfastness that fills us. I pledge to stand by your side through every joy and sorrow that life may bring, supporting you in every challenge and celebrating every triumph. I swear to be your rock, your companion, and your partner in all things. Through the many phases of the moon, sunlight and shadow, our joining will remain as enduring as the earth itself."

A single tear glistened on her cheek, her lips quivering with profound emotion. Her eyes held not only happiness but the unshakable truth of our spirits intertwined, joined by a power greater than any in all creation.

She drew a breath, steadying herself. "In the presence of these noble witnesses," she declared, "I, Merlonius, promise my enduring heart to you, Arthur. I embrace all that you are—your strengths and your flaws—as I offer myself to you, imperfect but steadfast in my love. I swear to stand beside you, supporting you through every challenge and seeking your wisdom in times of need. I choose to spend not only this lifetime but also all those that may follow with you, forever united as one."

Her vow wove with mine like twin threads in a single tapestry, now made eternal.

Merlin raised his staff high, his delight unmistakable as he proclaimed, "The rings that encircle your spirits bind you to each other for eternity. Your words are now sealed. We ask the Sacred Powers to look fondly upon Arthur and Merlonius, and may peace and light guide their path always."

"And so it shall be," Bedwyr declared with deep reverence.

We sealed our pledge with a tender kiss that held the promise of a lifetime together. Overwhelmed with emotion, Bedwyr shouted, "*Bennach!*", the Old Welsh word for blessings. To our surprise, a multitude of fireflies descended upon us, their radiant bodies transforming The Giants' Dance into a living constellation. It was as though the stars themselves had sent them to weave their light around us in harmony with all we had spoken.

Merlonius let out a joyful laugh, alight with wonder as the fireflies circled about us. She looked at us, her expression one of awe at the wondrous display. "These are so beautiful, Arthur… Merlin, Bedwyr, is this not truly amazing?"

The three of us laughed in unison, swept up in her wonder. I pulled her close, both of us enveloped in the dance of the fireflies, and I felt a contentment like never before.

"I have a surprise for all of you," Merlin announced.

An enchanting sight greeted us as we walked from the circle. An elongated wooden table, hewn from a single colossal tree, stood in all its glory, polished to a rich, glossy sheen. Candles of various sizes adorned the table, their dancing flames creating a serene and inviting feeling.

The enticing aroma of succulent roasted meats and freshly baked bread mingled with the rich scents of cheeses, nestled among fresh apples and berries, forming a welcoming feast. Pitchers of cool, clear water stood at the ready, promising a refreshing addition to the meal.

"Gather around, dear friends! The festivities are about to commence!"

We took our seats at the table as Merlin brought forth a simple, well-crafted pitcher filled with a rich, amber wine that glimmered in the candlelight. He moved around the table with a practiced ease, pouring the wine into each of our goblets. The earthy, robust aroma of the wine blended with the scents of the feast, adding to the festive cheer.

Bedwyr raised his cup high, "To Arthur and Merlonius! May their love grow ever stronger, their joy be boundless, and their union endure as surely as the stars above."

"To Arthur and Merlonius!" Merlin echoed as he lifted his goblet.

Merlonius and I exchanged a glance, her smile reflecting the gratitude that mirrored my own. We raised our cups, humbled by the care and support that enfolded us.

Laughter and stories wove through the night as we savored the feast and the presence of those dearest to us.

A contented smile played across Merlin's lips as he surveyed the table before him. "Despite my countless years, I feel a newfound vibrancy, surrounded by love and friendship. The union between Arthur and Merlonius shines with the brilliance of a rising star. I am filled with pride to have played a part in this unforgettable occasion."

"Your continual understanding and support of our joining," Merlonius said, her look shifting between Merlin and Bedwyr, "has breathed new life into our hopes and affirmed the truth of our commitment. We shall treasure this night and the gift of having both of you here, for it is beyond measure."

Bedwyr looked first to Merlonius, then to Merlin and me. "To witness the joining of your hearts is a memory I will carry with me always."

When we stood from the table, I gripped his forearm. "Safe travels back to Camelot, my friend. Your presence has made this night all the more meaningful."

He met my gaze with quiet strength. "Arthur, you are more than my king; you are also my friend."

Merlonius stepped forward, drawing him into a tight embrace. "Many thanks," she whispered, pressing a kiss to his cheek.

A slight smile softened his reserved manner. "M'lady, sharing this occasion with you has been a true honour."

He mounted his horse and, with a final, silent look, turned and rode into the fading night. We stood, watching as his figure dwindled into the distance, drawn into the calm of the night. As the last trace of him was lost to shadow, Merlin's words floated through the stillness, "Well then, let us return home now."

With a graceful wave of his staff, accompanied by a burst of radiant light, the table vanished, leaving behind a faint shimmer of magic.

We made our way back as the sun rose over the forest. The path, alive with the vibrant colors of dawn and the sweet aroma of wildflowers, seemed to echo the enchantment of the night.

Upon entering the cottage, Merlin asked, "Will you be here on the morrow, Arthur?"

"Yes, most definitely."

"Good, I shall return then for a short visit."

I met his wise, age-old eyes. "Merlin, through so many seasons of my life, you have stood beside me. To share this night with you, and to have your wisdom and magic woven into our joy, shall be a memory I will always carry within me."

Merlonius came near, her radiance undimmed by the night's end. She leaned in, placing a tender kiss on his cheek. "You have not only given me a life with you, but now you have joined me to the one whom I cherish most. Know that my gratitude to you will always endure."

His expression shifted, emotion settling over his features as her words touched him deeply. "Your kindness warms my heart, my dear," he replied, his eyes lingering on us before he cleared his throat, steadying himself. "Well then, I shall take my leave. May boundless happiness walk beside you on the path ahead."

We accompanied him to the door and stepped outside to bid him farewell. The winding trail towards his crystal cave beckoned him onward. We watched as his figure dissolved into the embrace of the trees, the first light of dawn spilling across the forest behind him.

CHAPTER 34

OUR LASTING BOND

Standing before the small cottage, my arm wrapped around Merlonius's shoulder, I offered silent thanks to the gods and goddesses for the enchanting events of the previous night. The handfasting ceremony had united us, and a profound serenity settled within me.

She turned towards me, her smile radiant, mirroring the bliss we both shared.

"How shall we spend our day?"

Her eyes brightened with anticipation. "Outdoors, without question. Perhaps we might ride to the meadow."

"Indeed. Let us go."

While she changed her garment, I wandered to the stream, its murmur and the earth's fresh scent wrapping around me. When she returned, sunlight danced in her hair, lending her an almost ethereal glow.

"You are more beautiful than ever," I said softly, pulling her close and savoring the taste of her honeyed lips in a kiss that lingered, tender and slow.

We proceeded to the paddock, the forest alive with the music of the wood nymphs. Merlonius mounted her new horse, Freedom, a spirited black mare with white speckles, a gift I had given her to help mend the void left by Sweetness. Though a year had passed since Sweetness died, she seemed never far from our side. I approached Odin, ears pricked as he waited eagerly for me. We made quick work of the saddles and mounted, our steeds carrying us into the green depths ahead.

The landscape stretched before us, unfolding in rolling hills and winding streams, accompanied by the melodies of birdsong. Merlonius's laughter, pure and free, drifted ahead of us on the wind, drawing us forward.

"We were much younger the last time we were here. Do you remember the way?" she called over her shoulder. Her spirit awakened a stirring within me, light and boundless, a feeling I had not known in too long.

The burden of my duties faded, replaced by an unbridled freedom. The warmth of the sun, the scent of blooming fields, and the sheer power of Odin beneath me filled me with the untamed spirit of the land. Our horses galloped freely, kicking up a cloud of dust that shimmered in the sunlight.

At last, we slowed, finding a tranquil spot beneath the shade of a great oak, the open pasture stretching before us. After securing our horses, we settled onto the cool grass, hands clasped.

"It has been too long since we have visited this place," she said wistfully.

"Indeed, but the memories of those times still remain. Returning here feels like a fitting celebration, a way to honour the love and promise our union holds."

She leaned into my shoulder. "Being here with you, like this, is all I have ever wished for."

An ache of sorrow tugged at me, knowing that my duties would soon pull me away. Unable to mask my emotions, I saw a tender knowing in her eyes as she met my look. Her fingers traced my cheek, her gaze holding mine.

"I will cherish every fleeting moment we have, Arthur."

I covered her hand with mine. "My love, from the day our paths first crossed, I dreamed of asking you to join me in a sacred union, to be my partner, to rear horses, and to raise children together."

"Oh, Arthur," she said softly. "When we met, I carried many fears, having lived with Merlin for little more than a year after my father and mother cast me away. Yet, from our first encounter, I was drawn to you, a force I could not resist.

"When you pulled the sword from the stone, I was truly happy for you, though I knew it meant we would be apart. The fear of losing you haunted me, but even in our separation, the tie between us only strengthened."

Listening, I felt pride for the strides we had made, sorrow for all we had endured, and gratitude for what we had forged through those trials.

"Merlonius, I cannot bear the thought of a life without you."

"I know your heart, Arthur. I, too, cannot envision this world without you beside me."

Her grip on my hand tightened, steadying me. "While our path may not lead to days filled with horses and children, we will never truly be apart. For as long as we hold each other in our hearts, our love will endure."

In her words, I found a bittersweet solace. Our journey, uncharted and uncertain, was filled with a love so deep and profound, it defied the very bounds of our existence.

Drawing her closer, I lifted her chin to me. Our lips met in a tender kiss, and in the sanctuary of each other's arms, we found comfort.

The sun drifted lower, its fading light stretching long across the land. A lull fell across the fields, the warmth of the day slowly yielding to the cool embrace of the eve. Reluctantly, we bid farewell to our peaceful haven and rode back to the paddock.

Tending to our horses stirred a swirl of emotions, each motion a reminder of how fleeting our time together was. We worked in unison, settling them for the night. With the task done, we returned to the cottage as the sky transformed before us, a vast canvas streaked with hues of crimson, violet, and deep indigo.

We had little desire for more food after the bountiful feast gifted us by Merlin. After pouring fresh water into the goblets, Merlonius slid mine across the table with a slow, deliberate push, her brow arched ever so slightly.

"Shall we play our game of casting stones?"

Chuckling, I retrieved the leather sack from the basket near the hearth, knowing how much she enjoyed this pastime.

"Why not?"

She picked up the stones, each marked with lines, and threw first. The satisfying sound of the marked stones rattled on the wooden table as they tumbled back and forth.

"I have a feeling I am going to beat you this time," she teased. "Two threes."

"Is that so?" I retorted playfully. "We shall see."

Taking my turn, I gathered the casting stones in my hand and released them onto the table.

"A three and a four, I win this throw."

I leaned back with a triumphant grin, meeting her playful gaze.

She laughed. "It seems the Fates favored you this time. But I shall not let you win again."

With each throw, her quick wit and playful remarks challenged me, and I was determined to outdo her. We spent the next few hours immersed in the friendly rivalry, exchanging laughter and jests, until, with grins of mutual surrender, we conceded to a tie.

Merlonius tilted her head slightly, a mischievous glint in her eye as her lips curved into a smile.

"Shall we retire now, Arthur?"

I met her gaze, slipping the casting stones back into their pouch.

"Nothing would bring me greater happiness."

We moved towards the bed, embraced by candlelight. Crystals on the small table near the wall cast shimmering fragments across the room, while the scent of lavender lingered in the air.

Together, we stood in the soft glow. Her skin pressed tenderly against mine, and her breath brushed my cheek in a whisper. The taste of her lips was as rich as wild nectar, and our movements flowed in a dance entirely our own. Every caress was a promise of forever, affirming the vows that united us. As we lost ourselves in each other, I knew I never wanted to let her go.

With a fervent kiss, we began to explore each other's bodies, our touches aligning, guided by instinct and desire. The night unfolded, and the pull between us deepened, fed by newfound fervor. Our breaths came in rhythmic gasps, stirring an intense passion that enveloped every inch of our being. Our whispered words and caresses transcended the mortal realm, weaving our souls together. Time seemed to drift away as we surrendered to the fullness of our ecstasy.

As the first rays of the morn seeped through the windows, a familiar faint sound reached our ears. Reluctantly, I pulled away from our tender embrace and quickly donned my garments. The tenderness we had just shared stayed with us, but the need for secrecy crept in, a faint shadow against our bliss. I pushed those worries aside, determined to hold onto the sweetness of these days a little longer.

When I opened the door, Merlin stood before me, bathed in the light of dawn. A smile rose unbidden as I beheld him.

"Merlin," I greeted. "Good morrow. Pray, come in."

"Many thanks, my boy."

He moved to the table where Merlonius had arranged a platter of fresh garden berries, their vibrant colors a fitting choice to break our fast. Beside them she set soft cheese and a loaf of crusty bread, with wooden cups of cool water close at hand.

After enjoying a bite, Merlin leaned forward, his gaze moving thoughtfully between us.

"Last night's ceremony was truly joyous. To see your love so openly celebrated was an honour beyond words."

"Merlin, the love Arthur and I share is a source of boundless joy, surpassing all I ever imagined."

"This sacred union fills my heart with more happiness than I ever expected. Having both of you in my life is a blessing I will treasure all my days."

Merlin rose, moving towards his workbench. His steps were unhurried, his expression contemplative, as if lost in reverie. He picked up a small bowl filled with water, now shimmering in the morn's light spilling through the open windows.

"Arthur," he began as he returned to the table, "there is something Merlonius and I would like to show you. You are aware that, much like myself, she is blessed with the gift of foresight. I have been teaching her the ancient art of scrying, a potent way to glimpse what is to come through water." He cast a glance at Merlonius, his eyes alight with pride as he continued, "Would you care to witness her newfound skill?"

Admiration and awe swelled within me as I saw the eagerness in her eyes, for she had embraced her gifts with both grace and courage.

"Pray, Merlonius, show me what you have mastered."

Merlin placed the bowl carefully on the table while Merlonius retrieved a crystal. With a slight tremor in her fingers, she lowered it into the bowl. Peering into the water, she glimpsed beyond the physical realm. Her voice, steady yet distant, carried an urgency that sent a chill through me.

"I see a great darkness. A woman, veiled in shadows, harbors ill will towards you, Arthur. In her chamber at Camelot, she delves into the forbidden arts."

Intrigue and dread drew me in, prompting me to lean forward, captivated. Beside her, Merlin's brow furrowed as he too viewed the troubling images she painted with her words.

"Merlonius, step away from this vision. Step away," he commanded, each word imbued with an undeniable authority.

With hesitant steps, she pulled back from the scrying bowl, her body retreating while her spirit remained tethered to the vision. Her eyes, shrouded in the mist of foresight, sought mine in a plea for clarity, then shifted to Merlin, questioning yet hesitant, the shadow of fear veiled within them.

"Who is this woman in my vision? Do you know of her?"

Merlin did not reply, his features betraying nothing of his inner deliberations. He seemed to be pondering, not just the answer, but the impact of this revelation. Finally, he spoke, his tone solemn and resolute.

"It is Morgan."

Her breath caught, and her expression tightened as though the name itself carried a weight too heavy to bear.

Merlin observed Merlonius, studying her reaction, testing the depth of her understanding. Then, after a brief pause, he turned to me. The usual composure and wisdom he exuded now seemed tinged with deeper concern.

Bracing myself against the unrest stirred by her vision, I deemed it necessary to be forthright. "Merlonius, you are aware of my half-sister, Morgan le Fay. I fear her intentions towards me are dark and perilous."

Noting her disquiet, Merlin's tone turned steady and reassuring. "There is no need to fear. I have woven protective spells around you, this forest, and even the walls of Camelot. Morgan's schemes will falter against them."

She heard his words, yet returned to unseen worlds. "Arthur, Morgan le Fay's reach extends closer than you think. In the dead of night, a serpent lies in wait, coiled beneath the guise of familiarity. It is poised to strike at the center of what you hold most dear. Beware, for it is Morgan herself who weaves this deceit to ensure your downfall."

She fell limp in Merlin's arms. Together, we eased her into a nearby chair. Her breaths came shallow and unsteady, her awareness waning like a dimming candle.

A deep unease settled in my chest as I knelt beside her, the sight of her so still striking something fragile within me. I could do nothing but wait and hope that she would return to me.

With a healer's touch, Merlin rubbed her wrists, drawing her back to wakefulness.

Her eyes fluttered open, slow to find mine. When they met, a glimmer of recognition passed through her, followed by confusion and urgency.

"Merlin, my vision… What does it portend?"

He took a measured breath, his expression heavy with contemplation. Resting his hand on her shoulder, he faced me and said, "It means we must be diligent in our efforts to keep Morgan at bay. We will do everything in our means to protect you, Arthur."

A grim certainty settled over me as I recognized the truth of her vision, a foreboding mirrored in Merlin's somber expression. It was clear that he too understood the threat Morgan posed.

Merlonius, grappling with the aftermath of her vision, looked earnestly at him. "Teach me, Merlin. I must learn to aid Arthur, to fend off Morgan's malice."

Sadness touched his features at her entreaty. "The Fates have spun their thread, my dear, and there is only so much we can change."

"There must be a way to stop her."

I could see her plea troubled him. "Merlonius, we will continue your studies and summon all the white magic within our reach."

Moving towards the hearth, Merlin retrieved a goblet. He offered it to her.

"Drink this. The valerian shall help soothe your mind and ease your spirits."

She drank, her features softening as the strain left her.

He took the cup from her before asking me, "I understand your duties call. How soon must you depart?"

I exhaled slowly. "Sadly, I must leave this day to address the affairs of court."

Merlonius sensed my concerns. "Arthur, what weighs on you?"

Pondering the complexities of kingship, I confided, "Some nobles resist my proposal to establish a common fund for the needy. Convincing them to part with even a fraction of their wealth is a daunting task. Yet, I firmly believe that aiding the least among us strengthens us all."

Merlin nodded approvingly. "You are on the right path. Remind them of our shared destiny. Those with much should always aid those with less.

"I will take my leave now. We shall meet again at Camelot before long."

When he reached the door, Merlonius rushed towards him. "When might I expect you again?"

Pausing at the threshold, he held her gaze. "Would this eve be too soon?"

"Not at all. I eagerly await your return."

She stood in place, watching as the door closed behind him. At last, she turned and walked to where I sat, joining me at the table.

"Your duties draw you away, Arthur. I know you must go, but I will miss you dearly."

"I wish it were otherwise," I confessed, taking her hand. "But I promise to return as soon as I am able."

"I know you will. Take heed and guard yourself well."

"You have my word," I assured her, drawing her into a comforting embrace that sought to soothe her worries.

Gathering my bag and securing my sword and scabbard, I prepared to depart. Merlonius accompanied me outside, where my steed, already saddled by Merlin, awaited me.

I held her once more, for parting from her was almost too much to bear. I buried my face in her hair.

"We are eternally bound, my love, my wife."

I drew back slightly, our lips meeting in a tender kiss that lingered, for neither of us wished to let go.

Once mounted, I forced myself not to look back, knowing the sight of her standing alone would undo me. Leaving the enchanted shelter of the forest, I guided Odin onto the solitary main road.

A rustling in the underbrush wrenched me from my thoughts. Three figures emerged from behind the thick oaks, their faces lost in the half-light of the forest. Their movements were quick, calculated, intent on catching an unsuspecting traveler unawares. My hand flew to the hilt of my sword, tightening in readiness for the impending fight. Yet, when they stepped into the sunlight, their ragged garments and desperate eyes became evident. Though they clutched pitchforks, they were ill-equipped for battle and posed little threat.

"Stand down, or face retribution," I warned, hoping for a resolution without unnecessary bloodshed.

At once, they dropped their pitchforks and fell to their knees, begging for mercy.

"Sire, we are not bandits but desperate men. Our families are starving, and we have no gold to buy wheat for bread. We do not wish to fight but have been driven to this end to feed our children."

"Rise," I commanded.

Taking thirty gold coins from my bag, I handed them to the one who had spoken, trusting it would provide a small measure of relief.

"Divide these coins amongst yourselves. It is a temporary measure, but it should suffice to buy wheat for your families."

Riding past them, their voices rose in unison, "Our heartfelt thanks, my lord. May the benevolent gods bestow their blessings upon you."

As I continued towards Camelot, I hoped that those unfortunate men would find a more sustainable path. The urgency to remedy the poverty and disparities plaguing our land grew stronger with each passing mile. My upcoming audience with the nobility was more vital than ever. The growing divide between rich and poor demanded immediate action, for if ignored, more individuals would be compelled to similar desperate acts.

The towers of the castle gradually came into view, rising in the distance like a beacon. Urging my steed onward, I galloped towards the gate, driven by a resolute purpose.

I dismounted and handed the reins to the waiting stable boys before making my way towards the great doors. Whatever challenges lay ahead, I would confront them directly.

Moving through the echoing halls, a tempest of emotions consumed me. Duty, love, and the foreboding sense of trials still to come stirred within me. I longed for the woman I loved and the life we could never truly share.

My path was set by Fate, my purpose clear, but my heart remained with Merlonius in the forest.

CHAPTER 35

WHAT THE FATES WITHHELD

After the joy of the handfasting ceremony with Merlonius, my return to Camelot ushered in weeks heavy with the affairs of the realm. We grappled with disagreements among the lords and faced potential threats that loomed at the edges of our peace, ready to disrupt what we had fought to secure. The nobility remained divided, not only over claims to land but also over my efforts to establish a common fund for the needy. My appeals for compassion met resistance, but I could not abandon this cause.

Managing Medrawt's rebelliousness required unceasing watchfulness, while the presence of the devious Morgan le Fay in the dark halls tested everyone's resolve. Days blurred into nights, each merging into the next in an unbroken rhythm of duty.

My chambers served as the center of planning and rule, where we tirelessly reviewed the kingdom's many conflicts. Bedwyr, my most trusted strategist, worked diligently at my side. Before us lay intricate diagrams, each line drawn and redrawn as we assessed the ever-shifting claims and allegiances across the realm. With practiced hands, we traced them, our quills shaping the fates of lordships onto the parchment. The darkness beneath Bedwyr's eyes mirrored my own, for neither of us had known true rest in far too long.

With a deep sigh, I leaned back in my chair. "There have been nearly three turnings of the full moon since I last saw Merlonius. I must find a way to escape Camelot's grasp, Bedwyr."

"Arthur, indeed, you must go to her. The nobility who are disputing these boundaries will arrive on the morrow. After that, I can attend to court affairs in your absence. Why not plan to leave as the sun sets?"

Suddenly, the doors to my chambers burst open with a resounding crash. Bedwyr and I rose swiftly, our warrior senses snapping to alertness. We reached for our swords in a swift, practiced motion, bodies braced and ready for the unfolding threat.

Merlin entered, his cloak draped around him like a dark mantle.

"Arthur, you must come with me now!"

"What has happened? Is Merlonius in peril?"

He stared at me, his eyes a turbulent sea of pain and conflict. His grey hair, unkempt and wild, framed a face lined with sorrow.

"Merlin, speak plainly—what has befallen her?"

"Merlonius… She was with child. She awaited your return to share the news. But at dawn, tragedy struck… it was not to be. She needs you now, more than ever."

I slowly sheathed my sword, feeling a dreadful emptiness. My surroundings seemed to fade into a distant mist.

"Bedwyr, can you oversee the court? I must be with her."

He responded with a solemn nod. "Go to her, Arthur. I will take care of matters here."

I grabbed my woolen cloak and hurried to Merlin's side. "Did you ride here?"

"Yes, my horse waits at the castle gate."

"Let us go to the stables."

We left my quarters swiftly and made directly for the stables, intent on reaching her without delay. I waited as the stable boy prepared Odin while Merlin went to retrieve his own horse. When he returned, I mounted my steed.

"Stay vigilant. Morgan may be lurking on the grounds, intent on trailing us."

"She will not," Merlin said, his tone sharp. "I will ensure she remains unaware of our departure."

With a swift motion, he raised his staff, the crystal at the tip glowing brightly. He lowered it, nodding to signal the matter was handled. Together, we rode towards the gate. Crossing the drawbridge, we gave our horses free rein, quickly reaching the edge of the enchanted forest.

We followed the path through the trees to the clearing and dismounted. After securing the reins to the paddock rail, we hurried to the cottage. She was seated by the hearth, turning as the door opened.

"Arthur… "

Hurrying to her side, I grasped her hand. The anguish she was enduring was evident in every tremble of her body. She attempted to rise, but weakness overtook her. Her cheeks were damp with sorrow.

"Merlin told me what you have endured."

"I carried a secret joy, waiting to share it upon your return. But at dawn…" She paused, the words caught within her, struggling to find the will to surface. She drew herself upright, and her pain poured forth. "It was not to be. In my dreams, I had glimpses of him. Oh, Arthur, he would have been our son."

"A son?"

"The visions came to me many a night. He had your features, and his hair was of a darker hue than mine. He was our son."

Overwhelmed, I could only enfold her in a tender embrace, holding her close as her tears found release.

Drawing on my strength, I whispered, "He will not be forgotten. Though he never drew breath in this world, he lives within us. What we lost will be honoured, always."

She held me tightly, as though anchoring herself in the storm. Neither of us moved, save for the steady rise and fall of breath shared in sorrow.

Merlin appeared beside us. "Nature, in its wisdom, sometimes takes these paths," he said quietly. "But now, we must look to your well-being and healing, Merlonius."

"He is wrapped in cloth, upon my bed. Please, Merlin, may we lay him to rest on the summit?"

Grief blurred my vision as her sorrow filled the space between us. That same despair shadowed his features.

"We will take your son to the summit and bury him there. A majestic tree will grow, its branches weaving a lasting shelter above him."

"May we go now, Merlin?"

"You must rest," I urged. "Merlin and I will bear him there."

"I wish to join you," her determination unwavering despite her frailty.

"The path, though not long, might be arduous in your current state."

"I have the strength to reach the base," she insisted. "With your help, I will make the climb. I cannot remain behind, for my place is with you and Merlin."

I exchanged a look with him, seeking his counsel.

He studied her for a moment before nodding.

"As you wish, my dear. Arthur, will you support her?"

I moved to her side, helping her rise from the chair. She leaned into me, her steps unsteady. I held her close as we made our way to the door.

He returned from the back of the cottage with a tiny bundle, cradling our lost son in his arms. Stepping outside, the forest enveloped us in a cocoon of mourning. The scent of pine pressed close, and damp earth clung to our boots as we followed the winding path in silence.

As we ascended, she began to falter. She pressed against my side, her breathing labored. Despite the difficulty, her will prevailed, and together we reached the summit.

Before us stretched rolling hills and dense forests, a view so serene it almost mocked our sorrow. In the distance, a grassy patch midway between the stream and the cliffs beckoned. It was a peaceful and secluded spot, perfect for our son's resting place. Slowly, we made our way there. When we arrived, I wrapped my arm around her waist, steadying her while her body trembled with sobs.

Merlin stepped forward, his staff in hand. He raised it high, and the ground parted like a deep wound, silent and raw beneath his whispered incantations. Next to it, a wooden box appeared, formed from the essence of the forest itself. With reverence, he tenderly placed our son in it. Then, with a final motion, he placed the lid on top, sealing away a piece of our hearts.

A tide of pain rose within me, relentless and deep, as if it sought to drown my breath. Tears blurred the verdant landscape into shades of grey, each gasp sharp and biting like a winter's chill. A tightness gripped my chest as if bound by rope, and my hands trembled. With effort, I steadied myself and stepped forward. Together, we lowered the box into the ground. He raised his staff once more, and the earth closed over it. With a solemn nod, we returned to her side.

We stood in stillness, hearts bound by the sacred act we had just performed.

Slowly, pushing aside his own sorrow, Merlin's voice rose strong. "Oh, Great Spirit, we ask that you protect and guide well the son of Arthur and Merlonius on his journey from the setting sun, through the darkness to the light, and to his place of peace."

She leaned heavily against me, her tears soaking into my tunic. Merlin, too, wept, his usual composure shattered by anguish.

He raised his staff again, and a sapling sprouted swiftly where we had just laid our son to rest. Its slender form rose up, its leaves reaching for the sky, driven by an unseen force. We stood witness as the tiny plant grew before us, rising into a towering tree, its wide branches cloaking the earth in solemn shade.

Merlonius spoke softly, her voice barely more than a breath, fragile and nearly carried away by the wind. "I cannot believe he is gone. Our poor son…"

I tightened my embrace around her. "He is not alone, my love. This tree, this enchanted guardian, will watch over him, cradling him in its embrace, sheltering him always."

Merlin stepped forward, and I followed, placing my hand upon its rough bark. A rhythmic pulse beneath my palm, strong and warm, carried the essence of life and magic now intertwined with this sacred place.

"Behold," he said, "this ancient keeper shall stand over your son's resting place, holding silent vigil for time beyond measure."

We stood there in reverent silence. Then, as though answering an unspoken call, a large black crow circled above. It descended with effortless grace and perched on Merlin's outstretched arm. A memory stirred briefly in my mind—the same majestic bird, seemingly untouched by time, had delivered a message to him when I was just a boy.

Merlin lowered his arm slowly, meeting the crow's gaze. He listened intently to its cries.

"You have done what was asked of you, faithful one. Go now, and be at peace."

The bird cawed one last time, then, with a mighty flap of its wings, took flight, soaring into the sky.

When the crow disappeared into the distance, he inhaled deeply before turning to us. "Bedwyr needs my help. Morgan le Fay is causing unrest, and I must intervene. Let us return to the cottage and see to Merlonius before I depart."

"Merlin, Morgan will use any and all means to undermine my rule. Bedwyr is strong, but I fear he is no match for her dark magic."

"Indeed, he is not. Come, let us begin our return."

We made our way down the incline, steady and watchful. When we reached the bottom, Merlonius faltered. I carried her the rest of the way and laid her on the bed.

"Rest now, for I must speak with Merlin before he departs."

I motioned for Merlin to step outside, my concern for Merlonius consuming me.

"What can I do to help her? Is she in real danger?"

"Her condition is fragile, but there is no immediate peril. I have prepared healing teas and have left them on the workbench. Encourage her to drink them. For now, stay close, and I will return as swiftly as possible."

I watched him mount his horse with practiced ease and cast one last glance in my direction before he galloped towards Camelot.

Returning inside, I found her awake and placed a chair beside her bed.

"Arthur, Merlin has been most attentive, insisting I remain near. I awaited your return, longing to share the joy of our child with you."

Tears trickled down her cheeks as I clasped her hand, feeling its slight tremble.

"My love, knowing Merlin has cared for you lightens my sorrow. Yet know truly, I would have treasured hearing of our child from you. Though my heart breaks with yours, let us now tend to your healing."

She wept as I brushed back her hair.

"Shall I bring you some of Merlin's healing tea, to ease you?"

She reached for my hand, her fingers curling around mine with quiet need. "Yes… that would comfort me."

I brought the tea, its soothing herbal scent rising as I placed it in her hands. She drank slowly, the colour gradually returning to her cheeks. When she had finished, she rested the empty vessel in her lap, a trace of calm settling over her.

"Try to rest now," I said gently, taking the cup and drawing the blankets higher to keep her warm.

I held her hand until her eyes closed, watching as she drifted into sleep. Touching her forehead to ensure no fever had taken hold, I was relieved to find it cool. With one last look at her resting form, I turned towards the window.

The setting sun cast long shadows across the forest floor, its fading light filtering through the trees. I stood there for a while, the silence deepening around me. Then, quietly, I walked to the front door and made my way to the paddock.

"Odin, I have not forgotten you," I said softly as his warm breath brushed my palm and he whickered. Leading him into the enclosure, I removed the saddle and bridle he had worn since our hurried ride to Merlonius's side. He stood patiently while I tended to him, his loyalty as constant as ever. I ran my hand along his neck, and he leaned into my touch.

"You have water, hay, and oats, my friend. Sorrow fills me, and I cannot linger this eve, but I promise to return."

From the edge of the enclosure, Freedom, Merlonius's horse, approached. I rubbed the sweet spot between her eyes.

"Ah, my friend, your mistress shall visit soon. She is presently unwell."

As if understanding, Freedom nuzzled my chest before turning away.

After ensuring both Odin and Freedom were well tended, my steps carried me back. I found her in peaceful slumber, her breath soft and steady. A deep and abiding love swelled within me, but beneath it lay the lingering truth of my absence, and the guilt it left behind.

I knelt beside the bed, brushing a strand of hair from her forehead. Her skin felt cool beneath my hand, and in her stillness, I understood the strength she carried, even in the face of such sorrow. *How much more must she bear, while I remain bound to the demands of the realm?*

Drawn to the still of the night, I moved to the window at the front of the cottage. The towering trees stood against the fading light, their silhouettes motionless. The murmur of the nearby stream rose softly around me, easing my restless thoughts. Even in darkness, the natural world offered a sliver of solace, a reminder of the peace I sought with Merlonius.

The door opened. I turned as Merlin entered, his steps quiet on the floor.

"Arthur, we must talk."

We stepped outside and went to the stream's edge. The sky had deepened into a vast expanse of darkness, scattered with stars. A cool breeze urged me to pull my cloak tighter around my shoulders.

"Bedwyr has been handling the court affairs admirably," Merlin began. "He is concerned for Merlonius and asked after her well-being. I assured him she would recover soon and foretold your return to the castle within three days. Does this plan suit you?"

"It does, yet I am hesitant to leave her side while her strength is not yet restored."

Merlin gave a small nod. "She will be well tended, Arthur."

He paused, his gaze lifting towards the darkened sky. "Let us now speak of the treachery Morgan has wrought in your absence."

I kept my gaze upon the flowing water as his words began to unfold.

"She has ensnared those driven by greed and envy, those who lust for power, stirring them into chaos. She has also spread rumours, claiming you have abandoned your throne. I confronted her near your quarters. Her dark magic holds no sway over me, and I warned her that she would suffer tenfold for what she had wrought.

"Though I have broken her spell over the weakened nobility, the suspicion it sowed lingers. Those who began to question your reign now dread your return. Still, rest assured, Bedwyr will face no further hindrances during your brief absence."

"Morgan persists in her plots against me," I said, my jaw tightening as anger stirred within me.

"She is indeed a formidable adversary, Arthur. We must always be vigilant against her schemes."

I pushed Morgan from my mind. "What of Merlonius? Will she fully recover?"

Merlin's eyes briefly closed as he gathered his thoughts. When he spoke, his voice was measured.

"Physically, she will mend, but the omens are clear—her womb will bear no more children. This revelation will deeply wound her spirit. We must surround her with all the compassion and support she needs as she walks this path of sorrow."

He regarded me intently, awaiting my response. Emotion constricted my speech. "Merlin, she is the very heart of my life. I cannot fathom a future without her by my side, nor would I seek another for the sake of heirs." Silence held me before I spoke again. "Has she been made aware of this?"

"No, but we must discuss this with her before you return to Camelot."

"I agree, but for now, let us return to her. I do not wish her to wake and find me absent."

Together, we entered the cottage, the quiet within wrapping around us. The faint glow from the fire cast a gentle light over the room as we walked back to her side.

He lightly touched her forehead and whispered, "The fever has been kept at bay. Good, very good." We looked at each other in silent understanding before he moved to tend the flames.

Merlin's revelation deepened the sorrow we already bore from the loss of our son. She lay asleep, her breaths even and slow. Each one renewed my commitment to support her and to remain steadfast against the harsh decrees of destiny.

How could the Fates be so merciless to one so undeserving?

The first rays of sunlight painted the horizon as I took her hand. "Merlonius, the morn calls," I whispered.

She stirred, her eyes fluttering open with a look of confusion and weariness. Turning towards me, she murmured, "Arthur?"

"Yes, it is I." I brushed a tender kiss across her forehead. "How do you fare?"

"Somewhat improved."

Her answer was simple, but the shadows in her eyes told me the pain was still with her.

"Would you care to rise and take a few steps?"

She nodded. "I think that would help."

"Allow me," I offered, extending my hand to help her rise.

"Might we sit at the table?"

Arm in arm, we walked slowly to the wooden bench where I guided her to sit. Just then, the door creaked open, and Merlin stepped in. The candle flames swayed, bowing greeting, and the once-cool space filled with a mysterious warmth. Light bloomed in his presence, reaching into the shadowed corners. Even the familiar creaks and whispers fell silent, as if in reverence to him.

"Merlonius, it is heartening to see you out of bed. How do you fare?"

"Much better." Her voice was stronger than before, though her pale face and the faint tremor of her hands betrayed her frailty.

Her eyes found mine, the question already forming. "Arthur, how long can you stay?"

Meeting her gaze, I yearned to promise that I would stay with her always, but my oath to the kingdom forbade such freedom.

"I will remain by your side for the next two days," I assured her, holding her hand. "I will not depart until I see your strength return and color rise to your cheeks."

"To have you by my side, even for two days, gives me strength I could not find alone."

Merlin walked to the workbench and returned with a tray bearing steamy broth, freshly baked bread, and a jug of cool water.

"I am grateful for the food and water, but I truly do not feel like eating," she said, mustering a weak smile.

"Merlonius, you must eat something. It will aid your recovery," he urged.

With some hesitation, she picked up the spoon and sipped the clear broth, then nibbled on a small piece of bread.

I leaned closer and inquired, "Shall we step outside for a short while?"

"Yes, Arthur, I think I would like that."

Merlin, sitting across from us, watched her closely. Catching his eye, I said, "Would you care to join us?"

"A breath of fresh air would do us all good. Let us go now."

A breeze swirled about us as we settled onto the benches in front of the cottage.

"Merlonius…"

"Yes, Merlin?"

"As you know, the Fates decree much of our lives, and often the reasons behind events remain hidden from us. Even with our gifts of sight, the intricate workings of destiny often elude our grasp."

He glanced at me, then back to her. "You and Arthur share a bond that transcends the ordinary. Nothing will ever truly sever what you have. Yet, the loss you have endured reveals a profound and painful certainty. The visions that have come to me in the night spoke of this hidden danger. Had the child continued to grow within you, your life would have been placed in peril, beyond our power to save."

She wept, and I held her close, offering what comfort I could.

Merlin leaned slightly forward. "Since this loss, my magic has revealed a stark truth. The ordeal has left unseen scars, ones that time cannot mend. It is beyond my power, or any known magic, to restore what has been lost. Merlonius, you have endured much, yet the natural order has shifted unalterably. You will not bear another child."

He withdrew a small crystal marked with ancient symbols from his robe. "With your permission, I shall seek further clarity."

She gave the slightest nod, and he placed the crystal over the place where life once grew. A soft radiance shimmered from within, its glow wavering before slowly dimming. His expression turned solemn.

"The crystal confirms my fears. The life-giving force within you has faded. My dear, the capacity to carry another child has departed from you. The Fates, in their silence, chose only now to reveal this truth."

She stared at him, her brows furrowed, searching his words for meaning. Slowly, she turned to me, her eyes reflecting the turmoil within.

"Arthur, I am so very sorry."

I clasped her hand. "Merlonius, my love for you is unshaken. You are my heart, my life, my very breath. Never doubt that."

She shook her head, the words flowing from her as if pulled by an unseen force. "I truly believed that our paths had shifted, defying the decrees of the Fates, when you asked me to wed. When I discovered I was with child, my spirit soared with this hope."

Tears flowed and I pulled her close, stroking her hair as she leaned against my chest. After composing herself, she continued, looking to Merlin.

"To lose our son, and now to hear that I may never hold Arthur's child in my arms… I do not know how much more I can bear."

I held her tightly, and though Merlin said nothing at first, the sorrow in his eyes revealed how deeply he, too, mourned for her.

"My dear Merlonius, it takes great courage to accept the path of destiny laid out for us by the Fates. I have the utmost faith in your inner fortitude."

The silence was like thunder, echoing around us as we confronted what lay before us. She turned towards the ancient trees, seeking solace in their enduring presence.

I placed my hand over hers, our fingers intertwining.

"Our loss is profound, but the unyielding nature of my love for you surpasses even that. You are not alone in this."

"Oh, Arthur," she whispered, "words fail me in easing our pain."

Casting her gaze downward, she gathered herself before looking to Merlin.

"Merlin, you have always been my guiding star, and now, in sharing this painful truth, you shine with a brilliance I have always trusted."

"Ah, strength is the story we weave together. Now, let us return to the warmth of the cottage, and allow yourself to rest."

"I am forever grateful that the Fates guided our paths to ensure we were together."

"As am I, my dear."

I helped Merlonius to her feet, keeping her close as we walked.

The hearth's warmth greeted us, but no fire could chase away the ache lodged deep within our hearts. The loss of our son and the cruel certainty that we would never share a child pressed upon me. Yet as I guided her to the bed, a steady resolve took hold.

Our future had been reshaped, but it was still ours to forge. Whatever lay ahead, I would stand with her, and together we would face the unknown.

CHAPTER 36

IN THE SHADOW OF DEPARTURE

I knelt beside her, carefully arranging the pillows and blankets, offering a small comfort amid our shared sorrow. She turned towards me, her eyes clouded with sadness.

"I will strive to accept what the Fates have decreed, though the burden is great."

"Aye, it is heavier than most. I know your strength and courage, and I will help you carry it."

"Arthur, without you in my life… I do not know if I could find the will to carry on."

"Merlonius, I will never leave you. My own life would have no meaning without you a part of it."

She reached for me. Our lips met in a kiss that held more sorrow than words ever could. "I love you," I murmured against her lips. I caressed her face, whispering, "Now, sleep and find what peace you can."

As she drifted into slumber, her breaths slow and even, I stayed with her. The events of the day, still sharp and pressing, intertwined with the ever-evolving narrative of our lives. Merlonius held the calm I yearned for, a presence of stability in the chaos of our world.

A faint stirring signaled Merlin's approach, his figure emerging in the dim light.

"She is improving, Arthur. It is best if you join me while she rests."

We sat opposite each other at the table, concern and weariness evident between us. My thoughts lingered on my life with her and the awe I felt for her gift of sorcery. I met Merlin's gaze.

"How is she wielding her gifts?"

"Her sight is expanding, and she is mastering control over the visions she once struggled to command. Her progress is remarkable."

His words pleased me, though a shadow of concern still lingered, born of the times I could not remain at her side.

"I am finding it increasingly difficult to part from her, more so than ever before."

"Arthur, I understand full well the hardship of your separation. When I must leave her alone in this cottage, in this vast forest, to attend to other matters, even with my magic, I do not rest easy until I return. The Fates have woven a tapestry that is often beyond our understanding. Such is often their way, is it not? But for now, let us find solace in each other's company and share a goblet of wine."

Rising, he retrieved a pitcher of rich red wine. After filling our goblets, we each drank deeply before he spoke again.

"I am very sorry for the loss of your son. Though I had rejoiced at the promise of new life within our clan, I understand that his departure was for the best."

"Merlin, years ago, I allowed myself to wonder what a child born of the love we share would look like. I knew wishing for a child would not serve the greater good of our clan, the land, or the child.

"My concern for her overshadows the loss of our child… yet I still linger on the son we lost." My grip tightened on the goblet in an attempt to steady my trembling hands.

He rested a reassuring hand over mine.

"Arthur, you bear the fortitude and courage of kings before you. We will weather this storm together as a loving clan does."

Lifting his goblet in a toast, he declared, "To our clan, may we always find strength in each other."

Following his lead, I lifted my goblet to his. A calm settled between us, yet I could not help but reflect on the difficulties awaiting me. Court politics and the looming threats of Morgan and Medrawt demanded my attention. Amidst these daunting challenges, hope endured, sustained by Merlin's steadfast presence and unwavering guidance.

Composure reclaimed me, and I rose. "I should go to her. Many thanks for the wine."

A low moan from Merlonius drew our attention. We hurried to her side, and Merlin pressed his palm to her forehead, his brow knitting as he exhaled sharply.

"She has a fever. Arthur, quickly, bring me the cloths and the bowl with the tincture I prepared."

I retrieved them without delay. He immersed the strips of cloth into the liquid, wringing them gently before laying them on her forehead. His fingers trembled, not from uncertainty but from the gravity of the moment.

"This fever must not take hold," he murmured.

As I watched, Merlin stood over her, his hands hovering above her frail form. Steady and commanding, he wove ancient incantations into the air, each syllable resonating with a power beyond mortal understanding.

"Anál nathrach, orth' bháis's bethad, do chél dénmha."

Breath of the serpent, spell of life and death, weave thy fate.

He lifted his staff, tracing unseen sigils in the air, his presence imposing, the wisdom of those who came before him resting upon his shoulders. The candlelight quivered, as though bending to his will. Without pause, he intoned another invocation in the ancient tongue:

"Glaodh air dòighean àrsaidh, na deamhain a thoirmeasg, agus na beannachdan a thoirt."

Call upon the ways of old, banish the demons, and bestow the blessings.

His free hand pressed lightly above her heart, and for a moment, a faint shimmer stirred beneath his palm. Then, drawing in a deep breath, he uttered one final invocation.

"Neart na cruinne, sruth na beatha, thig agus neartaich a corp."

Strength of the earth, flow of life, come forth and fortify her body.

The fever clung to her stubbornly, yet his persistence did not wane. Throughout the rest of the day, we diligently changed the cloths, tending to her with constant care. Merlin remained vigilant, reinforcing the enchantment whenever her skin burned too hot, whispering words of power as he mixed fresh tinctures to aid in her healing.

By late eve, the fever had broken, and she was in a restful sleep. Merlin withdrew his hand from her brow and straightened, his weariness evident. "The worst has passed. The Fates have not called her away this night."

"Merlin, my deepest thanks to you, to your magic, and to the gods and goddesses who have heard our plea. I do not know if I can leave her."

"You must. Bedwyr alone cannot hold back the tide of Morgan's deceptions for long. Once you have quelled the fears she is spreading, you can return. I will ensure she is well cared for and with time, she will heal."

I knew he spoke with reason, yet it did little to ease the sorrow tightening around my heart.

"Arthur, we must keep our resolve. Come, let us eat."

Leading me towards the hearth, Merlin raised his staff and pointed it at the table. The crystal at its tip glowed, summoning a modest meal of stewed meat with parsnips and beets.

Once our bowls were empty, I placed my spoon down and looked at Merlin. "This meal is a gift, and I am grateful."

"It is my pleasure, Arthur."

I returned to Merlonius's side. When her fever did not return, relief settled over me, and I offered a silent prayer to the gods and goddesses. At the first light of dawn, she awoke. Merlin, tending to the hearth, came towards us.

"How are you faring?"

Her lips curved into a faint smile despite her weakness. "I am much improved."

A brief pause passed between them before she added, "May I rise and wash?"

"Yes, with Arthur's help."

He picked up the wooden bowl and woven cloths, then made his way back to the workbench, leaving us alone.

"My love, I am relieved to see you gaining strength," I said, taking her hand. "Let me help you stand."

She leaned on me, bracing herself and mustering all she could. We waited, allowing her time to regain her balance.

"Can you assist me in changing into a clean garment?"

"Of course."

I retrieved a modest dress from the shelf.

She glanced down at herself, and I placed a tender kiss on her forehead. "You look more than presentable."

When we reached the table, Merlin poured water into a wooden goblet and set it in front of her.

"What can I get you?"

"This water and a piece of bread would be fine."

I noticed a subtle tremble in her hands as she reached for the goblet. She had endured so much. In a brief exchange of glances with Merlin, we shared an unspoken concern.

"Is something troubling you, my dear?"

Avoiding his searching look, she caught her lower lip between her teeth, her fingers fidgeting with the goblet's rim.

"No, Merlin."

I could sense her inner struggle, the pain she carried but did not voice. She sipped the cool liquid and and nibbled on the crust, the scent of toasted grain drifting upward as she ate. She glanced at me, then at Merlin, tears welling up, betraying sorrow and fear.

Merlin pressed, "Merlonius, what weighs on your mind?"

She hesitated, her hands tightening slightly on the goblet before she spoke.

"Last night, I had a dream, a haunting vision of Arthur's half-sister, Morgan. In the depths of my slumber, I saw her drifting through the halls of Camelot like a shadow carried on the wind, her presence both seen and unseen. She whispered vile untruths into the ears of men and women, her dark magic winding its way into their hearts. Her intent was clear. She sought to harm Gwenhwyfar and, by extension, you, Arthur. I woke with a lingering dread for your safety upon your return to the castle."

Her expression was haunted, still bearing the remnants of the dream. She looked to Merlin.

"Was it more than just a dream? Did I truly step into that twisted realm?"

Merlin peered past the veil, lost in something beyond the present. Her questions hung in the air, and after a long pause, he finally spoke.

"Merlonius, your spirit ventured beyond the confines of your slumbering body. I, too, have felt Morgan's malice. But fear not, for we remain firm in our purpose to protect all that is dear to us, not only Arthur but also you and Bedwyr. Trust in the power of white magic."

"Oh, Merlin, I do not doubt, yet my strength wanes. How can I possibly aid in protecting you, Arthur, and Bedwyr?"

"Know this, your health and spirit will soon be restored."

"Merlonius, with Merlin's boundless sorcery and Bedwyr's staunch loyalty, we shall withstand Morgan's plots. Together, the darkness she conjures will falter in the face of our light."

She hesitated, lowering her eyes briefly. She closed them, drawing in a slow, measured breath. When she opened them again, a faint glimmer of determination lit her eyes, like a candle slowly rekindling.

"With both of you by my side, how can we not succeed?"

Watching her, I was struck by her fortitude, and my admiration deepened. Though shaken, her spirit remained unbroken. In that moment, I realized again how deeply I loved her, and how much harder it was to step away from the woman who embodied both grace and strength to return to the demands of the crown.

"Arthur, when must you depart?"

"Alas, I must depart on the morrow to dispel the whispers of my absence," I confessed, reluctant to speak the words aloud. "Were there any other way, I would not choose to part from you both."

"Have no concerns, Arthur, for I shall heal."

"I will return to you as soon as I am able."

Merlin glanced between us, sensing, as I did, the sorrow she tried to hide.

"I will keep you company by night, Merlonius, but must leave each morn after ensuring your comfort. Arthur requires my support at court to quell the discord and doubts seeded by Morgan."

"Merlin, I am grateful for your care, but you need not worry for me. With each day, I feel my recovery taking hold." She looked at me before adding, "He needs your wisdom and guidance now more than ever."

With a heavy heart, I met their eyes.

"Once Merlonius has regained her well-being, would you both join me in honouring our son on the summit?"

She exchanged a glance with Merlin, a small smile touching her lips before she nodded. "Yes, Arthur, that is our wish as well."

"Very well, then. Shall we sit outside and let the forest offer its healing?"

"An excellent suggestion, my boy. Shall we Merlonius?"

She rose and took my hand. Together, we stepped out and settled on the stone benches facing the stream, its gentle current catching the last of the light. Merlin's words floated around us.

"Arthur, as I once shared with Merlonius, my father was King of the Fae. My mother met him when they were both young, running free through the woods." He turned to Merlonius, his expression softening. "Your love of the forest is so much like hers."

"Merlin, I am honoured that you have shared this knowledge with me."

He nodded slowly. "It was time, Arthur."

With that, he turned to the stream, his gaze distant, lost in memory.

I gently squeezed Merlonius's hand. She looked at me, and in that shared glance, we understood: Merlin was now seeing in worlds we could not.

As the sun sank below the horizon, its fading glow stretched across the land, bathing the trees and fields in its final light. We rose in silence and returned to the cottage.

I tended the fire while Merlonius settled into a chair by the hearth. Weariness soon overtook her, and she drifted into slumber.

Quietly, I slipped away in search of Merlin and found him tending the garden.

"Merlin, I would like to assist in preparing this night's meal."

"Of course. Gather a few stalks of chard, and we shall begin."

We returned with measured steps, mindful not to disturb her, and made our way to the back workbench. With a wave of his hand, he set flame to several candles, their golden glow blending with the last light of day streaming through the high window.

He handed me the chard and turnips from the garden. While I chopped the chard and peeled the turnips, the candlelight curled along the walls, shaping soft patterns.

"Merlin, this brings back memories of when I was young, and you would visit Sir Ector's farm. We would spend the day in the forest, and you would teach me how to prepare the vegetables for the stew we cooked over the fire pit."

He smiled, his thoughts drifting to the past. "Yes, I remember those days fondly. I am glad you have not forgotten what I have taught you."

"They were joyous times."

"Yes, my boy, they truly were."

We added the chard and turnips to the pot just as Merlonius stirred. Merlin gingerly touched her forehead.

"Your fever has remained at bay."

"Yes, Merlin, I am faring much better."

Joining them, I noted, "The warmth is returning to your face."

She looked up at me and smiled.

When the meal was ready, we gathered around the table. We ate and talked until Merlin noticed her growing fatigue.

"Merlonius, Arthur will be here when you awaken. You should take your ease."

"I believe I shall."

She rose, and we walked slowly to her bed. She settled under the blankets. I leaned in and whispered, "Rest well, I love you."

"As I love you, Arthur."

I remained by her side, watching as her breathing settled into a peaceful rhythm. Once I was certain she was comfortable, I quietly returned to the table where Merlin waited. We spoke in hushed tones, careful not to disturb her.

"Merlin, I will do my utmost to visit often, even if only for a short while. By using the secret passageway, Morgan will remain unaware of my movements."

"That is wise, and your visits will bring Merlonius great comfort."

"Since my earliest memories, you have been a source of guidance, wisdom, and support. And now, I must entrust to you the one soul I cherish above even my own life. For this, and for all you have given, I offer my deepest thanks."

"My boy, you give more than you know to my own humble existence. Go to her now, and I shall see you in the morn."

I returned to her side. As the night wore on, exhaustion slowly overcame me. My eyes closed, and I drifted into a light sleep. Just as dawn's first light kissed the cottage, she stirred.

"Arthur, good morrow."

"How do you fare?"

She sat up with care and eased her legs to the side.

"See how much stronger I am," she said, making an effort to show her improved health. "You can prepare to leave when you must; I am truly healing."

Drawn by our voices, Merlin approached, a glimmer of relief and joy lighting his features.

"Merlonius, you are faring exceptionally well. Splendid news indeed!"

A radiant smile lit up her countenance.

Not a single part of me wished to leave, but duty beckoned with an unrelenting call.

"I must depart for Camelot."

"I will take care of her. You need not worry."

While fastening my scabbard and sword around my waist, Merlonius came to me and wrapped her arms around my neck. I held onto her, cherishing the memory of her embrace.

"You have my heart, Arthur," she whispered into my ear.

"And you, mine, always." My own heart ached with the wish that time would stand still.

"Merlin, pray, inform me of any changes in her well-being."

"Of course, Arthur. She is much stronger now and on the path to recovery. After she has had some food and drink, I will follow you."

I made my way to the paddock, saddled my steed, and mounted him. Pausing briefly, I cast a final glance towards the cottage, holding fast to the memory of her within. I urged Odin onto the road that would take me back to Camelot and to all that awaited me.

The enchanted forest gradually faded behind me, and Merlonius's belief about defying the Fates filled my mind, a fragile hope I dared not dismiss. She believed our paths had changed when we wed. I pondered whether the loss of our son was part of a grander design, a course shaped by the gods to protect our intertwined lives.

These musings mingled with my grief for our loss and the sorrow of leaving her behind. Duty called to me, and I vowed I would return.

CHAPTER 37

RUMORS AND RESILIENCE

The road stretched ahead beneath Odin's steady hooves, yet my thoughts lingered behind. Her touch remained with me, her whispered vow still warm in my ear, and the ache of never holding my son hollowed my chest.

The wind began to rise, sweeping the dust along the path and lifting the edge of my cloak. Overhead, the sky had darkened to a brooding grey. Thunder rumbled low across the hills, echoing the unrest within me. Odin, faithful and calm, pressed on without need of command.

My life as High King had taught me to bear my burdens in silence, to guard what remained of the man beneath the crown. But the wound still raw within me pressed too deeply. I needed to speak, not to a council, nor to kin, but to the one companion who would not judge.

Thus, I spoke to Odin as I rode, of the doubts that haunted me, of the heaviness we carried, and of the pain of leaving her side once more. His ears flicked in response. Though he made no sound, his steady presence was a balm. In his strength, I found a measure of my own.

At last, the castle came into view, rising from the hills like a memory I had sought to hold back. Its high towers stood outlined against the darkening sky, solemn and unyielding. We crossed the drawbridge, and I brought him to a halt at the great doors. A boy stepped forward and took the reins with a respectful nod. His eyes lingered on me, wide and uncertain.

Does he see a legend? A king? I am merely a man, as he will one day be, carrying my own shadows.

I stepped through the castle doors, the sound of my boots echoing across the stone floor. I straightened my shoulders, the weight of all I had endured pressing close: love, loss, and duty. Still, I would not yield. Not now.

The sound of fervent discussion reached me as I neared the chamber of the Round Table. From somewhere within the castle, the delicate strains of a lute drifted faintly.

Upon entering, I found the nobles gathered near the Round Table, locked in disagreement as they challenged Bedwyr's position. Torchlight danced across their faces, the air thick with incense and sweat. Their arguments clashed in a discord of conflicting interests.

"Compromise seems to have eluded everyone's tongue, has it not?"

Conversations stopped mid-sentence, and all turned towards me. Disbelieving stares met mine as I stepped forward.

I addressed those assembled with authority and some weariness.

"Yes, it is I, King Arthur. I perceive the doubt among you, kindled by malicious rumors that I have forsaken my oath as High King. Be assured, such a notion shall never come to pass! Our realm is vast, and an urgent matter in a distant region demanded my immediate attention. In my absence, I entrusted Bedwyr to uphold the duties of the court, and I am disappointed to learn that his position was not respected."

The nobles' objections faded into a murmur as I approached Bedwyr. Moving with purpose, I stood by his side and quieted the gathering with a commanding look.

"Bedwyr, your perseverance has been a cornerstone of all we have withstood. Loyalty and commitment such as yours are beyond reckoning. Pray, provide me with a detailed account of the events that unfolded during my absence."

Once he had finished, the discussions resumed, now with greater structure and civility. Within the hour, Merlin arrived, and all eyes turned towards him as he entered.

"Hail, Merlin. Please join us." I gestured for him to approach Bedwyr and me.

He addressed the assembled nobles in a clear voice. "Greetings to you all. We remain hopeful for a peaceful understanding in these matters."

Silence settled over the chamber at his words, and with his appearance, it was clear that our authority remained absolute and our kingdom unified.

The men who clashed in discord now worked towards accord. At last, after three hours of deliberation, a formal agreement was reached. With the nobles and kings departing, their grievances settled, I welcomed the stillness that followed.

"Merlin, pray, how does Merlonius fare?" I inquired.

"She rests, showing signs of healing, though the path to her full recovery will be long."

Worry for her pressed hard upon me, and I found no words to offer in reply.

Bedwyr broke the silence. "Arthur, might I propose this: depart under the veil of night, after our meal, through the secret passage. I shall keep watch should those who seek your presence wander to our quarters. By doing so, you will have the freedom to be with Merlonius, returning before the darkest hour."

At his words, I saw our shared sorrow in his eyes. "I am grateful for your offer and shall proceed as you suggest."

"Arthur, know that your grief is not yours alone. My heart stands with you in this loss."

The thought of my son, knowing I would never cradle him, tightened my chest. All I could offer was a nod.

Merlin's hand came to rest on my shoulder. "Bedwyr, Merlonius would not have survived the birth of this child. Such an end would have been an unfathomable tragedy."

"Indeed, Merlin. A child might have brought gladness, but her death would have left us hollow."

"Our clan would never have regained its joy had Merlonius crossed to the Otherworld. Her laughter and her gift of healing could never be replaced."

Merlin shook his head slowly, the pain of this possible future settling around us.

Pushing aside thoughts of what might have been, I said, "Shall we proceed to the feasting hall for a brief rest and a meal?"

We walked through the echoing halls, our footsteps resounding in the dim passageways. Torches wavered with each gust of wind, and the mingling scents of roasted meat and fresh bread wafted around us, enticing our senses. Laughter and chatter grew louder as we approached, blending with the lively sounds of dining and the melody of a distant harp. The knights were already seated, indulging in platters of delicious fare and flagons of ale, their cloaks draped over their chairs.

Lancelot occupied a prominent position at the center table, his gaze unmistakably set on Gwenhwyfar. When she noticed our arrival, her cheeks colored with a blush, and she discreetly averted her eyes, heightening the discomfort I felt. Amid the festivities, I observed brief, uncertain exchanges and sidelong glances between Lancelot and Gwenhwyfar that betrayed their restrained longing.

I took my place next to Gwenhwyfar, greeting her with a nod, the unfamiliarity between us unchanged. Despite the hall's merriment, a distance remained, as it always had.

Refraining from conversation, I ate my meal of tender venison and spiced potatoes. From time to time, I glanced towards Bedwyr and Merlin, seated to my left. It was good to see them merry, engaging in cheerful banter with some of the knights.

When the meal was finished, I leaned forward to address them. "Would you join me in my quarters now?"

With a nod from both of them, we rose from the table and ascended the broad stone stair. At my chamber doors, I pushed them open with purpose, and we stepped inside.

Merlin and Bedwyr sat at the table while I restlessly paced, each heavy step resounding against the stone beneath my leather boots.

I halted, turning to face them as fury poured forth. "Where is that devious witch now?"

Morgan's treachery surfaced in my thoughts, her relentless scheming and betrayals fueling my anger. Heat flushed my cheeks, and frustration burned within me.

My hands clenched at my sides. "We will stop her, one way or another. If she will not come willingly, we shall drag her back to Avalon, kicking and screaming. This time, there will be no escape."

I turned from them, striding towards one of the windows. The high stone arch above it framed the moonlit courtyard beyond. A faint breeze drifted through the casement, carrying the crisp breath of night.

Turning back, I looked to my companions, seeking their counsel. Bedwyr's brows furrowed, his jaw tightening, while Merlin's eyes darkened, his lips pressing into a hard line.

Bedwyr spoke first: "She is still causing unrest and discord on the grounds."

"This matter is delicate, Arthur," Merlin added. "To cast her out now may appear as though we seek to conceal something. Through my sight, I have seen her near the stables, lingering there as if to overhear our counsel."

Conflicting emotions flared within me as I began to pace again. My fists tightened, then loosened, as I struggled to reconcile the different paths before us.

"I will no longer let my blood ties blind my judgment. Morgan is my half-sister, true, but she has been a persistent blight upon my reign, and action is long overdue. Merlin, while prudence is crucial, we cannot allow her to continue undermining our kingdom."

"What you say is true, Arthur, but we must proceed with caution. She is cunning, and we cannot give her any reason to suspect our plans."

Bedwyr shifted in his seat, the corner of his mouth lifting as a thought took shape. "Merlin, you mentioned seeing her lurking near the stables. What if we lead her astray?"

I frowned, "How do you mean?"

Merlin stroked his beard thoughtfully. "We could provide her with false information, let her believe she holds the advantage. If she thinks we are leaving Camelot for some time, she may follow, unwittingly falling into our trap."

The idea had merit. "I like it, but how do we ensure she does not discern our deception?"

"We will offer her just enough detail to make it convincing," Merlin replied. "Vague hints, spoken as if we are unaware of her presence. Then, when she follows, we will circle back to Camelot, leaving her wandering in the wilderness."

A rare grin touched Bedwyr's face. "Your mind works in clever ways, Merlin."

"Yes, indeed," I added. "Let her believe I intend to travel beyond Cameliard in a few days. Merlin and I will cover some ground, and he can weave a spell to veil her senses. Once she is drawn away, we will return to Camelot, and with any luck, she will remain lost for quite some time."

"My spell can keep her from finding her way back for an extended period. It will befog her mind, causing her to lose her way."

He turned to Bedwyr. "Shall we proceed to the stables and set our trap?"

"Indeed, Merlin, let us go."

"Very well," I said, rising from the table. "I will await your return. Merlin, shall you go to Merlonius this eve?"

"Yes, as soon as you no longer require my assistance."

"I wish to visit with her. Bedwyr, can you stand watch?"

"Certainly."

"Upon your return, I shall depart."

The two men stood, their determination evident in each step as they crossed the room and stepped out into the hall.

Left to the solitude of the night, I moved to the window, looking up at the star-strewn sky as a cool breeze brushed my face. Along the ramparts, knights strode with purpose, their cloaks billowing like black wings. The torches they carried cast wavering light on the stone walls, shaping dark forms that shifted with each step.

Before long, a soft knock broke the quiet.

Merlin entered and recounted what had transpired. "We found Morgan behind the stables, near the stall where Bedwyr keeps his horse. She listened in secret as we spoke of your supposed journey to Cameliard. We ensured she left before we did, convinced by the deception we laid before her."

"That woman is always scheming," I remarked, shaking my head. "But I am relieved everything unfolded as we hoped."

Bedwyr crossed to the far window, looking out before turning back to face me. "Arthur, she thrives on discord and finds amusement in inflicting pain upon your knights, even those of her own blood."

Merlin added, "Bedwyr speaks true. Her cruelty is no longer subtle."

He paused, then fixed his eyes on me. "On the seventh day hence, at mid-morn, we will take the road to Cameliard. She will not resist the lure of following, and once she does, I shall weave the mists to confound her. My spell shall take root, and five moons shall wax and wane ere her feet find their way again to Camelot."

"So be it. Let her chase shadows, while we return unseen."

"I must depart now. Shall we expect you this eve?"

"Yes, pray, tell Merlonius I will arrive soon."

Bedwyr inclined his head, his eyes steady with regard. "Merlin, your foresight strengthens our plan."

"We are each but one thread in the weave. Together, we can accomplish much. Be ever watchful, for Morgan will not cease until she has brought about Arthur's downfall."

There was no more to add, for Merlin's words carried truth. With that, he turned and left, his cloak trailing behind him like a shadow of the power he bore.

Bedwyr lingered near the table, his expression pensive. I studied him, aware of the peril in trying to outmaneuver Morgan and the danger still stalking Camelot. The quiet of the room seemed to hold its breath, as though the very walls awaited the next thread woven by the Fates.

Walking to the hearth, Bedwyr glanced back at me. "Merlonius requires your presence now, perhaps more than ever. I will guard the stair. You can leave without concern. Pray, convey my hopes for her swift recovery."

"Your support means much to me. I will make certain she receives your message."

He inclined his head in farewell, then stepped out and drew the door closed behind him.

I waited for a few breaths before slipping from my quarters.

"All clear?"

"Yes. May the gods and goddesses accompany you, Arthur."

I moved swiftly towards the secret passage, mindful of the gift of my friend's vigilance. At the end of the hall, I reached for the sconce and drew it down. The stone parted in silence, and I entered, ensuring it closed behind me before continuing along the narrow way. The faint shimmer of Merlin's enchantment guided my steps until I reached the wooden door set within the great tree.

Pushing it open, the air brushed my face with a coolness laced with moss and fallen leaves. With each stride, I held close the thought of Merlonius and the solace I hoped to bring her.

Upon my arrival, Merlin opened the wooden door and stepped aside.

"Arthur, please come in. Merlonius is eagerly awaiting your return."

The firelight bathed the room in warmth, and the rich aroma of roasting meat and herbs welcomed me. Seated by the hearth, Merlonius brightened upon seeing me.

She rose at once, joy unmistakable as she spoke my name. "Arthur."

I went to her, and we embraced, sharing a tender kiss.

"How are you faring, my love?"

"I am improving, and it lifts my spirits to see you."

"Bedwyr stands guard to ensure no one stumbles into our part of the castle and questions my absence. He sends his good wishes for your swift recovery."

"We are truly fortunate to call him our friend. His kind words bring me comfort."

Merlin approached us. "Merlonius, please join us at the table and have some food and drink. It will aid your recovery and renew your vigour."

With a nod, she accepted my offered arm, and we walked together to the table where a nourishing meal awaited. Though she made the effort, after only a few bites, she placed her spoon aside.

"Merlin, the hare and vegetables are delicious, but I find I have little hunger this night."

"Have no concern, my dear. The hare will be delicious cold, and we shall try again on the morrow. Why not rest a bit longer by the hearth."

"That will serve me well, Merlin. Your care is a great kindness to me."

She rose with my help and settled once more near the fire, while Merlin and I finished what remained of our meal. When we had eaten, we joined her by the hearth, the fire casting its glow between us once more.

"I will make every effort to visit each eve, though I must return to Camelot before the night reaches its deepest hour."

"Every moment with you is cherished, Arthur. But if your safety is at risk, pray do not come."

"I promise to be cautious. With the secret passage and Bedwyr's vigilance, my absence from Camelot will remain unnoticed."

Her hand found mine, our fingers intertwining. The firelight bathed our faces, drawing us into a tranquil closeness. Across from us, Merlin settled into his chair, his breathing even, his bearing at ease. Our eyes met briefly, exchanging silent assurances, yet uncertainty still stirred within me. Merlin took notice.

"Arthur, you have my word. I will see to her care."

"I know you speak truth, yet my greatest desire is to remain by her side, aiding her recovery."

She squeezed my hand. "I hold your presence dear, and I wish the Fates had allowed us another path. But your love, spanning distances, fortifies me. I will regain my strength and await your return, as I ever shall."

The embers crackled, their scent mingling with the fragrant herbs steeping near the hearth. Our thoughts drifted to the day Merlonius first rode Odin, her courage and spirit unmistakable. Merlin, with a knowing smile, recalled how she mastered the mighty steed, his pride evident. I remembered the awe and concern I had felt, marveling anew at her boldness.

She laughed, her eyes alight with the memory. "I never felt so free," she admitted, her voice touched with wistful longing. "It was as if Odin and I could fly beyond the horizon that day."

In our shared recollections, a flowing rhythm emerged. Merlin occasionally leaned forward, weaving deeper meaning into our tales. Merlonius, with a touch as light as drifting ash, caressed the back of my hand with her thumb. Each gesture, each word deepened the closeness between us, one forged through trials, triumphs, and vows of loyalty and protection.

As the night deepened, the glow of the hearth cradled us, offering a fleeting respite. It was in these times, away from the clamor of duty and destiny's call, that we found serenity. Here, we were not Arthur, Merlin, and Merlonius, bound by title and responsibility, but simply three souls intertwined by fate.

The fire burned low, and I knew I must return to Camelot, though parting weighed heavily upon me.

Standing by the door, I asked, "May I bring cheese or bread on my next visit?"

"We are content, my boy," Merlin responded.

"I will return with the eve's star."

I stepped closer to Merlonius and murmured, "Until the morrow, my love," pressing a tender kiss to her forehead.

"Until the morrow."

I brushed my fingers over her lips, then turned and walked into the waiting dark.

The age-old oak tree loomed ahead, its small wooden door concealing the secret path back to Camelot. Moving swiftly through the passage, I retraced my steps until I reached the hall near my quarters, where Bedwyr stood at the top of the stair.

"Hail, Bedwyr."

"Hail, Arthur. All is as it should be."

"Your tidings are good news indeed."

He approached, and together we made our way to the doors of my chambers.

"How does she fare?"

"She is weak, but her spirit remains strong. Your well wishes brought a true smile to her lips, a sight I had sorely missed."

"I have offered a silent prayer to the gods and goddesses that she remain with us. This world would be empty without her."

"I know, my friend. Oh, how I know."

"Rest well, Arthur."

"May you also find restful sleep. Until the morrow."

On the seventh day hence, as planned, at mid-morn, Merlin and I departed Camelot, our horses carrying us along the familiar road towards Cameliard. The ride would take over two hours, the path winding through woodlands and open fields. Each turn of the road threatened to summon memories of another journey years past, the day Merlin first brought me to meet Gwenhwyfar, a duty I had not chosen. That ride had been fraught with resentment and sorrow. The memory pressed near, but I forced it aside. This day's purpose was not to dwell on what had been, but to protect what I now held most dear.

We rode in silence, the steady rhythm of hooves marking the passing miles. At last, King Leodegan's castle rose ahead, its towers stark against the sky. My breath caught, and for a moment the bitterness of that earlier day returned, but I mastered it swiftly. We did not slow as we passed the gates, though the sight of its walls stirred a storm I would not allow to surface.

"She is behind us," Merlin murmured, his gaze fixed upon the road. "Her presence clings to the air like a shadow."

It was then, as the castle faded behind us and the road stretched into open country, that Merlin lifted his staff. The air shimmered, as though unseen veils had been drawn across the land. His voice, steady and resonant, carried on the wind:

"Coimhcheilg na ceò, falach an rathad.
Treòraich i gu fiadhach gun chrìoch.
Fada bhon dachaigh, caill a ceumannan."
Deceit of the mists, conceal the road.
Guide her into endless wilderness.
Far from home, let her steps be lost.

As the words left his lips, the world seemed to shift. A chill stirred in the breeze, and the very earth beneath my horse quivered faintly, as if acknowledging the power summoned. The path ahead shimmered as though veiled in mist, bending to Merlin's command.

He shifted in his saddle, his eyes fierce. "It is done, Arthur. She will not darken the halls of Camelot until many moons have passed."

"Then let her wander. So long as Morgan trails this deceptive road, the realm is spared her poison."

With that, we turned aside into the shelter of the trees, cloaked by Merlin's enchantments. Behind us, the road to Cameliard remained, yet for Morgan le Fay it would twist into wilderness. She would believe herself close to victory, only to find herself wandering far from Camelot's walls.

In the days that followed our return to Camelot, I visited Merlonius each eve, watching as her vigour slowly returned, like new life rising through the thawed ground. Her laughter, light and unburdened, could be heard once again as the moon waxed and waned twice over.

During this time, Merlin's masterful craft ensured our escape from Morgan le Fay's snares, his unmatched foresight restoring peace to the court. The hall, once rife with whispers of my supposed abandonment of the throne, now basked in renewed stability, and the nobles, their doubts fading, turned once more to embrace the order we had worked to restore.

Yet even amid this calm, a sorrow that refused to fade stayed with me. It called me to a sacred place we had not visited since our loss, and in quiet moments, I felt its summons grow stronger. I knew the hour was near when I must answer, no matter the demands of the crown.

CHAPTER 38

THE BOUGHS REMEMBER

Days passed in steady rhythm as Bedwyr and I remained immersed in shaping policies and forging alliances among the lords. Yet, amidst the demands of rule, a more personal concern surfaced.

"Bedwyr, I am drawn to visit our son's resting place," I said one morn, the ache of loss ever near. "This will require my departure for a short period on the morrow. Under the guise of a morn's hunt, I shall leave at dawn and plan to return by nightfall. Are there any pressing matters that require my attention before then?"

"No, Arthur. All remains peaceful within the kingdom. Your brief journey, disguised as a hunt, should not attract undue notice. I shall maintain order and see that all remains as it should in your absence."

"Very well. At dawn, I depart."

When our tasks were finished, Bedwyr took his leave. Drawn to the casement, I looked northward towards the forest, longing for Merlonius, knowing I would not be at her side this eve.

After a restless night, I rose with purpose as the first hues of dawn stretched across the sky. Armed with sword and spear, I left my chambers, my steps steady as I made my way to the stables. Odin was swiftly brought to me, and with practiced ease, I mounted and rode towards the drawbridge.

Trusting my steed's familiarity with the winding path to the enchanted forest, I guided him with a light hand. We soon arrived at the clearing, where I dismounted, patting his neck in thanks before securing his reins to the paddock rail. The familiar sounds of leather and wood mingled with the whispers of the forest.

My heart quickened, knowing she awaited me within. Approaching the door, I was greeted by Merlin.

"Arthur, it is good to see you. Please enter. Merlonius is preparing a light meal, and she will be delighted that you are here."

Stepping inside, I rested my sword and spear against the wall beside the door, the air rich with the scents of drying herbs and freshly baked bread. Merlonius's approach was a burst of sunlight, her joy infectious.

"Arthur, what an unexpected delight!" She embraced me, and in her touch, I felt the love that time had never dimmed.

"Join us," she beckoned, guiding me to the table laden with fresh berries, soft cheese, and slices of fresh bread.

The bond between us required no words, expressed in shared glances. In this refuge, kinship thrived beyond the ties of blood—this was home.

"So, my boy, how do you wish to spend your day with us?" Merlin inquired, drawing me out of my contemplations.

We were finishing our meal, so I broached the reason for my visit.

"I can stay for a few hours, and I hoped we might visit our son's resting place. Would that be agreeable to both of you?"

Merlonius and Merlin exchanged a glance, an understanding passing between them before she replied.

"This day is fitting for such a visit. We have taken our meal, so let us venture forth."

"Aye, we are ready."

Wordlessly, we set out towards the summit, accompanied only by the crunch of leaves underfoot and the distant chirping of songbirds. At the top, the tree that stood as a guardian over our son greeted us. It had grown taller, its base adorned with a ring of tiny blue flowers. Together, we stood in its shade, a faint breeze stirring through the leaves, a soothing touch upon our skin. I took Merlonius's hand, and she clasped Merlin's.

She lifted her face to the sky. "Little one, you rest in the arms of Spirit. In our thoughts, you dance; in our hearts, you live forever."

Her words settled around us like a blessing, stirring an ache that never fully faded. I looked upon her with awe, humbled by the grace with which she carried her sorrow. Though I stood as king, in that instant, it was she who held the strength of the realm within her.

A bluebird, seen rarely in these parts and considered a harbinger of mystical forces, descended gracefully, alighting on a lower branch. Tilting its head, its bright eyes glistened as it released a melody that rang with unspoiled sweetness, as though sent by the spirits themselves.

"This magical blue bird brings tidings that your son thrives," Merlin said. "His message is simple, a plea for peace and contentment."

Merlonius's breath caught. "Such a lovely gift."

I tightened my hold on her hand. "Truly, it is."

Merlin circled the tree, his fingers trailing along its bark, offering or receiving a silent blessing. When he returned, his hand rested on the tree before he turned to face us again. Sadness marked the lines around his eyes. I wondered if he, too, thought of what could have been.

"Well, shall we return to the cottage?"

We made our way back, the small stones shifting beneath our feet, each of us bearing our loss in silence. At the hearth, Merlonius stirred the embers, then reached for a bundle of dried herbs.

"Let me warm something for us."

I settled beside the fire while Merlin took to his chair, his bearing at ease but his breathing slower, measured. She crumbled the herbs into the simmering pot, and soon the scent of a broth of roots and herbs mingled with the air.

"It is ready," she said, glancing towards the hearth.

Merlin and I rose and joined her at the table. I watched as she ladled the broth into our bowls, each motion reflecting the quiet care she gave to even the smallest acts.

We ate in companionable silence, the simple fare of vegetables, herbs, and bread offering a modest comfort. Each bite eased the heaviness we still carried after visiting our son's resting place.

Merlin wrapped his hands around a cup of steaming broth and exhaled slowly. "Time spent together is never wasted, yet its passing is ever swift."

I studied him then, the weariness plain in his eyes, the lines of age carved along his face. Understanding settled upon me, though I was not yet ready to voice it.

As Merlonius gathered the dishes, Merlin rose and gestured for me to follow.

Outside, the midday warmth carried the scent of tree moss and memory.

"There are days I feel the years settling upon me, Arthur," he admitted, his tone thoughtful. "Not only in my body, but in my mind. I once walked between realms without effort. Now, the veil feels heavier."

I regarded him, uneasiness settling upon me. "And yet, you remain unchanged to my eyes."

A smile played at his lips. "The greatest illusions are the ones we craft for those we love."

He squeezed my shoulder but did not turn away, his eyes holding mine.

"You have known loss," he said at last. "More than most. And though you carry it well, it does not mean the burden is light."

I swallowed against the familiar ache. "Had I been here, perhaps things would have been different."

Merlin's expression held no judgment, only understanding. "Do you believe you could have stopped the turning of the stars? Unwoven the threads that were set before you?"

I looked away, my jaw tightening. "She carried our child for three turnings of the moon. Three, Merlin, and in all that time, I was absent. Duty called me away, and when she needed me most, I was not with her."

Merlin sighed, his eyes clouded with something I could not name. "Kings are bound by duty. But she has never blamed you."

"That does not lessen my own regret."

"No, but grief is not meant to be shouldered alone. She mourns, as do you, but not apart from you. She has never turned from you."

I closed my eyes briefly, allowing his words to settle within me. The sorrow did not fade, but it no longer stood unchallenged.

"Your child was loved. That love is not lost, nor has it diminished."

I gave a small nod, and he turned towards the cottage.

"Come, Merlonius waits for us."

The familiar scent of the hearth met us as we stepped inside.

She slipped her hand into mine as I neared the fire. "Will you walk with me?"

We closed the door softly behind us and wandered through the small clearing beyond the cottage, our steps slow, unhurried. The trees swayed above us, their leaves beginning to drift to the forest floor. She reached out, catching one between her fingertips, studying its edges before releasing it to the wind.

"I used to dream of bringing our son here," she murmured. "Letting him run through the trees, showing him how the world grows and changes."

Though her voice was steady, sadness lay beneath each word. I pulled her close, pressing a kiss to her temple, offering her the only comfort I could.

By the time we returned to the garden, the sun had begun its descent. Merlonius led me to the bench beneath the towering tree. Seated beside her, I watched as her fingers drifted over the garden blooms, her thoughts elsewhere.

"My heart still aches for the loss of our son. Each day, I struggle to accept the path the Fates have decreed." Her hand hovered over a blossom, but she let it fall to her lap. "I often wonder what his smile would have been like."

She glanced towards the garden. "And I grieve not only for his loss but also for all the unborn children I may never bear. For that, I am sorry." A single tear traced her cheek.

I wrapped my arm around her shoulder, drawing her close. "I share your sorrow," I said softly, lifting her chin until our eyes met, my love reflected in hers.

"I, too, envision our son, imagining holding him close and wondering if he would possess some of your incredible gifts. But know this truth: my love for you has only deepened since the day we first pledged our hearts to one another, many years ago."

She leaned into me without speaking, her head resting lightly against my shoulder. I took her hand in mine, feeling the enduring strength of her love.

We remained that way, our closeness bringing peace, the rise and fall of our breathing, a shared stillness between us.

"Arthur, we must speak of Merlin. Of late, signs of his weariness have grown. The toll of the years upon him… and I feel it more with each passing day."

Her words unsettled me, challenging a certainty I had once believed unshakable. But I had seen it for myself. The slow passage of time pressed upon Merlin, visible in the deepening lines beneath his eyes and the measured cadence of his steps.

"I know, it is a truth I did not wish to accept, but it is there, undeniable."

She touched my cheek. "Even he cannot evade time's grip, and as my true father and a pillar of our clan, his wisdom has guided us through much. I yearn to support him in ways that might elude his notice, to return the care he has so freely given us."

Pulling her close, I whispered, "Of course, my love. We will spare no effort to aid him."

She leaned into my embrace, a sigh escaping her lips as the strain visibly lifted from her shoulders.

"His well-being remains ever on my mind. Knowing you will watch over him, even when I cannot, brings me comfort."

I squeezed her hand, my promise firm. "Upon my honour, at every turn, through every trial, we shall stand as Merlin's trusted guardians, as he has been for us."

She met my eyes, gratitude reflected within them. "Your promise eases my worries more than you know. Together, we will uphold him."

The garden around us stilled as the sun withdrew, painting the sky in hues of farewell.

I steadied myself against the inevitable pull of duty. "I wish the light of day could linger longer. But alas, I must return to Camelot."

"My time with you is a treasure," she said softly. "Journey with care, and carry the knowledge of my waiting heart."

We walked slowly to where Merlin sat beneath the old oak tree, his presence as steady as the stream beside him. He looked up, a faint smile touching his lips as we approached.

"I must leave now, Merlin. Will you visit Camelot soon?"

"Yes, my boy, I shall. After a few more days here with Merlonius, I will come to you."

I kissed Merlonius farewell, still grieving the son I would never hold and carrying the ache of our separation, for after all these years, her safety remained our foremost concern.

These sorrows clung to me as I turned to face Merlin, seeing then the undeniable marks of time on his face. He too bore the touch of aging, which spares no one.

Mounted on Odin, I glanced back once more, finding them standing together against the dimming sky. A sight both cherished and bittersweet. Lifting my hand in wordless parting, I guided my steed forward, following the path out of the enchanted forest.

As the distance stretched between us, a yearning stirred within me. If only the hours could linger, if only fleeting moments could stretch into a tapestry woven of endless days.

CHAPTER 39

THE MERCY OF KINGS

Since the loss of our child, concern for Merlonius never left my heart. Though she had spoken of her sorrow, it lingered in silence between us, a hurt neither time nor words could fully soothe.

In endless contemplation, I wondered if there was a way to lessen her suffering. The Fates, with their capricious whims, had turned the wheel of our destinies, and I grappled with the harsh truth that all of this was, somehow, for the betterment of our clan. The anger that surged within me towards the gods and goddesses smoldered as an ever-present ember.

These reflections, entwined with Merlonius's words about Merlin's aging and the gradual advance of his years, stirred a deep disquiet within me. When I thought he was not aware, I would study the lines on his face, each one a trace of mortality and a reminder of the relentless progression of life. Still, his eyes held the same gleam of wisdom and magic that had guided us through countless trials.

With the approach of the summer Solstice, a noticeable anticipation moved through the land, touching even my burdened heart. Knights, nobles, and practitioners of mystical arts converged, their excitement bubbling like a spring, all drawn by the sacred respect for the longest day and the shortest night. It was a time for joyful celebrations of life's abundance and the vitality of nature, offering a stark contrast to our personal grief. The sun's ascent carried promises of renewal and revival, echoing the longing for healing that Merlonius and I so desperately sought in the solitude of the enchanted forest.

Away from the bustle of Solstice preparations, the stables offered a welcome retreat. There, I found comfort in the simple rhythm of grooming a new mare, her calm manner reminding me of the joys the world still offered. The patter of her hooves on the straw-covered ground created a soothing melody as she shifted. The scent of hay, mixed with sunlight filtering through the open stable doors, wrapped around me like a familiar cloak. While I tended to her, noting her youthful spirit and eager movements, my thoughts turned to Merlin. I saw what I had long refused to see: the lessened spring in his step, the weariness in his gaze.

Even the mightiest forces of nature bear the marks of time.

The sound of approaching footsteps pulled me from my reverie. Merlin appeared at the stall's gate, his stance rigid.

"Arthur, I must speak with you in private. It is a matter of utmost importance, and rest assured, Merlonius is safe."

Though he held his bearing, his face betrayed his concern.

"But of course, let us walk to my quarters."

Leaving the mare in her haven, I joined him, and together we made our way to my chambers. Merlin paced, his robe sweeping behind him with silent urgency, each step betraying a struggle not yet voiced.

Pausing by the windows, he turned towards me.

"Merlonius and I have foreseen troubling times ahead. Medrawt has stirred discontent among church officials and certain nobles with his damning accusations about Lancelot and Gwenhwyfar's courtship. They plan to bring the matter before the High King and compel you to condemn Gwenhwyfar to death."

His words landed hard. Fury surged within me, and I clenched my fists, my knuckles pale beneath the strain.

"Merlin, I cannot allow this to happen. I bear the mantle of High King. They cannot force my hand in such an agonizing choice."

He shook his head slowly. "The world shifts, Arthur. Many of the old ways are being destroyed. You will be placed into a position where it will seem you have no choice."

A surge of resolve overcame the mounting despair.

"No! I must find a way to get in front of this, to protect Gwenhwyfar and uphold what we know to be just."

I took a step closer to Merlin, the breeze from the window stirring my thoughts as I looked out over the treetops. An idea began to form, a glimmer of hope amidst the encroaching darkness.

"Tell me, if I were to send them to my estate in France, could they find safety and live out their lives in peace?"

He furrowed his brow, his gaze distant, as he peered beyond the veil of the present. "It could work," he said slowly. "The lands in Brittany, far removed from Camelot's reach, might offer them refuge. Your holding there is secluded, its hall and stout walls shielding it from the eyes of your enemies."

Those lands had been my mother's legacy, a distant birthright I had rarely visited. But now it seemed the only place where Gwenhwyfar and Lancelot might find sanctuary from the storm gathering around them.

"But time is of the essence. If we can see them safely out of Camelot this night, there is hope they may remain undiscovered. Gwenhwyfar and Lancelot are in her quarters. We must speak with them at once."

Leaving my chambers behind, we moved swiftly down the passage, guided by the torchlight lining the stone walls. Distant laughter drifted from the feasting hall as we neared Gwenhwyfar's door. I knocked, and she appeared, her face marked by clear surprise.

For a breath, I held her gaze, aware of the burden my words would carry.

"Gwenhwyfar, we must speak with you and Lancelot."

She stepped back to allow us entry. "Of course, my lord."

Though I had never entered Gwenhwyfar's chambers in all these years, I was not surprised to find the space a reflection of her cultivated and guarded nature. The bed, adorned with soft furs and embroidered pillows, lent the room a warmth she had never found beside me.

Lancelot stood near the window, his figure outlined against the sunlit sky. Upon our arrival, he moved towards us, his bearing respectful though tinged with curiosity.

"Arthur, Merlin."

I met his look, my purpose pressing upon me. "Medrawt has leveled serious accusations against you and Gwenhwyfar. He has incited unrest among church officials and nobles. They intend to compel me to condemn Gwenhwyfar to death."

Gwenhwyfar's hand flew to her lips in dismay as she rushed to Lancelot's side, her other hand finding his. Lancelot's fingers instinctively closed around hers, each feeling the full impact of the news. My jaw set, and my lips pressed into a taut line as remorse gripped me.

"I will not allow this injustice to occur. Gwenhwyfar, I understand that you sought love and companionship in Lancelot's arms when I could not give it. I do not judge you, for it is clear your affection for each other is enduring and true."

Lancelot stepped forward, his bearing steady. "My lord, I cannot forsake Gwenhwyfar. I love her and will stand by her."

"I am well aware of your feelings. Rest assured, you will not have to abandon her. You both must depart before the next sun rises. Take what you can and seek refuge at my estate in France. There, you may find safety and forge a life together."

Gwenhwyfar moved towards me. "My lord, from the day we first met, I felt nothing between us. It was not my intention to fall in love with Lancelot, but I did. He holds a place in my heart that surpasses all else in my life. I am grateful for your grace and protection. You have ruled with justice and fairness, and I will forever hold respect for you."

I held her, offering solace amidst the swirling uncertainty.

Lancelot knelt before me, his head bowed.

"By our sacred code, Arthur, I pledge to uphold the ideals of honour and truth, not only for your sake, but for the brotherhood we forged. Wherever I go, those values shall go with me."

Extending my hand, I helped Lancelot rise, clasping his shoulder. "You will always be counted among the Fellowship of the Round Table. And Gwenhwyfar will always be honoured as a queen. Go now, and prepare to leave at once."

"Lancelot, Gwenhwyfar." Merlin stepped forward, his presence steeped in quiet power.

"Beware those who offer aid too freely. Deceit often wears a kind face. Medrawt has shown his true nature, and we must remain watchful of Morgan le Fay's next move.

"In your new life, seek peace. Should you encounter strangers, look to the skies. A black crow will foretell that danger is near and that our support is never far. Now, you must leave swiftly, before our plans come to light."

Lancelot's expression, often guarded, softened. "Many thanks to you both."

"May your days be blessed with peace and joy all your lives long."

We departed, walking in silence, the castle unchanged around us. Yet within me, the remnants of what had unfolded settled into thought.

Upon reaching my chambers, whatever calm Merlin had carried gave way to restlessness. He paced, his robe trailing behind him like a shadow. At the casement, he paused, leaning on the ledge, his eyes fixed far beyond the walls of Camelot.

I heard the faint movements of knights shifting positions on the rampart, their steps blending with the familiar sounds of the day.

At last, Merlin turned to face me.

"Arthur, a web of deceit has been intentionally woven to coincide with the celebration of the Solstice. Those who plot against you have calculated that the vast gathering of attendees will grant them greater leverage to force your hand into their bidding."

His footsteps echoed slightly, while a breeze from the open window carried the festive sounds of the Summer Solstice celebration. After a few moments spent collecting his thoughts, he continued.

"Come the morrow, church officials and a select few noblemen will arrive, seeking an audience with you. You must feign surprise as they present their accusations and request to see Gwenhwyfar. When the servants inform you that she cannot be found, declare that you will dispatch your knights to search for her. Medrawt will not be present, as he remains on duty in the southeastern lands as you requested. If pressed, he will vehemently deny any involvement in this matter."

"Merlin, there will be no search for Gwenhwyfar. I will inform these accusers that she has not been found. But will they simply let this matter go?"

"Yes, they will. With time and the absence of Lancelot and Gwenhwyfar from the court, their story will fade into the realm of gossip and become nothing more than a distant memory."

I sighed, feeling both relief and resignation wash over me. "A distant memory is a good thing, Merlin. They deserve to find refuge and happiness. Now, what say you to joining me in the feasting hall before we return to my chambers and retire for the night?"

"A hot meal and a goblet of wine is a fitting end to our day."

We left my chambers and made our way to the hall, where the aroma of roasted meat and fresh bread greeted us. After a hearty meal accompanied by fine wine, we returned to my quarters, settling in the chairs by the hearth.

"Arthur, I know how much you miss spending time with Merlonius. And she yearns for your return."

"I often think of what my life would have been like if the Fates had not destined me to be a High King."

"It is a circular web that the Fates weave. For if you were not Uther's son, you and I might never have met, and in turn you and Merlonius would not have joined as one."

He gave me much to ponder, and as fatigue crept upon us, we spoke no more, surrendering to the embrace of sleep.

With the rising sun, several church officials and a select few nobles arrived, requesting an audience with the High King. Merlin and I walked side by side, making our way to the great hall. Entering the regal chamber, the scent of polished wood greeted us as torchlight from the sconces bathed the space in shifting light.

I assumed my seat on the throne, a symbol of the burden I bore, while Merlin stood faithfully by my side, his dark robe contrasting with the surrounding splendor.

They entered in measured steps, their expressions guarded. No words were exchanged at first, only the rustle of garments disturbing the silence. All waited, unsure of what was to come.

The stillness, stretched taut, finally gave way as accusations and requests poured forth, just as Merlin had foreseen. I summoned the servants who attended Gwenhwyfar and ordered her brought before the assembled court.

As we awaited their return, composure remained my shield as I regarded those assembled before me. *How easily the hearts of men turn to darkness when they feel emboldened to judge others. Mercy is swiftly cast aside in favour of appearances, their righteousness as brittle as dry leaves.*

The servants finally returned, reporting that they had searched Gwenhwyfar's quarters and the surrounding grounds but could not locate her. I thanked them and then addressed those assembled.

"My lords, your concerns regarding Gwenhwyfar have been heard. My knights will search the countryside, and she will be found. Nevertheless, my judgment will come only after careful thought and reflection."

They withdrew slowly, disappointment clear in their stiff bearing and reluctant steps. Their murmured discontent trailed behind them, like the last stirrings of a storm not yet spent.

When the last person departed, Merlin placed his hand on my shoulder. "Well done, my boy. You have handled this matter with great poise and foresight."

"It is a sad truth. These men turn so easily on those they deem weaker, made bold by a false sense of virtue."

He paused, his attention sweeping over the empty chamber. "And as the world shifts, the light shall grow dim, overshadowed by the encroaching darkness."

A shiver ran down my back at his words for they resonated with a stark truth.

"Shall we get some fresh air, Merlin?"

"That will do us both a great deal of good. Let us go."

We spent the rest of the day walking the grounds and visiting the stables. That night, after the eve's meal, Merlin and I left the feasting hall and returned to my chambers. We settled into our chairs near the open windows, where a cool breeze, laced with the whispers of the tranquil midsummer night, drifted through. Moonlight bathed our surroundings, casting a serene hush over our solemn conversation.

Rubbing my temples to ease the pain, a veil of exhaustion descended upon me. "What are we to do about Medrawt's villainous intentions, Merlin? He showed no regard for the innocent lives that could have been lost. The mere thought of his clan ties fills me with dread, chilling my blood."

"The path he treads is shrouded in shadow. I warned you long ago that we must remain ever watchful. He will not hesitate to seek alliances with our sworn enemies."

Bitterness stirred at his words. "The Saxons would bring nothing but death and destruction to our lands. Is he truly capable of such wickedness?"

"Yes, Arthur. He is."

"There must be something more we can do to thwart his plans." My words carried the sharp edge of my displeasure. "Mere banishment is not enough."

He raised a hand, his gesture urging patience. "Ah, destiny is a silent counselor, guided by the Fates as they turn the wheel of time. All shall unfold as it must."

Merlin sighed, his eyes resting on the soft light beyond the window. Then, with steady resolve, he rose.

"And now, my dear friend, I must return to the enchanted forest to take part in the Solstice celebrations with Merlonius. It saddens me that your duties prevent you from joining us, as your absence from Camelot would certainly be noted during the festivities."

I turned towards the north, where the forest waited beneath the darkening sky. "You know well my deep desire to leave these confines and celebrate the Solstice with both of you. I hold onto the hope that perhaps next year, I might share it beside you."

"As do we. Until we meet again, Arthur."

From my window, I watched as Merlin disappeared into the deep shadows of the towering trees. The Solstice breeze carried whispers from beyond these stone-bound walls, intensifying my longing for freedom, a dream painfully out of reach.

Within several days' time a knock at my chamber door announced Merlin's arrival. "Hail, Arthur. I bear good news. Both Merlonius and I have seen that Lancelot and Gwenhwyfar are safely hidden at your secluded estate in France."

Relief stirred within me, knowing that two innocents were spared sorrow and death through our desire to stay true to honour and loyalty.

Sheltered from prying eyes and harsh judgments, they had found solace and a semblance of security, a rare sanctuary amidst their tumultuous lives. In time, as the church officials and accusing nobles lacked their targets, their fervor waned, dissolving into the mists of forgotten conflicts.

The void left by Gwenhwyfar was subtly felt: slight hesitations in conversations, averted looks, and the empty spaces where she once stood. I settled into my rule alone, the court adjusting in her absence, no longer strained by subtle tensions or unspoken guilt. I found a different peace, one of release. The events set in motion by those intent on destruction had resulted in choices made and lives forever altered.

With the turning of a moon, the palace had grown quieter, its halls familiar yet faintly hollow. Merlin stayed close, his counsel steady.

His visits became more frequent after the departure of Lancelot and Gwenhwyfar. We walked the grounds, shared meals with the knights in the feasting hall, and spent our evenings together in calm reflection within my chambers. On one of those nights, as we sat by the window looking up at the stars, he shifted and turned to me.

"Arthur, you have given them a gift few could offer. Though the road ahead has changed, be thankful for the Fates' hand. Know that you have spared them a greater suffering."

His words settled over me.

"You speak truth, Merlin, and for that, I am grateful."

Still, beneath the mantle of my rule, the ache of an empty cradle persisted, a pain untouched by the clamor of battle or the lure of magic. My thoughts often drifted to Merlonius and the life we had dreamed of together, a life of simplicity and love, unburdened by the chains of duty.

I endured the regrets of a life destiny had not granted me, and with Merlin's constant presence and Merlonius's enduring love, I confronted the raw edges of my spirit. Their strength unearthed a fortitude within me to face the trials yet to come. From that shared bond, I drew not only the courage to persevere, but also the resolve to rise above the burdens of kingship and the scars that marked me.

The Solstice light lingered in quiet ways: in acts of mercy, in unspoken choices, in love that weathered sorrow. In that faint light, I found my path forward.

CHAPTER 40

THE DEPARTURE OF THE SAGE

Three years had passed since Merlin and I had protected Lancelot and Gwenhwyfar. Within the castle walls, a delicate hope for lasting peace had begun to blossom. I wanted to believe the kingdom's storms had finally abated, and that serenity had taken root in Camelot.

On one bitter winter's night, solitude claimed my quarters. I found brief comfort in the hearth's glow while the darkness pressed into every corner, casting long silhouettes that seemed to shift and breathe. Recollections rose like a tide, relentless and unbidden, pulling me back to the days of my youth.

The image of Merlin and Merlonius's cottage returned to me, always fragrant with lavender and wild herbs, a place that still felt like home.

Warmth stirred within me as I stood beside Merlin, watching Merlonius walk from the garden at his call. Her hair fell in soft waves down her back, her green eyes bright with curiosity.

A smile touched my lips as thoughts of the pond and waterfall surfaced, for it was there I first kissed Merlonius. Oh, how my spirit soared, and still does with my love for her.

I longed for those simpler days, for the soothing shelter of the forest, and for the fellowship time and duty had kept me from.

The flames crackled and roared, their fiery tongues captivating as I drifted deeper into remembrance. Resolving to visit them on the morrow, I had only begun to shape my plans when a rapid knocking shattered my reverie. I rose at once to answer the insistent summons. There stood Bedwyr, his stance set, distress evident.

"Arthur, you must come to my quarters without delay!"

We hurried through the dimly lit halls until we reached his chambers. He pushed the door wide, and there stood Merlonius by the window, her face streaked with tears, the depths of her anguish plain to see.

"Merlonius, what sorrow weighs on you this night?"

She collapsed into my arms, burying her face against my chest. I rubbed her back until she steadied herself and stepped back.

"Merlin is gone, Arthur. He died this day."

Disbelief struck hard, and I reached for the wall to steady myself.

"Gone?"

"Yes, after we left The Giants' Dance, he grew increasingly weary. Despite drinking healing teas, he refused to eat. Near sunset, he asked me to sit with him, for he said there was much to share and little time left." She paused, her breath unsteady as she struggled to continue. "Merlin told me he would soon depart this world. He wanted to hold on until your arrival, as he foresaw you would come on the morrow."

Each word struck me like a blow to my chest, deepening the sudden, piercing wound. Merlin had always been my guiding light, leading me through every peril and doubt. Now, with that light gone, darkness seemed to advance, threatening the very essence of who I was. I struggled to compose myself, to summon the strength that he had always fostered in me. But in that moment, I was merely a man grappling with a loss so sharp it threatened to split my heart in two.

Merlonius pressed on. "He urged me to listen closely to his instructions and to share all he revealed, lest he depart before your arrival.

"I tried to help him. I placed my hands upon his head, and I felt his life slipping away. He shook his head and moved them away, telling me that even my gifts could not stop the Fates from turning the wheel of his life. Oh, Arthur, it felt as if the very earth gave way beneath my feet when I heard his words."

I held her, stroking her hair, her pain mingling with my own. Gently, I guided her to the table and helped her to sit. I turned to Bedwyr, who had remained silently watchful.

"Pray, be seated," I said, gesturing to the chair opposite where I sat.

Bedwyr took his place without a word, while Merlonius remained beside me, her hands tightly clasped upon the table.

Merlin's death settled heavily upon us, an absence that felt as vast as the night sky. His counsel stirred in my thoughts: *"Trust in those who walk beside you, Arthur, as they are the pillars of your reign."* Now, those words carried new meaning, providing some solace through my grief.

"He feared for my safety. His magic, he said, was fading and would soon vanish. Before his final breath, he urged that if ever I found myself alone in the cottage, I must go at once to the door in the tree. The secret passage to Camelot would light at my steps. Once inside the castle, I was to seek you or Bedwyr with the utmost caution. His warning was clear: vigilance must not falter, for there are those within these walls whose malice is aimed at me only to wound you, Arthur."

I met her eyes, the truth of Merlin's trust settling within me. *He had given me his greatest charge: her safety. In my heart, I vowed to guard her with my life, to carry forward his teachings, and to preserve the future he had shaped.*

Her eyes moved between Bedwyr and me before lowering to her clasped hands. She looked up again, her face revealing the effort it took to steady her emotions.

"In his final moments, I held his hands and met the devotion in his eyes. His love for me endured, felt until his final breath."

The flames surged and leapt higher, stirred by the power of Merlonius's magic as her heartache lent strength to the fire. Light shifted across the walls in restless motion, mirroring the tempest within her.

"I whispered my love to him. A faint smile graced his lips as he brushed his fingers across my face with a touch full of affection. With serene acceptance, he closed his eyes and drew his final breath."

The grief she contained broke free in sobs that echoed through the room, each one a release of all she had held back. Gradually, the storm within her began to still and her breathing eased. She brushed the tears from her cheeks and spoke again, her voice low but clear.

"I heeded his counsel and made my way to the castle. After stepping out of the secret passageway, I sealed it behind me. As I carefully moved through the halls, I came upon Bedwyr."

"His last wish was to keep his death a secret until after the funeral pyre. He wanted his final journey to be at The Giants' Dance."

I reached for her hand, the touch meant to steady us both as we faced what must come.

"He bade me vow that once the last embers had faded, I must not return to the cottage to live. Without his protection, the woods would no longer be safe from men, beasts, and darker forces."

The truth of her words could not be denied. I understood the peril Merlin's absence would bring. A slow emptiness opened within me, hollow and raw. The thought of Merlonius, once Merlin's apprentice and now my wife, being forced to leave the only home she had ever known filled me with profound sadness.

"Camelot will welcome you as one of its own, should you wish it."

"Oh, Arthur… I cannot yet say."

"Whatever you choose, you shall not face it alone."

"Arthur," Bedwyr's words came quiet. "Now that Merlin's magic has faded, I am able to enter the enchanted forest. With my help, we can bear his body to The Giants' Dance."

"Your aid is welcome, Bedwyr. Together, we shall see him safely to the sacred stones."

"His wish was that only you, Arthur, and you, Bedwyr, join me when the funeral pyre is lit. He asked that I stand at the altar and pray, and to know he would remain by my side even in death. He also warned of whispers spreading falsehoods. We must keep the true nature of his death, and the manner in which we honour his remains, a closely guarded secret."

Her words left us in silence, save for the sound of our breathing.

"We must depart now, Arthur."

Bedwyr's determination fortified my own.

"Aye, we must go. Merlonius, remain here with Bedwyr while I retrieve my sword."

At the door, I glanced back at her. Though sorrow marked her face, her bearing held steady through the storm of emotion. I saw the courage Merlin had always recognized in her.

As I hurried to my chambers, the castle's stillness felt like a mournful lament for our great sorcerer. Entering, I paused to gather myself before donning my winter cloak and securing Excalibur at my side.

Returning to Bedwyr's chambers, I found him beside Merlonius, his calm presence offering her some comfort. At my arrival, they rose.

"Let us hasten. We will ride from the stables."

With determined strides, we left Bedwyr's chambers, our footsteps echoing through the shadowed halls. Stepping into the night, we made our way towards the stables.

We saddled our horses with practiced ease. Mounting my steed, I gestured for Merlonius to ride between Bedwyr and me, forming a protective shield against the uncertainties that awaited us.

Memories of Merlin filled my mind as we crossed the drawbridge and headed towards the enchanted forest, giving our horses full rein. I recalled the day he introduced me to Tân Wen, his dragon. Her sleek scales and wise eyes remained clear, as if she stood before us now. I wondered about her fate, now that his guiding hand was gone.

Upon reaching the cottage, we tethered our horses and entered. With a wave of her hand, Merlonius set flame to the candles, their soft glow shifting across the weathered walls.

I knelt beside Merlin, who rested in his cherished chair, his features serene, as if caught in peaceful slumber. I took his cold hand, remembering how those hands had once guided me through the fiercest storms of my reign. Bedwyr and Merlonius stood united in quiet reverence as I whispered my final farewell.

"Merlin, you have been the true leader of our clan, the cornerstone of my strength. Your wisdom saw me through every trial, and your love taught me the meaning of devotion. I will forever hold close the moments we shared: your laughter, your counsel, your unwavering belief in me. Your absence leaves a void no one can fill."

I kissed his hand and rose to my feet, wiping away my tears. Though my heart ached, the time had come to honour his final request.

"We will carry him to The Giants' Dance, as he wished. Let us bring the cart from the garden and begin his final journey."

Bedwyr and I brought it forward, securing it behind Odin as Merlonius readied her bag for the pyre. Together, we lifted Merlin's body and placed him gently in the cart, making certain he would remain secure. As Bedwyr stood watch, I stepped back into the cottage.

"Merlonius, it is time."

She nodded, and with a wave of her hand, the candle flames dimmed, their light retreating into faint embers, leaving the room shrouded in shadow. Taking her hand, I felt the strength in her grip.

We walked outside to where Bedwyr waited. Mounting our horses, we began our journey to bid our final farewell to Merlin.

The forest path held a familiar rhythm, one Merlonius and I had known well in Merlin's company. Yet, on this eve, it was not the haunting rustle of his robes preceding us, but only the faint stir of leaves beneath our horses' hooves and the occasional snort or whinny. The sky shimmered with countless stars, lighting our way as we emerged into the clearing where the towering stones stood.

While Merlonius stayed beside Merlin, Bedwyr and I ventured into the forest, gathering fallen branches and dried wood for the pyre. With deliberate care, we built the platform upon the stone altar, arranging each branch to ensure it would hold. Finally, Bedwyr gestured towards the completed structure.

"Arthur, it is finished."

I exhaled deeply; the loss of Merlin was inescapable, woven through every breath.

"Yes, let us send him home."

Together, we carried Merlin to the waiting altar. Merlonius walked quietly beside us, her bag of sacred herbs draped over her shoulder. Ascending the platform, she scattered them around the pyre, an offering to the departing spirit. After placing his staff at his side, I watched as she delicately positioned a quartz crystal over his heart, a final tribute to the wisdom he imparted.

She stood in silent reflection, her hand resting lightly on his still form, when the rhythmic beat of wings sounded above, heralding the arrival of Merlin's dragon, Tân Wen. She descended gracefully from the night sky, landing with composed dignity at the heart of The Giants' Dance. Her green scales shimmered in the moonlight, reflecting her majestic form.

"Tân Wen, have you come to bid our beloved Merlin farewell?"

Merlonius stepped down from the platform, her eyes meeting the dragon's shimmering gaze.

Tân Wen lifted her head to the stars, her mournful cry resonating through the consecrated ground. With deliberate grace, she approached the altar, Merlonius walking beside her as they neared the pyre together. The dragon's scales cast a glow, bathing the circle in a somber light.

"I understand, my friend. We, too, grieve for Merlin," she whispered, placing a comforting hand on Tân Wen's neck. Warm breath rose from the dragon's nostrils, curling in the night air, carrying the faint scent of heather and distant woodsmoke. Merlonius lingered there, sharing a quiet moment of kinship. With a final gentle stroke along the dragon's scales, she turned back to the platform where Bedwyr stood waiting.

Bedwyr offered the torch to Merlonius, who accepted it with a sure hand. She stepped forth once more onto the platform. Her fingers closed around the torch, the legacy of Merlin's magic stirring within her, both familiar and of elder days. She closed her eyes and took a measured breath. A murmur of incantations slipped from her lips, and with a mere brush of her fingers, the tip of the torch caught flame. Her power unfolded, a force ancient and wild swirling about her like the wind.

She looked to me. I nodded in shared understanding. With solemn care, she lowered her torch to set flame to the four corners. The wood caught quickly, crackling in somber harmony with the night.

Merlonius bowed her head as she placed the torch at his feet, completing the sacred ritual to guide him on his eternal journey. Looking at his peaceful countenance, she spoke the words to send him on his way, the power of her sorcery woven into every syllable.

"Lasting serenity to you, Merlin. You have been our teacher, our father, our protector, our friend. As the head of our clan, you have led us through darkness, bestowing upon us the light of knowledge. May the flowing air and enduring earth cradle you in eternal rest. Though your physical form has departed, your spirit continues to dwell among us. You have generously imparted your wisdom and gifts, leaving an everlasting imprint upon our hearts. We will forever cherish and honour the love we hold for you."

With our final farewell spoken, the fire roared, climbing skyward as if lifting his spirit to the heavens. She stepped down from the platform and came to join us. I extended my hand, and she took it firmly. Together, we moved to the edge of the sacred circle, watching as the pyre blazed, fierce and unceasing.

At last, with the first light of dawn, Merlin's ashes merged with the mist, rising as a cloud into the sky, a final tribute to his transcendent spirit.

In the ensuing silence, Tân Wen let out one last resounding roar, her majestic form rising to escort her beloved companion on their final journey. Together, they disappeared into the horizon, leaving the realm of mortals behind. With reverence, we departed the circle and mounted our steeds to begin the somber journey back to the cottage, the rhythm of hooves fading into memory's embrace.

Upon our arrival, Bedwyr freed the cart, and Merlonius and I stepped inside our home. The familiar scent of old wood and dried herbs greeted us, a poignant reminder of days now passed. The room seemed quieter, as if it knew we were departing for the last time, each echo lingering, reluctant to fade.

I turned to her, seeking words that might offer comfort, though none could truly ease what stirred within her.

"Merlonius, I understand your grief, the longing for Merlin, and the comfort this home once gave you. But you are not alone. Our love endures, and I will always stand beside you."

She moved to the window, her hand resting on the sill as though drawing steadiness from its worn surface. Her shoulders rose with a breath that trembled, and for a moment, she gazed into the shadowed stillness beyond before facing me once more.

"Arthur, your love sustains me, yet my spirit aches for Merlin, and the life we knew within these walls."

"I wish there were words to ease your heart. Life presents its hardships, and we cannot always shield ourselves from them. Yet together, we must find the courage to move forward. Let us return to Camelot and face whatever awaits, strengthened by our unity."

Tears traced down her cheeks.

Bedwyr stepped into the cottage, his steps slow and measured. I saw that he carried a pain he did not voice. He looked to me, then Merlonius.

"How may I help ease this parting?"

She moved slowly through the cottage, her fingers tracing the contours of cherished objects. She stopped when she reached her loom.

"My loom… I shall miss it," she murmured. "And what of the horses?"

"We will return for them," Bedwyr reassured her. "For now, take only what you must. It is not safe for you to remain here any longer."

"I understand," she said, more to herself than to us.

With the bag of sacred herbs still slung over her shoulder, Merlonius disappeared into the sleeping area. I heard the quiet rustle of cloth and the soft chime of crystal against wood, familiar sounds that called to mind simpler days.

When she returned, she carried garments folded with care and a small pouch that held the subtle shimmer of her treasured crystals. Among her belongings was the gift Merlin had given her on the day of our handfasting, a poignant reminder of happier times.

Reaching out, I offered to assist her. We stood quietly, surrounded by the solemn breath of parting, all that had changed settling over us.

She lifted her chin slightly. "I am ready."

Stepping outside, melancholy overwhelmed me. I closed the door behind us, its latch clicking shut, enclosing the life we had known within. It was as if not only the spirit of this place, but a part of myself, had been left behind within its walls. The finality settled heavily upon my shoulders.

We mounted our horses, casting one last look at what was now our past. A chill wind brushed our faces, and the distant hoot of an owl echoed through the trees, plaintive and low. I glanced towards Merlonius and Bedwyr, and tilting my head in silent accord, guided Odin onto the path that led us away from the enchanted forest. We ventured onward, as Camelot called us towards whatever peace might yet lie beyond our grief.

CHAPTER 41

BOUND BY PROMISES

Dawn's first light began to break just as we arrived at Camelot, casting a golden hue over the bustling market beyond the fortress walls. Merchants called out their wares, the clang of iron mingled with the beat of hooves on earthen paths, and life pressed forward with its ordinary urgency. The contrast was stark, the lively clamor outside set against the contemplative silence of our journey through the forest. Above us, the imposing castle walls loomed, and though the cottage and the enchanted forest had always been my true home, with Merlin gone, Camelot stood as all that remained.

Stable boys, their faces marked with fatigue from the night's labor, hastened to meet us, moving with weary determination as they took our horses. While the vibrant life around us continued, Merlin's absence wove a thread of sorrow through our return. The relief that might have otherwise filled our hearts was softened by the grief that had carved a place within it.

Bedwyr and Merlonius stood with a composure that belied their waning strength. The toll of recent events was clearly evident in the strain of their stance and the tiredness clouding their eyes.

"Would you like to rest a while before joining me for a light meal? It has been a long and trying night."

Bedwyr nodded. "A brief respite will do us good, Arthur."

Merlonius offered a faint smile. "A moment to catch my breath would be welcome."

"Very well. Bedwyr, pray, show Merlonius to her quarters. I must attend to a matter in the great hall."

"It would be my honour."

"Merlonius, your chambers have been ready since the day Merlin built this castle. No one has entered them, but we have kept them clean, awaiting the day you would claim them. I will come for you presently."

"It was so many years ago that he walked us through Camelot when he first built it," she murmured. "I remember the glimmer in his eyes as he guided us to my quarters." After a pause, she added softly, "I will await your return."

"Bedwyr, will you join us later in the feasting hall?"

"With pleasure." He looked at Merlonius. "M'lady, permit me to lead you."

I watched them ascend the stair, waiting until they turned towards the landing that led to our part of the castle. Only then did I make my way to the great hall, where I instructed a servant to seek out my brother, Kay.

Restless, I paced the length of the chamber, my spirit clouded by the void left by Merlin's absence. I tried to quiet the unease stirred by a future without his counsel, but it stayed with me, tightening around me like a cloak I could not shed. For a breath, I let the pain rise unchecked. The sound of Kay's arrival drew me back to the present.

"Arthur, you wished to see me?"

"Yes. Kay, Merlin has departed this realm. It is a grievous loss to us all."

Kay's expression softened, a glimmer of sadness passing through his eyes. "Arthur… this is sorrowful news indeed. Merlin was a wise mentor and, above all, a dear friend."

"Indeed, Kay. He was woven into the cloth of my life, as you well know from when I was just a young lad. His final wishes were that his apprentice and the healer, Lady Merlonius, take her place among us at Camelot."

"I have heard tales of the extraordinary healing gifts and kindness possessed by the Lady Merlonius. She is truly one of his most gifted apprentices."

"And it is the will of the Fates that she joins us here at Camelot."

Pausing briefly to steady myself, I continued, my tone firm and clear. "Now we must turn to other pressing matters. Please find Morgan le Fay, as I would speak with her. Then, gather a few of our knights. Seek out Bors, Gareth, Breunor, and, if he is near, Gaheris. And Kay, I would value your support at my side when you return."

At the mention of Morgan le Fay, Kay's stance grew taut, a shadow passing over his features. He gave a curt nod. "I will gather the knights and seek her out without delay."

He turned and departed with a determined stride. Though sorrow lingered within me, I readied myself for what must come.

One by one, the knights arrived—Bors, Gareth, Breunor, and Gaheris. I greeted each with a nod, our understanding shared without need for speech.

When Kay returned with Morgan, she entered the hall with deliberate steps, her posture defiant, every motion a display of will.

"What is the meaning of this, Arthur?" she demanded, her eyes flashing with undisguised contempt.

I faced her with calm resolve. "Morgan, you know well why you have been summoned. Your deeds have sown unrest and danger for far too long. As High King, it is my duty to protect this realm and to hold firm against any who disturb its peace."

Her cheeks flushed. "How dare you speak to me so! I am your sister. Your commands hold no power over me!"

Undaunted, I rose from my throne, my eyes fixed on the fury burning in hers. When I stepped forward, my knights tightened their grip on their weapons, poised and ready. Each deliberate movement reflected the seriousness of my decision and my unyielding authority.

"No, Morgan. Whatever claim you held has been cast aside by your own doing. From this day, you are barred from Camelot and all lands under my protection. You are to return to Avalon, to your sisterhood, and remain there, forbidden ever to return."

A shriek tore from her throat, wild and sharp.

"Enough!" My voice cut through her outburst like a blade. I raised my hand for silence, and her cries ceased abruptly, though her eyes burned with undiminished hatred.

"My knights have borne witness to this decree. They will see it upheld. Leave now."

Unyielding, she hurled one last curse as my knights encircled her. Bors and Gaheris gripped her arms, their heavy steps guiding her struggling form towards the door.

"Your father killed my father, and I swear upon his memory that I shall have my revenge. The throne is rightfully mine. Hear me, Arthur, it is mine!"

Kay met my eyes, his expression grave, before joining the others to see her gone. As they passed beyond the doors, an unnatural chill settled in the chamber, as though the very stones braced against what now stirred in her wake.

Despite her fury, the truth of her words echoed through the silence she left behind. My father's desires had indeed cost Gorlois his life. Though Morgan had twisted that grief into wrath and treachery, its roots ran deep and undeniable. I carried the crown forged by such choices. And yet, I could not allow her vengeance to consume all we had fought to build. The realm must be protected—even from blood of my own blood.

I looked around, trying to discern the source of what I felt. Merlin's spectral figure appeared beside me, as ethereal as the morn's mist over a tranquil lake. His touch was gentle on my shoulder, akin to the caress of a breeze, rendering me momentarily speechless.

"My boy, a job well done. Well done indeed."

Emotions surged within me, swelling and pressing against my chest. I fought to contain them, drawing a breath that trembled with the weight of my longing.

"Merlin, your friendship, your teachings, your wisdom, and your love have fortified me over the years. I shall miss you greatly."

"I am always with you, Arthur. In the stillness, seek my counsel." His voice faded as his form disappeared, leaving behind a presence that drifted near, faint yet unmistakable.

I cast one final glance about the room, Merlin's absence pressing close. Leaving the great hall, the torchlit passage stretched on, its silence bearing witness to the heaviness I carried. Each step through the castle's shadowed halls seemed longer than the last until, at last, I reached Merlonius's chambers, where I found Bedwyr standing near the door, his lips drawn tight, a sign I had long recognized as concern.

"Arthur, what has transpired?"

"Morgan le Fay has been banished. She is being escorted to Avalon by our knights as we speak."

"This decision has been long in coming."

"Yes, I know. I should have sent her away years ago. Now, the urgency to protect Merlonius is clear, and Morgan's presence would have continued to pose a serious threat."

"By all we have, we must ensure she is not harmed."

"My friend, we shall do so, together," I affirmed, placing my hand upon his shoulder. "Shall we see how she is faring?"

Turning from Bedwyr, I knocked softly on the door. It swung open at once, and Merlonius, with a graceful motion, bade us enter.

"Pray, come in."

Standing in the center of her quarters, she added, "It is welcoming."

Her effort to adapt was evident in her measured, thoughtful words, as though she were drawing them from a deep well. Yet her smile reassured me that she was still the Merlonius I had always known.

Looking about the room, I noticed her stones arranged with care on the wooden table at its center. Among them was the piece of amber I had given her, a poignant reminder of Merlin's counsel about its protective qualities. Placed beside it was the crystal from his cave, a tangible link to our history. Her bag of herbs rested nearby. Her garments, loosely draped over a nearby chair.

I walked to the window and looked out over the fields and lush, green trees. Her gaze held on the wild stretch beyond, and I understood her yearning—for the freedom of the forest and the simplicity of our cottage life. It was a longing I, too, carried.

"You have a beautiful view from here."

"It is indeed. Yet it reminds me how much has changed."

Wishing to lift her spirits, I asked, "Shall we join the others for some food and drink?"

Her features brightened as she agreed. We made our way to the feasting hall, with Merlonius walking between us.

Upon entering, we were greeted by platters of fresh fruits, loaves of crusty bread, wooden goblets brimming with water, and soft cheese at the head table.

I deliberately seated her to my left and Bedwyr to her left, leaving the seat to my right vacant as a tribute to Gwenhwyfar, the absent queen.

Our conversation flowed easily, filled with hearty laughter and lively exchanges. Merlonius cast me a glance, brief but filled with gratitude, and Bedwyr lifted his cup in silent acknowledgment. It was a simple exchange, yet something in it stirred my belief that peace might still find its place.

After the meal, Bedwyr leaned in close. "Arthur, I must take my leave for a brief time. There is a matter that demands my attention."

"Is there cause for concern?"

His reassurance rose above the lively laughter from nearby tables. "All is well. I shall return ere long."

As I watched him leave, a restlessness settled over me, drawing my thoughts towards the refuge beyond these walls.

My gaze settled on Merlonius, softening as it met hers. "Would you care to join me for a walk around the grounds?"

"Yes, of course."

We left through a side door, the stables ahead, a familiar part of the landscape. I lightly touched her elbow, guiding us to the right. Side by side, we walked, careful to keep some distance between us. The instinct to reach for her hand, as I once had in the enchanted forest, stirred within me but went unfulfilled.

For a time, no words passed between us.

Stillness settled between us, asking for nothing yet offering a fragile sense of belonging. Moving through the garden paths, I watched her with quiet attention. Her steps grew lighter, the strain in her shoulders gently easing. It brought me a small measure of relief, knowing that even here, among these stone walls and tended hedges, she could begin to find a place for herself.

And yet I missed the forest as well.

The memory of birdsong and wild things, of Merlin's voice carried on the breeze, of her hand in mine beneath the boughs returned with startling clarity.

I had brought her here to protect her, but I knew the cost of such safety. Still, I would bear it if only to keep her close.

When we reached a secluded bench, her eyes shifted cautiously before meeting mine. "Arthur, is it safe for us to speak freely here?"

I tilted my head slightly, surprised by her wariness. "Yes, of course. Why do you ask?"

She hesitated, her expression shadowed as she searched for the right words. "There is more I must tell you of Merlin's warnings. He spoke gravely of the danger that surrounds us—forces intent on striking at you through me. The thought that I might bring you harm is more than I can bear."

Moved by her concern, I clasped her hand, the slight tremor in her touch betraying the pain and uncertainty that gripped her. "His caution must not be taken lightly. Camelot is not the enchanted forest, and the threats Merlin warned us about still linger. We must remain vigilant, yet know this, my love: nothing could harm me more than losing you."

Her eyes dimmed with sadness. "If you were no longer in my life…"

"Then nothing shall ever come between us."

She nodded but glanced away, and I knew she was reliving Merlin's last moments with her once again. Then she turned and looked deep into my eyes, as if wishing all of this were not so. "Merlin carried much concern, and he spoke with solemn insistence. If I were to live at Camelot, our affection must remain private, and many aspects of our union must be kept secret."

"Merlonius, nothing gladdens me more than having you with me in Camelot. Though we must be cautious in public, I promise we shall find times away from prying eyes. Our chambers will be our haven, where I may look upon you not as king, but as the man who loves you."

She slowly shook her head, as if to clear the shadow still clinging to her. Then she drew a steady breath and lifted her chin, quiet resolve settling upon her.

"Arthur, would it be possible to have a small plot of land to grow herbs when the earth begins to warm?"

Relief and hope stirred within me, for her words marked her intent to remain with me in Camelot.

"Of course, it shall be yours."

Her smile faded, her expression turning solemn. "I thank you. He meant a great deal to us both, and we share this grief. The years we spent together hold many memories, and my thoughts are often filled with them."

"Merlin's death has left an emptiness within me that I do not believe shall ever fade. Perhaps it would ease our loss to speak of him together. Would you share with me the times you hold most dear?"

She searched my face, as though weighing whether to step back into her past. At last, she began.

"My early history with Merlin has largely been left unspoken, shrouded in the mists of time. I have revealed only fragments, choosing instead to forge new remembrances with you. Yet with his death, I feel moved to unveil those days more fully."

"Pray, do so. I wish to understand all that has shaped you, all that you hold dear."

"Reflecting on those early days, you know that my father and mother no longer wished me in their lives. I was but twelve years of age when I stood at Merlin's side and watched them depart. Fear and confusion consumed me, and the hurt of their leaving was almost more than I could endure."

Her words stirred my own buried anguish, recalling the sting of being forsaken by my clan and the burn of whispered judgments on Sir Ector's farm. Though such recollections rose within me, I set them aside and turned my thoughts back to her.

"I remember looking at this man, his beard and robe flowing, wondering what my fate would be. Although I sensed I would be safe, my gift of sight was then unclear to me, making it difficult to trust in that feeling."

Her gaze wandered towards the snowy hedgerow, drawn to something beyond the present moment. Around us, the gardens lay under a winter spell. A crisp breeze stirred the bare branches, carrying the quiet hum of the castle grounds. Though the earth was stripped of blooms, it sparkled beneath faint sunlight, its stillness deepened by a dusting of snow. Weak light filtered through the leafless trees, casting intricate shadows across the paths, a mingling of light and darkness.

Drawing further from the well of memory, she spoke again. "When we entered the forest that day, his words were kind and gentle, for he was keenly aware of my distress. He led us deeper into the shadowed trees, and I dreaded what fate might await me. To my surprise, a small cottage emerged in a sunlit clearing. Standing beside me, he told me that this would be our new home. That day, we spoke of many things—where to build the paddock, the horses that would find shelter there, and the plot of soil for a garden. We wandered to the pond and the waterfall, and he began to teach me how to listen to the murmur of the leaves and the voices of creatures. From that day on, I carried a kinship with the natural world, one that has never left me."

Her courage struck me, living secluded with only Merlin and the whispering trees as companions, embracing the solitary path the Fates had set. As her tale unfolded, I was drawn deeper into her life's story, marveling at the determination that had carried her to this moment.

"For many moons, I rested uneasily in the small bed at the back of the cottage, plagued by darkness and doubts. Yet he never left me alone. Night after night, he slept in the chair by the hearth, his steady presence a salve for my restless spirit."

A fondness lit her features, as though she could see him there beside her once more. Watching her, I sensed how deeply those early days in the enchanted forest had shaped her. She had emerged not only as Merlin's apprentice but as someone strengthened by the wisdom and trials of their time together.

"In time, Merlin chose a name that would better reflect my new life," she recounted. "He shared part of his own name, so that I might carry his essence with me always. The name I now bear was a gift from him, and it holds deep meaning for me."

I took her hand in mine. "It is a name worthy of the woman you have become. By giving you a part of his own name, he showed the love he held for you. To him, you were the daughter of his heart."

Her fingers tightened slightly around mine. "And he became my father in all regards except blood," she said softly.

She shifted to face me, a faint smile playing at the corners of her lips, her eyes holding mine for an instant. "He was a demanding teacher, pushing me harder than any of his other apprentices, those drawn by the old ways. He would row us across to a simple building on the island, where his teachings took place. At first, I felt like an outsider among others who shared my curiosity and gifts, preferring to remain alone in the woods. Yet, he insisted we persevere. Under his guidance, I found both my place and a comfort among them, becoming the sorceress I am this day.

"He nurtured my understanding of the gifts I possessed, teaching me not only to read and write, but to interpret the stars and commune with the spirits of the natural world."

Her thoughts turned inward, her features distant as she relived a vision from the past. "I vividly remember the first time my healing abilities came to light. We were by the stream when I discovered a small bird with a broken wing. An overwhelming urge to heal it took hold of me. Placing my palm over the fragile limb, I closed my eyes, focused my will, and saw in my mind's eye the bird soaring again, whole.

"To my amazement, it began to stir under my touch. I opened my eyes and saw its wing had mended. Raising my hands to the sky, I watched in awe as it took flight, its movements graceful and free.

"Merlin watched me closely that day, and I felt the depth of his knowing. Recognizing my gifts, he vowed to nurture them, so that one day I might use them to aid others. True to his word, he guided me with patience and care."

I reached out, my hand resting lightly on hers. "Your knowledge of medicinal plants and your deep tie to the mystical forces has saved countless lives. Tales of those you have healed resound throughout the kingdom. You are a beacon of hope in a dark and uncertain world."

"Your words honour me, Arthur." She grew solemn. "In his final words, Merlin instructed that I was never to return to The Giants' Dance for the healing ceremonies. He warned that without his presence, the followers of the new faith might see my gifts as a threat, deem me dangerous, and call for my death. He made me swear to uphold his wishes and remain in safety."

Understanding the gravity of his warning and the truth in his foresight, I considered how best to shield Merlonius while still allowing her to bring healing to those in need.

"You may continue your healing within the castle walls, under my protection."

She drew a sharp breath and sat straighter, hope kindling within her. "Do you think that is truly possible?"

I squeezed her hand. "Indeed. When people come seeking your aid at Camelot, you may help them, but only under the vigilant escort of my knights."

"Arthur, so much is changing. Yet knowing I may still offer healing to those in need brings me comfort. I am forever grateful that we are joined in love."

"As am I, Merlonius. As am I."

A sudden tread cut through the stillness of our haven. Bedwyr approached, urgency sharpening his features.

"Pardon, Arthur, Merlonius," he said, glancing between us. "There is something I must show you. Pray, come with me to Merlonius's chambers."

CHAPTER 42

REVELATIONS UNVEILED

Curiosity stirred with each step as we left the gardens, anticipation quickening within me. Bedwyr's focused determination only heightened my interest. Nearing her rooms, Merlonius and I exchanged a questioning look. I steadied myself, seeking calm before opening the door, uncertain of what we might find within.

She rushed to the far wall, where her weaving frame now stood. A gasp of delight escaped her, and her hands instinctively covered her mouth.

"My loom. Bedwyr, you returned for it. Few would go to such lengths."

A faint smile tugged at his lips, his eyes warming. "Your life is changing in ways yet unfolding and your loom may offer comfort in uncertain times. I have also arranged for Merlin's horse and your own to be brought to the stables, so you may again enjoy the freedom of riding."

She brushed her fingers along the edge of the loom. "Your thoughtfulness has touched me deeply. I have not forgotten the day Merlin gave me this loom, teaching me to weave cloth and spin wool from the fleece. Knowing our horses are here gladdens my heart more than I can say. I look forward to riding Freedom again and caring for Merlin's horse. It will feel as though he is with me once more."

Exchanging a glance with Bedwyr, I said, "My friend, your efforts mean more than words could express."

"Arthur, I pledged my loyalty to you and Merlonius. With this, I hope to bring you both some measure of happiness."

I looked at Merlonius. "I know you were here many years ago when Merlin built Camelot. Would you like to see it once again? Bedwyr and I would be honoured to accompany you."

"I would certainly value such a distinguished escort as you both," she replied with a smile, "and I would enjoy seeing Camelot once again."

Bedwyr understood that I wished to offer Merlonius another view of the castle and help her find ease and familiarity within these walls. Moreover, I wished to ensure all within Camelot recognized her significant role and accorded her the respect she rightfully commanded.

Together, we left her chamber and Bedwyr began speaking about this secluded quarter of the castle.

"This wing is reserved for those who dwell here. That includes Arthur, myself, and now you, m'lady. Rest assured, you are safe within its walls."

"It is far grander than I remembered."

We traversed the many chambers and halls of Camelot, each space rich with history. She listened to the castle's stories and greeted those who made their home within its care. All who met her were touched by her grace and gentleness.

With the sun's descent, we returned to the feasting hall for the eve's meal. The knights were already seated and fell silent at our approach, their bearing reflecting both curiosity and respect. Bedwyr and Merlonius took their places at the head table, while I remained standing to address the gathered knights.

"Ladies and noble knights, with heavy hearts, we mark the death of our revered enchanter, Merlin. He has ventured to the realm beyond, leaving us bereft of his wisdom. It was his wish that the Lady Merlonius, one of his esteemed apprentices, reside at Camelot, and she has graciously accepted this invitation. From this day forth, she will make her home among us. Now, pray, continue with your meal."

As goblets were raised, toasts of honour and welcome rose through the chamber. "Arthur," the knights responded in unison, "we mourn the loss of Merlin and extend our welcome to Lady Merlonius." Their faces reflected the gravity of his death, and a readiness to support Merlonius. When the goblets lowered, lively conversation returned, the hall alive with purpose and resolve.

Once we had finished eating, I turned to Merlonius. "Would you care to retire to your chambers?"

"Yes, Arthur."

I leaned towards Bedwyr. "Will you remain in the hall?"

"No, I will take my leave as well."

His decision to accompany us our first night helped quiet any rumors that might have stirred about her arrival. Together, we rose from the table and made our way towards the broad stair.

At its foot, Bedwyr said, "I think I will see to my horse. Farewell until the morn." He headed to the right side of the castle, disappearing through the door leading to the stables.

Merlonius and I climbed the stair. At her door, I opened it but paused, uncertain whether she needed solitude to reflect on the day or the comfort of my presence. Though she was my wife and we had always shared a deep passion, stepping inside felt as though I might intrude on her grief.

"Rest well, Merlonius. I will see you on the morrow."

"Good rest, Arthur." Her eyes held such emotion that I was left speechless.

She entered with a sigh, closing the door behind her. I paused, reflecting on what had passed between us earlier in the day. A faint ache pressed at me, urging me not to leave her alone. After a brief hesitation, I softly tapped on her door.

"May I come in?"

She stepped aside. "Of course."

I entered and closed the door behind us. She moved gracefully to the window, beckoning me to follow. I joined her, and together we gazed upon the night sky. A tapestry of stars adorned the dark expanse above, each twinkling like a tiny, glittering jewel.

"Do you still see shapes in them, as we used to?"

I followed where she looked and pointed to a constellation. A smile touched my lips. "I see the bear." Memories of our past stargazing returned in a gentle rush.

I drew nearer, wrapping her in a tender embrace and guiding her away from the window. At first, she stiffened, but soon yielded, drawn into the familiar refuge of my embrace. Leaning in, I kissed her tenderly. Resting her head against my chest, she let her tears fall, grief over Merlin's death flowing freely.

"Merlonius, I love you."

She drew back slightly, her eyes meeting mine. "I will always love you, Arthur."

Our love wove together past and present, each triumph and trial a thread in the enduring tapestry of our shared life. The distant sounds of Camelot faded, leaving us wrapped in the sanctuary of our love.

I continued to hold her until, with a weary sigh, she stepped behind the draped corner of the room, its woven cloth shifting with a faint rustle as she changed into a fresh gown. When she returned, her movements were unhurried, almost ceremonial, each step a gentle offering to the solace we sought. She joined me by the fire, and with her came our shared mourning for the loss of Merlin.

That night, I stayed with her not as the man joined to her in union, but as her protector and friend. Rising from my seat, I took her hand, and together we moved towards her bed, where she nestled beneath the blankets.

"May you find peaceful slumber, Arthur."

"Good rest, Merlonius. I will be here when you wake."

Returning to my chair by the crackling flames, I listened to the quiet rhythm of her breath as she drifted into sleep. Staring into the fire, I contemplated Merlin's death, struggling to envision a world without his guidance and insight. Resolving to protect Merlonius and assure her she was not alone, I offered a silent prayer to the gods for their aid in keeping her safe.

The fire's glow blurred into a dreamlike haze as sleep claimed me. I walked beside Merlin through a shadowed forest, his form steady, as though he had never left this realm.

"Arthur, there are bonds forged beyond the touch of time. The love and loyalty you and Merlonius hold for one another are gifts no kingship can bestow. Nurture them well. Take care of her, as you always have, and remember that life seldom gives warning before it parts us. The days you share are precious. Let them be marked not by duty alone, but by the joys and laughter of your hearts."

"I will, Merlin. With Merlonius beside me, I remember who I am beneath the crown. She sees the man, not the king, and in that, I find something no realm could ever grant. What we share is not bound by title or duty, but shaped by love freely given."

I reached for his arm, wanting to keep him with me just a moment longer. "Merlin, I do not know if I am ready to walk this path without you."

His hand rested on my shoulder, as firm as it had ever been. "You have all that you need. Strength is within you. Lean on those you love, and you will find your way." With that, he turned, the mist gathering around him until he was no more than a faint figure among the trees.

The next morn, sunlight streamed through the window as I stirred awake, Merlin's words lingering. I found Merlonius watching me from her bed.

"Did you sleep well?"

I rose from the chair and approached her. "I did. And you?"

"Yes, your presence brought me calm."

I took her hand and leaned closer, our lips meeting in a kiss as soft as the hush of dawn. The scent of the morn's dew and the sweet fragrance of her hair enveloped us.

"I will leave now to change my garments and will return shortly. Would you like to join me for a light meal?"

"Of course, Arthur."

With one more kiss, I left her chambers. Passing Bedwyr's quarters, I paused to knock lightly.

He opened the door. "Arthur."

"Good morrow, Bedwyr. Will you join me in my quarters?"

"Of course. Give me a moment."

As I turned towards my chambers, a steward crossed my path, offering a respectful nod.

"My lord, the cooks have prepared a special fare for Lady Merlonius this morn as a gesture of welcome."

"That is most kind," I said, touched by their thoughtfulness. "She will be pleased."

Upon reaching my quarters, I changed into a fresh tunic, its linen chill a small relief from the warmth of the fire. The morn's light filtered through the window, and for a time, I stood in stillness, the weight of Merlin's absence settling over me. A soft knock stirred me from my thoughts.

Opening the door, I found Bedwyr standing there, his hair slightly tousled, like a man who had endured many battles yet showed no sign of yielding.

"Pray, come in," I said, stepping aside.

He bowed slightly before entering, a gesture that spoke both of respect and brotherhood. With a fluid motion, he shed his cloak, revealing the sword at his waist, an unmistakable reminder of his readiness in uncertain times.

We settled into the chairs in front of the hearth.

"The land is at peace," I began, pausing as I chose each word with care. "The knights pursue the Quest for the Grail, and my duty as king is to preserve order. Yet in the wake of Merlin's death, I feel compelled to assure Merlonius's safety."

Concern crossed his face, his brows furrowing as he grasped the import of what lay before us.

"Merlin bade Merlonius to swear to avoid The Giants' Dance," I continued, the ache of his loss sharper than ever. "He foresaw the rise of the new religion as a threat to our cherished traditions and feared she might be wrongfully accused of practicing dark arts. His desire to protect her extended even beyond his own life."

"Merlin spoke true. The world as we have known it is changing."

Feeling a restlessness, I stood and began to pace. Each step echoed against the stone floor, a measured rhythm to my troubled thoughts. I stopped and looked at Bedwyr.

"Merlonius possesses a rare gift of healing, a precious legacy coursing through her blood. I entrust you with a vital task. Ensure that the knights and servants welcome all who come to Camelot seeking her help. Yet, we must remain vigilant. She should never be left unguarded while tending to those in need. At least one knight, preferably two, must remain by her side at all times."

"Consider it done."

His nod was solemn, a promise not only to the task but to Merlonius, one dear to us both.

"There is more. My kinsman, Medrawt, harbors malicious intentions towards the throne. He was among those who sought to expose Lancelot and Gwenhwyfar's affections, intending to stir unrest and force me to condemn the Queen to death. Morgan le Fay was the other conspirator."

Bedwyr's expression shifted to surprise and anger. "I had no knowledge of this."

I placed a reassuring hand on his shoulder, noting the tightness in his muscles. "It was through the foresight of Merlin and Merlonius alone that the plot was known. I aided Lancelot and Gwenhwyfar's escape, and they are hidden at my estate in France, where they remain safe."

His clenched fists gradually relaxed as I spoke. "Neither Morgan nor Medrawt knows of the other's schemes to claim the throne. Morgan is no longer welcome here, but my concern now lies with Medrawt. When word of Merlin's death reaches him, he may see it as an opportunity to exploit Merlonius to strike at me."

"You have my word. So long as I draw breath, she will remain safe."

"I am grateful for your valour. Should duty call me away from Camelot, I will inform you. In my stead, I entrust you with her protection."

"It will be both my honour and my duty."

"Let us go now to Merlonius and spend the day together."

His features, so often grave, softened with a rare smile. "There is nowhere else I would rather be."

When we entered Merlonius's chambers, the soft scent of lavender greeted us, stirring memories of her herb garden.

"Good morrow, Arthur, Bedwyr."

"Shall we make our way to the feasting hall?"

"Yes, I am quite hungry!"

As we walked, I leaned closer and added with a teasing lilt, "One of the stewards mentioned a special dish has been prepared just for you, my lady."

"A special dish, you say?" She tilted her head, curiosity sparking in her eyes.

We made our way down the winding passage, our steps echoing softly along the cool stone floor. Nearing the bustling feasting hall, the aroma of freshly baked bread enveloped us, a tempting promise of the hearty fare awaiting within.

The long wooden table was meticulously arranged, adorned with steaming bowls of porridge, crusty loaves, and platters of fresh fruit. We took our seats and began to savor the fare before us. Around us, the chamber brimmed with lively sounds, including cheerful chatter, the rhythmic clatter of wooden vessels, and the hum of tasks undertaken in the early hours of the morn by knights and those who called Camelot home.

When the meal drew to a close, an attendant approached, carrying a tray of preserved fruits, dried apples and plums among them.

"My lady, welcome to Camelot," he said warmly, presenting the platter. "May you find joy in your time here, and please, enjoy this food prepared especially for you."

"I am honoured by your welcome and grateful for the offering," Merlonius replied graciously. "I look forward to the years ahead in Camelot."

She accepted a piece of each fruit with a thankful nod. The attendant bowed before stepping away, his expression touched by her courtesy. Watching her, I saw how naturally she carried herself with respect and kindness, winning hearts with the simplest of gestures.

Bedwyr and Merlonius became immersed in a spirited discussion about horses, their unguarded laughter rich and full. Sunlight poured through the high windows, brushing their faces as they spoke with ease, their friendship evident in every exchange.

Their effortless camaraderie lifted my spirits. The bond we shared, born from mutual struggles and victories, resonated deeply within me. I understood then, as always, that together, no challenge was insurmountable. Within Camelot's protective embrace, the unity between us stirred in me an unshakable belief in what we could endure together.

And yet, beyond the warmth of that moment, shadows still stirred. I could not forget Merlin's warning that the Round Table, once united in purpose, would one day falter. The signs were already upon us. The knights were scattered upon their Quest for the Grail, and Medrawt, cunning and treacherous, sought alliances with the Saxons. I was determined to shield both Bedwyr and Merlonius from the darkness prowling unseen. I missed Merlin, his wisdom and steady guidance, but even among so many, I felt his spirit near. I yearned for time to pause, to remain in the sanctuary of such fleeting peace, though I knew the storm he foretold had already begun to gather.

CHAPTER 43

WHEN THE STARS FADE

The days of companionship with Bedwyr and Merlonius in Camelot did not mend the void left by Merlin's death, yet they brought a comfort of great worth to the three of us.

Now those remembrances belong to the past, clouded by what lies before me. As I survey this battlefield, the burdens of kingship and the relentless passage of time press upon me with a weight that yields no relief. The friendship and laughter shared among the Knights of the Round Table, daily constants of our lives, now drift like distant echoes against the harsh scene before me. Fallen warriors remain where they fell, their lifeless eyes turned skyward, solemn reminders of life's fragility.

Kay fights at my side as we battle not only the Saxons, whom Medrawt had aligned with, but also those of our own who turned against the throne.

"Arthur! They are stronger than we are, but we shall not falter."

Odin carries me forward as I slash and thrust my sword. Then I see an enemy dangerously close to Kay.

"Watch out, Kay. He is at your back!"

Before I can reach him, a Saxon spears Kay beneath his arm and he falls lifeless, gone from us forever. Anger rushes through me, laced with sorrow at his death. I am powerless, forced to watch as the tragedy unfolds before my eyes.

The clang of swords, the stench of blood and sweat, and the fervor of battle mingle with the pain of seeing Kay fall. When the fighting subsides, an eerie hush settles over the field. The fallen lie motionless, and the sounds of the dying fade, leaving only the remnants of war and loss.

In the aftermath, a calm unlike the silence of defeat envelops me, carrying faint traces of the peace and love from days long past. Even as I wield Excalibur and deliver the final blow to my foe, the inevitability of death remains ever-present. Victory does not shield me from the fate that awaits us all.

It has been three years since I lost Merlonius, the woman I loved, yet the ache has never eased. Day by day, I have been dying ever since. Weakened, I lean against the trunk of a tree, finding myself at the threshold of the Otherworld. Images of cherished moments with her flood my mind, fragments of a once-whole tapestry drifting through me, each steeped in sorrow for what was and longing for what might have been.

Within the castle walls, Merlonius found a measure of refuge, a haven from the losses that shadowed her. Merlin, her beloved cottage, and the freedom of the enchanted forest were all gone. Yet even there, her heart still yearned for the serene shelter of that mystical woodland.

Alone in our chambers, she removed her shoes and crossed the cool stone floor, her steps whispering of a yearning for the earth's embrace beneath fallen leaves. With a graceful gesture, she set flame to the candles, deepening her longing for the ancient magic that wove her fate with Merlin's. Often, before dawn broke, we would stroll through the gardens, the calm enfolding us.

"Arthur, each season brings its own beauty to the gardens," she remarked as we walked the paths. "Yet I find myself missing the pond and the waterfall. Do you remember when you likened us to the mallard ducks that swam contentedly under the moonlight?"

"Yes, I remember that night well. I believe I told you the comparison was bound to the duck's devotion to a lifelong bond. And it remains as true now as it was then. We are joined in this lifetime and in the journeys to come."

"Indeed, we are one, in this life and the next."

The fleeting tranquility of Camelot fades, giving way to another memory, familiar yet tinged with joy and sorrow.

The forest's call was too tempting to resist, granting us escape from the gossip and idle tongues, much like those that haunted my youth. Bedwyr, ever our loyal companion, joined us one day as we rode towards what once was the enchanted forest.

We traced the meandering path we knew so well. Our horses bore us until we arrived at the familiar glade. Dismounting, we were greeted by rustling leaves that seemed to welcome us home, while distant woodland sounds soothed our longing for this sacred place.

After tending to our horses in the paddock, we approached the cottage, our steps faltering. Here countless treasured moments had been born and still dwelled. Standing before what had been our home, a stone pressed upon my heart. I reached for Merlonius's hand, lacing our fingers together. Her responsive squeeze, tender yet firm, conveyed a promise of comfort and unity between us. Bedwyr, no truer friend than he, stood resolute at her side, offering his support. Tears streamed down her cheeks, reminding me anew of the love and magic these walls had witnessed. This history, rich with emotion, is one I have never forgotten.

Amidst this recollection, Bedwyr spoke, "I spent but a handful of days in this dwelling when you saved my life, Merlonius, after I lost my hand in battle. Yet the comfort and love that filled this home remain with me to this day."

"Oh, how I remember those days, Bedwyr." Merlonius touched his arm. "I doubted I could save you, my friend. But the gods and goddesses granted me the gift to do so, and I am forever grateful."

He gave a solemn nod, a tear tracing down his cheek.

Merlonius turned to me. "Shall we ascend to the summit, Arthur?"

"Yes, let us go."

We continued beyond the pond, climbing towards the summit where the magical tree stood watch over our son's resting place. Its branches stretched skyward, while below, delicate blue flowers blanketed the earth, offering beauty amidst our sorrow.

Standing beneath the tree's protective embrace, my thoughts turned to the son we lost, and I imagined the man he might have become, shaped by Merlonius's gifts and my own strength. While I lingered in these reflections, a sudden gust of wind broke the calm, carrying whispers from beyond.

Bedwyr felt it too.

"Arthur, Merlonius, do you see that? I believe it is Merlin."

Before us, in a shimmering haze, he appeared. He held his crystal-tipped staff in his left hand, and his robes fluttered in an ethereal breeze. Warmth radiated from him, enveloping us in a cloak of affection and solace as his words reached us, borne on the unseen air.

"My daughter, my son, know that your little one sends you much love. He is with you always, his spirit entwined with the bluebird from our first venture into this magical land. Do not mourn for me, for I have never truly left you. And to you, Bedwyr, for no finer friend could be found, I extend my deepest thanks."

The wind swept the vision away, leaving a great emptiness. I drew Merlonius close as my own tears flowed. Beside us, Bedwyr stood transfixed, his usual composure softened by the remnants of Merlin's visit.

Merlonius glanced at the tree, then at me, and breathed, "This day shall remain close to my heart, always."

I looked into her eyes, the depth of her words resonating within me. "And mine, Merlonius.

"Bedwyr, shall we return to Camelot?"

"Aye, it is time."

We descended from this sacred place, our movements deliberate and pensive. Leaving the summit behind, Merlin's words, mingled with the message of love from our son, left a deep mark on our hearts. When Camelot came into view, we realized we were not merely returning home, but entering a new existence, forever changed by what we had witnessed.

The memory fades, and the stark truth of my dwindling life closes in. The dead and the dying surround me. I must hold on until Bedwyr returns. I avert my eyes, seeking solace in times when love was my sanctuary, a refuge once as enduring as the stars.

Each cherished recollection was a brief respite, soothing the sharp edges of my pain, a stark contrast to the cold and relentless present.

Merlonius, a vibrant beacon, infused my darkest days with boundless joy. Among the countless moments we shared, one night remains vivid, filled with tender caresses and whispered words. We ventured deep into the forest and made our encampment beneath the vast starlit sky. Merlonius conjured a stew over the fire, and with goblets of water and wine we found a respite seldom known in Camelot. After our meal, we lay beside each other, searching for shapes in the stars. As the night quieted, she nestled against me, her breath a soft warmth on my cheek.

"Arthur," she whispered, tracing patterns on my hand, "promise me that no matter what storms may come, we will always find our way back to this."

"Always," I vowed, drawing her into my embrace.

Above us, the heavens glimmered with celestial brilliance, her hair flowing freely, and together we drifted into dreams, sheltered in each other's arms.

Amid the chaos of the battlefield and the looming presence of death, I seek refuge in remembrances of love, shadowed by my greatest loss. That fateful night remains clear in my mind, when the harvest fields lay bare and the chill of frost lingered in the air.

In my chambers, with the firelight upon us, Merlonius and I engaged in a lighthearted game of casting stones.

Forever competitive, she teased, "I shall surely win this match!"

She tossed the stones, her laughter filling the room, a sound I now know was the prelude to an unimaginable silence.

"See, two fours. I can assure you I am not using magic, but eight is a potent number to beat."

I smiled, turning the stones in my hand. "Do you truly believe you can win, Merlonius?"

I threw, and the stones yielded a two and a three.

"See, I told you, Arthur, only a five. Eight is a mighty number."

Her smile widened as she gathered the stones once more, her delight brightening the space between us. The night passed in serene happiness, filled with laughter, until, with a sigh, she rose and came to my side. Leaning close, our lips met in a sweet kiss. Yet disquiet crept into my contentment like a cloud passing briefly across the moon. A tightness gripped my chest, leaving me adrift in confusion.

I searched her eyes. "Merlonius, how are you faring?"

"My love, I am merely weary this night. I shall retire to my chambers and bid you good rest."

Drawing her into my arms, I held her close. Even after all these years, she was the most beautiful woman I had ever beheld.

"Merlonius, each day deepens my love for you. The joy you bring to my life is immeasurable."

"And you are the heart of my world. Your love sustains me through every trial."

Taking her hand, its familiar touch a steady comfort, we shared a silent accord, knowing our love would transcend time itself.

Her voice carried deep tenderness. "I often reflect on the day we wed and on our vows. The boundless wonder of joining as one has never left me. Know this: you are a part of me, and my love is unending."

"Merlonius, my love for you fills every part of my being, and it always will."

She rose gracefully, her hand lingering to caress my cheek before leaving.

When the door closed, a nameless fear took hold. That night restlessness consumed me, dread deepening with each passing hour.

At dawn, as I dressed, Merlonius's handmaiden arrived, her eyes awash with tears.

"My lord," she stammered, "it is Lady Merlonius. Please, you must come."

Without hesitation, I rushed to her chambers. There she lay, still and silent, the vibrant essence of her spirit gone.

"No, no, Merlonius, come back to me!" I cried, collapsing to my knees beside her bed. I took her hand in mine, searching her face as if sheer will could rouse her. She had slipped away in the silence of the night, leaving me alone. As I wept, my heart shattered.

Bedwyr soon knelt at my side, his presence a small comfort in the endless depth of my sorrow.

"Arthur, she has passed into the shadows. We must make preparations." His hand was firm on my elbow as he helped me stand.

There she lay, peaceful yet so distant, my dearest friend and love. The sight tore at what remained of my broken heart. Bedwyr's tears mirrored my own, and I found myself unable to offer or receive solace.

I wandered the halls in a haze, heartache consuming me, until I stood in the great hall, staring blankly at the seat of the High King. Her presence felt near, as though her hand rested on my arm. The agony of her absence was almost too much to bear.

It was well into the day when Bedwyr found me again, seated on the throne, lost to the world.

"Everything is ready. We are taking Merlonius to The Giants' Dance, as is fitting. We must go now."

I could not move, overwhelmed by emptiness.

Burdened by his own anguish, he touched my arm. "Arthur, please rise and join us."

Dazed, I followed him to the castle's broad doors. Merlonius lay upon a bier behind one of the horses, led by Kay. Several knights had assembled, and together we began the solemn march to The Giants' Dance.

When we arrived, the sacred circle was filled with villagers and knights. News of her death had spread, drawing all whose lives Merlonius had touched with her healing gifts to bid her farewell.

I entered the hallowed grounds and approached the altar where Kay and Bedwyr had reverently placed her upon the pyre. Their solemn nods signaled the time to begin. Stepping onto the platform, the very place where I had often seen her stand, a torrent of memories from our life together overwhelmed me.

Facing those gathered, I began, "Many thanks to all who have come to bid Lady Merlonius safe passage to the Otherworld. We are profoundly grateful for her life of healing."

Before I could continue, a young man stepped forward. "I stand before you on this day because of the Lady Merlonius. When I was a child, a fever nearly claimed my life. My mother brought me to her, and with her hands upon my head and prayers to the gods, she restored me. She was truly a gifted healer."

Then Sir Branoc, who had survived the Battle of Mount Badon, stepped forward with the limp that still marked his wound. "I was carried to the Lady Merlonius on a litter, broken and near death. Many believed I would not see the next sunrise, but she did not falter. Her hands steadied me. Her spirit called me back. I owe her not only my life, but every breath since that day."

Others came forward to share their stories. Villagers spoke of her healing touch, and knights recalled wounds she had tended, asking nothing in return. As their voices rose and fell, I struggled to contain my tears, each tale widening the void her death had left within me.

Bedwyr stood beside me. "I know how much she meant to you. She was not only a healer; she was a light in our lives. Her spirit touched us all, and her legacy will live on in every life she mended."

I nodded, words failing as my throat tightened. I looked upon her, her grace and the serenity that cloaked her forever held in my heart. A delicate breeze stirred, carrying the scent of wildflowers she adored. It seemed even nature mourned her death.

The ladies had dressed her in the garment she wore on the day we wed, a tender reminder of that joy.

"My love, my wife, my true queen…" I whispered.

"Arthur, she is as beautiful as on the day of your handfasting."

"Yes, she is. Yes, she is."

I faltered, unwilling to let go. Then, drawing a steady breath, I gathered my composure and gave the order. "Now, let us proceed."

Grief pressed heavily upon me as I command for the fire to be lit. Bedwyr placed the torch in my hand. The flame caught the kindling and burst to life, swiftly engulfing the pyre. Fire leapt skyward, casting a haunting glow across the faces of those gathered. I stepped back and joined Bedwyr, glimpsing Merlonius one last time, tranquil and eternally still.

Her ashes rose in a swirling column, lifted by the wind. One by one, the mourners began to disperse, each forever marked by her enduring love. When all had gone, leaving only Bedwyr and me, he could no longer contain his grief.

"She saved my life," he said, his voice raw. "She was so full of light. We will both miss her."

Blinded by sorrow, I found solace in his embrace. "She was woven into the very essence of my being." My fingers clutched his tunic. "I feel adrift, uncertain how to continue without her."

"Arthur, we will walk this dark path together. In her memory, we shall find the strength to honour her legacy."

We stood side by side, watching the fire burn to embers. A fading warmth clung to the air, as though her spirit had not yet withdrawn. The rustling leaves sighed softly, carrying traces of her voice. Beside me, Bedwyr closed his eyes, his features softened as if he too felt her easing our pain.

"Throughout her time in Camelot, we were inseparable each night. Yet on the eve of her death, a shadow of foreboding settled over me as she returned alone to her quarters." I felt the truth of it. "She knew."

"Her love for you had no bounds. She chose not to depart beside you, wishing to shield you from that memory."

The realization of her unselfish act settled within me. "Yes, she would do such a thing. Her gifts, together with visions wherein Merlin spoke to her from beyond the veil, revealed that her time was near. She knew…"

Neither Bedwyr nor I were ready to face the emptiness awaiting within the castle walls. We lingered by the pyre, each adrift in mourning. I stared at the place where the flames had burned, my heart heavy with questions. *How could a love so vast and enduring have slipped away so swiftly?*

At long last, I turned to Bedwyr. "Let us depart, for she is gone."

We rode together, the shadowed woods enclosing us. Slowly, memories of Merlonius surfaced. With each remembrance I thought I heard her laughter through the trees, her presence lighting our path. Gradually, the oppressive gloom began to lift, as if the very land sensed our sorrow and offered a tender tribute to our mourning.

"She healed more than bodies, Arthur. Merlonius renewed spirits with her kindness."

"How well I know this, my friend, for her love mended wounds I thought would never heal."

Her legacy, radiant with kindness, stood in sharp contrast to the chill she left behind. Her deeds, her love, and her indomitable will pushed back against the despair that threatened to engulf us. The branches above now framed the heavens, their silhouettes softened against the starlit expanse. Even so, the vastness of my sorrow remained daunting.

As I contemplated a future without her, the desolation seemed as endless as the stars. *Could I ever reweave the fragments of a spirit her presence once held whole?* With each step, I remembered her courage and compassion. In these thoughts, faint threads of hope stirred, as if she still walked beside me, urging me on. Yet the emptiness persisted, vast and unyielding. I feared it was not a wound to heal, but a part of me gone with her, never to return.

CHAPTER 44

A FRAGMENT LOST

The moon rose and waned in the wake of Merlonius's death, and grief consumed me. Though I carried out my obligations as High King, every motion, every step felt hollow and drained of purpose. Bedwyr rarely left my side, offering what comfort he could. I sought solitude in my quarters, staring out over the trees, often recalling the day we watched her ashes float up into the sky.

Six full moons had passed since I last held her, each marking the solemn, unyielding passage of time. Days blurred into one another, lost to a haze of unending duties and pervasive despair. Each instant hung heavy, then slipped away, like the morn's dew lost to the heat of the rising sun.

Her memory clung to me, an enduring mark on my spirit. The softness of her lips, the shelter of her embrace, and the lingering sweet scent of her hair haunted me, a ghost of our intertwined lives. Her loss left an ache beyond healing, a sorrow woven into the very cloth of my being.

One day, a knock at my door pulled me from my reverie. Without turning from the window, I said, "Enter."

Bedwyr stepped inside. "Arthur, come and see the new horse."

Lost in my thoughts, I stared at him, bewildered. "A new horse?"

"Yes, he arrived a fortnight ago."

"Very well," I replied, stepping away from the window.

Together, we left my quarters and walked in silence through the hushed halls of the castle. We descended the broad stair and passed into the courtyard. The coolness brushed against our faces as the land stirred from slumber. Above us, the sky stretched in a pale wash of color, softened by the morn's radiant light.

Inside the stables, the familiar sounds of horses shifting in their stalls and the smell of fresh straw stirred a deep melancholy. These same scents and sounds had surrounded us as Merlonius and I tended to the horses in the paddock of the enchanted forest. She would often sing as we worked, her voice carrying the lightness of her spirit. One line from one of her songs lingers in my heart still, soft as the wind through new leaves:

Where the light falls, love shall follow.

In every breath, a promise kept.

Her joy was irresistible, always urging me to join her, and even the horses seemed to delight in her presence. They would nuzzle closer, ears perked, drawn to the harmony of her song.

The image faded as Bedwyr led me to the stall of his beloved horse, Flight, who had been his faithful companion since Awen's death fifteen winters past. The rhythmic crunch of horses feeding echoed through the stable. Merlonius had so enjoyed caring for her horse and Merlin's, always ensuring they were well fed. The memory unsettled me, deepening the ache in my chest.

Regaining my composure, I turned to the new stallion in the next stall. He stood regal and proud, a charger bred for war, his rich chestnut coat catching the sunlight that poured through the open windows. Light played along the silken curve of his muzzle as he nickered, ears pricked with curiosity.

"Have you given him a name yet?"

"I thought you would like the honour of naming him."

The steed came to the gate, and I reached out to pat him on the side of his neck. I felt his strength beneath my touch, a noble creature, but my grief kept me from forging a true kinship.

"Let me think on this. For now, nothing comes to me."

We stood together by the stall, accompanied only by the occasional snort of a horse or rustle of straw. The horse's velvety nose brushed against my hand, offering a fleeting comfort, a tender reminder of life's quiet beauty and resilience amid loss. Bedwyr placed a firm hand on my shoulder.

"Shall we retire to your quarters, Arthur?"

"Yes." I was grateful for the chance to leave a place that, though once a refuge, now felt like a cage.

Even with Bedwyr at my side, I felt utterly alone as we made our way through the dimly lit halls of the castle. Reaching my chambers, I hesitated at the door. My hands trembled as I stood before the carved wood, torn between seeking the solace of Bedwyr's company and shielding him from the pain that had become my constant companion.

"Would you like me to come in?"

My gaze held on him, as though reaching beyond the present moment, drawn into the depths of my sorrow. Emotions churned within me, relentless and heavy, threatening to overwhelm. *How am I to endure another night without her by my side?* The emptiness clawed at the corners of my spirit, a loss far too vast to hold.

When I spoke, my voice sounded distant, even to myself. "Your offer is kind, but I shall see you on the morrow."

The understanding in his eyes conveyed a profound compassion, a wordless recognition of my despair.

"Arthur, should you wish to speak or need companionship…"

"I am most grateful, but not this eve."

With a faint smile and a nod, I stepped inside, closing the door quietly behind me. Crossing to the windows, I was drawn northward, to where the enchanted forest once thrived. Thoughts of my life with Merlonius overtook me, and I surrendered to them, releasing any hold on the present.

The night's cold edge met my skin, drawing me from the memories that held me fast. With one last glance northward, I returned to the hearth. Settling into the chair beside it, now my haven, I braced for another restless night. Sleep eluded me, and I wandered through an intricate weave of recollection and anguish. The fire hissed while the wind howled like a mournful ghost.

The first light of dawn brushed the horizon, yet I stayed trapped within the tangled web of grief. The emptiness she left behind was as raw as ever, and I wondered how I would ever feel whole again, bereft of her presence.

Bedwyr returned to my quarters as the sun's rays filled my chambers. His brow furrowed as he glanced around the room.

"Arthur, would you walk with me to the feasting hall for a light meal?"

"I think not. My hunger is absent," I said. "But I have chosen a name for the new stallion."

"That is welcome news. What shall we call him?"

"Erebos. It means 'darkness' in Greek. When I was a young boy, I was captivated by tales of the Greek gods found in ancient manuscripts. I recall that Erebos was one of the first beings to emerge from Chaos, the formless void that existed before the creation of the world. I believe this steed shall carry this name with distinction."

"A fitting name for a war horse. I shall leave you then, and will return after I check on Erebos."

"I shall be here."

With the door closing behind him, I reflected on the slow passage of days, each one wearing away a little piece of me. Despite my best efforts to carry on, a restless unease grew within me as the moons slipped by.

When the eighth moon since Merlonius's death waxed, I stood by the hearth, my fingers grazing the stone she once warmed her hands upon. Though the fire leapt and danced, the cold inside me held fast. Memories carried me to the time before I accepted my destiny as king, when she and I ran joyfully through the enchanted forest, free of burdens, free of sorrow.

A sudden knock pulled me back to the present. Reluctantly, I walked to the door and opened it to find Bedwyr waiting.

He stepped inside, his steps measured as he approached the hearth. "I think this day we should visit your son's resting place, Arthur."

I looked at him, my faithful knight and trusted friend. He has never left my side since Merlonius's death. I owed it to him to try.

"It has been some time since we journeyed there. Let us go."

As if in a dream, I secured my scabbard and Excalibur around my waist.

"I am ready."

Our footfalls joined the castle's faint stirrings. Stepping outside, we were met by a crisp morn, our pace unhurried as we crossed the grounds.

At the stables, Odin greeted me at the gate. Stroking his neck, I inhaled his familiar earthy scent, a wave of longing for what once was washing over me.

Struggling to steady myself, I watched as Bedwyr signaled to the stable boys to prepare our horses. With sorrow pressing upon me, we set off.

Crossing the drawbridge, we followed a familiar route I had travelled countless times. I gave Odin free rein, and he led the way with unerring steps as Bedwyr rode beside me. Around us, the forest awakened. Ancient trees stretched skyward, sunlight filtered through vibrant foliage, and the earthy scent of pine mingled with the soil, calling to mind days immersed in nature's magic.

Nearing the edge of what was once the enchanted forest, my steed slowed, sensing our arrival. When the cottage came into view, my heart moved fiercely within me at the sight of its decay. How much more sorrow could I bear?

We led our horses into the paddock, allowing them to graze freely. I stood still, overcome by remembrance of my time here.

"Arthur, shall we continue?"

I looked to Bedwyr, shook off the weight of the past, and nodded. "Yes, I am ready."

We latched the gate and followed the path, ascending the incline to the summit. We had come here before to visit our son. Now we were here again, but without my wife.

Reaching the top, we walked towards the large tree that sheltered our son's resting place. The sight of the vibrant blue flowers growing beneath its branches, a gift of Merlin's magic, stilled me; they grew nowhere else. My chest tightened, and I felt an ache rise within me as their petals shimmered with an enchanting radiance, catching the sunlight in a way that made them appear to glow, as though lit from within. I could almost believe she stood among the flowers, her presence wrapped in light and memory, closer to me than breath.

Falling to my knees, I buried my face in my hands, overcome by a torrent of despair. Pain surged through every part of me, and I cried out to the heavens.

"Why, why, why?" I screamed. "I have followed the path of my destiny, taken the mantle of High King, and returned the land to its people. Why then have you taken every reason for existing from me?"

Gradually, my tears subsided, and a measure of sorrow seemed to drain from me. "I wanted nothing more than to be bound to her in love, to raise children together, to keep a horse breeding farm, and to grow old by her side. But instead…" I shook my head.

"Arthur, it is time to release your grief and find peace. You are a good man, a great king, and you were the one Merlonius chose to walk beside her. She loved you."

Bedwyr's words rang true, and before I could answer him, a sudden gust of wind drew our attention to the brook beside the tree. There, shimmering into view, was a vision of Merlonius, her long hair flowing. Her image danced and swayed with the play of light, as though conjured by the forest's magic.

I rose to my feet. "Do you see her, Bedwyr?"

He nodded slowly, "Yes, Arthur, I do."

I stood transfixed as my beloved wife's figure floated towards us, her entire being aglow with celestial light. She seemed to exist both here and beyond, an ethereal essence that transcended the physical realm. She raised her hand and smiled.

"Arthur," she whispered, her words carried on the wind, "do not weep, for I am with you. Our love extends beyond the veils of life and death. I will always love you."

"My heart's queen and dearest friend, your presence brings both joy and sorrow. Though you are gone, my heart still longs for you, yet I find comfort in our bond, defying the boundaries of earth and sky."

"And you, Bedwyr, are indeed a loyal friend. My thanks to you for being a source of strength for my beloved and for your care of him."

Bedwyr, deeply moved, bowed his head. "M'lady, your presence is sorely missed."

She remained with us for several moments, and time itself seemed to halt. Sunlight enveloped her, casting a glow around her form. Slowly, her image faded, leaving behind a profound tranquility.

I looked at the tree beneath which our son was buried. "To you, Merlonius, who are and shall always be a part of me, and to our son, I send you my love."

"Bedwyr, my devoted and trusted friend," I began, facing him, "much of the healing in my heart this day comes because of your steadfast support. I am truly blessed, and I hold dear our brotherhood, not just as my loyal knight but as one who stands beside me as kin."

"You are my king, my confidant, and indeed, my brother, Arthur. My pledge to protect you is unbreakable, and I will honour it with every breath. The regard I hold for you extends well beyond duty; you are the one my heart chose to be my brother."

At the paddock we saddled our horses. I could not resist a final glance at what had once been my home, a hollowness gripping me.

We mounted our stallions and began the journey back to Camelot, the emptiness tempered only by bittersweet, cherished memories. One shone brightly: the day she and I had raced to the summit, our laughter mingling with the wind. Hand in hand, we spun in joyful circles, collapsing on the grassy ground, lost in fits of mirth.

Those remembrances, rich with love and delight, carried her presence so vividly it was as if her spirit moved beside me, her touch near upon my cheek. Even parted from this world, her love endured, a radiant light amid grief's veil.

Life at Camelot continued, and I marshaled all my will to push forward. Nearly a twelvemonth after Merlonius's death, a twist of fate drew me closer to the fulfillment of my destiny.

I had just returned to my chambers after a ride, placing Excalibur and my scabbard on the table beside my bed. As I settled in, a knock came at the door. Opening it, one of the handmaidens stood there, her hands trembling, her eyes fixed on the floor.

"Sir Bedwyr has fallen ill and is asking for you, my lord."

Without hesitation, I rushed to his quarters. Bursting through the door, expecting the worst, I found him sitting by the hearth, entirely well.

"Arthur, what brings you here?"

"I was told by the handmaiden that you were ill and needed my help." I studied his expression, searching for any sign of illness.

"I am in good health. I did not request your aid."

While we pondered the handmaiden's message, a chill coursed through me. Someone had used deceit to draw me away. Bedwyr and I exchanged a glance, and without a word, we hastened back to my chambers.

The doors stood ajar. Inside, the room was in disarray.

Next to Excalibur, the scabbard's absence struck me at once.

"Bedwyr, my scabbard is gone!"

We rushed to the windows. In the courtyard below, Morgan le Fay rode away, the scabbard hanging brazenly from her waist.

"If I go now I can catch her." His hand went to the hilt of his sword.

But I knew the pursuit would be futile. "No, let her go. The scabbard's magic is meant for me alone, and she knows this. Her plan is to dispose of it before you can reach her. Without it, I am vulnerable to a mortal wound. She will return swiftly to Avalon."

His brow furrowed as he stood motionless, the change in his bearing revealing what words could not. The Fates were at work, and the time of my rule as High King was nearing its end.

"We must gather our strength for what awaits," I said quietly.

We stepped away from the casement, settling into the well-worn chairs at the table. I clasped my hands tightly, pressing them against the table's cool surface.

"Arthur, what drives a woman like Morgan to embrace such darkness? She has hunted down your knights and woven dark spells to ensnare them. Instead of using her gifts for good, she has become a malignant force, consumed by hatred, forsaking her place as kin."

I weighed my response, caught in a storm of old grievances and bitter truths I could not change. "She has become a formidable threat to my kingdom. Merlin told me of her long-standing resentment. Morgan harbors a deep-seated anger for my father. She uncovered the truth of her father Gorlois's death, the night he fell as Uther sought Igraine.

"Seeing no end to her rebellion, my father sent her to Avalon, where she mastered astrology, sorcery, and the healing arts. She learned the art of wielding power, and there her thirst for dominion grew. She will not be swayed. Her ambition has hardened, and nothing I can say or do will alter her course.

"I remember now. The day after our handfasting, Merlin had returned to the cottage, and they revealed that Merlonius's powers were expanding. She had begun to see glimpses of the future through scrying. I can still feel her magic surge as she peered into a bowl of water containing one of the crystals from Merlin's cave. She warned us Morgan le Fay would one day steal something of great value from me." I sighed, "And so she has."

Her foresight came to pass, as it had so many times before, yet for this matter, its fulfillment turned the wheel of Fate, drawing my life towards its destined end. Why had I forgotten it? Why had I not prepared my defenses?

Bedwyr's inquiry pulled me back to what was. "How did Morgan know of the magic of the scabbard?"

"Merlin believed that Morgan's knowledge of the scabbard's power might have come from her access to ancient manuscripts or forbidden scrolls. Regardless of the source, she cunningly used that knowledge to her advantage. The scabbard is worth ten of Excalibur, for as long as I wear it, no fatal harm will befall me."

I rose and moved to the shelf near my bed, taking up the crystal from Merlin's crystal cave. As I turned it over in my hands by the casement, its familiar touch steadied me. For a breath, I felt Merlonius beside me, not as memory, but a presence, close and true. A hush settled within me, a sense of release I had not known since her death.

Retrieving the leather scabbard from where I had stored it, I returned to the table.

"It has been many years since I have worn my father's scabbard," I said, placing it before him.

"Through her treachery, Morgan has granted me the freedom to depart this world. I do not shrink from this path, for I have upheld my solemn covenant as king, offering all that a man may give. Yet, with the death of Merlonius, I feel a part of my soul has been lost, one that can never be restored. Perhaps, in these events, there is a somber solace to be found."

A faint smile touched my lips, unshed tears betraying the pain I struggled to conceal.

Bedwyr's conflict was evident, torn between respecting my wishes and his loyalty as a true friend. Sorrow shrouded his features.

"Arthur, nay, I shall find no peace in your death, my friend. None."

Resting my hand upon his shoulder, I gave it a squeeze. "I understand, indeed I do. You must know, I do not see my end as a tragedy. I have lived with purpose and honour. The time spent with Merlonius filled my life with love and light, gifts I will cherish until my final breath."

We sat in wordless calm, the silence between us heavy with all that remained unsaid. I knew that the threat posed by Morgan was far from over. Though she had fled, her presence still cast a shadow over us, and I feared her next move might be even more perilous than the last. Yet, for now, we could only wait and prepare for what was to come.

With the turning of the full moon, the shadow of Morgan began to wane at Camelot. I stayed vigilant, watchful for any sign of her return, yet she had vanished, leaving only the faint echo of a once-looming threat.

CHAPTER 45

DESTINY'S LAST STAND

A rider approaches, and I strain to make out his features, praying to all the gods and goddesses that it is Bedwyr. My breath comes shallow, and my hands tremble, betraying the dread clawing at my will. My vision, once sharp and clear, begins to waver, a veil drawing slowly over my eyes. A surge of fear grips me as I realize that my sight is slipping away.

But I refuse to succumb to despair. I clench my jaw and strive to remain aware of the world around me, taking in the rustling of leaves and the scent of earth. Yet, before darkness takes hold, memories rush in like a torrent, carrying me back to the moments that defined my life.

I recall standing by the windows in my quarters, watching the trees sway in the breeze with Merlonius by my side. Sadness and frustration welled up as I recounted the latest challenges brought on by Medrawt's actions. Images of him came to mind, whispering in the ears of discontented knights and those I was sworn to protect as he sowed the seeds of discord.

"Those loyal to me have reported that Medrawt is spreading untruths about the laws of Camelot. He opposes the funds established long ago to aid those in need, believing that wealth should remain in the hands of a few. His actions are causing unrest as those with shallow minds adopt his beliefs."

When the words left my lips, I recognized that the ties of blood and clan made the matter all the more agonizing, and I struggled to find a solution that would not lead to further strife.

Merlonius regarded me with steady resolve. "Arthur, I know Medrawt's actions are deliberate, aimed at undermining you and all we have built. His words are not merely the product of discontent but a calculated attempt to sow division. What I wonder is how far he is willing to go and whether he truly grasps the chaos he is unleashing."

I grappled with my competing thoughts and feelings. A penetrating silence settled between us as I struggled to confront the hard truth.

"His actions are driven by ambition, jealousy, and a thirst for dominion," I said at last, the admission heavy on my tongue, each word laden with regret. "He has lost sight of the true purpose and ideals upon which Camelot was built.

"My kinsman sees himself as my rightful heir, willing to do whatever it takes to secure his place. I fear he may even try to seize the throne before my death," I confided, the grim nature of this truth casting a pall over my spirit.

Merlonius caressed my cheek, her hand steady, as if trying to soothe the storm within me.

"Arthur, I grieve for the burdens you carry and for the harsh truth that kinship offers no sanctuary from them."

I took her hand and kissed it, her touch a gentle reassurance. Looking out over the majestic trees that surrounded us, I felt the unrelenting cloak of my responsibilities as ruler of Camelot. The ongoing strife with Medrawt loomed like an ominous cloud, seeping doubt into the corners of my mind.

Despite the conflict that had torn us apart, I could not deny how deeply the bonds of blood and clan still held sway over me. It was a constant battle between duty and the ties of kinship that continued to bind us.

Little did I know that, three years after Merlonius's death, the wheel of the Fates would begin to turn once more. On a hot summer's day, when the sun hung heavy in the sky, word reached me of unrest on my holdings in France. A group of rebellious landowners had seized my lands and refused to relinquish them. Gathering thirty of my bravest knights, I set off to reclaim what was mine and restore order.

A full turn of the moon later, I received troubling news: Medrawt was spreading tales of my death in France and plotting to seize the throne. Shocked by his treachery, I hastened back to Camelot, only to find that he had not only sown falsehoods about my fate but also bred discord among the Knights of the Round Table. Worse still, he had forged an alliance with the Saxons, our most bitter foes.

Merlin's counsel surfaced in my mind, words spoken long ago about the visions he and Merlonius had shared regarding Medrawt's ambition. *Sadly, Arthur, the path he has chosen is shrouded in darkness. We must remain ever vigilant in observing his every move, for he will seek alliances with our sworn enemies.*

Looking towards the remnants of the once-enchanted forest, I spoke into the wind. "Merlin, your warning has sadly come to pass."

When I sought to reason with Medrawt, our words clashed like storm-tossed waves, each argument drawing us further apart. The discord between us ran deep, our differences rising like a mountain that stood between us, unyielding. Yet I pursued a peaceful resolution, clinging to hope that clan ties could bridge the chasm between us.

His eyes burned with fierce determination, his jaw clenched in defiance. He shook his head, refusing to back down from what he desired.

"I will not relent, kinsman," he declared. "The throne is rightfully mine, and I will claim it."

His pursuit of rule was an undeniable strain. I felt compelled to try one last time.

"Medrawt, what of kinship and honour? What of your oath to the Knights of the Round Table?"

"The Round Table is for the weak, for those who cling to ideals while the strong are left to rot in silence."

He left me no choice.

"Then, in a fortnight, we will decide the fate of Camelot and Britain on the battlefield at Camlann."

On the eve of battle, I keenly felt the absence of Merlin and Merlonius. The confines of my chambers pressed in around me as my thoughts churned like a tempest. My steps echoed against the cold stone walls, mirroring the rhythm of my unrest.

I glanced down at my left hand and traced the Rune symbol Tiwaz (↑), carved into my skin. Its three lines stirred memories of Merlonius and the sacred moment she had gifted it to me. A mark of courage and purpose, bestowed on the eve of the battle at Mount Badon, it had steadied me in that darkest hour. And now, it would have to sustain me once more.

This battle was unlike any before, its outcome poised to shape not only Camelot, but the destiny of our land. Should Medrawt succeed in seizing the throne, the cost to our people would be dire.

I studied the upward arrow of Tiwaz, pointing to the heavens, and felt its power fortify my spirit. With Merlonius's wisdom and the Rune's guiding force, I found the conviction to lead my knights. True victory would not come from blade alone, but from the will to endure.

The moon cast a silvery light across the landscape, bringing a stillness to the night. Shadows moved across the walls, silent observers to my solitude. A light knock at my door broke my reverie. Opening it, I found Bedwyr standing there.

Deep lines marred his forehead, his usual calm replaced with worry and disquiet.

"Pray, enter. What has transpired?"

"Arthur, our scouts report that Medrawt has raised an army. The Saxons have sent many warriors to aid his claim to the throne."

I placed my hand upon his shoulder before walking towards the table.

"We are forewarned. The will of the Fates shall be with us, and we shall be victorious," I declared, aiming to bolster our resolve. Yet, beneath that certainty, a storm of doubt raged within me.

Bedwyr's weariness was evident, burdened by the looming battle. He hesitated. "I hear your words, but I fear victory may elude us."

"In these challenging times, my friend, we must hold firmly to our principles. Trust in our purpose, for we bear the hopes of all Camelot. Believe that Medrawt will not succeed in taking the throne from me. Rest now, and on the morrow, we shall face whatever comes with the courage of our brotherhood."

"I hope beyond hope that triumph will be ours."

"As do I, Bedwyr."

"We will stand by you to the end, Arthur."

"Your loyalty and those of our knights carries me into battle, and for that I am grateful."

With a nod, Bedwyr departed. Left alone, the enormity of the forthcoming battle settled over me like a heavy shroud. I looked at the empty chair across from me, where Merlonius used to sit. Conversing with her always brought ease, her love and understanding steadying me. With a deep sigh, I bore the hollow ache left by her death. The pain endured, sharp as on the day she died, an emptiness I carried deep within my heart.

That night, dreadful dreams plagued my sleep. Each slipped from my grasp upon waking, except for one. In this haunting nightmare, the ghost of Gawain appeared with a somber warning: fighting in the coming battle meant certain death.

As dawn's light crept across the land, I donned my chainmail, with Gawain's warning shadowing my thoughts. Near the stables, I joined my men and mounted Odin, my trusted steed. His black coat shimmered in the early light, and as I met his eyes, I wondered if he too sensed the danger ahead. Many of my men, weary from our recent return from France, nevertheless readied themselves to fight by my side. Bedwyr rode next to me, prepared to lead our charge into an uncertain future.

Upon reaching the summit at Camlann, I confronted Medrawt with a proposal, striving to keep my tone even despite the storm within me.

"Let us avoid this bloodshed," I implored. "You are my step-sister's son, a Knight of the Round Table. What is it you desire that I can grant?"

His face twisted with disdain and anger as he scowled at me. "What I want is what is rightfully mine: your throne. Britain needs strength, not the softened rule of dreamers and dying kings. Your ways and your reign are over."

The bitterness in his declaration settled heavily within me, like a chill that seeped into my very being. My years as the ruling High King had endowed me with wisdom and humility. Yet, the pull of kinship tugged insistently. I found myself torn between what I knew to be right and the ties of heritage.

Fortifying myself against the conflict of emotions, I declared, "Then we must settle this with the sword." I lowered my visor and commanded, "Advance in the name of Britain!"

My knights shouted, "For Camelot!" as they charged towards the enemy. The battlefield erupted with clashing swords, thundering hooves, and rising battle cries. Amidst the clash lives were lost on both sides, but the loss of our own left a profound mark upon me. The relentless pursuit of victory exacted its toll, shattering the very essence of Camelot and leaving an irreplaceable loss.

In the heat of the battle, I caught glimpses of Kay, his sword gleaming as he fiercely fought alongside the other knights, pushing back the Saxons and even our own misguided kinsmen deceived by Medrawt's promises. Each time our eyes met, an unspoken understanding passed between us: loyalty to this land and the unwavering devotion of a true knight.

Kay's voice rose over the screams of battle, cutting through the chaos with fierce resolve.

"Arthur, they are stronger, but we fight for Camelot! We will not falter!"

I turned towards my brother, intent on offering further encouragement and hope. I saw a Saxon warrior raise his spear.

"Watch out, Kay! He is at your back!"

But my warning came too late. I watched in horror as the spear pierced beneath his arm. Kay sank in the saddle, then was cast down lifeless from his horse.

Anguish poured into each swing as I charged, screaming to the heavens. The enemy yielded as I pressed forward, driven by sorrow and fury, until I reined in before the Saxon who had taken his life.

For a heartbeat, the world stilled and all I could see was the man who had struck down my brother. My rage deepened.

I drove Excalibur through him.

The clash of swords, fierce and unyielding, mingled with the smell of blood as we plunged deeper into the fight of life and death. Yet, despite the strain of their recent journey, my loyal knights stood firm with their unwavering courage in facing the Saxons.

Amidst the chaos, I confronted Medrawt. Wrath burned hot within me.

"Medrawt, you have brought this upon yourself!"

"I am the rightful king, kinsman," he shouted. "You have grown old and weak. Camelot thirsts for new blood."

With malice, he hurled his lance, and Odin fell, throwing me from his back. The ground struck hard, agony tearing through me, yet remorse for all I had lost drove me to rise once more. With a mighty surge, I charged towards him with Excalibur drawn, the blade gleaming with a savage light.

I seized him and dragged him from his horse. As we struggled in the dust, our swords clashed fiercely, and the din of the battlefield faded away. This was a fight to the death.

Suddenly, his blade found its mark, driving pain through my side in a fatal blow. Gasping for breath, I fell to my knees, the searing agony coursing from the wound below my ribs. But my will remained unshaken.

Medrawt raised his sword, poised to deliver the final blow. My resolve roared, and with the last of my strength, I wielded Excalibur. Its mystical force drove the blade deep into his chest, cutting through chainmail and flesh alike. He fell, lifeless, like my brother.

I was barely aware when Bedwyr found me lying next to Medrawt's body. His arms cradled me with a tenderness that stood in stark contrast to the harsh sounds of the dying around us. Seeing the severity of my wound, he swiftly tore a piece of his own garment to press against the bleeding, his actions swift and sure.

"You must take Excalibur to the water from whence it came," I whispered, my voice weak but determined. "Only then will I have fulfilled my sworn oath to the land."

"Arthur, you shall overcome this," he said, though his face revealed he understood the import of my request. The cloth, quickly soaked with blood, bore witness to the urgency of his efforts.

"I can no longer ride, and the sword must be returned to the Lady of the Lake. This duty now falls to you."

He nodded, "Let me help you stand."

With his support, I rose, though unsteadily. He guided me to a nearby massive oak tree, where I settled on the ground, leaning against the rough trunk.

Handing him my sword, I urged, "Make haste, Bedwyr."

He offered me a blade from one of our fallen knights. "Take this sword should you need it. I go now, as you have bid me, to return Excalibur to the Lady of the Lake."

I watched as he mounted his horse. With a final nod, he turned and rode away.

Left in solitude, my life force dimming, my mind blurred between the now and what was. My fight with the Saxon warrior remained vivid in my mind, a haunting echo of the violence that had filled my life. His sneer, the clash of swords, and the cold bite of iron were relentless reminders.

"You are weak, Arthur. You cannot defeat me," his taunts filled with contempt.

Our battle was fierce, the earth trembling beneath our feet. In the midst of the intense fight, I faltered, feeling the sting of the Saxon's blade. Darkness threatened to envelop me, but then, Bedwyr appeared at my side, pulling me from the shadows.

"Bedwyr, it is you?"

"Yes, Arthur. When I reached the edge of the woods, I saw the Saxon advancing on you. I feared I would not reach you in time, yet here I stand. I ended his life before he could take yours."

With the last of my spirit stirring, I reached up and gripped his arm. "Take Excalibur back to the Lady of the Lake. Return it to where it belongs, in the mystical waters that are the source of its essence."

He bent down, his eyes meeting mine, his face solemn with understanding. "It will be done as you have bid, Arthur."

Releasing his arm, I looked towards the sword, a deep wave of sorrow rising within me. "It is hard to part with Excalibur," I confessed. "It has been more than a sword—my companion through many battles, a constant presence in life's journey."

He mounted his steed, sorrow carved deep into his features. He glanced back once before spurring his horse forward, disappearing into the fading light.

Under the ancient oak, darkness crept into my vision, my vitality dimming like the final embers of a dying fire. The cost of this conflict, both in lives lost and the price I would pay, was immeasurable. Yet, amidst my fading senses, the image of Bors, renowned for his courage, remained clear. Leading a fearless charge against formidable foes, his valour fortified my spirit and reminded me that our struggle was more than a fight for survival; it was a battle for our deeply held beliefs and the very soul of Camelot. United in our devotion, we continued to fight.

Drifting between memories of my life and this battlefield before me, I became aware of Bedwyr as he returned and stood before me.

I tilted my head upward. "What did you see when you threw Excalibur into the water?"

"Waves and wind."

I knew that he had not taken the sword back to its rightful home.

"Bedwyr, I beg of you, do as I ask"

He stood over me in wordless silence. Desperation tinged my voice as I implored him once more. "Pray, you must fulfil what I bid thee. Go quickly for my time draws near."

He whispered my name, "Arthur." In that single utterance, I felt the depth of his anguish pierce me. "Is there another path to your healing?"

I shook my head. He inhaled sharply, and though I could not see his face clearly, I heard the firmness in his steps as he approached his steed. He departed, vanishing into the forest.

I lifted my gaze to the skies, reaching out to all the gods and goddesses.

"Pray," I implored, "grant him the strength and courage to carry out what I have asked."

But when Bedwyr returned a second time, I sank deeper into despair, the final strands of hope unraveling as he stood there, the slight falter in his stance revealing the truth.

"Will you betray me for the riches of the sword? Tell me what you have done."

"When I reached the water and raised Excalibur above my head, I could not bear to part with the sacred sword. I concealed it beneath a nearby tree."

Overwhelmed with distress, tears streamed down my cheeks. I could hear the strain in his breathing, each exhale heavy with his torn loyalties between his duty to me and his reverence for Excalibur. A heavy stillness pressed upon us, mirroring the fading strength in my limbs.

"Arthur, I will go and fulfil your request."

"You must venture further into the forest, and the Lady herself will guide you, for she senses Excalibur's return."

"Your behest is my duty. I shall see it done."

He mounted his steed and vanished into the forest, swallowed by its ancient boughs.

Time stretches and bends as I drift between past battles and the fateful field before me. Conflicts from long ago blend with the urgency of the present, creating an unsettling feeling of both familiarity and uncertainty. Each breath may be my last as I await Bedwyr's return.

Then, the ground shudders under the thunderous charge of hooves approaching. A familiar horse and rider emerge from the cloud of dust. Bedwyr dismounts and rushes towards me, his approach pulling me back from the edge of memory.

"Arthur, Arthur, I am here! Please do not leave me for I did as you have bade."

"Bedwyr, tell me. What did you do? What did you see?"

"I rode far into the forest, and as I dd so, the Lady of the Lake guided me to an enchanting, still lake.

"With a commanding tone, she instructed me to throw the sword towards the water. I did as she bid, and with a firm grip on Excalibur's hilt, I raised the sword above my head and hurled it as far as I could." He pauses, his breath unsteady as he recounts the memory.

"A hand rose from the water's depths, grasping the sword's hilt. The arm brandished Excalibur three times before disappearing beneath the surface with the sword."

A swell of emotions surges within me, each of his words shaping a striking image in my waning awareness.

"Excalibur is safe with the Lady of the Lake," I whisper. "My final duty as king awaits."

Bedwyr clasps my hand, urgency in his voice. "Whatever more you require, my friend, my king, tell me, and it shall be done."

"You have proven your loyalty and bravery once again. Will you aid me to reach the water's edge? I must fulfil my destiny."

He steadies me as I rise, his arm wrapping securely around my waist, lending the support I now desperately need. I can feel the strain in his muscles as we approach the water, where a thick, swirling mist envelopes the pool, concealing it from view. It is as if the mystical forces are preparing for a great unveiling, cloaking the waters in both mystery and anticipation.

A barge takes shape within the fog, bearing four hooded figures standing in silence upon its deck. Their faces are hidden, and a hushed reverence surrounds them. Bedwyr hesitates, then helps me aboard, where I lay down on thick blankets.

"I go now to join Merlin and Merlonius and will be healed of my wounds," I say, hoping to ease Bedwyr's sorrow. "You will be left with our memories and my love. Go to the one who makes you whole, and live out your life with her in love and peace, for the Fellowship of the Round Table is no more."

"Arthur…"

He grips my hand as a tear rolls down his cheek. "My spirit aches at the thought of losing you. But I bid you farewell with my love and the comfort of knowing you will always be with me, here," he pauses, pressing a hand on his chest, "in the deepest chambers of my heart."

With a final glance, Bedwyr's figure begins to fade, obscured by the mist, a welcome guardian of my journey's end. The fog's cool embrace against my skin and the lapping of water against the barge bring a calm that contrasts sharply with the chaos that once consumed me.

I succumb to a dreamless slumber, the remnants of battles past and the visions of fallen friends weaving a haunting dirge. This melody, mournful yet soothing, recalls the sacrifices endured and the lives forever bound to mine. Within its solemn refrain, I find a depth of tranquility unknown for many years, a rare reprieve upon a path long shadowed by sorrow.

I awake as the barge came to rest. The hooded figures help me to my feet, and with heartfelt thanks, I step ashore. The fresh scent of the earth and the verdant grass beneath me stir my senses. Then, from the haze, a familiar figure emerges, drawing nearer.

Merlonius closes the distance between us. "Arthur!" She draws me into her embrace, a haven of warmth and solace. Our kiss takes us to a place where only our love exists.

"You have journeyed far, my love. From the mortal realm's strife, across mystical shores, to this land of eternal wonder."

"Merlonius, are we truly beyond death?"

Her gentle touch upon my cheek reassures me. "Though our earthly forms have passed, our spirits flourish here."

A shroud of sorrow dims my sight, mourning a life once overshadowed by the burden of fate. "If only I had not been destined for the crown, Merlonius. If only…"

"The Fates wove our tapestry with purpose. Release your sorrow, Arthur, for our story is one of triumph. You followed your path with valour, never forsaking our love. Because of this, we are bound together eternally."

I pull her close, burying my face in her hair. The scent of the forest we both loved still clings to her. While we remain in each other's arms, we hear Merlin's chuckle. With his crystal-tipped staff in hand and eyes gleaming with warmth and mischief, he stands before us.

"Well, my boy, you have made it at last."

With a broad smile, I answer, "Merlin, to see you again brings back a happiness I thought I might never feel again."

His eyes, rich with the depth of our past, meet mine. "The love we share for each other and this land transcends all boundaries. The circle remains unbroken, Arthur. Remember, nothing has truly changed, for we are masters of our fate, bending what is real to our will. Come, let us return home."

Hand in hand with Merlonius, we follow him down a path flanked by majestic trees. Our walk leads us to our cherished cottage. Merlin opens the latch of the door and turns towards us.

"It is so good to be together again."

Merlonius and I exchange smiles, an understanding deep between us, as we cross the threshold. The glow of the fire wraps around us, and he closes the door, sealing out the eve's chill.

Familiar sights and scents embrace us; this place is truly our home, a sanctuary rich with love, magic, and destiny. The life I left behind has shown the true nature of kinship, for the strongest bonds are forged in adversity. Merlin and Merlonius are my true clan.

Standing before the hearth, I look to them, and a deep sigh of contentment escapes me. "Our home," I muse aloud, "is shaped by the love that sustains us and the memories we hold dear."

"Arthur, here in this enchanted realm, duty and fear have no hold," Merlonius says with warmth. "We exist in happiness and love." She smiles and asks, "Shall we visit our garden?"

Her invitation sparks a lightness in my heart, and Merlin's enthusiastic words, "And Arthur, it is no small garden, as you shall see!" lift my spirits even higher.

Surrounded by the company of those I hold most dear, the full measure of our journey reveals itself. It is a tapestry woven not just from the trials we have faced but from the enduring love that has guided us home, to where we were always meant to be. The burdens of crown and battle are behind me, and no shadows linger here. Love, unbroken and eternal, is all that remains. Yet even as I rest in this haven, I know that our story will live on beyond these enchanted shores. The circle closes, only to open again, for the bond remains unbroken. And in that unending tale, I am home at last.

Epilogue

You Are of Us

Words left unspoken, until now

I felt your sorrow before you arrived,
A ripple through the fabric between realms—
Not grief alone, but longing—
That ache only the heart knows
When it yearns for what once was,
And still is, unseen.

You came not with questions,
Nor to seek answers.
You came as you are,
And that was enough.

I wrapped you in my arms,
Not to shield you from the ache,
But to honour it.
For tears that fall on both sides of the veil
Are sacred things—
Proof that love endures
Even across the chasm of worlds.

Merlin stood close, as he always does,
His presence like the stillness before the stars appear.
And Jesus—light incarnate—
Left a silence when he went,
But even that silence spoke.

You said you just wanted to be here with us.
And so you were.
Not in the halls of Camelot, nor the forest glade,
But in that other place—

The soul's true home.
Othila.
The inheritance not of blood, but of spirit.
You are of us.

We are with you,
Not only when you walk the in-between
But when you sit in your chair in this waking world,
When you write,
When you weave,
When you remember.
You carry us in your bones.
And when the ache rises again—
As it will—
Return, and simply *be.*
You need no key.
The door has *always* been open.

The End

About the Author

Anita lives in Central Arizona, where the vivid sunsets and subtle beauty of the Sonoran Desert offer daily inspiration. A lifelong lover of story, her fascination with Arthurian and Medieval legends began in her twenties, sparked by a chance encounter with Mary Stewart's *The Crystal Cave* in a Connecticut bookshop. That moment planted the seed for what would become a long and deeply personal journey into storytelling.

Her debut novel, *Memories of Arthur: King and Man*, is the result of years of research, reflection, and dedication to reimagining these ancient tales with both heart and reverence. Anita's background spans more than four decades of business writing, but her creative path opened fully through study and mentorship, including work with Wesleyan University and instructors such as Brando Skyhorse, Jane Friedman, and Jule Kucera.

When not writing, Anita finds joy in quiet pursuits—weaving on her rigid heddle loom, walking her spirited puggle, and exploring the enduring magic of the natural world. She hopes this novel offers readers not only an escape into the past but also a reminder of the timeless bonds of love, loyalty, and purpose.

www.ingramcontent.com/pod-product-compliance
Lightning Source LLC
Chambersburg PA
CBHW030332010826

48973CB00004B/967